what people are saying about *the eves*

"Brilliant! I laughed, I cried, I learned. What more can you ask for from a novel?" –Kathy Myerburg

"Even after I finished *The Eves,* I kept wondering about the characters and their laughter and their hard conversations. I especially miss being able to check in with Tobias." –Bill Wild

"An incredibly riveting story. The characters, and the vivid descriptions of people, places, and events, immediately draw you in. This is a book I could not put down." –Marilyn Kessler

I just finished *The Eves* and I'm sitting here with a flood of emotions going through my entire being. This is a gift of a book. The songs quoted, with listen links, are spot on and a special bonus. Totally, this is a movie in the making. Oprah needs to read it! Every woman on our planet needs to understand that her story is a priceless gift to the next! –Tammy Barnett

"This is an engaging book. The characters are fully drawn and interesting; the storyline connected me from the start, the movie can't be far behind." –Nicholas Kuffel

"A novel filled with style, dignity, and humor. A tightly and smartly written book, every word counts!" –Antonia Moreno Essig

"I enjoyed turning every page, until the last one. This is a book that we will be talking about for a long time." –Bette Blitzer Mills

Enjoy Jessica's
journey!
[signature] 10.2020

the eves

a novel

also by grace sammon

Battling the Hamster Wheel™ Strategies for Making High School Reform Work
(Corwin Press, 2007)

Creating and Sustaining Small Learning Communities:
Strategies and Tools for Transforming High Schools
(Corwin Press 2008)

the eves

a novel

grace sammon

Cover design by Ivica Jandrijevic
Cover illustration by Elena Brighittini, artstation.com/chwee
Author photo by StephanieDubskyPhotography.com
Interior layout and design by www.writingnights.org
Book preparation by Chad Robertson
Edited by Nancy Johnson

ISBN: 979-8-6489-4720-7
LIBRARY OF CONGRESS CATALOGING-IN-PUBLICATION DATA:
NAMES: Sammon, Grace, author
TITLE: The Eves – A Novel / Grace Sammon
DESCRIPTION: Independently Published, 2020
IDENTIFIERS: ISBN 9798648947207 (Perfect bound) |
SUBJECTS: | Fiction | Grief | Coming of Age | Family life | Aging
CLASSIFICATION: Pending
LC record pending

Independently Published
Printed in the United States of America.
Printed on acid-free paper.

The Eves is a work of fiction. Names, characters, places, and incidents
either are the product of the author's imagination or are used fictitiously,
and any resemblance to actual persons, living or dead, businesses,
companies, events, or locales is entirely coincidental.

The links suggested in the Overture and Coda
are suggested for your enjoyment not for purposes of monetization.

24 23 22 21 20 8 7 6 5 4 3 2 1

With much love, gratitude, respect, and remembrance for
Josephine Theresa Caruso Sammon
Nearly two decades after your death, you still have reach!

To the two best contributions I have made to this Earth,
I love you beyond measure.

For my husband, patient, kind, and ever positive that it will all work out.

You are all my dash.

contents

overture

Your children are not your children.

And though they are with you yet they belong not to you.

You may house their bodies but not their souls,

For their souls dwell in the house of tomorrow, which you cannot visit, not even in your dreams.

Excerpted from **Our Children**
— Kahlil Gibran

Listen to it performed in its entirety by Sweet Honey in the Rock:
https://youtu.be/HCVvoL_F5gA

eighteen hundred square feet and a cat

S onia, Erica, and I drive in silence to my house, the roof of the convertible still down. The smell of earth and manure seeps from our clothes and mingles with the crisp Autumn air. Today provided so many images, statements, textures, and people to think about. Our silence is wrapped in the warm glow of Erica's camera from the back seat as she flips through the hundreds of digital images she has shot.

I'm unsettled and can't quite describe it. I've dropped out of so much. I've avoided being with Sonia, especially when she has her fifteen-year-old daughter, Erica, with her. I've avoided being around the energy, self-righteousness, and the sense of immortality of youth. I find that it scrapes too much at the wounds on my heart.

Sonia drops me off and deftly makes a three point turn on the street made narrow by cars parked closely on either side. I climb the three steps to the door of my row house. I kick today's still-virgin, plastic wrapped Washington Post to the side of the porch. There, it joins weeks' worth of unopened newspapers and an assortment of empty paint cans I've been intending to trash. Before I can get the key in the door Sonia has stopped in front of the house. As she sweeps the one wisp of errant hair back behind her ear, she reaches for a lipstick. Looking in the rear-view mirror she says "Jessica, I watched you today. You did not put your hand in the paint or leave your mark, but I saw you trace the hands of the others. Enough!" she says, cutting off whatever she thinks I am about to say. "Jess-cee-ka," she clips, her eyes now piercing into me. "This hiding from the world stops today. It is decided. You will write about that place."

It was an emphatic statement.

Revving the car, she is gone in an instant, with only an eye roll and a shrug of shoulders from Erica in the back seat.

As soon as I open my door the heat from the waist-high, silver-painted radiator hits me. Gabler raises her head just long enough to acknowledge me before she curls back up on the shelf over the radiator. She is twelve pounds of cat, and nearly fourteen years of age. She's a beautiful Tabby, but Gabler now pales in comparison to her theatrically-strong, Hedda Gabler namesake.

Roy Gillis, my general contractor, has a soft spot for cats. He has not only built her the shelf to perch on but also a rather attractive little flight of stairs to help her get to the warmth of the radiator. Like everything Roy does, it is methodical and done with great attention to detail. The little staircase matches my main staircase exactly, complete with banister and newel posts. The fact that these two pieces sit "kitty corner" from each other isn't lost on me. It was a sweet gesture.

I peel off my sweatshirt and toss it on to the bicycle parked at the foot of the staircase. There, it joins an array of clothes that don't ever quite make it upstairs. I toss the house keys into the bicycle basket where they sink to the bottom of an oleo of odds and ends. As I head down the hallway towards the kitchen, I almost realize that the place is in more disarray than I'd like. I'd also admit, but only to myself, that there's probably something wrong with my being in the house less than a minute and the fact that I am already in the kitchen pouring vodka into a crystal tumbler. Neat, no ice, just the biting warmth of a double shot of vodka over which to mull the day and Sonia's parting comment, a mandate that I write about this day and the people we've met. It is an intrusive demand. I don't need to become one of Sonia's many personal projects.

Sipping my vodka, I turn and lean against the cabinets on the east wall of the kitchen, relaxing into the safety of this space, I see the note taped to the counter. Roy does this daily as he leaves. It will outline what he's done and where we need to go next with the renovation. Most days, I read them.

"*Jes,*" it begins. He's the only one who calls me that. To everyone else I am, and have always been, Jessica. Unless, of course, you add the always-a-warning-that-you-are-in-trouble middle name. "Jessica Marie" coming out of either parent's mouth was enough to make me stop what I was doing and coil with guilt, justified or otherwise.

To Roy, however, I was, immediately, just "Jes," not even bothering with the second "s." He must think I am a lot more uncomplicated and straightforward than I feel.

"Jes, the plastering on the wall in the hall is done."

"I've got the new kitchen door in. I also installed the up-dated humidity gadget for the space over the windows in the dining room—I'm glad we found a better home for the orchids than the floor of your bathtub. ☺ You've probably noticed that already."

I hadn't.

"Oh, by the way, I ignored you on the crown molding in the front parlor. Think you are wrong on that, but we can discuss. It got late so I am walking over to Columbia Rd. and picking up Cuban. Should be back in about thirty minutes. I'm counting on you being hungry. No obligation to share a meal, but we can talk about the next stage of the renovation if you want. Meanwhile, if you are reading this, you beat me back, go look at the parlor. RLG (6:37p)"

6:37p. Roy is nothing if not precise. He is also patient. I started this project nearly a year ago thinking I could quickly and gracefully sail through a complete renovation of my hundred-year-old quintessential DC row house, all 1800-plus square feet of it. The idea was that it would help me renovate my spirit. It's not turning out that way. Too many memories.

I have to admit that what we have accomplished, however, is lovely. I've wanted to preserve much of the 1900s feel of the house while I upgrade it to a place of elegance and comfort. Comfort, what would that look like?

The kids and I moved here over 20 years ago, after the divorce. When I first looked at this place it had been leased out to college students for decades. Layers of paint later, it still looks like they live here. Ryn was just two-and-a-half and Adam was an ever-so-tiny three months old. Washington Capitol University had hired me to work in its undergraduate division. With that one bit of security, I left my husband James behind in Sarasota to continue running his plastic surgery practice, to work on the commission planning the regional medical school, and to pursue his desire for youth and beauty—both his and others.

I chose this house, in an area that was once considered an "outskirt suburb of Washington, DC" because it was within walking distance of good schools, was in a diverse neighborhood, and because I could be at the National Zoo pushing a stroller within minutes. The streets are heavily tree-lined, and you can imagine a different era as these row houses began to spring up. In the 1900s, Helen Hayes, First Lady of the American Theater, grew up here, so did Walter Johnson, one of the legends of the original Senators baseball team. The neighborhood is listed on the District's historic registry as one of the '*original escapes* from the city.' *Escape* sounded exactly like what I needed after the divorce, and I've cherished my ability to do just that these last three years. What did Sonia accuse me of? Hiding? Ridiculous!

Feeling the vodka warm me, I ponder Roy's note and review our progress. The first-floor renovations included taking down some walls and starting on the installation of a bathroom. These are the only spaces I've really let Roy and his workmen address in detail. I love the new space between the kitchen and dining room. Roy captured exactly what I imagined. Now that we've taken down the west wall of the relatively small kitchen, it opens to the large dining room forming a wonderful space for entertaining. If I entertained. The entire south wall of the dining room, to my left as I look out from the kitchen, is shared by eight-foot-tall windows and a built-in window seat that runs the length of the room. Roy's built in a clever hot house with a humidity function across the top of the windows for the orchids. Orchids, outrageously prized here, and ridiculously simple to grow in Sarasota. For decades, a friend of mine there kept sending me varieties. Keeping them in a humid bathroom kept them, mostly, alive.

Roy has divided the kitchen and dining room spaces with low cabinets, opening on either side into each room. For the counter tops he has found the perfect piece of stone. "Catholic church altar white" or "tombstone white" marble was what I requested. He found the piece with just the slightest striations of black. It feels thick to the hand as well as, somehow, to the eye. Around the rim there is a pencil-thin groove, pleasant to run your hand around, and useful in catching spills. Three small hand-blown blue glass lights dangle above the counter with sufficient light and a dimmer on the wall to control for mood. Roy argued for four, I insisted on three. The counter has just enough overhang on one side that three leather-topped stools slide neatly underneath, opening the possibility of *three* people sharing a space, reading the paper, eating. Even so, I usually eat in the upstairs office or in the parlor.

Walking through the dining room, I marvel how Roy has beautifully refinished the doors separating it from the front parlor. He's even been able to preserve the original push-in light switches, top for on, bottom for off. I slide open the heavy pocket doors. I am sure that Roy has closed them for effect so that I will be impressed at his work from today and a room transformed.

The room smells earthy, transporting me to days when my father did home projects. Sawdust shavings are swept neatly in a pile to be vacuumed up later. The bed I've brought down from upstairs, the bottom of one of the kid's trundles, is to my left, neatly covered with a drop cloth. I sleep in here most nights now. The piano to the right is one that once belonged to my parents. A fireplace, with its twin above in my bedroom, hasn't worked since the kids were little. There are piles of papers and boxes and Gabler's kitty litter tray in a corner. If you could ignore all this, you would notice that Roy was exactly right about the crown molding. It is the perfect touch. It provides the elegance of a distant era and it brings your eye up to the really wonderful twelve-foot ceilings that give the small room a sense of classic enormity. I am learning that Roy sees what I cannot.

He rings the bell announcing his arrival before walking right in. His signature, "Greetings, greetings," and a quick, "Hello beast," directed at Gabler, come wafting in along with the smell of spices and chilies, meat, and rice. He's a bundle of energy. At 65, it seems he can't sit still for a minute. He quickly eyes his handiwork in the parlor, gives me a wry smile, and heads straightaway to put the bags down in the kitchen as he babbles.

"Hey, how was your day, did it work out as planned, what was Erica's reaction to everything, are you hungry?" These, all separate questions, rush out of his mouth as one run-on sentence before I have a chance to answer any one of them. He continues, "I bought yucca frita with garlic sauce to share, seafood paella in saffron sauce for you, black beans and pork for me. I also bought wine, but see you have water. Should we eat here at the counter or did you want to sit in the parlor and admire the molding?"

He winks after his last sentence. It's all streams of consciousness for him. I haven't said a word since he's walked in and he already has the meal laid out so we can help ourselves. I opt for paper plates versus china and unwrap the plastic forks from the restaurant. I hand him a bottle opener and a wine glass. With his back to me, I pour myself more vodka.

As he bustles about and babbles, lathering butter on the warm Cuban bread, I wonder if he is another Sonia project or an add-on to mine? Sonia was his first client and she has passed him around to others. Roy's business, "Gillis Custom Remodeling: creating homes of grace and classic style" is only a few years old. He used to be one of the chief executives at Morgan Mac Brokerage before it tanked along with the rest of the country's economy. He's amazingly even in demeanor for having weathered the trauma of those days. I suppose the golden parachute he received cushioned the fall and gave him the excuse he needed to leave the industry and his third wife. His soft New England accent comes out when he uses specific words making him sound, in part, like the man in the old Pepperidge Farm commercials I remember. Sonia tells me he's classically trained in music, speaks German fluently, and seems to know his way not only around carpentry, plumbing, fabrics, but also women. He seems far more complicated than a "Roy." He should carry a name like Jonathan, Garret, or some such.

Roy's already sitting at the dining room table, back to the kitchen, when I go and join him facing the parlor, the large windows, and orchids behind me. I utter my first words. "The molding looks great. Thanks." I'm only slightly aware that although he's been working all day, he's taken the time to wash up and comb his hair. I still have manure on my sneakers.

He starts to get up to get more wine, asking me if I want more water, and if I had noticed the work on the first-floor bathroom. I interrupt him as he babbles, telling him, "I'll get it. Let me pour the wine, you got dinner."

I pour my vodka, before his wine. I didn't, of course, notice the bathroom. How did I get by until now with only one bathroom? I toilet trained and raised the two kids with just one bathroom on the second floor. I remember, silently, how we stayed upstairs for weeks on end playing Candyland in the hallway, rushing to the potty at the right moment, until they got it right. The transom skylight in the bathroom illuminated their efforts day and night—an odd, yet comforting feature that I want to make sure we keep intact. Somehow, we got by with the one bath through all the high school parties and after-school hanging out. Yet, Roy's idea of a downstairs bath was a good idea, mostly because of my current sleeping arrangement.

Rejoining him at the table he wants me to consider redoing the two top bedrooms as the next project to be tackled. "Not yet," I say as simply as I can.

"Then next up," he says, "is finishing the front hall. I've taken down the Post-It Notes stuck on the back of the front door so I can scrape and refinish it the same way we did the doors to the parlor. I also assume I can move your bike-turned-coat-rack to the storage in the basement."

There is suddenly no air in the room. I try not to reach across the table and grab his shirt collar when I ask, "Where are the notes from behind the door?"

"Easy, Jes, I put them all together and put them in your office." I can tell he senses the controlled panic in my voice. I excuse myself and take the steps two at a time, round the landing, pass their bedrooms at the top of the stairs, pass the bath, my bedroom, and launch myself into my office at the front of the house. There is a folder neatly labeled "Notes from back of front door." Inside is the stack of stuck together notes. I pull them apart desperate to find it. It's in the middle, a two inch by two inch yellow Post-It-Note. Two words, in pencil, in Adam's childhood handwriting, *Out biking.*

Oh, God, when will the pain stop rushing in? I clutch the note and know Roy's standing behind me waiting for an explanation. Before I can begin, I walk past him, the bath, their bedrooms, the landing. I head down the stairs practically tripping over the bike at the foot of the stairs, on my way to the kitchen. I have the decency to pour him a glass of wine before I pour myself a drink.

I walk back down the hallway toward the front door. "This note stays here. Please." I say, handing him the note, inhaling deeply, and leaning against the bicycle to slip off my sneakers.

Dinner ruined, he puts the note, deferentially, on the back of the door, walks down the hallway to the kitchen, quickly disassembling our meal, and tending to the trash. I pick up my glass in the dining room and move to the parlor bed. Minutes later he joins me. The silence painful, he sits across from me on the piano bench and waits. The vodkas give me the excuse to retell the story that Sonia knows all too well.

"I'm sorry," I begin. "I know it's a small thing. You'd have no way of knowing. It's difficult." I gulp. I inhale. "My story goes like this. I met James while I was in college. He was in medical school and teaching undergrad Biochemistry at Incarnation University near Sarasota. I was his student. I knew there were other students he dated, but I wanted to believe what he saw in me, and what we had, was different.

"If you could ask him, he'd say that I kept him waiting for sex.

When he threatened to move on to someone else because I wouldn't sleep with him, I gave in. I was a virgin. It sounds so stupid to say that now, as if it mattered. But, do you remember? It once mattered. Back then, even the decision to have sex 'out of wedlock' mattered. It mattered who you 'gave' your virginity to. He was considerably older than me, and experienced. I wanted to believe that he knew best."

Roy shifts uncomfortably on the bench. By now I don't care. Once started the story erupts out of me.

"I got pregnant and he insisted on an abortion. He'd set it up with a friend of his from medical school. He wasn't willing to risk his Catholic school fellowship being jeopardized by the indiscretion of an out-of-wedlock pregnancy. It was in an era where abortion was just becoming legal, state by state, across the country. I went, alone, to his friend's office, but couldn't go through with it. I can remember having my left hand on the doorknob and tracing the letters on the door with my right finger, 'Dr. Patrick Tasco, OBGYN.' I turned around and left. Later, I lied, telling James I'd gone through with it but had not used Tasco, using instead a reference from a friend of mine. I then quickly applied for a semester abroad and later gave birth to a son in Norway.

The dark and gloom of Oslo in mid-December matched my mood. When it came time, I left my son behind for adoption. Only Sonia knows that someplace out there I desperately hope there is a Derek or Sven looking for me.

"When I returned, James and I simply picked up where we left off. I never shared the secret that we had a child. Together James and I had a history. Three years later we were married. We were, I thought, pretty happy. There were the typical doctor-wife tensions of my husband always being too busy, working late, and having the hospital staff fawn all over him. I suppose I should have known things were going on, but I thought being invisible was what I deserved. Incarnation is a teaching university and a hospital, so he was able to continue his teaching as he practiced medicine. He developed the plastic surgery specialty at just the right time as sunbaked Florida women wanted to balance youth with the ever-desirable tan. There were many occasions where I suspected his drug-prescribing practices, as well as his own abuse, but there was nothing I could put my finger on."

Listening to myself, I sound bitter. Roy sits in silence twirling a ring on his right hand. I take this as permission to continue.

"We waited a while, before we had children. Cathryn came first and quickly turned into the ebullient and talented 'Ryn.' Then just over two years later, Adam slipped into our lives, as simple a delivery as you could imagine. He was quiet and peaceful. Observant from birth. They inherited the best and the worst of both James's and my characteristics, I suppose. They were also more talented than either of us put together. To me they were pure joy.

"Our marriage lasted 10 years on paper, a lot less if you think of how separate we were. We divorced shortly after Adam's birth. Later, it never seemed to matter that James was nearly $100,000 short in child support or that he had so many women in his life. It was over. I am sure we each have our own versions of this tale. However, I do think we remained a team, both worked at being good and present parents to our kids.

"The divorce was hard on Ryn. She knew at a very sensate level that she missed her dad and his nighttime storytelling, and the comfort of toys left behind in Sarasota. For Adam, it was always more primal. He was just so damn little. I remember before he was born being embarrassed as I waddled through the divorce proceedings awaiting his birth, feeling utterly rejected. Afterwards, my mother moved in with us for a while. That helped so much. I never properly thanked her for getting all of us through. The years just went too fast."

I get up. Roy follows me to the kitchen. There is just a slight lift of his eyebrows as I pour another drink. He declines my offer of more wine. Returning, I try to drag a chair from the dining room into the parlor so he's more comfortable. Ever the gentleman, and motivated I am sure by not wanting to scrape up the floors, he takes the chair from me and carries it in.

"The kids and I, the *three* of us, did all the regular things families do—go on vacations, take music lessons, play sports, have friends over. We had routines and traditions. Each year, on the first crisp autumn night, a night like this one, we'd take blankets and comforters onto the roof of the porch just outside my office window. When the city quieted a bit, we'd listen for the roars of the lions from the zoo. Really. Three miles from the White House, but under a mile from here, we could hear lions. You still can if it's the right type of night and the wind is blowing from the west. We never ceased to marvel that we could hear them.

"School seemed easy for them, inheriting their father's brains, not mine. Our house was the 'drop over after high school spot.' Everyone could walk here from school, and they did. Living here the kids quickly picked up on the languages our neighbors spoke, especially Spanish. It probably set the stage for the work they would choose as adults.

"I can't say there was any huge drama in being a single parent. Even with James living so far away, they saw him quite a bit. I guess it's never enough, though, when you are the 'other' or absent parent. They were always hungry for him. His wealth allowed for him to travel up here quite a bit and he'd usually stay with us. If he wasn't here for holidays, the kids would go there. If he wasn't dating someone at the time, I'd stay with them in our old house on Casey Key.

"Ryn, Adam, and I, the three of us, were about as solid as it gets as a family, both with and without James. We were so honest with each other. They knew, mostly, about my past and I knew more about them than most moms knew of their kids.

"When I was at work, and Adam was out riding his bicycle, he'd leave me the Post-It-Note. It's just always been there, on the back of the door, moved to the front of the door when he was 'out biking.'

It let me know he was out, but that he was coming home." I say this looking toward the front door, assuring myself it's still there.

"For my fiftieth birthday they gave me this." I get up to get my iPod from the kitchen console, enough of an excuse to pour another drink. I don't bother to offer him wine. Handing him the iPod. He looks at me, at it, and flips it over. Inscribed, it says simply, 'For a Rock Star Mom. Love always, Ryn and Adam.'

"Next thing you know, they are all grown up and old enough to be running a small nonprofit their dad helped them establish. The purpose was to help inner-city youth get a solid education and into college and careers."

Resettling on the couch, I simply continue with my story, "We were divorced twenty-three years when rumors of the federal law-suits began to surface. James called me asking for my silence and support. I knew so little of his work at that point I was surprised at the call. He wanted to see if he could get all the legal matters handled without going to court. I had no desire to see him suffer, then, so I was passive for a long time. I grew more concerned when the inves-tigators called. Through just one of their seemingly offhanded ques-tions I put all the pieces together. James had been dispensing con-trolled substances, defrauding health-care benefit programs, and was involved in wire fraud. The investigators wanted to specifically pros-ecute on five cases in which deaths had resulted. James faced life in prison. The enormity of that stunned us all. But it was the wire fraud charge that tipped me off to a greater danger. Ryn and Adam could be implicated and harmed."

For the first time, Roy interrupts me. "Jes, I get it, it's complicated. I don't want to be rude and interrupt, but you don't have to go here."

Ignoring him, I feel my anger rising. "Don't you see? I realized that James had been channeling money through the kids' nonprofit, putting them at the risk of being charged on multiple counts. I wasn't sure how this part of the prosecution would proceed, but my own lawyer made it very clear that Ryn and Adam could take the hit for much of this. At every visceral level possible I was set to protect them. Protect them from prosecution and protect them from the knowledge that their father had thrown them under the proverbial bus. He was more than willing, in my opinion, to pass on his own guilt to them.

"I really believe the kids were oblivious to all of it, as kids should be, about some parts of their parents' lives. I wanted more than anything to figure out a way that I could both unravel the kids from James's situation and to keep them from knowing that the whole basis for their nonprofit was a fraud. I was working on this when James told them that I was going to be deposed in the case. The kids called to ask me not to testify, as if that could happen once, I was subpoenaed. They called me from Adam's house in Ohio and asked what I knew, and if I could tell half-truths if it was bad. I told them I couldn't. They said they loved their dad and didn't want to lose him.

"I said that I thought it was going to be a really hard trial and that they should hold off on coming to the depositions. I told them that I was going to tell what I knew, the illegal abortions dating back to the mid-'70s and the drugs, and the other practices. I didn't want them involved. Ryn railed at me first. She wanted to know how I could hurt her dad, a man she so admired. She wanted to know if I was doing this to get revenge on her dad for making me abort my baby. "Maybe your dead baby is more important than your live daughter," she wailed.

With that, I began to feel the flood of bile in my throat and my fists clench.

"Adam took no time going for the jugular either. He wanted to know if this was all revenge for the divorce. Both of them asked me to stay out of it. They were coming to counter my testimony. They would prove that their dad was innocent.

"They decided to drive through the night in order to make the depositions. They called me as they came through the Allegheny

Mountains to ask me again not to testify. I could hear the rain pounding the windshield. I said, without elaborating, that I had no choice but to testify. I wanted them to just concentrate on their driving. I hung up with an, 'I love you and be safe.'

"They must have called James right after that. Ryn assured him that they were driving fast, even with the huge storms all night. They assured him that they loved him, that they would be there on time to watch their mother be deposed. A gigantic thunderclap interrupted their call.

"James loves to remind me of this conversation and that he was on the phone with them when Ryn ran off the road hitting the tree. As if his own pain could add to my own. Adam died instantly. Ryn took a little longer.

"I didn't testify, but James was still convicted on all counts. He was sentenced to twenty-five years to life imprisonment. It didn't matter. I had my own sentence to deal with, life without my children."

Finished, I look up at Roy.

"*Out biking,* almost four years, he's not coming back."

Silence. The air is heavy.

Roy's face is pained. He's still holding the iPod, staring at it and then at me. He moves to the bed-turned couch and puts his hand over one of my shaking, balled-up fists. I think he is going to lean in to hold me.

"Stop. You need to go. Please." I said. Again, "You need to go."

"I am going to go, Jes. I'm not sure what you were thinking. I just wanted to say I am sorry and thank you."

I'm relieved to hear the door shut as he leaves, more secure in knowing that Adam's note is on it. I don't even check if Roy locked the door as I pass it and move the bicycle away from blocking the hall closet. On the bottom of the closet is a wooden chest I've taken from my parents' house. Even to me it looks like a coffin. On top there is a thick sealed envelope. Inside, I gently take out the baby clothes and the few pieces of their artwork. I flip through the crewel work muslin squares that Ryn and I started as part of a quilt project in Girl Scouts. We had promised to make the quilt together, but we ran out of time.

Tomorrow really isn't promised, I think as I feel the panic rising in me.

I'm digging now. I know what's at the bottom of the box, just on top of their birth certificates. Two separate small pieces of paper with their tiny, paint-dipped three-year-old handprints. Adam's is red, Ryn's blue. Their names are written under their hands, protected forever by clear contact paper. On the back of each print their pre-school teacher has cataloged how many times they were line leaders, or did the weather, or helped with snack and such. There is a notation for "upstairs" and "downstairs" with counting hash marks next to them. I have no memory of what this can mean, and I can no longer ask. I trace their handprints over and over. I lay my hands over theirs, and then hold them to my heart.

Sonia needs to be less observant, no, I didn't trace the handprints earlier today. Maybe she just needs to let me alone. We're supposed to be friends. I'm not one of her projects! I carry my children's hands with me, returning to the parlor and lifting the iPod from where Roy left it. In the kitchen I pour vodka, tuck their handprints under the iPod console, slip the iPod into the console and hit play. I have the presence of mind to check that the door is locked as music fills the house. Roy has taken care that I am safe, locking the door behind him. I reach to pick up the obese Gabler. At least for a while tonight she will be happy to exchange the warmth of the radiator for that of my body. I don't even bother to pull back the drop cloth as I slump to the bed, trying to stifle the wail rising in my throat.

yesterday: forty acres and a mule

When I wake, the bitter taste of last night's drinking coats my mouth. Knowing that I don't remember all that was said the night before I make my usual mental note that I should probably drink less. Gabler is calling me to the kitchen for her breakfast. Noisy cat. While I wait for the coffee to brew, I see the handprints, unremembered from last night. Damn.

Turning from this reality, I try to gather my thoughts and experiences from yesterday. I want to catalogue them as closely as I can remember. I'm not yet ready to give Sonia her due, but I know her well enough that there is always wisdom in her words. She knows me well enough that she's raised the challenge of writing. It's my trigger. I love the feel of the words flowing through my fingers on to the keyboard, appearing on the screen. Creating a story where there was nothing. Always surprising myself at the result.

I give each of the handprints a quick kiss and tuck them under my iPod, grab my coffee, take the stairs to my snug little office, and begin. Closing my eyes, inhaling, I try to be grateful and at peace. Letting the good parts of yesterday flow through me again.

Title? Sonia's Project? No. Who is the audience for what I will write? Unknown. I decide to write about yesterday in the present tense. I take a moment waiting for how the day will unfold on my screen. How to begin? At the beginning! Deep breath and my fingers glide:

It is an October, picture-post-card-perfect Washington, DC, morning. I come bounding, or what I consider "bounding" these days, down the steps of my Hobart Street house. Sonia is leaning against the car waiting. The sky is finally blue again, after months of summer gray. The air is crisp. Sonia utters an equally crisp, "Why is it that you are dressed like that? How many times do I have to tell you, Jessica Barnet, when you are dead, they will not care what you said, they will remember only how you looked!"

"Good morning to you, too," I say, handing her a cup of coffee for the quick trip to Anacostia, then down to Martinsburg. Sonia, many, many years my junior, driven, flamboyant, lovely. She's come out of her way to pick me up. It's 7 o'clock am. She has already talked to the people in Martinsburg, checking on the details of the day. She's printed off some materials for me to review, and run three miles on the treadmill, undoubtedly laying out plans for her next academic article as she ran.

Even with the convertible top down, she's arrived with every hair in place. She has her hair tightly wrapped in an Evita Peron-like bun at the nape of her neck, yellow and black shirt, black designer jeans, black boots with yellow laces, and new white work gloves with yellow trim tucked neatly into her right rear pocket.

It doesn't matter that our goal for the day is to harvest an acre of land. Sonia is all about making a statement. When she speaks, she is strong and decisive. Her words, as well as her gestures, cut the air, ensuring that inflection, body language, and message are all in concert. She has the same Latina charisma I imagine in her fellow countrywoman Evita.

By contrast, I am dressed in black sweatpants with a hole at the knee, sneakers, a T-shirt with freshly splattered coffee, and a university sweatshirt tied around my waist. I look pasty and pale next to Sonia in both skin tone and attire. My accomplishments this morning entail making the coffee and leaving a scribbled note for Roy, asking him to hold off on the crown molding for the front parlor. He's frustrated, I think, at the slow pace of the renovation. But the molding is just one more decision I can put off until tomorrow.

Erica is in the back seat of the Saab listening to music, the ever-present camera at her side. She gives me an "it's too early" sullen nod but she will come alive by mid-morning, a replica of her mother's animation in every respect. Sonia was very young and unmarried when she gave birth to Erica. It was the last unplanned thing she did.

Sonia and I are unlikely friends from graduate school. She is way ahead of me in career plan and accomplishment. She's already put a few years behind her as Doctor Sonia Cortez. She teaches at Martinsburg Community College in Calvert County, Maryland. She is also Dean of Special Projects—official and otherwise. Each of these projects is geared, in part, for the greater good and, in part, for the good of Sonia. She is, like I said, all about making statements. The energy and the clarity of purpose she brings with her are among the many skills that I believe will eventually position her for national office.

I assume I am one of her special projects, for which I am, begrudgingly, grateful. You can understand why she's focused on me. Ever since the trial, it's been too easy for me to crawl under a rock. My dissertation, "Mitochondrial DNA: Our Mother's Story," still sits in the same spot it did a few years ago. I know I am selling the University and my students short—coasting on old lectures. I've quit almost all activity, avoid almost everyone, and I'm already thinking of cancelling the trip I just booked to go on an African safari.

It's more than the added pounds of the past years that make me sluggish and slow to act.

Today, I am convinced Sonia is weaving me neatly into a plan I don't yet understand. It's part of her "get Jessica out and about program." She's mixing that with a small army of college students she's gathered to bring inner-city youth into new experiences. First, we head into Southeast DC, along Pennsylvania Avenue, decidedly away from The White House. Passing the aging RFK stadium, former home of the Washington Redskins, former home to the Nationals, and current home to the DC United soccer team, we cross the river, unassumingly, into Anacostia. It is one of the poorest, primarily African American, and most historically interesting parts of the nation's capital. Here, Fredrick Douglass and Booker T. Washington and the Black elite of the 1890s made their homes.

At Anacostia High School we meet up with a "cheese bus" and thirty brown- and black-skinned high school students. The kids hate these buses. They know the difference between the buses with air conditioning and Wi-Fi for the kids from the affluent Upper Northwest, DC or Potomac, Maryland and the busses waiting for them today. These school buses are old, the color of Velveeta cheese. Sonia has selected them for a reason—to remind Erica that it's not about the Saab or the Mercedes. Sometimes life is a cheese bus. It gets you there all the same.

We ride the short thirty-two miles down Pennsylvania Avenue away from Washington and down Rt. 4, across the District line into Maryland. Martinsburg is literally on the rim of the nation's capital, and worlds away from it.

It's an odd thing, I think, how the city evaporates so quickly in every direction from Capitol Hill. Within an hour, sometimes less, you can be in the horse country of Virginia or the tobacco and farming fields of Maryland. As the nation's capital falls behind us, other things too fall away from the group—the high school students are showing less posturing bravado and the college students are talking in more relaxed tones. Erica, finally awake, is multitasking, chatting about greenhouse emissions and the effects of farm runoff on the watershed, intermittently snapping photographs, and checking out the high school boys. All the while her hands are articulating through the air exactly like her mother's.

Our destination is a series of buildings and farmland nestled in Martinsburg, part of Calvert County, Maryland, just north of Calvert Cliffs. Sonia is giving me the background. Established as an independent parcel in 1868, the land was given to Tobias and Delores Thatcher, newly freed slaves, by relatives of Oliver Kelley and his niece Caroline Hall. The gift fell nicely in line with Kelley's desire to support the establishment of The National Grange Project.

Sonia is surprised by my blank face, which gives away that I know nothing of this project. Like many people who come to the US from other countries, she knows more US history than those of us who were born here. The Grange came into existence, she says, not-so-patiently, and in footnote-like fashion, following the American Civil War in an effort to unite citizens in improving the economic and social position of the nation's farm population. She precisely paints the picture of a group of seven men, assisted by Caroline Hall, sitting around a plain wooden table planning to create an organization that would become a vital force in American democracy. Sonia, as in all things, is adamant that these first "grangers" were people of vision, with faith in God, their fellow man, and the future. Today, over a hundred years later, The National Grange building still sits across the street from the White House and is the only privately held building on the block.

"I am surprised you do not know of this," Sonia clips and continues. "Today we are going to a spot where the earliest grangers coupled their vision with a gift to the Thatchers. It was part of the legislated '40 acres and a mule' promised to freed African slaves giving them the opportunity to plow and own their own land.

"You know, I assume, that that legislation was ill-fated, seldom enacted, and quickly repealed. In fact, it never applied in Maryland, but Tobias and Delores benefitted from the spirit of it and they agreed with 'Mr. Oliver's' and 'Miss Caroline's' intent for the National Grange Project. They decided to call their exactly forty acres, simply, 'The Grange' and they named the mule Oliver. I am not sure if this was out of respect for Oliver Kelly, or because Tobias and Delores recognized his stubbornness. Regardless, from that day to this, the land has stayed in the Thatcher family.

"When we get to The Grange you will see the rolling hills, the outbuildings, and the edge of the cliffs leading to the sharp drop to Chesapeake Bay. The story goes that because of a soft spot in that first Tobias' heart, and the firmness of his Last Will and Testament, there has been, and always will be, a mule named Oliver at The Grange. There has also always been a Tobias.

The man you will meet today is the great grandson of the first Tobias. His daughter, and her partner CC, take care of much of the operation now, but, as you will see, it is very much a place where new beginnings take shape.

"Tia and CC are an interesting pair. I do not think that Tobias imagined 'white' or 'being a woman' on the list of attributes for his only daughter's partner. At close to ninety, however, he is happy to turn over the reins and see The Grange slip into a new set of hands. He's come to accept Tia as she is, and CC as she is. In so doing Tobias has had to accept that the Thatcher bloodline on this land is coming to an end."

At this point, the bus takes a jarring left turn off of Rt. 4 and makes its lumbering climb up the gravel drive. Comments from the students pull Sonia away from my introduction to The Grange. The high school students' comments of "there's nothing here" and "how come it's so empty" are sandwiched between wide-eyed anticipation and "what do people do out here."

It's evident, in an instant, how far we are from what we know.

As we come off the bus we are met by Tia—a pretty, middle-aged, round, coffee-colored woman. She's patient as she waits for us to get off the bus, and patient still until we are quiet enough to be welcomed. She and CC work in unison. They've done these harvests for years. We are given our mission—to harvest one acre of land surrounded by buckwheat. The students laugh at the word *buckwheat*, their only association being with the wild-haired, ebony-hewed character from *The Little Rascals*. The plant surrounding our designated acre couldn't be more of a contrast to that—two feet high, deep green foliage, delicate white flowers.

Tia waits for the students to settle down again and points out that there are adjacent acres, but the goal is to have us work this one acre, reap the harvest, and package the cornucopia of our work into baskets and boxes for donation to the Anacostia Food Pantry.

Students who have come more appropriately dressed for the mall than the acreage are quickly and effortlessly refitted with work boots, overalls, gloves, and the like. Sounds of "But there's nothing here!" fall way to sounds of amazement as huge carrots and softball-sized beets are pulled from the warm earth. Rows of beans of a hundred hues, now dried on their stalks and vines, are pulled, filling buckets. Car tires, stacked tall to protect the peppers from the wind and to keep in the heat, are carefully dismantled and the last of the crop finds its way to baskets.

Hundreds of garlic bulbs are pulled from the drying shed and the buckwheat is threshed for later milling. There is laughing and singing, along with groans, as the weight of our efforts is pulled to the edge of the field.

Erica is everywhere, taking pictures.

We break for a lunch of vegetarian chili made entirely from this land's harvest. Tomatoes, beans, corn, peppers, and spiciness ground from the pepper seeds. The students are so hungry they quickly stop asking why there isn't meat in the meal. The warmth of the chili is most welcome. Once we have stopped working, we feel the nip of the October air settle in. One by one we notice a golf cart careening over the fields headed straight for us.

Tia announces that Tobias will be joining us for lunch. At eighty-seven, he is no longer able to drive a car, but the golf cart suits its purpose. He uses a cane to get from the cart to some bales of hay that lie about. Despite a sense of age, he looks strong and healthy, as if the cane is only a temporary aid.

"Welcome to this place," he says, with a gentle timbre in his voice. There is something in his presence that undemandingly demands respect. The students give him their attention. I take in the beauty of the darkness of his skin and the dry, work-wornness of his hands. He continues.

"My father, and his father, and his father before him, and others before them, farmed this land. The first land records about this place go back to 1670, a time before presidents, a time before there was a United States." He waits to see if the enormity of that sinks in on his audience. "I own it now, although I am not really sure you can own a place like this. Certainly, the Native Americans who walked these fields before 1670 knew that," he says with a chuckle. "I've always thought we are more like caregivers, tending the earth while we walk it. This land will be here long after we are all buried under it. For over two-hundred years now this land has been worked by Blacks both slave and free. I'm honored you're here with me today—welcome."

As he talks his eyes run over the land as gently as if he was caressing it. "There's a lot of history here. It's amazing what can result from a single gift. My great-grandparents were given the original parcel of forty acres of land. Over time my grandfather and then my father bought what used to be the plantation house and an additional thousand acres or so. We lease a lot of the land out, but somehow, it's still all connected. My father did well by the work of those before him and did well on his own. He made sure we all got an education and made sure we all knew the value of hard work."

He readjusts himself on the hay bale and continues pointing to a house in the distance. "The original plantation house over there is the last of its kind in Maryland. You might not notice it, so I'm going to point it out. The house is laid out in the shape of a cross. The architects wanted it to symbolize that here we are committed to the land and to God. The house has got a porch, turret towers at the four corners, and a rear staircase. I always liked a house with a rear staircase.

"You probably didn't notice the old store on the corner of Route 4, just before you turn up the drive. We run that, too, and try to keep it both efficient and what CC here would call 'charming.' We're also building a new house over there for the ladies. You'll meet them later. The new place will be kind to the environment and made, in fact, out of straw bales like you are sitting on. Before you leave you should go over and see the progress we're making. When it's done you won't know that the frame is grown from these fields and covered in stucco made from our clay.

"Despite the history of the place, we are not really so much about preserving the past as we are about looking at the future. I say this so that when you see my mule Oliver over there at the milling post, you will understand that it's not about being quaint or historic. Oliver can do the job. It saves us using electricity or gas. Come spring he'll be out here helping plow the earth. There are pigs and chickens over by the main barn, and llamas and sheep by the smaller outbuildings. We've got bees over on the far side of the fields. They seem to be a simple insect, but they are endangered and that's a bad thing for all of us.

"The buckwheat that surrounds this field has a job to do. It pours nutrients into the soil, keeps the weeds down, and serves as a nectar, a food, for those important bees.

"We call all of this, together, The Grange, partly because of a man's idea for a project, but mostly because my great-grandfather liked that the definition of the word "grange" is more than just a farm. A grange is a farm but also the residence and outbuildings of a 'gentleman farmer. A 'gentleman farmer'" he repeats with emphasis. "Not bad for a freed colored man. But I've gotten to talking too long. We still have work to do today. So, I'm honored you came. Thank you for coming. I'm glad you took the time."

As Tobias heads back across the fields in his cart, I quickly make the timeline matches of The Grange and my Hobart Street, Mt. Pleasant home. Both can tie their development to the Calvert and Carroll families and their status as "Lords Baltimore." It struck me as funny that as The Grange was getting started in the mid- to late-1600s not only had my area of DC not been developed yet but Washington, DC, itself would not be created until 1791. Even at that, my neighborhood, just three miles from The White House, wouldn't see what we would call "development" until the 1900s.

When Tobias is out of sight, I join in the work of boxing the vegetables, raking back our acre, spreading it with manure, and gently putting it to sleep for the winter. As we finish up, we carry the baskets of beans to the barn. I instantly love the feel of the place as we cross the threshold. The original planking has been worn by many a man and mule. Inside there is a modernized space powered by wind and sun. Twenty car batteries are nestled in the wall, taking nature's charge, and passing it to lights and fans. Inside there are long wooden tables in a work area. At the far end, behind glass, there is space for Oliver.

On each of five tables there are large wooden bowls put out for our use as we shuck and sort the beans. At four of the tables there is a woman serving as a table host to the students. They seem ancient to the students, and very old to me. They must range in age from seventy to one hundred.

This meeting, too, is part of Sonia's planning. Over the casual activity of detaching beans from their pods, we will bridge lifetimes.

As the students spread out, I go to one of the tables that seems slow to fill. I am assuming some of the students might be avoiding it due to the large Rottweiler at the old woman's side. She seems cold, detached, solid, like the barn beams. Not the kind of woman that is going to gush over or work to engage her audience. As I sit, she is already responding to a student's blurted out question, "What are all you old people doing here?" I think the question comes out rudely, but in fact there has not been one bit of problem with the kids all day. I'd like to think that I am unprejudiced, that I would not have assumed the worst of these kids, but I guess, at least in part, that isn't true. They've worked hard all day, laughed, been so open to this very different experience, and now, with many of them raised by their own grandparents, they are probably more comfortable than I am in sitting with these old women.

Our table host begins. "You are probably-*a* wondering who we are. We all-*a* got here from different places and for different-*a* reasons," she is saying. Looking around the room, she takes in each table and continues, "You should not-*a* leave here today without getting to know us a bit. We have not always been old, and each of us has a story. Our host then nods her head toward Tia, CC, and Tobias standing by one of the tables. "Tia and CC—her given name is Cynthia, you've already met. Tia owns this place with her father. She's-*a* fifty years old. Black, but more in coloring like her mother, I think. CC is a nurse by training. She and-*a* Tia met while on an eco-tour in Costa Rica twenty years ago. The two of them quickly reordered their lives and-*a* made the commitment to live, as openly as they could, together. CC is Irish and about-*a* sixty-five, I think."

Our host continues, "Jan Kiley, the Black woman over there, wearing the Bob Marley sweatshirt, is seventy-seven. She is Tobias' wife's cousin. You can't see all her tattoos, but they are worth seeing.

She and Tobias' wife Joan went to Howard University together. Joan, she died-*a* last month."

I pull my eyes from Jan Kiley with her arms alternately flailing the air and resting akimbo at her hips. In our table host I hear the hint of an Italian accent. I'm distracted by the accent for a moment as I'm pulled to thoughts of my own mother. I pick up the cadence of her speech and the insertion of the *"a"* in front, and sometimes behind, some of the words.

She continues, "The white-*a* woman over there is Deirdre Stalzer. She's eighty. The other white woman over there is Margaret Mary Wright, she used to be a nun. She's older than Tobias by some years. In-*a* her nineties. She's smart as a whip and so is her tongue. It's never been clear to me how she got here, but it's probably worth asking.

"The only other of us who lives-*a* here is Sydney Blackstone. She's come here before her time. She's in her late forties. She has cancer and isn't feeling well tonight. We'll see how that turns out, by the by. The doctor who bought Tobias' medical practice thought it would be good for her to a recover here. Yes, that's right, Tobias is a doctor," she responds to their shocked faces. "He doesn't need to announce it to people. He'd think it amusing to see your surprised faces. He met Tia's mom, Joan, when she was a freshman at Howard University. He was already graduated and pre-med. He's taking her death pretty hard.

"Several years ago, Deirdre approached Joan with the idea of opening The Grange for others to live. She liked the idea and a plan for expanding the work of their farm to include the opportunity for residents to live together in community. Margaret Mary came next, then me, Sydney, then Jan. I think we all believe a place like this would surpass our spending the rest of our days in a nursing home or with the fear of winding up in one.

"Some of us have children we are close to, but most don't expect to, or want, to spend their time with them.

"I was-*a* chairman of the board of the City Council when the application for permission to zone this spot for communal living came up. I was about to retire and had already determined that living in such a place as this would be more interesting than countless rounds of bingo, old movies, and armchair aerobics. It didn't appeal to me to live a life where someone else determined that I needed a low-salt diet or no alcohol. Besides, I didn't-*a* want to live so alone anymore. The original entrance requirement for residents was simply a desire to stay active and to contribute to the world, and mostly to not let ourselves be bored to death. Finances helped, but that wasn't an up-front requirement. I recused myself from the vote but lobbied for it. The motion passed easily.

"We are very old. Separately, we have-*a* lived a sum of five hundred and eighty years. My-*a* name is Elizabeth Jacobi, I am eighty and this," she says, leaning heavily into the Rottweiler, "is Pavarotti. He's about the most loyal thing I've known in life and he's a huge help to me now." The dog leans into her and takes his black tongue and wipes it across her face.

Elizabeth looks directly and intently at me. "As I said, we are old. This means we have good stories if you are willing to listen." I'm unnerved, somehow, by her look and turn away to take in the activity at the other tables. "Whatda ya hafta do," I hear her say behind me.

The conversations continue, table to table, as students work to separate bean from pod. I imagine that each of the women is telling some version of Elizabeth's story as the beans are shucked and sorted. Bowls fill. My own hands slow as I run them through the colors—this bowl is filled with beans that resemble Shamu the whale or the Asian symbols for Ying and Yang, this one with beans that are half maroon and half white, these others are tiny and as black as ebony, and these are the color of polished walnut. Some will be stored for food, some will live again and be replanted to produce a new generation of beans for next year's harvest, and some make their way into my pocket.

We are done. The food is all catalogued and weighed. The empty pods are swept from the floor and gathered for the pigs. Everything that fits under the seats on the bus goes to the Anacostia Food Pantry for the needy, and will, undoubtedly come to some of these students' tables though that organization. Everything else goes to the store parking lot at the corner of Rt. 4 and The Grange road. There, those in want and need can take it freely. "It's about a single gift," Tia says as we get ready to leave.

There is one final ritual, however. CC asks for us to reassemble in the barn. I notice her sneakers as she walks us up the gentle slope of a staircase to the barn loft—rainbow laces, pink-soled bottoms.

In the loft, the light shifts. Each wall is covered with a kaleidoscope of palm prints and illuminated by gallery-quality track lighting. Hands— different sizes, different colors—hundreds of them. CC explains that years ago she and her nephew traveled to Denmark and had a layover in Reykjavik, Iceland. It was a long layover in a small airport. A sign in the lounge invited journeyers to leave a comment or make a draw- ing on the wall. Her young nephew noticed that many people had traced their hands. The two of them overlapped their four hands, traced each one, and wrote the date. Hoping that those four prints still mark the airport wall, CC brought the same idea to The Grange. She solemnly invites each of us to leave our mark upon this place, as we had upon the land, and as we must upon the earth. I watch as boisterous voices become hushed, and as hands are gently dipped into bins of wet paint and then reverently touch to the walls.

Tobias, now standing at the bus door, silently nods his good-bye to each of as we leave.

That's it. Six pages done. I make a note to flesh out a character sketch of those I met today, or maybe it will just unfold and I will get details over time. Yesterday was a lot to take in.

Rolling my neck, I just breathe. Sonia *might* be right. Not right about me hiding, that's ridiculous, but there is something to write about here.

first, we walk

Two days later Sonia erupts into my parlor. I haven't bothered to change clothes or shower since she admonished be
for hiding. It's not important to me. I've got hours before I
have to be at the University, and at least a few hours before Roy
shows up to work.

Clearly, she's disgusted that her plan hasn't instantly taken hold of me,
somehow transforming me into what she thinks I should be. "Jessica,"
she says, emphasizing all three syllables distinctly, "Jess-cee-ka."

I raise my eyebrows, not wanting to give her the satisfaction that
I may, indeed, have taken her suggestion and written. I can feel her
chastisement of me rising anew and have the distinct sense that she
wants to add my middle name to the statement.

"Jessica, I have told you, *this is enough*." She is close to irate.

"There are many days of *Washington Posts* to trip over on your porch. It is amazing the neighbors have not called the police to check to see if you are still alive. Today, you will do several things. First, go take a shower and put these on. We are going walking and I am not going with you the way you look." With that she hands me a Nordstrom's bag filled with fully color-coordinated sports bra, panties, socks, and a running outfit with appropriately coordinated shoes.

"Sonia," I begin, "I can't have you do this. I'm fine. Look, I'll grab my sneakers and we can walk if that makes you happy."

"Jess-cee-ka Ma-rie." I actually giggle at the sound of this, but I now know she's serious. "You will shower and put these on. Perhaps, my dear, if you begin to look like you can crawl out of this prison it will happen." With that she moves to my kitchen to make coffee.

After showering and drying my hair I don my new outfit and feel ridiculous. The bright colors and yoga-like running outfit only exaggerate my weight gain. I feel overly coordinated in blues and grays and pinks, an over-stuffed version of Sonia. There is little arguing with Sonia at this point, or actually any point. I head downstairs. She has Roy's marble countertop set with placemats and china. Sliced fruit has magically appeared on the plates and *The Washington Post*, sans plastic wrapper, is lying there, inviting me to read.

"Sonia," I try to protest, but can't help laughing. "You really are a stubborn bitch you know."

"Do not speak to me right now," she says, showing me her palm. "I am reading the paper."

We sit in silence as we each read through several sections of the paper, making occasional asides about government, both local and federal. Here, in DC, they are the same. After a while, she says "Crossword?" with a fun, yet manipulative grin.

"Don't push it, Sonia. If you came here to walk, let's do it." I counter.

"Sudoku?" She laughs and questions me, rising from her stool.

"This is good." Sonia states. "Today we walk. You look very good.

Remember what I said, when you are dead no one will remember what you said, they will remember only how you looked!"

As the two of us begin our walk we talk about the work on the townhouse. She asks about Roy, and if I am happy with his work, and what I think of him. I love the work but have little opinion of him other than his quirky preciseness and ever up-beat attitude. Although he has been at my home for months, we have never really talked beyond the other night. I am honest, as I always am with Sonia, telling her that I shared the story with Roy and that I regret it. Vodka, stress, embarrassment, devastation—my theme. I should have left well enough alone and let him draw his own conclusions at my panic.

I discern a slight cringe and a small disapproving shake of her head, but Sonia doesn't really seem to be listening. I marvel anew at the ease with which she seems to do *everything*. She's chatting away about her work, a man she's thinking of asking out down at the community college, and her work at The Grange. She's talking about Erica and being on schedule for getting herself emotionally prepared to have Erica gone and off to college in a few years. She wonders aloud what it will be like not to see her daughter all the time.

I notice she catches herself here.

"There's really no way to be prepared for them to be gone, you know," I tell her.

I am surprised at her barbed reply. "Jessica, apparently you do not remember that I know your *whole* story. I know what you felt in losing Ryn and Adam. However," she states, waving her finger from high to low, "I am someone who believes that in large measure we can write our own stories, change the endings.

"That is why I demand your help at The Grange. This is a very fascinating place to me. There is something very magical there. We have this historical place and we have these interesting people. I believe we have this unique opportunity to make a difference. I feel as if this concept, the women living together, is there, but, also, not quite focused. More needs to happen. I think they need your help."

Sonia is almost yelling at me, pressing some point she feels is lost on me. "Jessica, I do not understand why you do not see what I see. These women each have a story to tell, I can feel it. You have a deep interest in women's history. You should be hungry to hear their stories. They are old but not in the way I thought being old would be. They are vibrant. Jan is just, what is the word that you use? "A hoot." She defies anything I thought of as what growing old looks like. Margaret Mary is a master quilter—you have your unfinished squares. Elizabeth has something brewing, something unspoken, but I can't put my finger on it. Deirdre and Sydney, I don't know well but they are part of this puzzle.

"Then there is Tia and CC, they've been doing this harvest project for a few years, and I've seen how it changes people. There's probably grant money there, and stories to tell. Tobias and Tia have the land and the store. They are struggling with how best to coordinate all the many changes that are going on there. You are struggling. It is clear to me. These are all dots and you, the disconnected Jessica, must connect them."

"Sonia," I manage to fit in before she continues. "No one could ever accuse you of being oblique."

"I am asking you to do just two things. First, I have left for you an envelope from Erica. It is under this morning's paper. After you look at this, call Tia and set up a meeting with Tobias. He will have to give you permission to allow us to interfere." I smile at her choice of words. "Do not think you need to know where this is going before you start, Jessica. This trip will end where this trip ends, but it cannot begin unless you are willing to start."

When I don't respond, she's exasperated. "I am too tired of you, Jessica."

We've walked through tree-lined streets, crisp with fall air, past closely parked cars, our feet rustling through fallen leaves, yet the only sense and sound that I am aware of is that of the pit I feel in my stomach, and the sound of Sonia's last words echoing in my head—she's *too* tired of me.

We continue in silence for quite a bit, something I imagine is quite hard for Sonia. We turn onto Columbia Road for the last leg home and we fall, naturally, into the small talk of friends. We lament that The Omega restaurant is no longer on the corner. Best black beans, ever. We lapse into nerdy professor talk about demographics and how the neighborhood, Latino for decades, has become more diverse even in its "Latino-ness." We are enveloped in the smells coming from the restaurants as they prepare to open for lunch. There's a peace to this, a natural rhythm.

Later, with Sonia gone, the house smells, welcomingly, of coffee. Pouring another cup, I slide the envelope out from under *The Post* and join Gabler on the sun-drenched window seat. I'm used to reading Erica's papers for school and anticipate it. Her witty writing always needs editing. She is the victim of "texting" and the verbal shortcuts of her generation. But what greets me instead of a paper for school are photographs. Surprisingly, they are in black and white, a stark contrast to the colorful Erica. There is nothing stark about the photos, though. They are deep and inviting. Rich in tone. They make you want to trace your fingers around the edges and in the shapes. This young woman has captured the feel of our recent day together with an eye I didn't anticipate. There are silhouettes of arms holding up huge carrots against the fall sky. A student's hands splayed in the rich earth, dirt under the nails. Shadows on walls. Tobias' feet and the foot of his cane. Young hands caressing bowls of beans. Steam coming off bowls of chili. Mud- and manure- covered bus tires.

And the women!

CC's swollen-legged, sneakered-feet, ascending the staircase to the loft. Jan's head thrown back, in profile, in a howl of a laugh. One of the other women's arms, all hangy-down-upper-arm skin, around a much taller shoulder. A set of eyes creased and crinkled. Breasts, large and heavy. Elizabeth's huge hand tugging on Pavarotti's ear.

One of the photos makes me catch my breath. It's of a single empty chair with two unmatched hands gripping the back of it. One, clearly, Tobias' hand, I recognize the age and gracefulness of it. The other, I assume, is Tia's. The focus is so sharp you can see tension in the photo. My mind leaps, trying to fill in a blank. This chair was filled by someone else at previous harvests. Surely, Tobias' wife, Tia's mom, had sat here. What was her name?

What had Elizabeth said? Tobias' wife had died just last month. Tobias and Tia, tense, uneasy, not wanting to take her chair. In this frame Erica has brilliantly left space for her lost image. Erica, too, sees what I do not. I stare at the blank space left by a woman I will never meet. I imagine she invisibly greets me, and the name comes to me. "Joan."

I flip quickly through the rest of the pack and there's not one photo of a whole person, and no full-on faces. Fascinating.

Picking up Gabler I take her and the photographs to the dining room table. Spreading the photos, I look to see what's there, what is missing, what is the story that is being told. I ask myself, "OK, Erica and Sonia, what do you see that I do not?"

I make a few notes on the back of papers left by Roy.

Sonia has pushed two of my big buttons. First, she said she needed my help. I owe her much, and the thought that she is "too tired of me" is painful. Secondly, she has tempted me by making this a women's history project, a journey of discovery. It's been way too long since I had a hunger for that.

Gabler circles and makes herself comfortable among the photos and Roy's papers. I go to the phone to call Tia.

joan

On my way to meet Tobias I try to frame my still unclear thinking. I want to appear clear-headed and purposeful when we meet. Sonia says they need help. Help doing what? I know I'm supposed to convince him to let me and Sonia "intrude." But intrude to do what? To allow me to ask questions, write about his land, interview the women, and write about them? Document their stories? It's not a very focused request.

Maybe I should first try to build common ground with Tobias as a man of science. As a doctor he would probably "get" my obsession with DNA, but it isn't exactly a conversation starter.

My "nerdy DNA thing," as Erica calls it, began in undergrad school when DNA really began to be understood. My particular interest began when they discovered that a part of each woman's DNA, the mitochondrial DNA (mtDNA), is passed from a mother to her offspring equally, male and female, sons, and daughters. However, only the daughters carry that same DNA successfully into reproduction and the next generation. Her son's mitochondrial DNA does not make it through fertilization, and so her genetic footprint does not carry to her son's offspring. Meanwhile, her daughter carries her mtDNA to her daughters, and her granddaughters carry to their daughters in an unbroken chain.

Most surprisingly, regardless of the size of our world, or our diverse cultures, experiences and preferences, scientists have determined that there are only nine differences in this mitochondrial DNA across all of humankind. They can reach back to pre-history and can link us to our nine ancestral mothers. Nine, just nine. Passed to us only by our mothers, and carried forward only by our daughters, I can't help but to believe our stories, like our genetic helix, are closely intertwined. There's even talk in the research of one day being able to identify a "Mitochondrial Eve" by being able to trace the mtDNA back to the origin of humanity. It doesn't matter to me whether this happened by the hand of God or pure evolution, I love the idea of a Mitochondrial Eve.

What I wonder most about is who were those nine women, what are their stories? Why their DNA? Did they have any understanding of their uniqueness? I guess it is a "nerdy DNA thing," as Erica tells me. But, with such a small number, how closely related must we be, as women, to almost anyone we meet?

Despite its awesomeness, I doubt DNA is the place to start with Tobias. History, then. I would love to learn more about The Grange and get a sense of place. And the aged women, they will have stories! I can ask for stories of the war, civil rights, and immigration, of Ellis Island, and of a whole history of the women's movement—their breaking of glass ceilings, or they're not caring to do so. I'd love their perspective on how America has changed. Maybe I can capture what they would want to leave behind for the next generation. Thinking of my own mother, maybe I could capture the conversations they wish they had had with their own mothers, or those they would want to have with their children. This approach feels more comfortable.

Throughout the hour or so drive, I retrace the ride down Route 4 and, predictably, as DC falls behind me, I reconnect with the land. I've made the trip down to this part of Maryland so many times. Although greatly changed from even a few years ago, the shopping malls and housing developments haven't quite erased Maryland's rich history as a major tobacco grower. Tobacco growing, once the highest paying cash crop per acre in colonial times, has virtually stopped here after the big tobacco companies paid the farmers to stop growing it. Sad to me, the land is now mostly sold off to developers making places like The Grange as unique as Sonia says it is. However, tobacco barns, drafty buildings that appear to be ready to collapse, still dot the increasingly hilly landscape as I drive south. At this time of year, the tobacco leaves have been harvested and will hang to dry for another month or so before they are ready. It's probably lost on most, but as I drive past the towns of Upper Marlboro and Lower Marlboro, I appreciate that this is the real Marlboro County, and that the tobacco leaf is still at the center of the county flag.

Driving south, the landscape rises. Off to my left, invisible from the roadway, I know there are the cliffs that tower over the sparkling Chesapeake Bay. I used to bring Ryn and Adam when they were little to collect sharks' teeth and chase sand crabs. We'd come this way to explore the nuclear power plant and to wonder at its hydroponic gardens. There's a road sign suggesting "Visit Historic St. Mary's." It's just a bit further south. This was the bus route for the mandatory fourth grade school trip to learn about Maryland state history. The trips, the bus rides, the chaperoning, those were very good days.

I find myself recalling the docent's speech about George Calvert, the first "Lord Baltimore." Escaping England's persecution for his

Catholic faith, he came here to a settlement he called St. Mary's and claiming the land as Mary's land—Maryland. It was 1631.

Fast forward two hundred and fifty years. Make friends with Indians, displace Indians, establish a colony, grow tobacco, fight a revolutionary war, establish slavery, fight a civil war, abolish slavery, give Tobias and Delores Thatcher land. Fast forward one hundred and forty some-odd years and four generations. We've arrived at today.

As I near Martinsburg and the small bend in the road, I'm still not clear on an approach. Just north of the power plant, the road sways gently east before swinging west and continuing south to the end of the of the peninsula. There was a small town here. Now, however, the only landmark for what was the center of Martinsburg is the small market across from the turn to The Grange. Glancing over at the market, I make the left onto Tobias' road and property. I drive up the gravel path past the field we just harvested and think of it as gently resting for the winter. Coming to the house, I decide to wait a minute before exiting the car.

Deep breath, one step. I hear Sonia's oft spoken words, "Things either work out, or they make a good story."

Okay then, here we go.

The house is, as Tobias described, large with a wraparound porch encircling the cross-shaped footprint it makes on the site. Tia has told me to just enter by the side door and call out. No need, I am immediately in the kitchen. Pavarotti, lying at Elizabeth's feet, raises then lowers his head. His size seems to have doubled in this smaller space. Tia is mixing something in a large wooden bowl. My quick impression of the room is that it's a truly splendid space for cooking and sharing time. There's the genuine feel of the original house but with all new appliances, Sub-Zero fridge, great lighting that mimics old gas lamps, both wood and granite countertops and a deep, trough-like sink. The cabinet tops are decorated with vintage items—an old wash basin, baskets, and a milk jar. Next to Tia, on the counter, is a good-sized piece of Native American pottery to hold kitchen implements.

As they both greet me, I realize I am grateful that Elizabeth is here. Even the shortness of our meeting at the harvest gives me a sense of familiarity that eases the knot in the pit of my stomach.

Tia warmly invites me to sit as she hands me coffee and asks me directly if I've decided how I am going to approach Tobias.

"Actually, Tia, I thought I'd start with you. You seem to be the go-to person, at least according to Sonia. So, I thought it would make sense to start with you. I have to be honest—whatever Sonia has in mind isn't clear to me.

"On the drive down, I thought of a lot of options and then I settled on you. I know your mother just passed and I know what a hard time I had after my mom died. I'm wondering if you'd tell me about your mother. It can't be that common a story for an African American woman of her day to have gone to college and graduate school and also to be a huge landowner. It isn't that common for a bi-racial gay couple to be living openly with the parents of one of the partners. And I'm wondering if there isn't some slant on a mother-daughter story we could capture."

I can tell from her face that I've said this all exactly wrong. It sounds like I am here to make a documentary. "Tia, I'm just trying to figure out what Sonia and Erica see here and figure out my place. Here's what made me come."

I open the folder I've brought with me and slide Erica's photo of the empty chair across the kitchen counter to her. She takes it, gently tracing the chair.

"Jessica, there are those with a story here," Tia says, "but I'm not one of them, and theirs are not mine to tell. Like I mentioned on the phone, you have to start with Tobias."

Elizabeth shakes her head at Tia's words and locks eyes with me. "You come-a with me. Tia doesn't mean to sound so harsh."

Elizabeth flips her palm from a flat position to one of a raised palm. Without her saying a word the Rottweiler is on his feet. She grips his harness and he pulls forward enough to help her stand. "I will take you to Tobias."

Elizabeth, with a limp, and Pavarotti close by her side, leads me through a small maze of narrow hallways. She nods her head in the direction of the room on the right and tells me that Tobias will be waiting. With some difficulty she turns to leave me. She puts her hand, briefly, on my shoulder, and sighs, "Whatda ya hafta do."

The room I enter timidly is a tidy art studio filled with strong, crisp light overlooking the ridge of cliffs. You can see the great Chesapeake sprawling for miles ahead of you. Tobias appears to be asleep in a soft, floral upholstered chair. Even asleep he establishes a presence. Dark skinned, freckled. Old, but also, somehow, ageless. Short, trimmed beard. Closely cropped hair, receding hair line. Elegant hands folded in his lap. His lanky legs outstretched and crossed at the ankles. I don't want to disturb him so take time to get a sense of the room. It is clearly a woman's room, the floral upholstery, the daintiness of the few knickknacks. There's a picture of what must be Tia as a baby, and one more current of Tia with a lamb in her lap and CC holding the harnesses of two llamas. Next to the easel there is a sepia-toned picture of what must be a very young Tobias. He's in a smart Army uniform, casual, field service cap placed dapperly towards the side of his head, tie tucked into the shirt just between the third and fourth buttons. I reach for it and hear behind me, "I'd appreciate it if you wouldn't touch that."

Tobias is awake. As he sits up, he takes his wallet from behind his head, takes his cane from the side of the chair, stands, and tucks the wallet into his back pocket.

"I'm so sorry," I tell him. "I didn't mean to wake you."

"It's alright," he says, looking around the room as if bringing it into focus. "I'd come in here most mornings and watch her paint.

This is such a peaceful spot that I'd sometimes fall asleep. Joan, my wife, liked things a particular way. She didn't want to put any slipcovers on the chairs to protect them from my hair oils. I took to putting my wallet behind my head. Been doing it for decades.

"Sorry, I was asleep when you came. Welcome. It's Jessica isn't it?"

I understand in an instant why he's asked me not to touch anything. He doesn't invite me to sit in the other chair. So, we both stand, Tobias listening patiently as I go through pretty much the same spiel I gave Tia, hopefully more tactfully. I talk about my stream of consciousness in the car, minus the DNA side of things. I feel like I'm still not finding the footing I want. I can't read his face. I end flatly with stating that I think I am supposed to come and help in some way and I know I need his permission to do that.

After a bit, he moves to the bay side of the room with long low bookcases under a full wall of windows. He pauses, just for a moment, to stare out at the bay, wide enough here to extend as far as you can see. Turning, he sits upon the case and smiles.

"Jessica, I appreciate you asking my permission, but Joan and I always wanted this to be a place where everyone felt comfortable, where everyone felt they were at home. Like I said the other day, we never really felt we owned the land, more like we just get to use it while we walk this earth. We wanted the type of place where Tia's friends would want to come after school and have sleepovers. We accomplished that. Now I will admit that I never imagined all this communal living, but that too seems to be turning out pretty well, although it will be a lot better when the other house is done.

"I am sure there are things you can help with, I am sure there are things you can learn and document about these women, and this land. But for me, even with all our generations on this land, the most remarkable thing was simple. Joan.

"I'm sorry I snapped at you about not touching that old photograph of me. We can talk about my time in the Army and being 'colored' back then sometime if you think it's of interest. But Joan was the one who really made all this happen and it pains me more than I care to say that she is not here. Doesn't seem right. Will never be right.

"Her laughter would fill this house. Every touch here is hers. But, as the others came, naturally, things had to shift around. This room was hers and I want to leave it exactly as she left it. I don't even like the way that sounds, but I like the feeling that I can sit here and wait for her and she can come in at any moment, pick up a brush and paint.

"Her love of this place was so simple, pure. She gave birth to Tia here because she wanted the next generation of Thatchers to be born on this land like all the others before her. I think that's why she kept Tia's baby picture so close. She welcomed CC, too, and loved her well.

"I think you would have marveled at her. Behind you there are some paintings of her. She's captured herself pretty well."

Turning I see there are a series of three fairly large paintings. Each is of a woman in a near identical pose. Full face to the artist. Broad brimmed straw hat. Coffee colored skin. Intense, piercing, smiling eyes. Narrow, flat, nose. Closed-mouth, content smile. There's an inscription on the frames, but I'm too far away to make them out.

I actually gasp, she is so beautiful. The eyes so perfectly set as to meet your own as you meet her.

Each of them is painted decades apart. I gawk at them as I hear Tobias saying that she gave him the first one when he returned from World War II and they came here to visit with his family. He was twenty-nine, Joan seven years his junior at twenty-two. The next was for their thirty-fifth wedding anniversary. She had just completed some work at the local community theater. She would be roughly my age. The one on the far right she painted just six years ago, on their fiftieth anniversary. They had renewed their marriage vows. It had been Joan's idea. She was seventy-four then, eighty when she died. The paintings are so honest. She is beautiful in each and she has not hidden her aging. The signs of aging I've already come to notice in myself, lines, the under-chin slackness, the sagging jowl, slightly wilted breasts. In the last picture her shoulders are slightly rounded and there is a small scar on her right cheek.

Inexplicably, I feel my eyes fill with tears.

"Tobias, she's lovely."

"Indeed, she is the most perfect woman I've ever seen. Met her, fell in love on the spot when I looked into those eyes, and I never looked away. Selfishly, I'm the one who should have gone first. Sheer mathematics would have led me to believe that. That, and she was just so alive.

"I don't like being left behind like this. I always thought we'd be together until they folded my hands in the box. I worry we didn't do enough for her, but Tia, CC, and I, we did our best. She had that same great smile on her face as she passed into eternity.

"I'm told there were four hundred people at her funeral. I can't say that I noticed. I was just focused on making sure she got safely and gently tucked away. It was a beautiful service and the community did right by her. Afterwards, we took her body to where generations of Thatchers rest. Mr. Oliver and his niece Miss Caroline are up there, too, but not with the colored folk. They have their own gated area. But as far as I can tell, none of the generations of Black folk who worked this land wanted a fence to keep them in.

"We wrapped her in a shroud and covered her with one of Margaret Mary's quilts. Some of the boys from the community college helped us put her on the wagon. I drove that mule Oliver as gently as I could, not trusting anyone else to give my love a smooth ride. I drove her from the church, by the house, past the sheep and llamas, over to the cliffs to look out on the bay, and finally, to her resting spot. I may have imagined it, but those llamas in with the sheep stood tall as she passed.

"Still, there's no way to drive a mule and a wagon across this land

and have it be smooth and I cringed at every bump. We placed her up there, just in the ground, no box, just as she wished.

"It's hard to think of her there, not because she's dead but because her body is so still. She was always so active, so involved in the church and the schools, always heading a committee, inviting folks here to work, to stay if they needed. She got involved in the community college, did some teaching, but mostly she mentored the young faculty there. That's how we really got involved in so many of the projects we run. She was always thinking, always being creative and always trying to get people involved. She loved to golf. Not a lot of Black women in that sport. She thought of building a small executive course on this land to get more Black girls involved in that, too. Probably one of the few projects we never embarked on before she died.

"Mostly, she was a woman of great faith. I like to consider myself a religious man, but she had something special in that department. She faced her illness and all the treatments, pain, and nausea that went with it with more grace and dignity than it deserved.

"She was already sick when she painted that last painting, but none of us knew it. I don't know if you noticed the scar at the top of her cheek."

I want to tell him I noticed the scar, but I don't want to interrupt.

"The priest called up from the church to tell me she fell down there, and the paramedics said she broke her hip and cut her cheek on the pew as she went down.

"It hurts to be a doctor and to have taken that at face value. I never thought that it wasn't the fall that broke the hip. It was the hip that broke and caused her to fall. She had bone cancer and we all missed it for almost four years. I pledged 'first, do no harm.' Well, I never harmed her, but missing that diagnosis still feels like I did. Only real regret of my life, really.

"I've seen a lot of people die, in war, in my practice. I've never seen anyone so peaceful about it. Her cousin, Jan, you met her the other night at the harvest. Jan was kicking and screaming and angry at the Lord to be losing Joan. Not Joan. She was at peace from the moment she was diagnosed. Now don't get me wrong, she wasn't hurrying off this Earth, but she felt God had a plan. At the end, when the pain got bad, I told her I could up the morphine, make it go away, let her rest, let her go. She took my hand and smiled that great smile and told me that the Lord and his Mother would come for her in their own time. I envied that faith.

"She told me she was content. She knew that her programs were going well. She liked that we had the nursing students from the community college come up and help her, check on her. She was giving of herself even then. Husband for a doctor, 'daughter-in-law' a nurse, and all those students. The best we did was to ease her journey. Tia took to calling us 'death concierges.'

"She said she was happy that Tia was well loved and productive. She said she was grateful to have had a man who so faithfully loved her for so long. I was humbled and grateful for that.

"She sure loved Tia and CC. She's the one who started calling her CC. How Joan picked up twenty years ago that Tia and CC were, *uh*, partners, eludes me. She'd insist that CC stay over when she first visited, and she insisted that Tia and CC not put up a charade. I was never sure if it was because of her faith in the Lord, or despite her relationship with the church, but she said Tia was our daughter, our only child, and there was going to be nothing that would interfere with that.

"'Tobias,' she would say to me, 'Don't be an old man. You need to go with the flow on some things.' That would make me laugh. *Go with the flow?* I hadn't heard her, or anyone, say that in years. I'd laugh, but 'flowing' wasn't easy for this old Black man to do sometimes. Having Tia and CC together was one thing that was hard for me. Don't get me wrong. Cynthia is a good woman. I knew being a mixed couple wasn't going to be easy, and I certainly knew that being 'queer' wasn't going to be easy. Maybe the hardest part was I just knew there would be no more Thatcher babies on this land. None of it was easy, but Joan made sure it was right in the end.

"Those last few weeks before her death we'd sit in our room and talk about our earliest days together. I knew the meaning of bitter-sweet in those moments. I loved talking with her about our first apartment, the colors of the walls, the dentist we rented it from—he was taking a big chance on renting to colored folk in that neighbor-hood. Joan and I came a long way together.

"That last week before she died, she called her friends and said goodbye. She called Jan and said she was going to miss her. She told her that she was more than a cousin, she was a best friend. She asked Tia and CC to get her address book out and she sent a dozen people flowers and notes of thanks.

"Then, she lost consciousness, and we watched her die.

"Jan moved here when Joan got sick. It was a shame she was away visiting her daughter when Joan died. I imagine she will stay with us now, even with Joan gone. It's nice to talk about Joan with her. Tia's not really ready. I think she thinks if we don't talk about it, we can ignore it, that the grief might go away. I don't see that happening."

I move to look more closely at each of the paintings. Even with my back to Tobias I can feel him watching me.

"So, you see Jessica. I'm trying to go with the flow now. I like the projects and this place. I like being here, close to Joan. However, this is not a place I could have anticipated or planned. I am an old man. God willing, I won't have too long to wait before He calls me home to be with Joan again. I know a lot of things Jessica, but the most important is that the love of a good woman sustained me.

"So, in answer to what you are to do here, I can't say. Go with the flow. This life is not a dress rehearsal. It's a journey and I think our job is to do it well along the way. Joan would welcome you here for what-ever reason, and I do too. Take a minute and look around. If you don't mind, don't touch anything. I'll meet you in the kitchen in a bit."

I thank him and return to the paintings. Six decades of Joan look back at me. Closer now, I can see subtleties I didn't notice before. Each has a different background that clearly is just out of focus enough so as not to distract from Joan's image. The first portrait is set in front of the bay. The second is in front of a theater marquee of some kind. The last, in front of what appears to be a small country church. Each of the frames has a painted saying in what my Catholic grade schoolteachers called "Palmer Penmanship." Joan's was a perfect italic painted script. In sequence they say, "Go with the flow," "This is not a rehearsal," and, "To thine own self be true."

I jot down each of these expressions on separate pieces of paper so I can think about them later. I am awed. I feel a hush surround me. Then, as I meet her gaze in each of the portraits, I say aloud, "Hello Joan, I'm Jessica. I am so very honored to meet you."

I keep Tobias waiting well more than a bit.

hamlet act 1, scene 3

The drive back to DC is a blur. I try to focus on the morning, sights, sounds, senses. Formulate questions. Connect dots. What happens instead is I just sit with the feelings and try to name them. Edgy, intrigued, eager. Uncomfortable, curious. Haunted.

I drive, obliviously, a route I've taken hundreds of times. Up Rt. 4, the increased density of the urban sprawl, pick up Massachusetts Avenue, quick dogleg around the Capitol and Lafayette Park, north on 16th, left on Hobart. Home.

The insistent Gabler greets me at the door and I scoop her up.

"OK, cat, I've got a few hours before I have to teach my evening class. You deserve some attention." We head for the window seat to sort through the mail. I toss the folder from this morning on the dining table and the three notes I made spill out. I'll straighten them later.

The weather has changed, dark clouds gather, temps have turned raw. The shift in daylight always alters the feel of the space in the house. I've never been able to describe it well, but the whole feel of the place changes in these dark, pre-dusk autumn and winter afternoons. It's, somehow, somber. That feels about right for right now.

"Greetings, greetings!" Roy joyously comes through the door.

"Hey, Jes, I'm glad you're home. I saw your car. Probably should have knocked or rung the bell. Maybe you want me to do that, maybe you don't. Did you have a good morning? I thought I'd come by and clear off the front porch. I'm going to need the space to store the rest of the crown molding and paints. Would that be OK? I'm also going to move your bike. I want to get started on refinishing the hall and closet doors. Assume we are still set on the same colors?"

All the while he's in motion, moving the bike, checking which doors close smoothly and completely. Gabler hops off the window seat to great him and he scoops her up. "Hello, Beast."

"Roy, you exhaust me! Sit for a minute. We can go over next steps. I wasn't really giving you my attention the other night. About the other night..."

"Jes, it's OK. I appreciate you sharing. I have no comment on it other than I'm sorry." Putting Gabler down on the dining table, he says, "I left the paint chips here on the table. Can we go over them one more time?"

He sees my three notes as he looks for the paint chips. "Is Erica reading Shakespeare's tragedies for school?" He holds up "to thine own self be true."

In response to my quizzical look he pronounces, "Hamlet, Act one, scene three."

"You do impress me, Mr. Gillis—business mogul, entrepreneur, craftsman, golfer, tennis player, *and* Shakespearean scholar?"

"I wish, Jes. Other than playing Tybalt in *Romeo and Juliet* and

Laertes in *Hamlet,* I've never read or seen any Shakespeare. My mother used to say it all the time, 'to thine own self be true.' She always told us the words were from the Bible. She was wrong, but people are always mistaking quotes that we use as from the Bible. Actually, lots of them are Shakespeare's.

"The quote is from such a cool scene in the play, it really stands out. Polonius is known for his long-winded speeches. His son, Laertes, me in the play, is trying to get away from his father and escape to Paris. Polonius just can't help himself. He wants to give some parting advice to his son. Typical of kids, Laertes has no patience for him."

Roy strikes an authoritarian and ominous pose.

"Polonius: *This above all: to thine own self be true, and it must follow, as the night the day, Thou canst not then be false to any man. Farewell, my blessing season this in thee!'*" He continues, "Laertes: *'Most humbly do I take my leave, my lord.'*"

Roy gives a sweeping bow and exits the dining room in grand Shakespearean style.

"I've just added 'actor' to your credits, Mr. Gillis," I call after him, laughing, delighted at his portrayal. He's also just saved me the Google search I was about to do on the phrase. I'd heard it many times, and I *had* thought it was a biblical reference.

Roy re-enters, as if on cue, and I ask, "So, what do you think Polonius was trying to say to his son? Is he talking about honesty? Lying? Some deep introspection?"

"Well, the way my drama teacher, Mrs. Spires, explained it is that Polonius feels a sense of urgency. His son is leaving. He doesn't know if he'll see him again. Despite Polonius actually not being the greatest of guys, he wants to send his son off fortified with wisdom. In his leaving, Laertes carries with him the reputation of the family.

"Polonius is certainly saying be honest in your actions and deeds. He's also talking about being loyal to your family and yourself. Take care of yourself first. Know who you are at your core. Be true to who you are supposed to be. Live a proper life. Polonius thinks himself very wise. Like most kids, then and now, Laertes isn't interested in listening to the message. Simple."

"Is it really that simple, Roy? You seem to see things so, *um*, straightforwardly."

"Most of time things are, Jes, unless we muck them up. Hey, I just came by to clear off the porch. I'll be back to do the rest of the work later. I've got to get going. *Um*, you're not saving those untouched *Washington Posts* on the porch for a special purpose, are you? Can I borrow a trash bag for some of the materials on your front porch?"

I stand, amazed at his constant patter, and benevolently and mockingly say, "'Neither a borrower nor a lender be' Roy Gillis. Jesus Christ to the Apostles. Ha!"

"Sorry, Jes, it's also, actually Shakespeare, also Hamlet Act I, Scene III, and cooler still, actually Polonius. Part of one of his long-winded speeches. Ha, back at you! But I will bring you more trash bags."

Taking the bags from under the sink he closes the door gently. I can hear him whistling and the *thwack* of the still-wrapped newspapers slap against the concrete as he tosses them into the bag. *Thwack, thwack, thwack, thwack.* No wonder Sonia had noticed them.

There's still time before class to make some notes. Picking up the folder, I say, "Come on Gabler, let's go to the office." Together we mount the stairs, she more spritely than I despite her aged legs. She meets me at the end of the hall and is already on the windowsill as I enter.

This used to be their study room, a place to go do homework. It's a snug room. I've kept the almost child-sized desk and made it my own years ago. It sits between the two tall, paint-caked window frames with glass that rattles in the wind. They open onto the roof of the little porch I told Roy about the other night. I crack open the window not blocked by the cat. The radiator has always made this room too hot. I can still hear Roy working below. Now there is the methodical *swish, swish, swish* as he sweeps the porch. I wouldn't have thought of that, I would just lay the materials on the porch and cover them with plastic. Maybe, if I had any. Roy, I am sure, has already measured out and pre-cut exactly the size of protective plastic he needs, and has it on hand, and is ready to weight it down with the right materials to secure it in the wind.

He's pretty quaint. Interesting guy.

Settling into my desk, I open my folder, Erica's "empty chair" photo is still on top. I'd retrieved it from Tia, with an apology for mucking up our first visit. I lean over my desk to pin the photo to the corkboard between the windows. Talking out loud, I say to no one, "OK, I get it, Erica, Joan's left a void. Sonia, what do you have in mind for us to do here?"

Sitting and putting my feet on the desk, leaning back, "Joan, is there a story untold here? Is there more you want said?" I open my tablet and begin notes. Night comes so early at this time of year. Even after all this time, it stuns me—4:30 and pitch dark in DC in winter. Sarasota, not till after six. Realizing that if I don't leave now I'll be late for class, I jot one last note. *Figure out the beginning, then, go with the flow.*

Getting ready to leave, I notice my bike has been removed from the front hallway. Roy's taken all the materials previously draped across it and placed them, nicely folded, on the stairs, with the basket contents placed on top. Locking up, it's evident that Roy has the porch perfectly neat, a perfectly precise tarp is covering the molding supplies, and the recycling bins are missing. *I'm sure he's found a place for them,* I think, as I rush to car.

At the first red light I text Sonia, *"Awkward start with Tia, but a really good day. Do you have time for a walk tomorrow? I need to figure something out."*

Instant response, *"I'm there. S."*

C

From: JMBarnet@google1.com
To: TiaThatcher@TheGrange.com, CC@TheGrange.com
CC: DrTobias@TheGrange.com, SoniaCortezphd@Martins-
   burgcommunitycollege.edu
Subject: Follow Up
7:38 PM

Dear Tia and CC:

Thank you both for all the time you have taken with the phone calls and emails and all the back and forth as we work at setting up my next trip to The Grange. I particularly appreciate the conference call we did with Sonia. She's largely responsible for helping with the increased focus.

I want to recap next steps here. Please take a look and see if I've got it right. I've also attached a draft of the oral history questions. May I ask you to give them to the others? This way, they will have time to think them over before I come down.

Here's what we've summarized:

A.   There are six community projects currently in the works: 1) The Yearly Harvest; 2) The Quilters; 3) The Wool Project; 4) The Mercado Mikado - (the corner store, I think you call it the M and M); 5) The link with Martinsburg Community College; 6) The new house. While these are all operational, there has not been time to document them and, we've agreed that there is room for some improvements.

B. In addition, the sum of these projects at The Grange, and the decision to create a communal living situation, needs to be documented. In our research we haven't been able to find any similar kind of co-op (for lack of a better word). That is significant. It might garner some national attention and might generate grants.

C. You wanted to create a "to-do" list for yourselves - including a review of the various projects to see if they are appropriately set up from a business, legal, and economic perspective. You'll need to consider if creating a nonprofit makes sense and is possible. I might be able to help here. I know a bit how nonprofits work.

D. We have determined that at least some of the women think the oral histories are a good idea.

E. I will come down for a meeting and you will coordinate the times. We will start out informally, just to get a sense of things, and then I will meet individually with at least Jan to start a history, Deirdre to discuss wool, and Margaret Mary to discuss the quilts. Elizabeth will decide later if she wants to chat. Sydney has had a rough week on her chemo, and we will let her decide if she's up to being part of any of this.

F. You will check with Dr. Allison (Ali) Beck, Dean of Student Services at Martinsburg to see if she has time for me to visit with her at the community college to discuss that connection. Once you get me a time, I will check with Sonia to see if she is also available.

It looks like we have everything covered. Tia, again, I apologize for being so wrong-footed as I started out last time. I hope this approach feels more comfortable.

Please let me know if I've missed anything. Please note: I've copied both Sonia and Tobias on this; the latter in order that Tobias is fully in the loop and can have us change direction if he likes.

Tobias, we are being more structured, but, I promise, we will go with the flow!

–Jessica

Hit [SEND].

From: JMBarnet@google1.com
To: ElizabethJ@TheGrange.com
Subject: Thank you
8:15 PM

Dear Elizabeth,

I wanted to drop you a quick note of thanks for your kindness the other day when I was at The Grange. It may have seemed like a small thing. You and Pavarotti walking me down the hallway to Tobias in Joan's studio may have seemed like a small gesture, but it really got me out of an awkward situation with Tia, not to mention, eased me into Tobias. That was a big help as I get my footing around this exciting, but still vague project. I also want to thank you for the suggested questions you sent up. I think they will make a great start for interviewing the other women, AND YOU!

As you requested, I've sent them on to Tia and CC without an acknowledgment that they were your suggestions, or the fact that you are the one urging me to write their stories.

By the way, I really enjoyed meeting you at the harvest. My mum was Italian and listening to you reminded me of her and so many of my relatives! Plus, my grandmother always used to say "what do you have to do" the way you do. I had forgotten that. Thanks for bringing up that memory.

Please check with Tia on the schedule she's set up. Hope to see you soon.

–Jessica

Hit [**SEND**].

From: JMBarnet@google1.com
To: SoniaCortezphd@Martinsburgcommunitycollege.edu, photo-
bug@google1.com
Subject: Thank you
8:20 PM

Hey Sonia and Erica,

Erica, I haven't had a chance to tell you how amazing your photos of the harvest are! Pretty impressive. Really moving. Thank you, more than you know, for sharing them. I've got the one of Joan's empty chair over my desk. Yes, Erica, I figured that out.

Sonia, you can see from the other E that things are in pretty good shape for next steps. Thank goodness Tobias has this "flow" attitude and Tia doesn't seem all that into creating something specific. A lot less pressure. Thanks, lots, for this.

Don't feel you have to come to the Allison Beck meeting, but you are, of course, more than welcome.

And, yes, I did find my dissertation files on my old laptop and yes, I've made an appointment with the Dean. If Erica wasn't included in this email, I'd tell you what a pushy thing you are 😊. See you on our walk tomorrow. Erica, see you at dinner. Soon!

Love,

–Jessica

Hit [SEND].

From: JMBarnet@google1.com
To: Cathryn8561@aol2.com, Adam8561@aol2.com
Subject: I miss you

Dearest Ryn and Adam...

I stop typing and stare at my still hands on the keys. Thoughts, not words, spill over the screen.)

I get up from my desk, "Whatda ya hafta do, eh, Gabler? Come on downstairs. I know, I know, I've kept you waiting a long time for dinner. We're usually in the kitchen a lot earlier than this."

Down the hall, past their bedrooms, around the corner, down the stairs, past the closet. Roy's taken the door off for sanding and refinishing. Memory chest visible on the floor. There's progress on the roughed-in bathroom under the stairs. Gabler, ahead of me, meowing loudly for dinner. Pour vodka. Feed Gabler. Pour vodka.

Opening the back door for some fresh air I see the "missing" recycling bins. Roy must have thought this is a far better place for them than the front porch. I make a note to ask Roy if he can replace the steps from the porch to the yard. I've thought they were too rickety for years. The way these houses are set on the property makes it so my first floor is actually a whole story above the yard. The basement opens to the yard. These kitchen steps go a long way down. Fixing them is a good idea. I also need to ask Roy if he knows a good landscaper. The rear yard is a bonus, but it really needs attention.

It's a fairly warm night. DC is so funny this way. You can have all four seasons in a single day at this time of year.

"Hey, Gabler, after you are done, come back upstairs. I'll be on the roof." Pour vodka, go upstairs. In the office I grab the quilt from the back of the chair, open the window and crawl out on the roof above the porch. It's not lost on me that this is not as easy for me to do as it once was.

Leaning back into the room I grab my glass and pull the side chair over making it easier in case Gabler wants to hop up and come through and join me. It's been years since I've been out here. Impossible not to remember the storytelling and the campouts or the time Adam decided to disobey a punishment, for what I can't remember, and sneak out of the house from up here. I'm so lucky to have found this spot. Leaning against the wall of the house I take in the sounds of the traffic on 16th Street, people walking below, and music coming from somewhere over at Columbia Road. Big city, small town, cozy neighborhood. Safe. Still an escape.

Gabler joins me, nestling against me for warmth. We sit quietly together. A gentle breeze is coming from the east. "No sounds from the zoo tonight, Gabler. We need a west wind for that."

Eventually, we go back in. I look at the computer screen. "Dear Ryn and Adam,"

Hit [**DELETE**].

the grange project

Tia and CC have arranged a schedule that has me going first to the community college to meet Dr. Beck. In order to maximize time, I've taped four "notes for the ride" to the car's dashboard.

Allison Beck: focus on the link between the college and The Grange. Why did it start, what are the goals, how does she measure success, where does she see expansion?

The Grange: Take tour with Tia and Tobias, get a sense of the sum of the parts. Ask to see the new construction, the cemetery, the cliffs, the sheep and llamas, the rest of the land. Listen to what they say as we tour. Be like Erica, make snapshots in your head.

The Women: Get Deidre's take on the wool project and Marga-
ret Mary's on the quilts. Besides Jan, is there anyone interested
in doing the histories?

(Elizabeth's) Questions: What is your earliest memory? What
do you remember from a story your mother or grandmother told
you? What brought you the most joy? The most regret? What
would you want your gravestone to say? Who is one person you
would like to have a conversation with from your past? Are you
religious—more so or less so than in your youth? Are you politi-
cal—more so or less so than in your youth? What fills your days?
What is most surprising about being your age? What would you
say is your finest accomplishment? What do you want to leave
behind when you die? Do you have children? [Note to self:
What's going on with Elizabeth and her urgency for me to do this
project and capture these stories?]

I'm hoping they don't want to talk too much about their children
and focus more on their mothers, but I am thinking that the im-
portance of the story here is what gets said and what gets listened to
between mothers and children. While it sounds wrong in my head
to think of them as accomplishments, I'd certainly count giving
Adam and Ryn to this earth as the best thing I've done, so, I better
be ready for the women's responses.

I'm still mulling all of this as I near Martinsburg and The Grange.
The little market is there on the right. I decide to stop for coffee
before heading the few miles down the road to the college. Like the
house up the hill, there is a core of an original building with addi-
tions. It still has post boxes for a few residents, but the community
college's post office has largely taken over for this area. The front
porch is worn and echoes footsteps from long ago. I like how the old

bell, displaced as you open the door, peals as it must have for generations, announcing arrivals and departures.

Inside the market is lit with dust-filled, slanty sunlight coming through the small windows. Light operetta music plays in the background. There are two college-aged students behind the counter absorbed in texting, or tweeting, or Insta-something. However, both manage a, "Good morning" and, "Can we help you?"

"Just looking around for a bit, I'm going to grab some coffee now, that OK?" They are already reabsorbed as I look around. There are the expected things, coffee, water, sodas, and cigarettes. Newspapers: *Calvert County Times, St. Mary's Times, The Washington Post,* and *USA Today.* An assortment of snacks, various and sundry items, not quite a general store. And the unexpected ones—beautiful skeins of wool, dyed in rich colors like cranberry, blueberry, onion, and pea. There's both lamb and llama wool. There is produce—fresh, canned, and dried. The wool, and most of the produce, has "The Grange" label on them.

Neat.

The music switches from operetta to opera and back again on a playlist loop of some kind. I pick up a jar of the dried beans with a soup recipe attached, refill my coffee, and head to the register. There is a large quilt hanging on the wall behind the counter. Although it's asymmetrical in design it has a distinct pattern. Rt. 4 runs from the top to bottom of the quilt. The fields, house, cliffs, and Chesapeake Bay are off to the right. This market, then more fields, and what I think is the Patuxent River sit at the far-left edge. The stitched words "Mikado Mercado" circle the store in the same Palmer penmanship hand I recognize from Joan's frames. Along the bottom, in a different hand, it says "you are here."

"Great quilt," I say to the kids at the counter. "Surprised at your choice of the opera music."

"Oh, Dr. Tobias asks us to play it until at least eleven. Most of the oldies have come through by that time. Plus, he says that a place with a name like this should be playing all Gilbert and Sullivan. You notice the name on the quilt? Two of the oldies made that when they changed the name two years ago. Kind of a cool name too. The Thatchers had a contest for the name change. A Spanish lady from the community college put this one out there. *Mikado* because it seemed every time she came in that operetta was playing and 'Mercado,' the Spanish for market. She said the *Mikado* would drive her nuts and she'd wind up singing it the rest of the day."

I pay with my credit card and use my finger to sign the screen when asked. Ha, *fingeriture*, they called it. A finger signature, who knew? The technology is a stark contrast to the circa 1900 National Cash Register machine alongside it.

Getting in the car I look up at the Mikado Mercado sign.

Sonia. Ubiquitous Sonia.

Martinsburg Community College sits just back from the road and is a large sprawling campus. Like most colleges of this type, it's become increasingly important to the community. State universities, like Maryland, are harder and harder to get into and frequently require getting a two-year academic base at an institution like this before entering a full college or university. Many of my own students have come through Martinsburg, too. Driving by some of the buildings it's clear that the trades are also well represented. The automotive, HV/AC, horticulture, and health science buildings are clearly labeled. The main campus building holds the student center and all the student services. The Dean's wing is off to the left. I pass Sonia's office, door closed. It's okay that she can't make the meeting.

The door to Dr. Allison Beck's office is ajar. Tapping lightly, I open the door to two people standing close together behind the desk, looking out the window. The sense that I've interrupted something immediately dissipates as they turn to me with broad welcoming smiles.

Allison is a tall, big woman. Big, but not heavy, very fit-looking.

Irish-Middle European complexion, reddish gold hair, about my age, maybe younger. The Black man, I learn, is Officer Gene Martin, Director of Campus Security. He is, by every measure, perhaps the most stunningly handsome man I have ever seen, distractingly so. Young Denzel Washington in-the-flesh beautiful.

With ready smiles and quick handshakes, they come out from behind the desk. We quickly introduce ourselves. Gene leaves abruptly.

Despite his speedy exit I still have the sense these are both people you like instantly. I've always marveled at that instant likability some people have. How do they do it—make you feel both instantly at-ease and eager to spend more time with them?

"Oh my, he's stunning." I blurt out, embarrassed that I started on such a superficial level. "I'm sorry if I interrupted."

"Not at all, Gene is a very attractive man. He gives me regular reports on campus security and identifies students with specific problems who need special attention. He's a pretty amazing guy. I'll be very sad when he leaves us for a new job in the coming year.

"Come in and sit down. I'm so excited that you are going to be working with all of us. Sonia talks about you all the time. You are going to be a great addition to the team!"

I didn't know it was a "team" and Sonia talk about me "all the time"? She's barely mentioned Allison to me other than she helps connect students up to Sonia's projects. Odd.

I lay out my series of college-related questions for Allison, and she fills me in on the goals of the community service involvement. As she talks, I take in the neat and orderly office, multiple Post-It-Notes on a calendar board, and a display case filled with Baltimore Ravens paraphernalia. Allison begins.

"It started as a simple collaboration with Sonia. She needed to create some special projects for the American Studies major. I knew about the Thatchers through Gene. It was an easy match. You probably didn't notice Gene's last name, 'Martin.' He can date his family back generations to when Samuel Martin, the largest land and slave owner in the area, bedded one of his slaves, producing Gene's bloodline. It happened all the time, of course. With the exception of Gene and his two nephews, all the original Martins have moved on leaving Gene's family as representative of Martinsburg's heritage. His and Tobias' family go back to that time.

"Do you follow football? Gene played a short while for the Ravens before an injury sidelined him. Anyway, he and Tobias have an arrangement about the Martins' use and leasing of acres from The Grange. He helps out up there often—he helped bury Tobias' wife, Joan, last month." She seems wistful.

"Back to how this all started. What we noticed in the first project was how energized the students were when they got to apply what they learned in real-life situations. We also saw that when we identified students at risk of failing or of getting into trouble, the experiences, including the simple exposure to a set of 'other mothers' really seemed to make a difference. You probably know what it's like, how you can tell your own children one thing a dozen times and they don't hear it or do it. Then suddenly someone else says the same thing and it's brilliant!"

I groan silently as she continues.

"So, I just started expanding the projects and the experiences. Sonia thinks I'm bossy. I tell her I just have better ideas!"

She says this so easily, and with such mirth, and with the absolute conviction that she is right.

"I really got focused when I read a *USA Today* article about regrets and aging. Reading the headline, I anticipated that as we age, we regret the loss of our looks, mobility, friends dying, and things like that. I was dead wrong. What the article pointed out was that the regrets were not current. Older Americans mourn events that are decades old. They regret a road not taken, a talent not followed, a missed chance, a relationship that wasn't fixed. Older Americans want peace of mind more than anything else. Sure, they worry about the other things too, and they worry about money and family. But most older Americans reported that it was the old regrets that mattered.

"I thought, if I can provide an array of experiences to the students, they can make better choices. I'm thinking, better choices, fewer regrets. It's reverse engineering in a way. I want our young students to turn into content old people.

"I went to Sonia and told her that I thought it would help the oldies at The Grange if we started getting more students involved up there. I think that is the first time she told me I was 'bossy.' I knew it really was a good idea. The *USA Today* article went on to say that if, as we age, we fill our lives with purpose and meaning, we have less time to ruminate about the past and are more satisfied in the present. That seemed pretty straightforward.

"Mostly, I want to be connected to The Grange because I like the spirit of the place. Don't get me wrong, I'm not interested in taking my place among the oldies, not yet anyway, but with my own parents gone I find myself surprised that I like the sense of having these older adults in my life. I've asked myself whether it's because it makes me feel younger to be around the oldies, staving off my own aging, or because I like the people and a sense of history. I think it's both.

"My husband, Malcolm, and another contractor are doing most of the work on the new house. Have you seen it yet? It's splendid. I'll be over there this afternoon picking him up. If you haven't seen it yet we'll give you the grand tour."

We finish up with some data points about the number of students involved over time and a promise to see each other this afternoon.

Sitting in the car I make some notes about first impressions and open questions. I can't decide if this is becoming more simple or more complex as I learn the ever-expanding cast of characters. Regardless, I'm sure there's a complex story here, and I'm pretty sure I'm not on anyone's team.

jan

"Going with the flow" happens rather immediately. I get to The Grange House and there is no general meeting or gathering as planned. In fact, it appears no one is home with the exception of Jan. Sleeves rolled up, I see the start of the tattoos Elizabeth alluded to when we first met. They are intricate and mono-chromatic against her brown skin. Symbols and totems I don't understand run up and around her arms. She's in the kitchen, singing with, what can only be described as, "wild abandon." Dolly Parton's "Travellin' Through" accompanies her. The smells coming from the bubbling pots, nothing short of amazing.

"Good morning, child, come right in!"

We've barely met, and I am her "child." I recognize that it's a customary, colloquial statement in the Black community, but still,

I'm mindful of it. It feels kind.

"I went over your questions and think they are a good start. After losing Joan I've been giving these kinds of questions a lot of thought. Can you hand me one of those spoons?"

As I approach the pottery jar crammed with wooden spoons, I ask if she thinks they have enough of them.

"Now, *that's* an interesting question and there's an interesting answer. It seems, in deciding what to bring with them to live here, most of the women brought their wooden spoons. Lots of them were their mother's or their aunt's. The olla is something I gave Joan years ago. It's an antique from the Hopi pueblo in Arizona. I worried that it would break. But Joan insisted that these jars were made to be used. I love all the spoons crammed in, multiple cultures and cooking histories jumbled together. Imagine how many meals were made with these, how many mothers' hands held them. What stories they could tell!"

She continues, "I love stories and I love food. I think this Hopi olla, with its spoons, would be a great cover for a cookbook. Maybe I'll get around to that someday. It would be good if we could match spoons to recipes."

Rapidly, I agree and make two notes—one adding the question about what did you bring with you to The Grange, and one about Jan writing a cookbook. "I'd love a picture of that. The way you describe it, there's already a whole back story here through the spoons."

Jan jumps right back in. "I'll take a picture and email it to you. I've got a new Photoshopping program from Erica that I can play with and adjust how the light hits it."

"Really, you Photoshop?" I ask.

"I didn't say I do it well. What I do well is garden and cook; and cook for a lot of people. You should stay for supper."

"So, what's on the stove?" Her response won't matter. I'm made hungry already by the aroma.

"Lime and curry chicken in tomato paste sauce, stir-fry cabbage with carrots and canned plums, and mashed potatoes. If we finish early enough, I might make a pie. CC brought in the last of the apples this morning."

We go through the list of questions first, just to confirm that she wants to, or is willing to, talk about all of them. I quickly realize this won't be short question and answers, at least with Jan. I already want to ask her what she brought with her, why the tattoos, and, if there's any significance to the Hopi jar. I want to know if I am wrong, or if I have created a stereotype, that country music, à la Dolly Parton, isn't exactly a *Black thing* (if there is a "Black thing"). I'm pretty sure these questions will have to wait. Jan wants to talk.

Turning down the pots on the stove, Jan invites me to her room in the turret on the second floor. The room is accessible only up a winding stair making it undesirable to the rest of the women. Jan explains that she still has the legs for it and the daily sun rise and east-facing view inspire her. I'm winded and my knees are screaming by the time we get to the top. Although she took the stairs slowly, Jan hasn't skipped a beat.

The room is cramped. There's an oversized bed that must have been assembled here, with an air mattress—the only one able to make it up the stairs. There's an armchair and a low stool being used as an ottoman in front of it. Like Joan's studio, there are bookcases below the turret-surround windows. These are filled with Native American pottery. On the two walls that are useful for pictures there are a dozen paintings. Horses in darkness silhouetted against a pale moon, horses with Madonna-like women with babies riding bareback, and there are sunrises.

"Joan did most of these," Jan says, as she sits down on the low bookcase, inviting me with her hand to sit on the stool. "This one is the first she gave me. We were teenagers. She was trying to capture the story that is always told about my mother's birth. Joan loved it. She felt it made me quite exotic! She and I are related on our fathers'

side. My mother was Indian, Hopi, specifically. I'm what they used
to call red-boned—a mix of 'redskin' and 'negro.' I am that, and
more. It seems that that term, along with 'high-yellow,' are deroga-
tory terms now, but we never thought so—it was just a way of describing who we are. I was red-boned, Joan, a mix of Black and
white, more high-yellow.

"Anyway, the list of questions you sent down asked about my earliest memory. It is my mother telling me the story of her birth on
the pueblo in Arizona.

"Sit, Jessica, and I will tell you. In my mother's culture, a good
storyteller is one with a story bag of oral traditions, someone who
collects and remembers stories from long ago, someone who sees that
a story is being created every minute, right in front of your eyes. My
mother was such a woman. My mother would sit us down in front
of her. She would sit on a low stool, legs open wide, elbows on knees,
leaning into us." Jan assumes this position, leaning deeply towards
me, and continues, "My mother would then say, as if casting a spell,
'Aliksa'i, it is time for a story.' In Hopi 'ali' means something like
delicious, good, delightful. As children, we fell under her spell, ea-
gerly awaiting what came next. Following tradition, she would always tell us if the story we were about to hear was true or made up.
These are her words, Jessica.

"'Aiksa'i.' This is the story of how I was born. This story is true. I
was born close to midnight on the pueblo in Arizona. The wind blew
and the coyotes yipped, yipped, yipped, announcing my arrival. Because we had no Hopi word for 'apportioned lands,' we borrowed
the Spanish word 'pueblo' to describe the land our people had pop-
ulated for a thousand years and the white man had so recently 'given'
to us. The pueblos, like the white man's allotted reservation lands, were
supposed to be neatly drawn lines to bring peace, while providing pros-
perity for the white man. But it was still a restless land. Still, the soldiers
came. They still come. One of the women had the back of her legs

slashed by a soldier's sword as she was walking the road the week before my arrival. It was too dangerous for us to stay. So, it was, in our house made of stone, with dirt floors, clean and swept, and with a small kiva in the corner for warmth, that I came into this world. I slid from my mother easily, but only after a full day of labor. My first wails were accompanied by deep inhales of the pungent smoke from the pin-ion-wood fire. The other women tended to my mother and me as my father readied the horses. He then lifted my mother, as gently as he could, on to a horse. The woman handed me to her with a bless-ing. Then, my parents rode into the night. And, so it came to be that I was baptized at midnight on the back of a horse as we fled."

Jan laughs and her eyes sparkle. "This is my earliest memory, me and Joan listening at my mother's feet to this story. I just can't think of a more auspicious start to person's story! Of all the things you wouldn't want to do directly after childbirth, I imagine, horseback riding is right up there.

"Child, you look skeptical. What I can tell you is that all Hopi true stories start and end the same way. I wish I could remember the words she'd say. I never bothered to learn the language my mother would gladly have passed on. But always at the end of a true story she would say the words in Hopi and then translate 'this is not hear-say, Jessica, this is really true.'"

I am humbled. "Oh, Jan, I wish I was a better writer! Your mother's beginning indeed makes a very good story and both you and she tell it beautifully."

"What I wish Jessica, is that she had written it, or that I had taken the time to capture all of her stories, or that my children would have been interested. It didn't seem important to me until after she was dead. And, since I barely see my children, I imagine neither my mother's story, nor mine, are important to them. My daughter Brenda used to come here. She and Tia used to be close. I'm not sure what happened to that, but families are funny places, aren't they?

"We didn't see much of my mother's family and I have no other real Hopi roots, although my mother made sure I was a bona fide, card-carrying Indian. She and my father moved to Baltimore so he could work on the railroad. Decent work for a Black man in those days, but very far away from the pueblo.

"In answer to your question about whom I would like to most speak with, it would be my mother. At my age I understand, and regret, the many hurts I caused her, big and small. I wonder at the hurts and joys I didn't even know I caused, as I watch myself and my daughter spar and miss opportunities together. I wish I had been a better daughter. I wish my daughter saw what I now see. I would give an awful lot to see my mother sit, where you are, on her stool and whisper '*Aliksa'i.*'"

Chills run down my arms as Jan reaches between her legs and into the bookcase picking up a piece of pottery, caressing it. "It's one reason I bought this 'storyteller.' It's by the Cochiti clay artist Helen Cordero. She was actually a bad potter. She could not quite get the coiling right for pots, so she made these figures instead. This one is in remembrance of her grandfather, braids going down his back, children climbing all over him. He was the storyteller in her family. I think she got the idea from Cochiti lore around 'singing mothers.' Her work was so wildly popular with tourists and collectors that they were copied, adapted, and rapidly manufactured by many tribes and vendors. In answer to a question I think you want to ask, what I brought here was my mother's stool, the one you are sitting on, and this collection of paintings and pottery. These were the things that mattered." She leans further toward me, offering me the figure. Taking it from her it is surprisingly light, has an old dusty feeling, it makes you smile.

Elbows on her knees, she says, "Jessica, I tell you this, our stories are important. This is not hearsay. This is really true."

just for today

My mind is too full, after talking with Allison and Jan, to process one more interview. I beg off a discussion with Deirdre. I need time to clear my head. I'm surprised that it feels like I have been sitting far too long today. A walk will do me good. Pointing me to a path that will lead me to the new construction, Jan assures me that if Allison shows up, she will let her know that I'm at the new house. As the door closes she calls out for me to invite Malcolm and Ali over for dinner, and shouts to Deirdre and Margaret Mary, asking them to peel and core the apples, and set the table.

The wide path runs behind the house along the top of the cliffs. Ahead to the left there are lines of white fences dividing and then subdividing broad sections of acreage. The path dips into a canopy of huge linden trees. Small twigs and branches, snapped in the wind, crunch under my feet. Off to the right, so close, the Chesapeake Bay. It's a unique perspective being up here. When I had the kids, below, hunting crabs and sharks' teeth I had no idea what sat atop the cliffs.

It is cold, the wind, strong off the bay! I increase my pace, almost to a jog, until I come across an animal pen off to my left with a dozen or so large, almond-colored sheep. They are heavy with wool, huddled together in a corner of the pen under a huge leafless tree. What seems like miles of fence runs down toward Rt. 4. As I walk over and lean into the pen, two llamas, clearly not happy at my sudden approach, run over, stomp their feet aggressively, and spit.

"Really? Really?! Oh, *yuck! Yuck! Yuck!* That's disgusting," I shout into the wind at the nonplussed llamas. Turning to try to wipe the green, odorous slime off my shoulder with my sleeve, I see a golf cart bumping along the path in my direction.

"Good afternoon, we haven't met yet, I'm Deirdre. Jan said you'd be walking this way and I thought with the wind and the cold you might want a ride. Oh, I see the llamas got you. Sorry about that. They are just doing their job, guarding my sheep."

She reminds me, instantly, of one of Sleeping Beauty's three plump little fairy godmothers. Cute, flighty, humorous. A bit magical.

"Nice to meet you, I'm Jessica. Guard llamas? Really? Pretty effective, and this is pretty disgusting."

"I know, but they do the job of keeping predators away from my sheep, stomping and spitting. I keep them up here now, under the trees. My last llama got struck by lightning in the lower, more open pasture. It doesn't help to be the tallest in this crowd."

In response to my stifled giggle, she continues, "It's OK, Jessica, you can laugh, everyone does.

"You can wash up at the new house." She looks absolutely lovingly at the animals. "They are beautiful, aren't they? This is a good flock. The wool has been extraordinary this year, and we're getting good results with the llama fiber as well. More about that later. Just let me toss these two bales in the pen." With that she gets out of the cart and removes one and then another diminutive hay bale from the back, tossing them gingerly into the pen. "Cute hay bales, eh? Luckily, Gene Martins' people make them up for me or I wouldn't be able to tend the herd the way I like. Come on, hop in. I'll ride you up to the new house."

We travel the path for a short distance, through the trees, and see the new house straight ahead. I apologize to Deirdre for not meeting with her earlier today, explaining my overload and the need for a walk. I tell her I want to talk to her about how she got the idea for all of this. She graciously says we will have time to talk, and that she's not surprised if I found Jan a little overwhelming. She babbles a bit about the sheep and knitting and how surprised and delighted she was when her children and grandchildren gave her the two llamas last Mother's Day.

We come to a bumpy, jostling, stop in front of the house, with the two wheels on my side just off the path. The west-facing house is a large, oblong shaped, stuccoed house, with deeply slanted tin roofs. Great eaves overhanging the wrap-around porch.

Deirdre says, "Malcolm will have to explain all the mechanics of the place. All I can do is point out the wind towers over there and the obvious design features. The roofs, gutters, and drains go into containment bins to collect rain and melting snow. There's also some, oh, what's the word, special water system. It's frustrating to keep losing words at this age. Anyway, the water is used and cleaned from all parts of the house, even the toilets—it's used, reused, and also used for the plants. I'm not sure I'm comfortable with it—oh, wait, 'gray water' system! It's called a gray water system. Sorry, senior moment! Lots of those in this crowd!

"We will see about the water thing. Oh, and there's something called a composting toilet that sounds just dreadful! Luckily, CC has installed both the composting toilet and a traditional one in response to our protests. There are solar panels on the west-facing roof, and we now have an entire field of solar panels below, something about getting this house 'off a grid.' There's also a garage in the back with a covered walkway so we can get to the cars and golf carts. Goodness knows some of us, who shall remain nameless, shouldn't be driving anymore!

"We like Malcolm's design. Poor dear, it hasn't been easy for him to please all of our interests, and CC's absolute demand that all the materials be, drat, what does she call it, oh, from 'sustainable' materials.

"The big bare landscaping beds here are being plotted out now by Sydney, Jan, and the horticulture students from the college. Poor dear, Sydney's had a rough week, so tired of the chemo. She wants this bed to be pretty and medicinal. She has a good list of what will grow well here and be perennial. I'm so glad Sonia and Ali asked her to do this!

"Anyway, here we are. Go ahead, hop out and walk right in. Malcolm's wonderful. He can show you where to take care of the llama spit. He will be eager to show you around. Jan asked me to remind you to invite them to supper, and I hope you'll stay."

Leaving the cart, I choose the gently sloping wood ramp up to the corner of the porch rather than the wide central stairs at the front door. The front door is extra wide and there is almost no sill between porch and the house interior. Clearly, this place is being designed, seamlessly, to accommodate the women as they age. Walking through the doorway is inspiring. Open, airy, filled with light. No furniture yet. Jimmy Buffet music is coming loudly from the back of the house. Warm wood tones are everywhere. There's a great room, alcoves, and what appears to be six-bedroom suites, three to the left, three to the right. One on each side has a private bath, while two share a "Jack and Jill" connecting bath.

There's a large loft overhead adding to the dramatic effect when you enter the great room. Ceiling fans are circulating counterclockwise, sending heat back down to the rooms from the ceilings. There are also rooms in front of me on a second floor.

Walking across the great room, I slide open the door I suspect might be an elevator. "Eureka," I say aloud.

"It's an elevator, not gold," says the voice behind me. I'm met by a broad smile and a laugh. "Jan texted that you would be up here. I'm Malcolm. Did you survive the ride with Deirdre?"

He is a man's man, someone comfortable in his own skin. Sandy-blond hair with a tan that I just assume is perpetual. There is no stress about him. He's dressed in cargo shorts and a Caribbean-look Tommy Bahama shirt that contrasts strongly to the brisk fall air outside. He smells sweetly of a man that has worked all day. The equally sweet smell of rum comes to me from the glass he is holding in his left hand, pencil in the other. Like his wife, he is instantly likable. I'm comfortable with him. I let myself think how nice it will be to get to know him, and Ali, and Gene.

With a sweeping and examining eye he looks over the room and explains that the floor is cork, the doors and paneling bamboo. "The front porch, railing and benches are from recycled carpet fiber, totally termite resistant, but they look just like wood. NyloBoard—who knew? I was skeptical about all the sustainable materials until I see them and the rich wood grains and lustrous, stone-like looks.

"Did you notice this, above the elevator call box? The other contractor put in this recycled clear plastic panel so you can see that both the interior and exterior walls are straw bales. I'm sure Tobias told you about that. The straw is grown here on property and is baled. We assemble it and synch it together. We cover it with clay stucco we make from harvesting the clay from fields. Makes for a very well-insulated house! The roof is aluminum. If Deirdre mentioned it, she'd say it was tin. She forgets. Aluminum is safer for the water table and run off. Did you notice the big eaves? I think they keep the over-all feel of the building more in keeping with the period of The Grange main house. They also serve to protect the walls, help with snow removal and with the solar elements we need."

He pauses, noticing my shoulder and sleeve. "I see Deirdre's lla-mas got you. Come into the kitchen and wash up. I'll turn down the music some. The kitchen has worked out really well! The floor is re-claimed wood from local barns. The cabinets look like walnut, but they are eucalyptus. The countertops are my favorite. The material is bet-ter than granite, has the same look and feel. It's what they call 'pa-perstone.' Amazing to me, its recycled paper. I like it because, while it looks like granite, granite gets so cold. This stuff seems always lus-trous and warm to the touch. Beyond the kitchen there's a solarium.

"Over here we have the battery closet. You saw something similar in the barn. Here we can turn on and off sections of the house or the whole house if it's not in use for a period of time. All energy-efficient appliances, of course. I think we've come awfully close to CC's goal of being kind to the earth, not taking any of its dependa-ble resources. Come over here and I'll show you on the spec sheet how the gray-water system works."

I don't think I've said a word, taking in the feel of the place, the sheer idea of it, running my hands along the recycled paper-turned-granite-like counter tops, noticing all the attention to detail.

Simultaneously with us moving to the large kitchen table and the spec drawings the back door of the solarium blows open to Ali and behind her, Roy's "Greetings, greetings!"

Roy? Really? How much have I missed? Ali and Sonia being BFFs? Roy, working here too? Of course, he's the "other contractor" Ali mentioned. The attention to detail, the panel revealing the straw bale construction, that's pure Roy. With the arrival of Roy, I suddenly feel like a fish out of water. There are too many dots that I'm not connect-ing. I gratefully accept Ali's invitation to take me back to The Grange house, leaving Roy to finish up some specs with Malcolm.

The drive to The Grange house takes us through the solar fields and through Ali's glowing description of Gene and the Martins' fields. Ali shows me the Martin house and describes it, inside and out. She shares how Tobias bought additional property some years back when the rest of the white Martins' descendants were leaving. She adds that Gene leases it, bartering products and services with Tobias.

When we get back to The Grange house, once again the aromas are enveloping. I'm momentarily surprised to see Sonia and Erica here. Perhaps, nothing should be surprising me about The Grange. Deirdre, and a wan brown woman with a headscarf—who can only be Sydney—are playing Mah Jongg. Sydney is Shari Belafonte- or Halle Berry-beautiful, even with the effects of the chemo.

Jan states that cocktail hour has started, and I should help myself. I pour myself a vodka, feeling Sonia's eyes on my back.

I get hellos from everyone and introduce myself to Sydney. She gives me a sincere welcome, saying she looks forward to talking with me.

Walking over to Jan, I tell her I marvel that she's already got a pie in and out of the oven. She replies by telling me that when she's in a pinch Roy has finally convinced her that Pillsbury pie crust works just as well. She tells me he uses it himself when he's in a hurry.

"I didn't know he baked, too. Pretty impressive. Hey Jan, I'd love to stay for dinner, but I really have to get back. I totally forgot about my cat."

"Aunt Jessica, Roy told me to tell you he took care of Gabler before he came down today," Erica comments.

Of course, he did, Erica, I think. "Thanks."

My escape route is cut off. I try to become invisible and simply help Jan prepare for dinner. I hear Tobias tell Tia he'd take his "highball" now as he joins CC on the couch. Funny, I haven't heard that term since my own father died. Dad liked a whisky or bourbon and ginger, served in a tall, or "high," glass. There's a railroad connection to the name "highball," too, something about the pressure in a steam engine, but I can't recall what it is.

The Mah Jongg players finish up. Soon Malcolm and Roy come over from the new house. I try to spend time with the haughty

Margaret Mary, whom I have barely met, but quickly return to ask Jan about needing any help. Roy is clearly comfortable here, like a host, trying to make sure everyone has a beverage. Deirdre is talking to CC about the llama fiber. Sydney and Ali are chattering away with Jan about the homeopathic garden as Jan continues her cooking.

It is time for our meal, and I wait to sit until others have taken their places. Pavarotti helps Elizabeth to her feet. Tobias takes the table's head. CC to his left, Tia to his right. Immediately, they are holding hands. Sydney takes her place next to Tia. Margaret Mary next to CC. Deirdre next to Sydney. Elizabeth next to Deirdre. Ali and Malcolm sit next to Margaret Mary. Sonia pulls Erica back until the rest of us sit. I take a place next to Elizabeth. Roy, Sonia, and Erica fill in. Erica takes the place at the foot of the table, to Sonia's raised eyebrows.

I look around. Thirteen at table. Unlucky, unlucky! My mother never let us be thirteen at table. She would cite the superstition about Jesus Christ and his twelve Apostles at the Last Supper. Since that dinner of thirteen, the omen goes, one person at such a table will die in the coming year. "Dinner didn't work out very well for JC," my mother would say. As I chuckle to myself, remembering my mother's sense of humor, it sounds like this is the type of thing I can share with Deirdre when we chat.

Looking around at the ages of the diners, of course, someone will be likely gone in the coming year. But who? It's an old superstition, but it still creeps me out. Unlucky.

Sydney asks us to bow our heads. As the rest of us join hands, Sydney speaks.

"Just for today, I will not be angry. Just for today, I will not worry. Just for today I will be grateful for every one of my blessings. Just for today I will work honestly. Just for today, I will be kind to every living thing. Amen."

Just for today.

$$e^2$$

From: SoniaCortezphd@Martinsburgcommunitycollege.edu
To: JMBarnet@google1.com
CC:
Subject: What is wrong with you?
8:00 PM

Jessica, what is the matter with you? You practically bolted from the table, even before the dessert. I would not have even let Erica up to leave the table as quickly as you left moments ago. Really, you frustrate me.

I will see you in the morning. Tomorrow we pick up the pace to a run and you will explain yourself.

Sonia Cortez, PhD
Dean of Special Projects
Martinsburg Community College
Sent from my iPhone

Hit [DELETE]. Sip vodka.

From: JanKiley@TheGrange.com
To: JMBarnet@google1.com
CC:
Subject: Spoons
9:36 PM

hello, Jessica,

Attached, please find the photoshopped picture of the wooden spoons. I think it shows quite well. If you like it, you will need to give Erica some credit. She helped me get the tones and lighting on it after you left tonight.

Until we see you again, tell stories! - Jan

Hit [**REPLY**].

Write a quick thank you, view and print the really nice photo, sip vodka.

Clumsily retrieve photo from printer, pin to cork board. Sip vodka.

From: AllisonBeckphd@Martinsburgcommunitycollege.edu
To: JMBarnet@google1.com
CC: SoniaCortezphd@Martinsburgcommunitycollege.edu
Subject: A favor
10:17 PM

Hello Jessica,

I am so glad we met yesterday. Now that you are on the team, if it's not too much to ask, on your next trip down can you stop at the Mikado Mercado (M and M) and order a sandwich or a salad or something? We are trying a new project out with our struggling culinary students, keeping it simple, but offering them the opportunity to get a feel for providing some food items. Just go in and order and give me your impressions. I've copied Sonia here as it was her idea.

Thanks, and, like I said, welcome to the team.

Xxoo, Ali
Dr. Allison K. Beck
Dean of Student Services
Martinsburg Community College

Hit [**REPLY**]. *Sure, Ali.*

Pour vodka.

XXoo and 'team?' I don't think so, my friend.

From: ElizabethJ@TheGrange.com
To: JMBarnet@google1.com
CC:
Subject: Tonight
11:45 PM

> *Dear Jessica,*
>
> *Thank you for staying for dinner tonight. I enjoyed our conversation. It is making a difference, I think, to the others, that you want to do this work. But, are you happy doing it? There is a sadness, I think, about you. I hope you are alright. If not, "Whatda ya hafta do?" ☺*
>
> *Fondly,*
>
> *Elizabeth*

Indeed, Elizabeth, Whatda ya hafta do?

Close iPad, pour vodka, and head to the parlor, just for tonight.

next steps

Determined to derail Sonia's anger and scrutiny, this morning I am up early, coffee on, newspaper picked up from the front porch and open on the kitchen counter, as if it is being read. I am sitting on the steps of the porch, fully "Sonia-like outfitted" just as she jogs up the road to me.

"Parking was difficult this morning. I am down at the end of the hill. Why are you out here on the porch?" she pants, slightly.

"Good morning to you, too, Sonia. Coffee first? It's ready, or we can head out. I want to tell you about my discussions with the Dean."

She takes the bait and I feel I am, at least momentarily, off the hook for leaving early last night. Today, the walking has moved to a jog, but the pace feels good and familiar from too long ago. I tell her about the email confirmation I have from Dean McManus assuring me that all my credits still hold, that all I need to do is update the research findings, and that he will help me put together a new dissertation committee. He and I have set a tentative timetable for one year from this upcoming January to finish up, hold my orals, and have, finally, my doctorate. I ask Sonia her opinion, knowing that she will, willingly, give it. She confirms the timeline is a good one, but she urges me to schedule my oral defense before the holidays so I can really enjoy the break. She wants to know more about my thinking on what research updates are demanded. I'm struggling now with breathing, jogging, talking. Sonia isn't the least bit winded. In order to get my breathing back under control, I toss her some questions.

"Tell me about you and Allison. I didn't know you were BFFs. She certainly talks about you all the time. You, and Gene Martin, and Roy. How did Roy get all up in the mix?"

Before she answers we jog a bit more. I am assuming she's noticed my shortness of breath. Then, she stops. "Jess-cee-ka, you sound like a jealous child. Do not mistake people who work well together with friendship, and do not believe what people say to be true, as true. You should know this yourself. Allison and I are not friends."

Before I can ask her to explain, she bolts ahead of me, calling back to me, "Come, we are almost to your house. This has been a good start at a run for you."

In pace with each other, again, I feel oddly gleeful, chosen, special. Ali and Sonia aren't friends. I hadn't even realized that I was jealous of Allison. Stupid, but I was. I didn't like how familiar she was with talking about Sonia. But how could you not be friends with a woman like Allison? I'll find out more about that at another time. For now, I am childishly happy. Sonia and I have been each other's "go-to" person for a long time. Along with everything else that happened, I can't lose her, too.

"Come, Jess-cee-ka, pick up the pace. Just to the top of the hill."

Then, her shriek. I hear it as I fall. "Jess-cee-ka!"

Crash. It happens in an instant. My roll-over ankle snaps, and I'm spilled onto the sidewalk. Nauseous, feverishly hot, I try to pull myself together on the sidewalk. Sonia is at my side. I tell her quickly, "Hey, don't freak out. I'm going to pass out, but I'm OK."

A few moments later I'm back. "Sorry about that, Sonia, same old injury. Crap! This hasn't happened in years. My ankle just rolled and snapped. It's going to be a bad sprain. Damn, this hurts! I should have worn the ankle brace if we were running. Stupid! I was due, but it hadn't happened in so long, I'd forgotten. Can you get your car and drive me the rest of the way?"

Back at my house, Sonia has me set up on the window seat, orchids overhead, left leg elevated, ice pack on ankle, Gabler in my lap. She's retrieved the crutches off the back porch and has them at my side. We are sitting sipping coffee.

Worried that Sonia will want to discuss the events of last night, I hijack the conversation by sharing that the materials for my Africa trip have arrived and that I will be leaving just before Christmas in three weeks. My ankle should be fine by then. If not, it's the excuse I've been waiting for not to go. I point to the complimentary duffle bag, tickets, and the final packing and immunization check list I've left on the dining table last night. I feign excitement at all of the above as Sonia flips through the materials.

"You have highlighted items. This is good. I did not know that you should not wear blue or black because of the Tsetse fly. And it is probably good to know that the lions do not like red. However, I do not like this suggestion that you wear lots of gray and black. This is very, very dull and will leave you without making an impression on anyone. You must think about this." She pauses. "You are very brave to do this, Jessica. This is a good thing to do.

"Now, we need to talk about why you should have stayed last night." Here it comes. I've dodged the rapprochement bullet as long as possible.

Surprisingly, Sonia launches into a totally different topic. She's in rare form today.

"It is always good to hear the women talk. I like, very much, watching Erica interact with them. It is so funny the things she does not know. Last night someone brought up an appreciation for the new refrigerator. Then someone else started talking about how the ice man used to bring ice to the house. Deirdre recalled how her mother would put a triangular sign in the window that had the numbers five and ten on one side and twenty-five and fifty on the other, depending on how much ice they needed. She recalled how the ice man would carry the block of ice up the apartment building stairs with huge ice tongs.

"They all were very amused when Erica pelted them with questions. 'Was there really a job called 'ice man?' How much ice could fifty cents possibly buy? Why did the man need to bring ice?' And, 'Why did Deirdre's family need to have ice delivered? Why didn't they just make it in the freezer?' Tobias was kind and explained that ice wasn't 'made' in those days. There was no electricity to do that. Ice had to be harvested. The only thing the ice box did was keep the ice from melting. He gave Erica the type of history lessons I love. Telling her about how the 'frozen water trade' came about in the early 1800s, about sixty years before Tobias' family was given the original forty acres. I love how he always puts things in the context of his land.

"Tobias told us that the ice on the near-by St. Mary's River was sold on occasion, but most of the ice came from ponds and waterways between New England and the Hudson River in New York. In a minute Erica is using her iPad, pulling up the online encyclopedia and looking at maps and pictures. Each of the oldies had a story about ice, ice machines, ice skating, and so on. Erica said later that we should call these things 'her-stories' and that you, Jessica, should hear them and write them down. Jessica, this simple talk about a refrigerator led to bigger topics. This is what we must discuss.

"This is why I was angry that you left. The conversation was exciting, and I wanted you to hear it. I know you do not think you have a project, but it is unfolding now. It is what Jan says, this is unfolding right in front of your eyes! You do not see that you have started this, with the exception of your error with Tia, people like you, they want to talk with you.

"Tobias said he'd like to spend more time with you and take you around the property, show you the cemetery, introduce you to the mule. Sydney, I think because she is wasting time thinking she is dying, wants to talk to you very soon. Margaret Mary, for me a woman very hard to understand, said she would meet with you. Oh, and Allison, she just oozed about how wonderful you are. Looks like you, too, will have a new BFF," she says with a slight barb in her voice. "However, what I am most excited about is that Tia and CC said they wanted to talk with you. I did not think that would happen after you made such a mistake at the first meeting."

"Gee, Sonia, how do you *really* feel about that," I ask her, marveling at how she can both charm and annoy me at the same time.

Sonia's phone beeps with a message from Erica, *"M, tell J re contest! cu l8r."*

"Erica wants you to know that the women have decided that they are tired of calling the new building 'the new house.' They want it to have a name. They are opening a contest like they did for the M and M. I, of course, expect to win this. However, Erica insists that you, too, should enter.

"Jessica, what Erica asks is unimportant. I have something more important to talk to you about. Do not worry your head about naming that place. I will take care of it."

I laugh out loud at her.

"Silence, Jessica," she says sweeping her hand in the air. "I tell you, this is important. I need to settle something with you before you go to Africa.

"Yesterday," she says, newly serious, "I was at The Grange House because I was working with Elizabeth to redo my will, make a power-of-attorney, health care proxy, living will, and all the other documents should I be incapacitated or die."

"Are you kidding me? Sonia, you are like, thirty-what, and the healthiest person I know!"

"Hush. Jessica, I think about all the women there, and I think about Sydney. She's not that much older than I am. I need to make sure Erica is OK if something happens to me.

"I have written that she will be yours," she says gulping. "I have written that you will take care of her. That you will love her and guide her. I trust you to make sure she will remember me. Not only what I wore, but what I said."

She says the latter with an attempt at humor. This may be the only time I have ever seen Sonia close to tears.

"I need you to do this, Jessica. It is written."

Speechless.

"Sonia, I can't. I'm not good at it. *You* know that. I failed so badly with Ryn and Adam. She deserves better, she deserves you."

"Jessica, do you think I would do this without talking to Erica? Yesterday she spent the afternoon learning about all the documents, how they are used, and when they would need to be used. She understands that there are three years before she is eighteen and can execute this all on her own. She also understands that she will need someone to help her, and she wants that person to be you. She was so clear yesterday, saying how she has missed the 'you' before the trial. I think she knows you have avoided her. Maybe I am just being her mother here, but I think she knows it is because it feels too much like being all together again. We both miss the old Jessica.

"You did not fail Ryn and Adam. I know the mother you were to them. Creative, fun, generous. You drove the carpool, were the Scout leader, planned the trips, made adventures, and introduced them to care for people with less than they had. James did not do that, you did. You planted gardens on Mother's Day, gave them their first jobs. There were art projects and music lessons. You paid for everything when James left you in the lurch and the child support stopped. I do not understand why you did not do what I told you and tell them. They should know what their father did, and that their father was ready to hang them out to dry.

"Do you remember the time one February, it was freezing out, way too much snow, and we were so tired of winter? You put Bob Marley music on, turned up the heat, and lit the fireplace. You invited us over and we all got in our bathing suits, put beach towels on the floor and had a 'we need summer' party?

"In high school you were still there with their activities. In college you were the one that drove them across country, set up their apartments. There was such joy in how you parented, and they turned out to be amazing. You know that. I would want that for Erica, and she would too. You have the room. Jessica, it is time."

"Sonia." I can't speak.

"Jessica, I have written this. Please, for me, let this be true. I want this. If I have an accident and become incapacitated, if I die, I need you to make the decisions for me. I do not want Erica burdened with that. You, above all, will know what to do."

Then, the tension is broken. "Greetings, greetings!" Roy.

Sonia and I break into peals of laughter. She, most uncharacteristically, kisses me on the top of the head, saying she has to run, that she will see me soon, and that she is glad it is my left foot that snaps, because I can still drive to Martinsburg and help "your new BFF, Allison," out on her new project.

Without a pause, she gives Roy a peck on the cheek as she darts by him, telling him that he should be nice to me today because I have finally run, and because I will not be doing it for quite a while.

Unlucky. Lucky. I am both.

oh, would some power the giftie gie us, to see ourselves as others see us

Sonia whisks out the door, a new promise between us, as Roy deftly moves around my kitchen, launching into a running monologue. "Jes, sorry about the leg. Sonia texted me to pick up ice packs. I'll put them in the freezer. I bought one of those medical freezer packs too. Hey, Jan sent up this piece of pie from last night for you. You should have stayed through dessert at least. It's really neat watching all the dynamics unfold down there."

"Good morning, to you too, Mr. Gillis. I understand that we have to add 'baker' and 'baker-cheat' to our list of your skills," I kid him. "Get some coffee and join me. You have me captive this morning," I say to him, indicating the crutches and ice. "This is the time to go over the renovations you recommend, and, perhaps, for you to tell me about the rest of your skills so they are not always a surprise to me."

He pours coffee and joins me on the window seat, Gabler moves from my lap to his. I realize I've barely studied him in all the months he's been here. He's taller than me by a bit. I'd guess six feet, yet he's somehow compact, neat. Today he's wearing simple jeans, expensive belt with a Southwestern-looking buckle. An outdated, but attractive, plaid shirt, cuffs rolled at the sleeves. I don't think I've ever seen him in a coat or sweater. He's just this side of handsome. I like watching his hands move, and like the sound of his voice as he enumerates his attributes.

"Well, let's see, I make five dinner meals, period. Well, actually only the entrées. I like to bake cookies and pies. Yes, I cheat, on occasion, with Pillsbury pie crust. I play the trombone and the trumpet. I like watching all sports. I play tennis and golf and would love to play football again.

"Oh, that reminds me, Malcolm and Allison are watching the Ravens game on their boat Sunday. It's supposed to be a warm weekend. Their boat is a great spot to hang out. If it gets cold, they will turn the heaters on. I don't think we will be moving the boat out into the bay unless we get a very early start.

"By the way, Ali seems quite taken with you. They asked me to invite you to come. Just a head's up, Allison doesn't like to be distracted during the game, so not a lot of chit-chat. They always have a crowd. Ali is an amazing cook, so there will be lots of food, and more than enough alcohol. What do you think? Would your leg make it impossible? I could help. Think about it. You don't have to decide now."

I'm ready to decide but have been given a "get out of jail free" card by Roy's lack of a need to make an on-the-spot decision and by his quaint rambling.

He continues. "Let's see, what else about me. I worry, all the time, about almost anything. I have three boys. Well, grown men, really. I wish I was closer to each of them, but that's not on any of their agendas. I'm more content than I have ever been. I've done pretty much everything I've wanted to do, except have a lasting relationship with a woman.

"I'm pretty constant, Jes. What you see is what you get. What about you?"

"I don't know, what do you see, Mr. Roy Gillis?" I regret the question the minute it comes out of my mouth. Reaching for the crutches I decide to deftly move the conversation in a different direction. Roy, solicitously, wants to help me move, tripping me up in the process.

So much for deftly! "It's OK, Roy, no need to *help*." I gasp and giggle, as I right myself out of his arms. "I've got a few things to do in my office. I've got to scoot upstairs, literally. Every time this happens, I can't quite manage the steps and the crutches, so I wind up bumping up the stairs on my behind. The first-floor bathroom should have gone in years ago. Roy, if you could, just take the crutches up to the top of the stairs, I can get it from there."

He, of course, obliges, taking the crutches as I bump up the stairs. I get the crutches at the top of the stairs and go to my office. I don't remember printing and posting the picture of the spoons and the pottery but straighten it now on the cork board. I send a few emails to my students, and one to Sonia, "*I am awestruck, thank you. Yes, of course, I will do this. You had better not make me need it! I love you, both of you. Tell Erica.*"

I line up my next set of meetings at The Grange, one with Sydney and, nervously, set up a conversation with Margaret Mary. I make a note to bring my disconnected quilt squares with me. Maybe the quilt will be a starting place for us. I'd much rather start with Tobias. There's something about him that keeps calling me back. I just want to spend more time with him. I decide to shoot him an email, not letting on that I know what was said last night, I ask if he can give me a tour of the full property and if he will, please, take me to the graves.

I get back to the top of the stairs ready to descend, pausing at their bedrooms. Is it time, as Roy says, to let Ryn and Adam's rooms be redone? Their rooms are too much like they left them, and not enough like how they would be if they still came and used them. Erica, here? The price of that is too much to bear.

Bump, bumping down the staircase on my bum, crutches under one arm, I am not anticipating Roy, Gabler in his arms, ready to ascend the stairs and ready to answer a question I posed twenty minutes earlier.

"Jes, I don't know you as well as I'd like, but this is what I see. I think you are complex. I think you are wicked funny, smart, and quick. You go to sarcasm a bit too readily, but it is never at anyone's expense. I've never seen you be cruel or cross. I think you have a good eye for detail and appreciate fine things. I like the way you always have interesting factoids. I think you drink more than the average bear, and that you have your reasons.

"I think it's a very good thing that you are walking and running. If it's not too forward, I like the changes I see in your body as a result of it. I think you are beautiful. I think, if you let yourself, you will make a difference at The Grange. I think it will make a difference in you. I have been watching you for almost a year now. I have not pushed, but after watching you the other night at dinner, hanging out on the edge, with so much to contribute, I want to push, a bit. I watch as the others react to you. I don't think you see it. They want to be with you. They want to tell *you* their story. They see an amazing you. So do I, Jes.

"I think there is a back story. I think there is something you are leaving out. I hope you trust me with it. I think you deserve this house, finished. I think you deserve to be loved. I think you deserve to be happy. I'd like to be a part of that, with no demands."

This all feels like an uncomfortable confluence of events. Sonia, Roy, the notes I've begun to make from the interviews with the others. This is sooo not supposed to be about me, way too uncomfortable. Move on, change focus.

"Well, I do declare, Mr. Gillis, I think you flatter me." I say in my best Scarlett O'Hara impersonation, hoping to make light of all this.

"Jes, there are just times in our lives when odd things come together, in a good way. I hope this is one of them." Turning from me and going back down the stairs, he says, "Come on Beast. Let me feed you so the Southern Belle can rest her ankle."

Dumb struck.

I decide, clumsily, to re-ascend the steps, dragging the crutches with me as I hear Roy, below, feed the cat. He shouts up that he sees my Africa trip information has come. He adds that he thinks it's really brave of me to go on this adventure by myself.

Do I have a choice? In my office, email screen up, I take some travel-sized vodka bottles from a drawer and pour them into an abandoned, empty coffee cup from some time ago. I carefully type in their email addresses, knowing from the non-profit website they are still operative.

Dear Ryn and Adam,

I love and miss you beyond measure. I wonder each day how you are. The thought of you spending one more Christmas away from me brings me sadness beyond words.

I do not know how to say I am sorry in more ways than I have already done. I am going to Africa in a few weeks. It is as far away as I can think to go without wanting, or expecting, you with me.

Sadly, I know, too, that you will be with me even there, as you always are. While in Africa I would want to see you marvel at what we would see. I would want to lie in our tents and listen for the roar of lions. I would want to, simply, build more memories together.

Everyone is telling me how brave I am to go to Africa, alone. I'd love to discuss that with you. Would they be saying that if I was headed for Paris or Rome? Do they say it because it's Africa, and if so, what does that say about perceptions? Do they say it because I am a white woman, travelling to the 'dark continent?' Does this raise questions of racism and classism because of Black people, or poor people, or because there are lions and tigers and bears? Oh my!

Now, I am just being silly. There are no tigers, and I'm not sure about bears. I just miss our debates and your humor.

Brave? Bravery would mean admitting that you didn't die in the crash, that you've just chosen to be dead to me. It is just too hard to stay here and face another holiday, knowing we could be together, but will not be. It is not the going that is brave. I am going to hide. I am a coward. Bravery would mean staying and facing the silence between us. Bravery would mean accepting that it is, somehow, ok, and that someday, you will forgive me and come.

It's been three years now. I miss you each moment.

I know you will visit your dad this holiday. He always makes sure I get multiple pictures of you during your visits. I'd like to think he is trying to be kind, but I know it's to bring home the fact that, even in prison, he gets to be with you, and I am excluded. That sounds harsher than I mean it to be. You all look delightfully happy.

I hear Sonia's voice in my head. "Jess-cee-ka, do not sound like an old bitter woman. Bitter is ugly. Bitter is something you choose. Better sad and angry than bitter, Jess-cee-ka. No one wants to be around bitter."

I delete the last paragraph and go for trite.

> Adam, you have grown so tall! I love the beard, you look really handsome. Ryn, it looks like you are growing your hair long again. I'm wondering if you ever braid it. You look very fit in your last picture, like when you run marathons. I am running again or was until this morning when my roll-over ankle snapped, again.

Again, I hear Sonia editing my words. "Do not try to get their sympathy. You will look manipulative." I leave it that I am running again.

> I am sorry for everything. If I could take it back in an instant, I would. If I could have taken the fall for your dad I would have.
>
> I cannot understand that you have chosen this path of erasing me from your lives. I wish I could tell you my side of the story.
>
> Merry Christmas. Be safe, have fun. I loved you from the moment you first grew under my heart. I will love you even after it has stopped beating.
>
> - M

Wait.
Hit [**DELETE**].
Wait.
Breathe.
Bumping down the stairs, I round the corner on crutches. It's early in the day, I eye the vodka bottle. Roy's on the back porch. Leaning against the countertop, I ask him what he is working on.

He says that he noticed the porch and back stairs really needed to be replaced so he was taking measurements. He adds that he has set up an appointment with a landscaper to discuss salvaging the yard.

Of course, he has. Putting the vodka bottle under the counter, I ask him what time I would need to be at the boat on Sunday in time for us to pull out into the bay and still catch the pre-game show.

He's promised a crowd. I can still hide.

the dash -

Over the next few days I take advantage of my injury. The messed-up ankle has provided the opportunity to get a good start on the doctoral dissertation research up-dates, easier, and far less engaging, than I would have thought or hoped. My mind is elsewhere. Finally becoming *Doctor* Jessica Barnet doesn't seem important.

Being laid up has also given me the opportunity to do the Africa trip preparations I fretted about being able to get done. I've down-loaded books to read—*West with the Night* and *Into Africa: The Epic Adventures of Stanley and Livingstone.* Also the PBS biography on the famed archeological family, Louis and Mary Leakey and their son, Richard. I've watched Robert Redford and Meryl Streep in *Out of Africa* at least three times.

"I had a farm in Africa…" is the opening line of the movie. Erica does quite a good and dramatic imitation of this, making Sonia and me laugh and delight in her talents. *"I ha-d a fa-rm in Af-ri-ca,"* Streep's character says it, and her life unfolds. I try to imagine myself transformed and wonder what that would look like.

The possibilities at The Grange also keep tantalizing me. I've made a chart of all The Grange women's names and ages, my initial observations, anything that I feel is important that they have said, or I have learned. I try to remember what Elizabeth said that first night as we sat in the barn and put her descriptors of the women in the boxes.

It felt right to include Tobias and even Joan in the chart. I've left blank squares, not knowing if others, like Gene Martin, should be included. That, of course, opens the possibility that the story, however it unfolds, should also include Sonia and Allison, and Malcolm. And Roy?

Roy? He keeps rumbling around in my head. I certainly averted what looked like a pretty direct request to get together. He, being a gentleman, let me side-step the issue, literally. Not so easy to do on crutches. I smile at myself and keep ruminating. What's going on with him, all these months at the house and suddenly a shift? What's going on with me?

Clearly, when I told him *my story* the thought crossed my mind to have sex with him. That would have fit the pattern—drink vodka, drink more vodka, have sex—one more way to avoid dealing with the fact that it is easier to pretend they are dead rather to admit to myself, and others, that they are really just dead to me, and they choose each day not to be with me.

Easier to tell this lie, than admit to the truth. I botched the most important of relationships. I've been judged and condemned by my own children. I've lost them in the process. So much easier to tell the story, see others' shock, have them understand my pain. It is as real as if they were dead, worse, really.

This way, it's nice and tidy. Easier to tell my story than deal with the endless questions about what happened, why don't you see your children, are they coming for the holidays, are you going to visit them, did the kids call for Mother's Day, what's this one doing, where is the other living. Endless. Easier to tell this story than watching others judge me or feel their scorn. Scorn followed with a touch of leprosy-like avoidance. I saw it all in the first year. Someplace in the middle of year two I made up the story. It didn't even feel like a lie.

How could I even figure out what a relationship with Roy could look like? I can just see me opening the conversation, *Oh, Roy, by the way, you know that whole thing about the kids and the car…?*

Oh, what a tangled web we weave, when first we practice to deceive. Who said that, Shakespeare? I don't think so, someone Scottish, I think. I should ask Roy, he would know.

Roy, again. I've gotta stop that. I don't *do* relationships. I haven't really since James and I divorced. Another bad idea, I should have dated, given the kids role models, created a new family. I didn't date because I didn't want to worry about bringing a man into our lives. I had to be sure no one would ever hurt either one of them. It's probably more true to say I didn't date because, simply, I loved the three of us. *Three.*

Shaking all of this out of my head is important. Sydney didn't want to wait for a face-to-face meeting. I've arranged to do a Google "Hang Out" with her today. She, apparently, uses and prefers the Google video chat options in her work. Already familiar with Skype, this is one more technology thing I have to master. Thank God for Erica. She's got me all set up.

Judging that it's late enough in the day, I go to the kitchen and only pause for a moment before grabbing a coffee cup and pouring the vodka. I've got time to go over my notes before Sydney calls in. I'm trying to capture the messages, themes, and lessons each person seems to impart. I've written questions, wonderings, and "thoughts for the ride" in the squares and margins of my chart. The "thoughts for the ride" was supposed to be "thoughts for the run," helping me focus, along with my ever-present music playlist from the iPod the kids gave me. I've been trying to increase my running endurance. I'll have to put that off for a few weeks.

I set up for the video chat at the kitchen counter. I can get a better height to the camera, the light comes in from behind, I don't look so old, I can put my hand on my chin, hide the jowl that seems to have suddenly appeared, and be closer to the vodka.

While I wait for Sydney to initiate the chat, I go over my emails. Allison and I have been emailing back and forth. Malcolm has been checking the weather. Unseasonably warm. One o'clock game. If I can be there by ten "The Captain" will get us out on the water, down the river, around the tip, and up to an anchorage on the cliff's side. Allison assures me that I should bring nothing, that she always has too much food and too much to drink. Reading into this last bit, I have to assume that she is referring to the number of available beverages, but maybe she, too, overdoes it, on occasion.

She's told me that on the boat tomorrow there will be me, Roy, Sydney—if she's up for it, Tia, and CC for sure, and, possibly, Tobias. Between six and eight of us then. Not quite a crowd, but enough. Interesting, she hasn't included Sonia.

She's warned me, as Roy did, that she doesn't like talking during the game, but that if I want to chat there are multiple decks and plenty of room on the boat. "Wear something purple," she demands. There is also no rooting for the other team, apparently.

It's almost time for Sydney to initiate the call. I pour just a bit more vodka, and settle in for the chat, realizing I'm nervous. In all likelihood, she's dying. Thirteen at table. How do I frame this conversation?

The computer prompt rings right on schedule and Sydney's beautiful, soft face, appears on my screen.

"Hello Jessica! Thank you for doing this today. I've really been eager to talk to you. How are you?"

We exchange pleasantries. She comments on the surprise of seeing the orchids over my shoulder, I tell her how easy they are to grow and that I'm pleased that she will be boating tomorrow. I tell her that I have no set agenda for our conversation but that I've made some notes. I know she already has the set of questions. I invite her to begin and study her face and mannerisms as she speaks. I peek over her shoulders to take in what her room looks like. Soft colors, great artwork, comfortable feel. She begins.

"I don't have the luxury of a lack of focus and purpose right now, Jessica." She says this ruefully, she's not scolding me. "This is my second round at 'the attack of the brain cancer.'" She says this like it's a sci-fi movie title.

"I've completed the therapy. Now we have to wait and see if it works. If it doesn't, there's only one more option. It sounds ridiculous. If the cancer isn't killed off, they will actually inject the polio virus directly into my brain. Seriously, what mad scientist makes these things up? Anyway, I'm on a short leash, and I know it. If things go south, I'm prepared, not like Joan, but prepared. My kids will come. I will be fine.

"But, I'm also angry. I know that's common, but that doesn't matter. I am so angry. I am afraid. I feel powerless. I hate it. I grab every opportunity I have to reclaim myself. I feel I lose my way far too often.

"You know, this is all made more absurd because of what I do for a profession." I prompt her to tell me about that and she continues. "I'm a 'life coach,' really, a *life coach*. Someone who has clients that come to her with goals or no goals, skills, or no skills, and together we create a plan, set goals, acquire skills, and build the life they say they want. It's not therapy. I don't have the time, or the skill, for that. Life coaching is simply focused work, taking charge of your life and positioning it for happiness and success as you define it. I do most of it electronically, in email, blogging, and videoconferencing, like this. I've been able to continue with most of my clients while here at The Grange, except on the really bad days. But there's a cruel irony being in this situation and being a 'life coach,' don't you think?"

I agree, feeling both curious and vodka relaxed. I ask her how she would treat herself if she came to herself as a client.

"I've thought about that—good question. I'd want to know what I want to accomplish, what goals I have set. I'd want to know if I thought I could accomplish them, or what I would need to accomplish them. And, honestly, I'd come up blank. I'm content with what I've done. I love my kids and grandkids. Oh, don't look so surprised. I married stupidly young, but we succeeded at it. We defied the odds for teenage marriages succeeding, especially for young Black kids. I worked for DC schools for many years. We had four children, two boys, two girls. Howard worked for the Justice Department. He was killed in the line of duty, a drug bust, nearly twenty years ago. The kids were tiny. Luckily, among the amazing things you can say about the Black community is there is almost always a strong family and extended family. I miss my husband to this day. He'd be very proud of the children, especially how his boys turned out to be fine men. I have five grandbabies. I am not ready to leave them. I am blessed that they all live up in Anacostia, near the 'Big Red Chair.' They visit me most weekends.

"When I think of what more I'd like to do, I wonder why it matters. I'd like to read more history before I go. I'm fascinated by Frederick Douglass, his mixed-race ancestry, the work he did shortly after this grange came into existence. There's no record that he was ever here, but I'd like to think he came, maybe with his second wife, Helen Pitts."

Knowing nothing about this I urge Sydney to go on. "I don't really know much about her other than she is responsible for the Douglass museum in Anacostia, and that Helen graduated from Mt. Holyoke, was a suffragette and, as a white woman, was the subject of much scorn in both the Black and white communities. Her marriage caused her to be estranged from her parents.

"I identify with that since I don't speak to my own parents. I've been thinking a lot about trying to fix that. I could toss out the lure of my dying in front of them, but I'm not sure it's that important to me. As a life coach, I can tell you that the number one goal of older parents is to improve or fix the relationships they have with their adult children. I fantasize that it might be important to my own parents to get reconnected, but I cut them off long ago. Do you know, Jessica, that parents who are estranged from their children are suicidal at ten times the national average?"

I tell her, "I didn't know, but I'm not surprised." I understand exactly what she is saying at very visceral level. I sip from my coffee cup, and prod her with "what did you learn from your mother that you remember now?"

"Most things about her make me angry. I've got a list. On the positive side, I remember, when we were little, she would always tell us that in each day there will be many occasions to say 'please,' and 'thank you,' and 'I am sorry.' She would add, 'See those things, say those things, often.' I've tried to do that with my life.

"I guess that's what I've been thinking about. I'm waiting for my mother to say she's sorry. One of the reasons I haven't contacted them is that the research shows that parents who really want to reconcile with their children go to them and do the big apologetic, apologizing for everything under the sun, not even knowing what they are apologizing for, failing to see what their own children experienced. I don't want her coming here all fake apologizing. I want the real thing."

"Boy, Sydney, I get that, and that you are angry." I am not proud that I'm happy she's moved the conversation away from her own idyllic situation with her children and grandchildren to one of pain. It's a much more comfortable place for me to be. I imagine her as the petulant child waiting for a parent to apologize.

Without the details, I can only wonder what Sydney's mother needs to apologize for, what was her experience? What did her mother do that Sydney cut her out of her life, taking, presumably, her dad with her?

While I make notes Sydney unexpectedly explodes. "Did you just say that you 'get that I'm angry'? Damn you, I started that way, or weren't you listening? Are you so self-absorbed in your little project to have missed that? Let me be clear, I am angry at everything. I am God damn angry at being sick. I am angry at the failure of medicine. I am angry that I am going to miss my children's and grandchildren's lives. I am angry that I feel I need a mom right now and don't have one. I am even pissed that I am pissed. If I have to be sick, I want to be freakin' Mother Teresa or Job, dealing gracefully with life's adversity. Angry, angry at everything," she mutters composing herself.

"I try to be grateful for this place and that the old women are trying to make a home for me. Instead, I find myself irritated at each of them. Deirdre is annoyingly perky, prancing and dancing among her llamas. Jan is always trying to make everything all right—as if that will keep Tobias, Tia, and CC from realizing that Joan is actually dead. Margaret Mary, haughty, overpoweringly strident, skeptical, has an opinion on everything.

"And, if I have to listen to Elizabeth sigh one more time her stupid 'whatdoyouhaftado' I'm going to scream. Could she just freakin' ask a question? We'd all gladly have her 'go on the vacation' she wants. She can have mine for goodness sake! I hate that they all seem to have time left and I don't. I hate that a polio injection to the brain might be my best freakin' shot at survival. I even hate this stupid project, Jessica," she says almost sneering and leaning into the screen.

"What the hell do you want from us, some great life lessons that you can catalogue and fit into a doctoral dissertation or book, some words of wisdom from the old, the dead, and the dying that will heal whatever the hell is wrong with you?

"One of your stupid questions is 'what will your tombstone say.' If I died today it would simply say 'She Was Pissed.'"

Her energy spent, she finishes with, "But that's not how I want it to end. I'd like to have the anger behind me. I'd like to think it's not too late to have a man I love at my side. I'd like to think that the little dash between the date of my birth and the date of my death symbolizes a life well lived between those two events. I want the dash to matter. But, just for today, I am so maddeningly irate."

We close, awkwardly. She apologizes, I do too. I tell her I hope we are OK for tomorrow and she says it will be fine. She's exhausted.

Her image gone from my screen, I get up, dumping the rest of my vodka/coffee cup into the sink, thinking about our apologies. Thinking about how many more there may need to be. I've been so caught up in my own pain I never once wonder what Ryn's and Adam's experience of these years apart have been like. Do they miss their mom? I ache for them.

Turning on my iPod to the *Mama Mia* soundtrack, I putter about as the music fills the house. I turn it louder. Alternately, singing and swaying on my crutches, until that certain song makes me stop in my tracks with grief, "slipping through my fingers…."

"To a Rock Star Mom. Love always, Ryn and Adam."

Really?

I stop by the front closet to pull out Ryn's quilt squares from the chest in the front hall. I don't remember leaving their handprints on top of the chest. Pausing I trace them. I then select two orchids from the dining room humidifier, one with small yellow blooms and one with bold violet ones. Packaging them in therma-sealed bags, along with instructions on how to keep them easily healthy, I will give one as an apology to Sydney, one as a hostess gift to Ali. I'm not sure what she drinks, but I remember the smell of Malcolm's rum at the new house. I've picked out a "sipping rum" for The Captain to enjoy while we motor over to the cliffs. My tidy packages placed by the front door, I set the alarm on my phone.

My meeting with Margaret Mary is scheduled for stupidly early in the morning. I'll need to be up before dawn to get ready, make the drive, do the interview, and still get to the boat. The ride home will be late. I make a note to take care of Gabler before I leave. Head to the parlor, just for tonight. Push Gabler to one side, and nestle in. I fall asleep wondering if Sydney is OK and thinking about the dash.

food for thought

I've fussed more than I want to admit in getting ready for the boat. Put on clothes, changed clothes. Put my hair up, take my hair down. Put on makeup. Put my hair back up. I think the ankle swelling has gone down enough, and the ankle feels good enough, to forgo the awkward crutches. Gingerly, I slip on my RocketSoc® ankle brace, check that the ankle will hold, and change my clothes again.

Sydney's words about Margaret Mary echo in my ears on the drive south. Strident, haughty, skeptical, opinionated. My notes say she's the one Elizabeth said was a former nun. I'm forming an image of Mother Superior from some movie, maybe Sister Aloysius from *Doubt*. I'm dreading our meeting.

Remembering, at the last minute, that Ali has asked me to stop into the M and M, I swerve in, carefully climb the stairs, and am greeted by the little bell as I enter. The menu is modest, a few breakfast items, some sandwiches, and a salad bar. Music from *HMS Pinafore* is jauntily playing. Appropriate for the boat outing later. I grab a cup of coffee and tell the culinary student behind the counter that I need a sandwich for later in the day and ask for tuna salad on rye toast with lettuce. I observe, as instructed by Ali. The student washes her hands. Good. Tells me they don't have a toaster. I suggest that she ask the program to provide one. She indicates that would be good, as a lot of people ask for toast.

Hmmm. Then, we get to the lettuce. She tells me that they don't have any. I stare at her for a moment. "*Um*, maybe I should just get a salad?" I say to prompt her thinking. When she doesn't react but says she will get me a to-go plate, I ask her to tell me about the salad bar. She starts telling me "lettuce, tomato, cucumbers…" and then, the light bulb goes off!

"Hey, I could get you some lettuce from the salad bar and put it on your sandwich!"

Brilliant! She's so proud of herself! My sandwich wrapped up, I hobble down the steps and she calls after me, apologizing for the lack of toast. The little bell echoes its good-bye to me. Thank heaven for teachable moments! I'll report to Ali that basic problem-solving skills and a toaster could help. I leave in a much better mood.

Elizabeth and Pavarotti again greet me as I enter the side door. Elizabeth is listening to the news on an Italian TV station. We exchange pleasantries. I ask to put the sandwich in the fridge. The house is quiet, so I assume most everyone is still in bed. Elizabeth corrects me. CC, Tia, and Deirdre are out tending to the animals, Tobias is probably up at the cemetery with Jan, and Sydney is out by the cliffs doing yoga. I've carried the orchid for Sydney into the house and placed it on the counter so Sydney doesn't have to carry it back after the boat. Elizabeth suggests, with a raised eyebrow, that

I finish up my coffee, telling me that Margaret Mary doesn't allow any food or drink in her room.

"Really?"

I comment again that I'm surprised how early everyone is up. Elizabeth assures me that while they are all early risers, Margaret Mary rises before dawn each day to say Lauds. *Lauds?* Surprisingly, I remember this from the nuns and my old Catholic school days—these are the earliest of morning prayers, said as part of the Morning Office. "Really?" I say again, "Wow! Lauds, I'm surprised I even remember what they are, more so that people still say them!"

"She prays, prays a lot. Maybe enough for you and-*a* me!" Elizabeth winks and we both giggle. I feel conspiratorial.

With a quick "up" to Pavarotti, Elizabeth laboriously rises from her chair with his help. The two of them escort me to a door located under the large front staircase. I'm assuming it's the loo or a closet. Elizabeth, with a cock of her head, tells me that Margaret Mary picked the smallest room in the house, a former slave's room. She suggests I ask her about that. Shrugging her shoulders and motioning to the door she indicates I should enter, turning, I hear her mutter the now familiar, "Whatda ya hafta do."

Knocking softly on the door I hear Margaret Mary, clear New England accent, "Come."

When I enter she is, literally, rising, slowly from a prayer—kneeler placed below a two-foot-tall statue of Jesus the Christ Child. Raising her hand slightly, she indicates that I should wait a minute before speaking. The room is narrow, dim, one small high window at the far end. It is stark, but comfortable. There's the kneeler, an easy chair by a diminutive bookcase, a small desk and straight-backed chair. A single bed, neatly made with an off-white chenille bedspread, is placed on the left wall. Hung over it is a quilt with children's names and multi-hued faces, and images of bikes, baseballs, books, campfires, ice skates, and sailboats. In the center is a likeness of the Jesus statue.

I decide to start with the quilt. She sees me noticing it. Inviting me to sit in the easy chair, she folds her ninety-plus-year-old body into the straight-backed desk chair and looks me squarely in the eye. Even in the dimness, and at her advanced age, she has the most dazzling blue eyes I have ever seen. She begins, "Miss Barnet, we will talk about the quilt by and by, but, if you would be so kind, please let me start. I understand that you are interested in doing oral histories of those of us who live here, and perhaps in doing a historical perspective of the land itself. Is that correct?"

She sounds precise, she sounds like someone capable of hearing my doctoral orals. Depending on how things go, maybe I'll have her read my dissertation and she can challenge my thinking. I can't imagine that I'd be any more intimidated at the oral test than I am now. I remind myself this is voluntary. I don't have to be here.

I mutter that the oral histories are where I think the project is going but that I'm not exactly clear on what the final product will be. I drag Tobias, figuratively, into the fray, telling Margaret Mary that he seems to think I can just wing it, go with the flow, until project clarity suddenly arrives.

Her eyes have not left my face. She seems to want to say, "We are not amused," but I continue. "To be honest, I think you probably all have amazing stories. I'd like to hear them, learn from them, and share them. For example, what is one of your earliest memories?"

"Miss Barnet, what difference could that possibly make to you? If I told you that one of my earliest memories is of my large family returning from Mass on Sunday mornings and having the house dizzyingly filled with the smell of roasted chickens and potatoes and that that single memory brings a smile to my face nine decades later, would it matter?

"Given that we had to abstain from all food and liquid for at least twelve hours prior to the Holy Sacrifice in those days, just entering the house would make your mouth water. In winter we would immediately sit down to eat. But, oh, in summer! My mother would pack up the meal. My father would carry it down the steps of our apartment and, quite creatively, tie the bundles to the engine of the car to keep everything warm, directly to the engine, quite inventive, quite ingenious. Funny to think of that now. My father would then return to the apartment, line us up, carrying whoever was the youngest, and off we would go for a day at the beach.

"Those are my earliest and best childhood memories, but other than being a delightfully quaint and dated story I cannot see what difference it can make, Miss Barnet."

"Please. Please call me Jessica, it makes me uncomfortable to have you to refer to me so formally."

"So be it," she says looking away from me for the first time. "The lack of formality today is something I mourn, along with the lack of good sentence structure, and the loss of Walter Cronkite and his peers as TV newscasters."

I'm not sure if it's permissible to laugh in her presence but I find her statement wonderful and want to remember to write it down later. For now, I am unsure if I should be addressing her by her last name or her first. Instead, I simply state, "The memory you shared is delightful and it gives me such a great picture of you…"

Again, she raises her hand, indicating silence. She finishes my sentence, "A great picture of me *when I was young*?

"Jessica, close your eyes." I do so. "Think about yourself. Is the image you create of a woman near sixty, with a slightly sagging jowl line, a hint of gray, and with lines on her face and veins clearly visible on her hands?" She must notice I wince. "Let me shift to something more comfortable. When you think of any one of us here, what do you see? You see our age, how our bodies sag, how it takes us a bit of time to get up from prayer. You are surprised when you learn that we do things like Photoshop." She sees my body wince and recoil. "Yes, we talk about you when you are not here. There are not a lot of secrets when you live like this.

"Keep your eyes closed. You imagine yourself as very young next to us, somehow giving you a feeling of youth and immortality. You note our gray hairs and our agedness. You are ready to write our histories because you think our lives are over and behind us. You think that we are 'done.' Open your eyes.

"Am I that far from the truth, Jessica? Have you made notes about us?"

Feeling as if I have been caught passing notes in school, I tell her that I have. She asks to see them. I hesitate but hand them to her. A look of self-satisfaction, indicating that she is exactly correct in her assessment, crosses her face before her eyes return to mine.

She closes her eyes and continues, "I am shocked, when I catch my reflection in a mirror or store window. I don't recognize, and want to deny the sag of my neck, the spots and veins on my hands, the soft flabbiness of my breasts and stomach, the lack of pubic hair." She sighs. "I am shocked because when I close my eyes, I see a young and able woman. I am still in my thirties, maybe forties. I see the convent, habit, and sisterhood I left behind in order to adopt children and be a mother. I see myself adding baby and child after baby and child, raising them on my own, biking and ice skating with my children. I see myself doing that still with my grandchildren. Creating, along with my brothers and sisters, one large, closely connected clan. I see me as still capable of doing all those things represented on the quilt. I like to think that I simply choose not to do them. Those faces and names on the quilt above the bed are my children, grandchildren and great-grandchildren."

She opens her eyes and chuckles at the look on my face.

"See, I have surprised you. It seems that you are easy to surprise. You have made predeterminations about us. We are not, as I fear you believe, done our lives. We have probably had all of our firsts, our first dates, first cars, first loves, careers, deaths of close loved ones, life threatening awakenings, and so on. I am not convinced, however, that we are 'done' or even done *all* of our firsts. The rest of what time we have left would be entirely boring if that were the case. Jessica, as long as you hold these preconceived notions of us you will never get to the truth of any of us.

"When we are all together in the common areas, I do not see old women. I see the girls we once were. Jessica, I think your approach to this project is quite wrongheaded, quite wrongheaded.

"I see I have confused you. It is just food for thought. Do not write the stories about the beginning of our lives because you have judged that we are already at the end them. Jessica, *once upon a time we were girls, and we still believe we are*. We are still very much alive. In many ways we are at a beginning, to not understand that is wrongheaded.

"Come and sit by me and show me what you brought with you. I think Sonia mentioned quilts."

the tug

A quick glance at my watch has me reluctantly begging my leave from Margaret Mary. I offer thanks and apologies and ask if I can come back soon. I want to show her the quilt squares. She asks if I want to leave them with her. I almost do but I don't want to part with them. She's no longer intimidating, instead, there is something about her that is captivating. I want to ask her about so many things.

Wrong-headedness? Food for thought, indeed.

Back in the car, the GPS is leading me thirty minutes south to Solomons Island. I've never been there. A quick internet check describes Solomons as a picturesque island town nestled between the Patuxent River and the Chesapeake Bay. "Nestled" brings up cozy images and the web images are just that—a busy marina, replete with restaurants, shops and art galleries, boats full-sail, families, and strollers. Established in 1867, population 2,000. *Maryland Seaside* magazine lists it as one of "America's Happiest Seaside Towns."

I'm eager. Being truly happy would be great, but today, just for today, I am grateful. It is a perfect day for being out on the water. It's one of the things I miss most about my life with James, and Florida, being surrounded by water, being in it and on it. James was such an able seaman. Even when our sailboat heeled far to one side, I felt safe. Life was always on the edge with James. I suppose I should have known.

Pulling into the Island Harbor Marina, I luckily find a parking space close to the boat slip. The marina is perfectly situated in what James always called "good water," minutes from the open waters of the Patuxent River and the Chesapeake. You can be sailing or cruising in no time.

From the car I can see Roy and Ali sure-footedly gamboling about the bulwarks of the boat, checking lines and fenders, making sure the decks are dry. They are outfitted in purple Ravens' athletic shirts. A small black dog runs behind them, between them. I can see Malcolm in the pilot stand, also sporting purple, presumably loading charts, checking weather. Nice boat. I'd estimate a forty-five-foot-long trawler, in the same class as cabin cruisers and tugboats. Probably two full berths in the fore cabin and a queen bed in the aft captain's cabin. There are probably two heads, a full galley and great room. I count three tiers of decking, one behind the pilot house up top, a large deck behind the great room and a small one just below that at the aft. I note there will be good sunbathing on the fore of the ship. As my eyes lazily take in the boat, I realize it's been too long since I've been in a marina.

"Permission to come aboard."

"Permission granted! Good morning! What's with the brace?" calls out Malcolm as he leans out of the pilot's window.

My hands are full with rum and the orchid. I am grateful that Roy leaps down to the dock to help me aboard. Ladders, I hadn't counted on the ladders for getting aboard, and moving from deck to deck. This is more difficult than I anticipated.

Ali comes down the ladders frontwards and quickly, both thanking me and admonishing me for bringing anything.

"Come on, let's get you settled, ice on the ankle and a beverage in-hand before the others get here. It will be nice to chat. Remember, no talking during the game."

And so, the day unfolds. Beverages in hand, with a mental note to not overdo it. Allison and I sit amicably and chat. I report my experience at the M and M, and she says she will take care of the toaster and talk to the culinary instructor. She says it's discouraging about the simple problem-solving skills and adds that she's gotten similar reports from Gene.

I tell her about the upcoming Africa trip. She shares her and Malcolm's plan to fly to Ft. Lauderdale and cruise over to the Bahamas during the college's long break. I can hear Malcolm and Roy up top talking about the course we will take and the odds for today's game. I move on to tell Ali a bit about my conversation with Sydney last night and my hope that it doesn't cause any part of today to be awkward.

This is feeling fun, like we are girlfriends, chatting lightheartedly. Outside of Sonia, I don't have this. Because Ali's just mentioned Gene, I ask her, since she's friends with both Sydney and Gene, what she thinks of my idea of trying to set them up together.

Her tone changes immediately, "That's not going to happen, and please don't mention Gene today."

There it is again, the sense of something, just beyond my grasp of understanding. Awkward.

CC, Tia, Tobias, and Sydney arrive together. CC and Tia in matching purple shirts, Sydney in purple leggings. Even the black dog is sporting a Ravens' bandana. Tobias and I are colorless. At least I gave Sydney the yellow orchid, saving the purple one for Ali.

"Have you met the beast?" Roy wonders as he pops down from above, the dog under his arm. "This is *Oso*, the Schipperke." He plops Oso down on my lap, takes drink orders for the others, and moves on.

I ask Ali about her dog and she tells me how he was a present from Malcolm. "The breed name is said *skipper-key*. Malcolm will tell you they were bred as barge dogs, rat finders, the Captain's or 'skipper's' dog. However, Sonia and I looked that up and the breed is actually Belgian, and they were used as herders. I guess it doesn't matter. Malcolm gave him to me because their listed traits include being stubborn, mischievous, and headstrong in temperament. Like Sonia, Malcolm seems to think I'm bossy," she giggles. "He seems to think I deserve a pet that will show me what that's like!"

"That's right," Malcolm joins us and kisses her. "Everybody ready to go? I've got the engines up and running."

Although I am clearly the only one that hasn't been here before, it is comfortable to be aboard and with these people. Malcolm and Ali, the instantly likeable, make everyone comfortable. It's a party boat, the conversation is easy. Malcolm, ready to launch, puts the American flag on the stern, and invites Tobias up top for the view and to drive. He asks Ali and Roy to get the lines, and with a joint, "Ay Cap'in," they do so, and we move out. Ali's ability to be both hostess and first mate is impressive. Roy is ably pulling in, coiling, and tying off the lines and fenders. He left "sailor" off of the list of attributes.

CC, Tia, Sydney, and I move to the open-air deck, Ali is checking on food, and the three men collectively maneuver the trawler out of the harbor towards the bay. As we get settled, I have the chance to say to Sydney that I am really glad she was up for coming today. I try to say it with enough emphasis that she knows I mean, not just in general, but after our conversation last evening. She thanks me for the orchid. Tobias shares that when he and Jan came back in this morning, they both commented on the sweetness of the small pale-yellow flowers. This opens the opportunity for CC, her hand around Tia's waist, to talk about when they first met in Costa Rica.

As they share the story of their eco-trip, they change before me. They become young women in their early thirties and forties. They tell us, as if it was yesterday, not twenty years ago, about meeting at the airline's executive lounge in Houston. CC was flying from Boston, Tia from Baltimore. They share that while they didn't have their "gay-dar" set up on purpose, it was pretty easy to scope out the other and strike up a comfortable conversation at the bar. It delighted them to discover that they were on the same flight into Costa Rica's capital, San Jose, and, better yet, on the same eco-tour down from the mountains to the Pacific Ocean and into the national parks.

"CC, rather manipulatively" says Tia, "got up from the bar, went to the airline desk, and without telling me, had my seat switched to be next to her in First Class."

"What can I say," CC laughs in response "I wanted to get to know her. Ah, the benefits of being gay and having more disposable income than the rest of America."

Tia continues, "It was a pretty magical trip. The plants, the animals, even the insects awed us. The really startling thing for me was seeing the orchids. I can still remember our guide talking about them and being awed that they seemed to grow everywhere in the trees. There are…"

"…fourteen hundred varieties," CC interjects, finishing Tia's sentence. "We saw one tree with eight varieties. Our guide was a little orchid obsessed. I remember she talked about how they live on fungus, and… damn, what did she tell us was the one thing humans can eat from orchids," she asks looking at Tia.

"You can remember that there are fourteen hundred varieties of orchids and you can't remember what is harvested from the small yellow one?" Tia kids her, taking her hand.

"I know," Ali announces triumphantly, returning to the deck, carrying a tray of appetizers. "Vanilla!"

"Correct," pops in Sydney. "Small yellow orchid, green stringbean liked pods. Dry them, ferment them, and eureka, vanilla!"

"And you know this how," I ask her.

"Well," inserts Allison, "I know it because of cooking. Vanilla is stupidly expensive when you think about it, despite the fact that we probably all have a small bottle in our pantries. I wanted to know why. Reading up on it, I found out that of those fourteen hundred varieties you mention, CC, about one hundred and fifty of those are the pale yellow ones that produce vanilla beans, but that only two types bear enough quality 'fruit' to be used commercially. On top of that, it takes six months to develop the product."

"It's cheaper than chemo," Sydney interjects to inquisitive looks. "Vanilla is the second most expensive spice, but it's cheaper than chemo. You probably all know it came first from Mexico, the Spanish gave it the name, meaning 'little pod,' but they learned of its anti-inflammatory and anti-carcinogenic properties from the Mayan and Aztecs. The alternative health doc I go to uses it to inhibit the growth of cancer cells.

"It was a good present, Jessica. Thank you."

"You are welcome." With that, there seems an instant peace between us. "So, what's the first most expensive spice," I ask her.

In unison, Ali and Sydney respond, "Saffron." Ali quickly adds, as if competing for the bonus round, "from the pistils of the yellow crocus."

Sydney shares that her doc uses this too as an antioxidant and as an antidepressant. I admit that I have neither vanilla nor saffron in my pantry.

As CC and Ali settle in for the pre-game show, and Tia and Sydney head up-top, I work my way to the deck on the stern to better sense being on the water. We head north and pass the Drum Point Lighthouse. I know where I am. It no longer serves its original purpose, but it's beautiful and unique 'screw-pile' design can't help but make you smile. We are passing Calvert Marine Museum. I imagine a small Ryn and an even smaller Adam running through the exhibits.

"A penny for your thoughts," Roy interrupts.

"Just remembering. Roy, thanks for asking me to come today. And, for all your patience with me on the house. Really."

"Need anything, Jes?"

"Nope, I'm fine, really," and I am.

We sit in relative silence watching the bay and the coast. Occasionally, I am aware of the commentary from the television, Ali's prognostications for the game's outcome. CC admitting—to Ali's horror—that today she has to root for the Patriots. "Them there are fighting words," Malcolm calls down from above.

The boat's running motors slow, then stop as we come to anchor across from the Cliffs. So, so, so good to be on the water.

Everyone, with their varied levels of football enthusiasm and the very clear intent to be avid, silent fans, moves in to watch the game. By half time, with the score determined by everyone, except the loyal Ali, we move to various spots on the boat for cleanup, quiet conversations, and the enjoyment of being on the water. Everyone is very sweet about my foot, and I am shooed off, gratefully, to simply sit at the stern, as Malcolm reverses our route. I am delighted when, from behind me, I hear the deep timbre of Tobias' voice, "May I join you?"

Once he's settled in the other deck chair, he slides down, and places his wallet behind his head. He tells me how he used to play on the beach under the cliffs as a child and how Joan loved to take Tia and her girlfriends to play there, how Joan had been a Girl Scout leader and had campouts under the cliffs, and how Joan and Tia would walk the beach hand-in-hand, even into Tia's adulthood.

"She's a good woman, too, don't you think," he asks me, eyes closed.

I'm not sure if he's referring to Tia or CC, but the word "girl-friends" seems to have prompted his comment. "Seems to be Tobias. Was it hard for you to, *um*, 'go with the flow'?"

"Harder than I would have thought, I'd have to admit. Even now, I sometimes find it easier to think they are just good friends, rather than…." He pauses. "*Lovers*."

"Hard to always understand the decisions our children make, eh, Jessica?"

I stare at him, his eyes still closed. Nothing in his serene body gives away that he is referring to my story.

"Indeed it is Tobias. Indeed."

He wants to know how the interview with Margaret Mary went this morning and I tell him about my nervousness and that she thinks I am quite "wrongheaded."

"That would be Margaret Mary, quick to judge, quick to share her opinion, but there is usually something in what she says to at least consider. Did she mention she taught CC in elementary school? CC remembered her as one of her favorite teachers and tracked her down on Facebook, somehow. They got in touch, next thing I knew she came here." Straightening himself in the chair, and returning the wallet to his back pocket, he scans the cliffs.

I remember all the times I brought Ryn and Adam here. So much closer and easier than negotiating the traffic and crowds of Ocean City and Rehoboth beaches. It always seemed a magical day when we three were at the cliffs. It would be nice to know if we were ever under Tobias' watchful eye, or if we, by chance, and without re-membering, played alongside Joan and Tia.

I'm trying to trace back specific times there as if I could conjure up some memory of a Black woman and her child, trying in vain to match up the middle portrait of Joan to someone I met. I'm still thinking, staring at the cliffs when Tobias asks me, "I should have asked before now, Jessica. How many children do you have?"

Before I realize it, "*Three*" comes from my lips, and my heart starts to pound.

We sit in silence for a while, as I try to slow the pounding in my chest. We are almost past the cliffs when Tobias says. "My grandfa-ther would take me out on his boat, and we'd sleep overnight about here," he says, pointing to the cliffs. "He would wake me and my cousins up with a clang of the ship's bell and announce 'The cliffs are awake! The cliffs are awake!' Then, tumbling sleepily out of our berths we'd come up top, not to watch the sunrise, but to watch the effect of it on the cliffs. Invisible in the darkness, then barely perceptible, they splendidly change colors throughout the day, but they are magnificent at sunrise. I've been thinking of my grandfather a lot of late. It's nice that he gave me the gift of thinking about the cliffs waking up. Something always calls me to the water, and something always pulls me back home," he shares.

"I can see how that happens." I respond and keep going, "There does seem to be something very special about this part of the world, isn't there, Tobias? Just this morning on the way down I was trying to put my finger on what keeps pulling me back here."

"Lots of us here feel that, Jessica. I know Malcolm does. He's a good man, solid. He feels that tugging you describe all the time, wanting to be on the water, needing to work the land because Allison is grounded here. Good solid name for this tug of a boat, don't you think? Most people think it's just a descriptor."

My blank looks shows that I'm embarrassed to admit that I didn't bother to ask or notice. "The Tug," he offers with a contented smile.

It's almost sunset when we near the harbor and a defeated Ali calls us up for final beverages. Gentlemanly Tobias and "The Captain" help me up. The day has turned cool, but it's still comfortable. Ali has the post-game show on low volume, ready to argue the referee calls as the re-plays are run. Tia, hand on CC's arm, seems to be suggesting that she should be both satisfied at the Patriots win, and silent about it.

Then, sweetly, and unexpectedly, there is the trumpet. Through the large front windshield of the great room there is Roy on the sun-deck, at attention, silhouetted against the fading light. Horn held high, he plays *Taps*.

Barley audibly, Tobias and Tia start singing. Sydney, soon, joins in.

Day is done, gone the sun.
From the lake, from the hill,
From the sky.
All is well, safely rest.
God is nigh.
Thanks and praise, For our days,
'Neath the sun, 'Neath the stars,
'Neath the sky,
As we go, this we know,
God is nigh.

Tears run unchecked down Tobias' and Tia's cheeks and she takes his hand.

Malcolm, Ali, and Roy bring the boat gently to rest in her slip. We all sit around, not wanting the evening to come to an end. Malcolm and Ali are staying on the boat for the night and invite me to do so to avoid the drive and to prolong the party.

Motivated by knowing I do need to make the hour and thirty-minute drive, I break up the party by saying I have to go. The others too move to go. Roy helps me off *The Tug* and to my car. I like the feel of my hand in his.

Tobias is leaning against his car as he waits for Tia and CC. He's looking up, smiling, and pointing. "That's Orion, the hunter constellation, largest constellation in the winter sky. My granddaddy would always ask us to find it. It's just been visible for a few weeks, and it will be gone by spring. Always makes me feel like my granddaddy is with me during these months."

I find the constellation easily. I used to point that one out to my own kids. Along with Tobias, I smile up at Orion.

"I know dad. That's Orion. Let's go," says Tia, holding the door for him. I wince at what sounds like the harshness of it.

eve

I t's been a long day. When I pull into Hobart Street there are no parking spaces close to the house. My ankle is screaming from use and managing the ladders on the boat. As I hobble up the steps, I hear the beep for a text message.

"I estimate you should be home by now. All OK? – RLG."

Smiling, I open the door, get greeted robustly by Gabler, move to the kitchen, grab one of the freezer packs Roy bought, pour a quick vodka, and head to the window seat before I text him back. "Yes, just this minute, uneventful, thank you. Ice pack on ankle, thanks for that too." I hit send, hesitate, and text again, "U looked pretty splendid today."

"You too. –RLG"

"☺"

"You left out sailor."

"Sorry about that. Didn't know you liked the water so much. – RLG"

"Soothes the soul."

Then, *"Liked the Taps, nice touch."*

"I don't play my horn enough. Having a drink? – RLG"

"No." I lie.

"Busy week? – RLG"

"Finishing up with my students, packing, no more time at Grange ☹. *You?"*

"Got to go to the new house, Malcolm thinks one of the eaves has a problem, some leakage at the roof line. 'Nite. – RLG"

"Nite, sleep tight."

Nothing back.

I sit, just enjoying the quiet of the evening and pull out my notes. *Mary Margaret's wrong-headedness comment is bothering me. I make more notes. Once they were girls,* she said – *they think they still* are, she said. The story doesn't end with them—*it begins with them.* Puzzle pieces forming the frame, not yet seeing the whole picture, but closer.

My text goes off, again. Smiling. Oh, not Roy, Erica.

"we r on our way, r u home yet"

"yes, all ok?"

"yes, want to bring you something."

"k," I type back, amused at how I teenage text.

Thirty minutes later Erica and Sonia arrive, having found a space right in front of the house. That's good. Sonia and I can switch out spaces when they leave.

"We brought presents," Erica announces. "Not for Christmas, I know you don't want that. These are for your trip. We have to open them on the roof!" I give her a hug, holding her more tightly than before. I may imagine it, but it seems she returns the hug more deeply than in the past. I'm grateful for it. Then she's gone, bounding upstairs, scooping Gabler up in the process.

As I look at Sonia with a "what's this all about" look, she says, maybe a little exasperated, "Jessica, this was entirely her idea. I love you, but it is not my idea of something I want to do late on a Sunday evening to come into the city and climb on your roof."

Handing me a huge thermos, she asks, "Can you manage getting upstairs with this?" To my raised eyebrows she says, "Don't get excited, no hot toddies. It's hot chocolate, it's a school night. I told you this is not my idea. It is way too cold to be out there without something to warm us."

I bump up the stairs on my bum, giving my ankle a rest, feeling the cold air blowing in from the open window in my office. Erica calls that she's taken the blankets from Ryn and Adam's rooms and their flashlights and that she's also grabbed the quilt from the office. By the time I am trying, clumsily, to get through the window and out on the roof, Sonia is behind me, bottle of Baileys Irish Cream and two glasses in-hand. "For old times' sake," she says with a wink.

From each side of the window they help me onto the roof and help me ease into place. Leaning against the house, we snuggle together, Erica between us, seeming a bit anxious. Sonia and I sip our Baileys-laced hot chocolate. Just like years ago, almost.

We gaze at the night sky through bare and stark branches. Then we hear it. The lions! Roaring into the night! A west wind!

"Yeah!" shouts Erica jumping up from between us. "I knew it. I've been watching the weather. I really need snow by the end of the week to close schools so I can miss my chemistry test. I saw the winds are coming from the west. I remember what you always say about needing the west wind and preferably a crisp night. Lions!"

Sonia reaches for my hand and we sit awhile just listening and watching Erica backlit by the streetlamp. No matter how many times I've been up here I love when this happens. The contrast between the traffic on 16th, the occasional chatter of people walking below, and, just within the edge of our hearing there they are, roaring into the night, calling out and answering each other.

"This is for you, Aunt Jessica." Erica bends down, handing me a package.

The first is a bright red T-shirt with a lioness roaring loudly. It's inscribed *Let us prey.*

"I'll be sure to carry this with me and put it on right away if the lions charge, Erica."

"This one too but open the card last."

Another T-shirt. Gray. They've done their homework. The front of this one has a multi-colored circle with a helix in the middle. "MtDNA!" I laugh out loud. "How nerdy did your friends think *you* were buying a T-shirt with this on it? I love it! Love both of you." The shirt's back has a series of what look like six wide, curved arcs. "Sorry, what are these?"

It is their turn to laugh. Sonia tells me that I will know when I get to Africa. Erica, mimicking exactly her mother's voice and intonations, "Because you do not know this, Jess-cee-ka, you must now wait until Africa to open your card."

After our laughter quiets we sit in silence for a while. Right before we are ready to go inside, I ask Erica if she sees him. She takes a minute, then looks up into the night sky and smiles her beautiful smile. She remembers! "Yes, Orion. I noticed him before. Hope he can make it snow!"

Inside, back in the heat, Erica crawls onto my bed in the parlor and falls asleep, leaving Sonia and me to talk over the two interviews and the day on the boat. I tell her about trying to set up Gene and Sydney, saying what a stunning couple they would make. "Let me guess" says Sonia, "Allison did not think this was a very good idea."

"She didn't, how did you know?"

"Everyone except you and Sydney would know this, Jessica. Open your eyes. Do you not see how Allison gushes over Gene? She and Gene had, or depending on the day, are having, an affair."

There it is. The thing just beyond my seeing it. I am an idiot.

"Jessica, even Malcolm knows this to be true. Malcolm came to me because I was one of her friends. I thought he was going to ask me to betray her secret, but he came to me already knowing. He wanted to talk through how to tell her that he knew. That he didn't want to put her through the ordeal of owning up to it. He wanted her to know that in life you don't always get second chances, but that he would give her a second chance.

"I think Malcolm would give Allison many 'second chances.' I even think Allison knows that she belongs only and always with Malcolm. This thing she is doing with Gene is just foolishness. This is why I cannot be her friend right now. She knows this. What the two of them together are doing makes no sense, and it is hurting others.

"Malcolm trusts, I think, that it will run its course, or at least change when Gene leaves the campus in the New Year. Malcolm must know that it's just too much of a temptation for both of them when they work together. This was not my story to tell you, Jessica, but you would only make matters worse if you meddle here."

Coming from the great meddler herself, these are powerful words. I'm so naïve. Malcolm and Allison look so happy, so at ease with each other. Feeling stupid, I switch gears and comment on the dog, Oso.

Sonia says thoughtfully. "I gave that dog his name. I think Malcolm gave her this gift to bind her more to him,"

"*Of course you did!* So, why 'Oso'?" I ask, expecting a profound answer.

"You are so silly Jessica, not everything is significant. He was very small and fluffy, like a little black teddy bear. Oso means bear. Simple.

We switch out the cars, wake Erica up, and say our goodnights. I check to see Orion's progress on his hunt across the night sky and whisper a good night to the lions and to Tobias.

Inside, as I wash up the cup and glasses. My mind swims with thoughts about the old women, of Ali and the temptations life puts in front of us, about the repairs on the eaves at the new house that Roy is doing this week, and my weird obsession with a mitochondrial Eve. Then, the text comes in. It's Roy.

"Who is driving you to the airport? – RLG"

"Sonia, I think."

'OK. Why are you up so late? – RLG'

"I'm answering your text ☺. Seriously, Sonia and Erica just left. We could hear the lions tonight. It was wonderful! I'm excited. I just got an idea for name of the new house...." I text, leaving out my idea, teasing him.

"Sonia think it up? – RLG"

"Nope. All me." I make him ask. Oh, god, I'm flirting.

"OK, tell me. What inspired you? – RLG"

"I actually started thinking about the new house as an entity, not just a house. You know, the way you do a boat. Then, thinking about the women, I realize each of them is a start to a story not the end of a story." Not wanting to admit I was also thinking of him, I type, *"I was also thinking about the house structural design and the big eaves that overhang the porch. Started thinking about how I find the place seductive, magical, a place for beginnings. What do you think about calling her The Eaves or even The Eves?"*

An immediate response from Roy, *"Brava! Entirely agree! Excellent! Sonia will not be happy. Both names are perfect. Hope the oldies love the names! – RLG"*

"Thanks."

"Let me take you to the airport. – RLG"

"Yes, please, thank you. 'Nite."

Yikes.

africa

Packing, end of semester grade reports, getting Gabler to the pet sitter, and compiling notes for The Grange project get out of hand. I make a resolution that when I come back in the New Year, I will get organized. I have piles upon piles of paperwork throughout the dining room and parlor. My office isn't much better. The bedroom is a disaster. I've left drawers open. Clothes are tossed and across the bed and on the little table and chairs at the foot of the bed. I've just finished packing and gotten my suitcases downstairs when Roy arrives.

As instructed by the tour company, I have the small duffel bag packed with essential items and three days' worth of clothes for a small safari side trip. My large suitcase is packed complete with fourteen days of clothing, camera battery charger, and gifts for local children.

I'm grateful for the ride to the airport and for Roy beside me. Something about going on excursions is always a bit easier when you have someone to chatter with before getting squarely and summarily dumped at the departure curb. I miss the old days when someone could take you right to the gate and be right at the gate eager for your arrival. So many images of long good-byes and quick, excited hellos! I'm feeling decidedly not brave.

Roy senses my tension but has no sense of the details and pain ever-present in my head. He tells me I don't have to go. I know I must. The gnawing pain of the last years, so much more intense at Christmas, makes the holidays, or sharing the holidays with others, unbearable for me and for them. I've thought and rethought trying to contact Ryn and Adam again, but decided it might upset their holiday. I am sure that James, mocking and taunting me, full of mean-spiritedness, will send pictures of an idyllic visit showing that, in the end, he has our children. As painful as it is, I will relish just seeing their lovely faces.

After the other night, our time on the boat and our texts, I am not sure how to approach Roy for a good-bye and simply wait as he hands my large suitcase to the skycap for check in. As he returns to me, he takes my hands and leans in to kiss me, slowly, purposefully. As I breathe him in, I relax, ready to leave behind my nagging thoughts and set out for adventure.

"Go have fun, Jes. Really. Enjoy yourself. I'll be here when you get back. Right here in this spot. I like you a considerable amount, you know." Before I can respond, he leans in, kisses me quickly, and is gone.

Tossing my small, tour-supplied duffel bag over my shoulder, I make my way from curb, through security, to the gate. I go through the bag and re-catalogue what I've been instructed to pack. I've left an extra day on the front end of the tour for any travel delays and in order to arrive in Tanzania refreshed. I go over the flight itinerary: Dulles, Frankfurt, Addis Ababa—Ethiopia, Kilimanjaro. I text Roy a thank you and send *"I love yous,"* and *"Merry Christmases,"* to Sonia and Erica. I turn off my cell phone. Then, I turn it back on. I text Ryn and Adam, *"I love you beyond measure. I hope your Christmas is happy and safe,"* and hit send.

I turn off the phone and tuck it into the bottom of the bag. For the next fourteen days it will be useless. No need for the international service option, there will be no calls.

The trip over is easy and uneventful. Upon arrival in Frankfort, I immediately miss my first connection. This poses the threat that even the window for travel snags might be lost. An historic ice storm is closing in and threatens closing down the airport for a few days. The news fuels a sense of tension, urgency, and doom throughout the airport. So far undaunted, I run between gates and airlines as each carrier promises me that they have booked me, rebooked me, and have transferred my luggage with each change. Five hours later, spent, I arrive in the Lufthansa Airlines' lounge seeking help. The line goes out the door, tempers are short. However, there are snacks and vodka, and the tension here, at least, is at a lower decibel than in the airport as a whole. Computer access helps and I'm able to email the tour company explaining my dilemma. When Lufthansa tries to close the lounge at the end of its long day we, the stranded, protest. Two days later I am still enjoying gummy bears and vodka and a host of really excellent food services. I see the narrow window for making the safari connection all but vanish.

The first small miracle happens in the middle of day two when the weather breaks and I get placed on a plane bound for Addis. Personally, I insist on calling it Addis Ababa, simply because it is fun to say, and it calls up images from a sixth-grade geography project of Haile Selassie and Ethiopian royalty. In truth, everyone else now calls it simply Addis. As I get ready to go to the gate headed for Addis, the gate agent tells me the connection to Kilimanjaro is frightfully close. She warns me to, run, run to your gate upon arrival.

Once we take off and before darkness falls, I look out the window and trace the boot of Italy from the sky, land of my mother's birth.

Flying through the night, the sense of adventure begins to give way to the sense of loss. It now seems foolhardy to be taking this trip to Africa, the one everyone thinks I am so brave to take. I feel decidedly un-brave as the stars go by the window. Then, as if I could reach right out and touch his belt, there is Orion straddling the equator. Tobias! Tobias' grandfather and grandfathers before that and right back to this African continent. Tonight, whatever time it is in the States, maybe Tobias will be looking up for Orion, and we will be connected. Deep breath. I am okay. Just for today.

The bouncy landing in Addis is met by a blurred cacophony of sights, smells, and sounds. I run out one secured gate and meet with security at another. If I miss this connection, I am in Ethiopia with no plan. If I make the plane, I still may have missed the connection to the tour. If that happens, I then have to figure out how to catch up. There is no time to think these things through, or to ascertain anything about the airport or the country's history beyond the barrage of sensate impressions. I make it to the gate and find it is only dimly concerning that when the guard takes a bottle out of my bag and I tell him it's water, he takes this at face value. He replaces it in my bag and sends me on my way without a thought to what the clear liquid could be. All passengers clear the gate and board a bus and head off down an unlit road, nothing visible on either side. The road is unpaved, made passable only by the tire ruts of previous voyagers. We travel for an extended period of time, finally pulling into a grassy area lit only by the bus headlights. The bus maneuvers in order to light our path to a very small plane for less than twenty passengers. This is now day three of travel and I have lost my sense of day and time and time zone.

The tired band of travelers arrives at Kilimanjaro, a tiny, one gate airport. It's two o'clock in the morning, the smell of fresh cut, heather-like grass fills the air. Those with luggage pass quickly through customs. The agent wants to go home. I am the one person left standing at the luggage carousel as it goes around and around, empty. I wait as if somehow the bag will make it on the next go-round. The customs agent takes my tour information and promises my luggage should arrive by morning, later this morning.

Not brave, nervous, I leave the tiny airport, hoisting my small duffel bag on my shoulder and make my way the few feet to the parking lot. There is but one vehicle, a dusty jeep, with threadbare tires. A tall, lean, Black man clad in a red tunic with blue trim and a large ceremonial necklace is leaning against it, a long rod in his hand.

He looks up from his cell phone and notices me, "Jambo, jambo! You must be Miss Jessica. Jambo! My name is Robert," he says, righting himself from the jeep.

"Jambo, salama," I reply to the most common of Swahili/Bantu greetings I have committed a handful of useful Swahili phrases to memory. As Robert launches into a full welcome, all in Bantu, I realize I have been in Africa a very short time and have made my first, of what I hope will be very few, blunders. I stop him, probably rudely, mid-sentence. I had forgotten that adding the "salama" is only done if you want to indicate that you speak Swahili. Gratefully, Robert lapses immediately and amicably into fluent English. More gratefully, I slide into the safety of rescue in the dusty jeep.

Explaining that it seems my luggage has failed to arrive, he loads only my small duffel bag and me into the jeep, assuring me he will check after the luggage. We drive through the still night to Arusha, the poorest place I have ever seen. We pass men with bows and arrows along the road. Robert educates me as we drive, indicating these are not hunters, as I guessed, but armed guards to protect, largely, the tourists. When we make the final turn into the tour-associated hotel, I am in a different world. Inside the fence, lush, well-manicured grasses surround idyllic, posh "huts." Immense trees encircle a large and prestigious manor house. The disparity between inside and outside the gate chafes at my sensibilities, but not enough to stop me from appreciating my accommodations.

Robert has escorted me to a perfectly lovely "hut" with a lighted path, air conditioning, mosquito-netted bed, a shower, and a note from the tour director saying she's already been on the phone with the airlines and they promise my luggage by morning, later in the morning. This is to be the theme of the next fourteen days of the journey. My ill-fated luggage will fail to arrive.

I shower, delightfully shower, and slide between the crisp cool sheets. Luxuriously in bed for the first time in an uncountable number of days.

By morning the tour participants assemble for the traveler welcome meeting. We scope out those who will be our fast friends by the end of the journey in the contrived false intimacy of tours. There are always "types" on these tours. I have been many of them—the newlyweds with their perfectly appointed themed outfits, the perfect family, the grandparents and grandkids, the single woman, the Germans—there are always Germans. This time, I am "the single woman." As anticipated, I'm a little harder to slide smoothly into the couples and family groupings. Everyone silently wonders why the single woman is here by herself. They assume there is a story. And, of course, there is.

Africa amazes. There is no amount of Nat Geo or PBS *Nature* that can prepare you for the sheer enormity of the savannahs, the herds of elephant families, your first giraffe looming over the trees, or for giraffes fighting—slapping and wrapping their necks around their opponents'. On Day One we are all "safari virgins" gawking at the massive herds of gazelles and elephants. By Day Five the gazelles go practically unnoticed as we focus on covering "the big five"—lion, elephant, Cape Buffalo, leopard, and rhinos white and black. The deadly Cape Buffalo and hippos abound. Zebra (said here with a short 'e' zeb-ra) and an array of the world's most amazing birds surround us at every turn. The cheetah are most elusive.

Each night we relax to a white gloved served dinner. At the close of the evening we are escorted to our private five-star-hotel-rated accommodations by armed guards, ensuring we will not be mauled by lions and such. The richly crafted raised tents are outfitted with hardwood floors and wrap-around porches, mahogany furniture with marble tops and brass fittings speak of unbridled elegance. Plush towels and robes hang in our elaborate bathrooms in what I imagine are the equivalent of the poshest of British touring train coaches. Flaps up or down you can hear the hyenas yipping in the night. I am treated to the sound of lions roaring most nights, and my heart aches for my tiny rooftop porch and the closeness of Ryn and Adam.

At dawn we are awakened to the tinkling of Robert ringing a small bell announcing that the birds are awake, that coffee or cocoa is being left on our porches, and the fire, bringing us hot water, is being lit under our tents. At the sound of the bells I think about Tobias and his grandfather and how the cliffs wake up.

Each morning, I pull from my duffel the same clothing, the only clothes I have. By Day Three, I've worn everything but one of the T-shirts Erica and Sonia gave me. Each morning, a proper British breakfast greets me, and we are on our way for the morning game drive. There are the occasional opportunities to visit a school or a market to purchase items. At each stop there are male merchants who overwhelming, and by some quirk, introduce themselves to us as Uncle Sam. "I am Sam," they say. "Remember my name, tell your friends, buy only from Sam, Uncle Sam."

Day Six. It is Christmas. Despite my upbeat façade of the last few days, it is just that, a façade. I am longing for Ryn and Adam, wondering how they are, wishing we were together, or at least in touch. They don't know where I am. Yet, stupidly, I expect that they will get in contact with me. After all, it is Christmas. The internet is a hard thing to secure on safari, even at this level of service. I annoy the kitchen staff by asking more than once if I can try their internet. I can't quite pull off the merriment of the group or the outrageously misplaced "White Christmas" carol music playing on a loop in the tent camp. I long for something more authentic than the white-gloved service and the seemingly staged visits to Bantu bomas, the fortified enclosures for homes and livestock. I beg off the morning and afternoon game drives. From my duffel bag I pull out Erica's still unopened card and the T-shirt with the mtDNA on it, my last remaining clean clothing item. I slip it on and sit in the silence of my luxurious porch in silence.

Before I have a chance to open the card, my solitude is interrupted by the tingling of a little bell at the end of the small path leading to my tent. "Excuse me Bwana Bibi, I am wanting to check that you are OK this Christmas Day." It is Robert, greeting me with the respectful Swahili greeting roughly translated as 'Boss or Spirit Woman.' He has his long staff in one hand, bell in the other.

"Thank you, Robert. I am fine. Thank you for checking. Why aren't you out on the game drive?"

"It is my day off, Bwana Bibi. I have the time to pray and to sit, and to check on you."

I am wondering if he has been assigned by our tour guide to make sure I have a good day. He comes closer but keeps a comfortable and formal distance on the path. "Robert, I am fine, really. Thank you." Somehow, this doesn't suffice, and he continues to stand in the path.

"Would you like to come up and sit for a moment, Robert?"

"No thank you, Bwana Bibi, but I will sit here for a moment." With that he easily collapses his enormously long legs into a squat, sitting on his haunches, sideways to me, and gazes out into the savannah. He seems content to keep silence with me. Minutes later, "Bwana Bibi, it is very brave for you to come to Africa by yourself."

"Robert, why do you say that? When I was preparing to come here many people said that to me as well, and I don't understand it. There really has not been one moment when I have not been well looked after, safe, well treated."

For the next forty minutes we engage in amicable conversation. All the while he is squatting and not meeting my gaze. He shares that it is rare for a single woman to come on safari. He tells me he is saving up for three more cows in order to make the requisite ten needed to be able to buy his bride. He wonders if no one had enough cows for me! He is intrigued by the idea that he could come to the United States and not have to buy a wife. Eventually, we wind our way back to the topic of me being brave.

"I think you are brave, Bwana Bibi, because in Africa you really cannot hide, and you cannot really be alone. In Africa you must know who you are, where you fit, where you are going. Africa is a very big place and we are only a little speck of it, but we are each a speck that must fit someplace. You must be very secure in this, very brave, to come here."

He continues, "The next two days are my favorite part of our journey. Are you anticipating it well? Is this why you have come to Tanzania?"

I have to force myself to focus on his questions, not really hearing them. I'm too taken aback by his statements about bravery. It's embarrassing to admit to him that I didn't have a specific reason for coming here. I leave out that I am hiding from the reality of my life. I tell him that I did very little research on this trip or the itinerary, just booked it because the brochures keep coming year after year and that I needed to get away. Far away.

"Ah, Bwana Bibi, tomorrow we are going to the birthplace of all civilization!" he says, hardly able to contain himself. "Tomorrow you will be in a very luxurious hotel that sits high above the Ngorongoro Crater, part of the Great Rift Valley that extends all the way to Israel and Mesopotamia, to Eden! To the Promised Land! It is one of our seven natural wonders. It is a most amazing place. It is clearly, a place that God created."

I encourage his enthusiasm and marvel at his faith.

"Bwana Bibi, it is the world's largest inactive, intact, and unfilled basin made from a volcanic implosion three million years ago. Your brochure will describe it as "the world's most unchanged wildlife sanctuary." As I said, I think it is a place for God. When we move to the Serengeti, you will be in the Great Migration. Your brochure will describe this as 'The World Cup of Wildlife,' but I am not really sure what that means. There we will see *rafters* of hippo, *crèches* of ostrich, *kaleidoscopes* of giraffe, *parliaments* of vultures, and *sounders* of wart hogs. There we will see *dazzles* of zebra in the hundreds and hundreds of thousands, only surpassed in numbers by the two and three times as many *implausibility* of wildebeest."

I stop him, amazed at his words. Words so richly cast and toned they draw me in, and I catch his enthusiasm. An "implausibility" of wildebeest. Rafters, crèches, kaleidoscopes! Really? What would Jan call all these descriptors? Ah, *delicious*! I ask Robert if he knows that we have very few words for what he is describing, mostly a flock for birds and sheep, or a herd of almost any other land animal.

"This is very limiting is it not, Bwana Bibi? What you will see in the day after tomorrow cannot be described with just the two words you use. Oh, and I have saved the telling you of the Olduvai Gorge. No white man walked here until 1892. Tomorrow, you will walk where the great Mary Leakey made her discovery. From your hotel tomorrow, go to the rim of the crater and gaze out. You will see that the hand of God, may His name be praised, indeed moved over the land."

With that he comes easily up to his full height, tells me he will bring me my dinner if I like, and thanks me for passing time with him this Christmas Day.

the crater

That night I finish the supper, and the very thoughtful side-car of vodka, brought to me by Robert. He tells me that the others saw cheetah on the afternoon game ride, and it is unlikely that they will appear again.

It is OK, Christmas was still, somehow, a full day. As I slip into bed, I remember the card from Erica that accompanied the T-shirt I am still wearing. *Aunt Jessica, Merry Christmas. Have a great trip. Take photos. Find Eve. Love, Erica (and mom).* Under her signature she has drawn the same six scratchy blobs that are on the back of my shirt. I'm assuming the Eve reference is to my nerdy mtDNA thing. You've got to hand it to Erica, she really listens. Between her note and Robert's words, today I realize that I should have done more prep in coming here and then remind myself that it is OK. I can go with the flow and simply experience what unfolds. Hopefully, Erica won't be too disappointed that there will be few photos. Camera separated from suitcase-packed charger worlds ago, my camera died on day two. Remarkably, the loss of it is freeing. I get to be "in the moment," face-to-face with the beasts, rather than separated from them through a viewfinder.

In the morning there is, again, Robert and his tinkling bell. I am already up, on my porch, and ready to greet him. Proudly, I say, "Jambo, habari ya asubuhi, Robert. Hello, good morning!"

He gives me a slight bow and a broad smile. "Jambo, *habari ya asubuhi*, Bwana Bibi. Today will be a most amazing day!"

It is Day Seven. As we near the hotel I am surprised, after all the driving, when our guide tells us we are only one hundred and ten miles from Arusha. She tells us about the Crater and reiterates many of the things I have learned from Robert. She adds that the Crater gets its name from the sound the Bantu cowbells make as the animals move in and out of the valley. Ngoro, ngoro.

Tonight's accommodations are everything Robert promised and more. As a proper hotel, they can do my laundry! My three days' worth of clothing has been stretched to the max and I welcome the opportunity to exchange everything I have for the plush hotel bathrobe as my laundry is being done. The tour operator apologizes that the luggage will now likely never arrive.

There is time to relax before the late afternoon game ride. I unabashedly walk through the hotel in my robe and slippers. I'm on my way to the infinity pool, (I like the sound of that) via the gift shop.

The gift shop is a more pristine version of the small markets we have visited. The shop worker, dressed in Bantu garb, asks if he can help me, introducing himself as Samuel. A more formal "Uncle Sam" for a more formal vendor setting. I laugh at his introduction and he wonders if he has said something funny. "Not at all Samuel, I am just so happy to be in a proper hotel and to get clean laundry."

Everywhere we go, everyone I meet has such pride in this land. Samuel is no exception. He helps me pick out a few items, and a very sweet multi-colored carved bird for Roy. It's of a Speke's Weaver, common here. They are the industrious builders of elaborate bottom-entry nests that hang from trees by the dozens. I pick out two different types of coffee bean necklaces for Erica and Sonia, and a few bags of the rich coffee we have been drinking each day. The big purchase is the tanzanite, the lustrous and lush deep blue diamond-like stone mined nowhere on earth but in Tanzania. A pair of stud earrings for Erica and a pair of teardrops for Sonia.

While he wraps up my purchases, I ask Samuel to tell me about the deep blue stones. He tells me, his voice full of mirth, that he assumes that the stone existed for a long time but was only 'discovered' in 1967, after his country became Tanzania. The name tanzanite comes, he knows I must realize, from the name of his country, but prior to 1964 there was no country. The country was made up of the lands of Tanganyika and Zanzibar. He continues with trivia that must be part of what he is told to share with tourists. The stone was named not by a geologist, or sadly, even by a Tanzanian, but by, and here he forgets the name, by the expensive New York company that uses the light blue boxes.

"You can't mean Tiffany?"

"Yes, Bibi, you are right! This is it, Tiffany, thank you. I can also now remember it was made the birthstone, whatever this really means, for December just a few years ago."

Samuel tells me he will apply my charges to my room and send my purchases ahead. As I begin to head to the Crater's rim, I spy the spoons. Hand carved wooden spoons of various sizes and hues, some with beads wrapped around their handles. I select six of them bringing them to Samuel to wrap and tell him I will slip a small one with beads into my pocket.

As Robert instructed, I go to the edge of the Crater and am stilled.

For nearly one hundred miles the world lies before me, tumultuous storm clouds and heavy rain hangs far out to the east. Yesterday, as he spoke, I was jealous of Robert's faith. Today, alone, fingering the smooth wooden spoon in my pocket, I stand at the edge of the world, on a rift that runs north through Africa and into the "promised land." The words of all my years of Catholic school training come rushing back. Margaret Mary and Elizabeth cross my mind as I, unplanned, recite aloud the words of the Old Testament: "In the beginning, God created the heavens and the earth. The Earth was without form and void, and darkness was over the face of the deep. And the Spirit of God was hovering over the face of the waters. My hand laid the foundation of the Earth, and my right hand spread out the heavens. When I call to them, they stand forth together."

The words of the New Testament come to me easily now as I continue aloud, "Humble yourselves, therefore, under the mighty hand of God."

Pulling myself away, I ready for the afternoon ride and exult in clean, crisp, freshly laundered clothes. We descend more than two thousand feet into the Crater and head to the Gorge. Our guide tells us the history of discovery and the ongoing research being conducted by the Leakey family today. She prepares us to visit the small museum just off site from where the studies are being done and encourages us to walk the trail that leads to a casting of the original prints.

Upon arrival, I opt to do the trail while the others move toward the museum and the inevitable gift shop. The trail is marked with the same six arc-like smudges from the T-shirt and Erica's card. I know now from the signage that these are the "Laetoli footprints" formed 3.5 million years ago and discovered by Mary Leakey and her team in 1976.

This is the place where Man first learned to stand erect and to walk into uncertainty. These fossilized footprints are the record of our oldest human ancestors. Formed when, *for the first time, three* individuals, one clearly larger than the other two, stood erect and, with a clear two-footed stride walked side-by-side, close enough to touch, over wet volcanic ash.

A woman and her two children? The long sought mitochondrial Eve? Eve and *her* children, I choose to interpret.

I am still kneeling at the site, tracing, and retracing the *three* pairs of footsteps, tears rolling down my face when Robert finds me. He bends to me, lifting me by the elbow, steadying himself with the staff. "Come, Bwana Bibi, it is time to stand up. Perhaps this is why you came to Africa."

re-entry

The rest of the trip unfolds much as Robert described it. To stand amidst the Great Migration surpasses every expectation. This annual clockwise trek through the great Serengeti from Tanzania to Kenya includes millions of animals following the path. We look like a speck amongst them.

At dawn on the last morning of the trip, we drive quickly across a submerged road with, what I know now is, a "rafter" of hippos eyeing the intrusive van. At the airfield we wait alongside our vehicles for a "kaleidoscope" of giraffe to move off the grassy runway. The trip happens in reverse—Addis, Frankfurt, and Dulles, all with smooth connections and without incident. Upon landing, my anticipation of getting home is soon dampened. As soon as I touch down, I turn on my cell phone connecting me back to—well, back to nothing from Ryn or

Adam and back to a disappointing text from Roy.

"Jes, I checked, and your flight is on time. Welcome home. Sorry, I can't meet you, have sent a car service. Text driver when you are outside baggage claim 555-747-1458. – RLG"

Really? Really? He said he'd be right here. I probably made all sorts of mistakes and misinterpretations with Roy. Or, worse, I scared him off. Now I'm just feeling foolish.

I have two hours in the customs line to mull this over before I text the driver. I was not smart enough to get the Global Entry thing done before I left so I could sail through the tedious lines. I use the time to mull over what is going on with Roy and to catch up with Sonia. She and I text back and forth, I tell her customs should not be taking this long given I have only the duffle bag and a small shopping bag. She tells me Erica says hi and she wants to see my photos. She catches me up on what's gone on for the last two weeks and I feel connected again.

When my driver pulls up, I realize Roy must be feeling really guilty about not picking me up. He's sent a stretch limo. The driver gives me a "good evening ma'am," opens the rear door, tells me he's taken the liberty of opening a bottle of champagne for me, and that I will find it and a glass, along with a few appetizers, on the table stand.

I feel ridiculous in the huge space of the limo but settle into soft jazz, interior lighting, along with food and beverage. The driver scrolls down the dividing window, asking if I am comfortable and if I have a preferred route into the city. At this time of night, it is probably fastest to do Rt. 66, or maybe the Beltway to Connecticut and down, but I opt for the GW Parkway and across Memorial Bridge, down Rock Creek, and home. I pour a glass of champagne and sip slowly. There was almost no alcohol once I got to Africa. I didn't want to pay for each drink separately and call attention to my drinking.

Returning to DC always gives me an appreciation I lose when I drive past the monuments every day. Coming across the Memorial Bridge, Arlington Cemetery now behind me, Potomac River underneath, the

Lincoln Memorial is lit in front of me. No matter what time of day or night you cross the bridge there are runners, many with "Marines" T-shirts. I can't wait to run again. My ankle feels great. The upside-downside of the safari was with sitting almost all day in the vans there was lots of time to rest my foot, but no chance to exercise, let alone run.

The driver makes the sharp right at the Lincoln, banking under the bridge and continuing along the Potomac, Georgetown to my left. He bears left to go behind the Kennedy Center and The Watergate, then the zoo. Almost there, I pour another glass of champagne. When the driver comes up Park Road and onto Hobart, I'm wondering how awkward things will be between me and Roy now that I've screwed up. As the driver double parks, I notice Roy has left lights on for me—nice. My lone little duffle bag is removed from the trunk and run up to the front door. The driver returns to open my door and give me a hand to get out. He demurs on taking my tip saying that Mr. Gillis has already taken care of it. "Of course, he has. Thank you," I tell him, picking up my shopping bag, unlocking and opening the front door.

"Greetings, greetings! You're here! Gabler, look who is here!" Roy's words greet me as he heads to the front door from the kitchen.

"Look who is here indeed!" I reply, feeling the broad grin on my face. Gabler comes to greet me. "Hey Gabler, how are you? Boy, do I have cat stories to tell you!" Then, to Roy, "I thought you couldn't pick me up."

He babbles, "Not if I wanted to have Gabler and dinner waiting for you. Here, let me take your bag upstairs. Did your luggage really never arrive? Sonia was so annoyed at this. I'm surprised she didn't call the airlines directly after you told her."

He looks handsome. Cordovan loafers, crisply pressed black "dress" jeans, cordovan belt, green denim shirt, sleeves rolled back at the wrists, just the way I like them on a man, watch with leather watchband, black onyx ring on his right hand.

I tell him he can leave the bag in the hallway or in the parlor, but he runs, literally runs, the duffel and the gift bag upstairs. We don't hug or kiss hello. I'm not sure if he's here just to greet me and is leaving or if he's staying for dinner.

The house smells fabulous, Italian red sauce, sausage, meatballs, and peppers. I snoop under the lids of the pots while he is upstairs. A large salad is ready to be tossed and garlic bread ready to pop in the oven. Yum! Plates, silverware, cloth napkins, and stemware are ready to go on the table, so I'm guessing he's staying. Good.

"Oh, Roy, you shouldn't have, but this looks and smells amazing. Thank you!

"Do you mind if I take a quick shower, I feel so skuzzy from the plane. I'll be fast. Then I'll set the dining room table."

"Take your time. I will be here, Jes."

The shower is perfection. All showers are not equal—the ones after a gritty day in the yard, childbirth, and travel, especially this trip, rank as outstanding. Toweling off, I hop on the scale. Yeah! I guess all the sitting was offset by the lack of alcohol. Down four pounds.

When I enter my bedroom, I suddenly realize that the house has been cleaned, really cleaned. The clothes from the bed, chairs and table have been neatly folded and put on top of the dresser. The bed must have clean sheets because you can tell it's freshly made. The carpet has vacuum marks.

I quickly pick a pair of dark brown jeans, hoping they will fit if I lie down on the bed and zip. This seems like such a teenage trick. I remember Margaret Mary's words. She's right. I feel like I might actually look like a teenager, not a woman of near sixty with a muffin top. Success! I button the button, pick a red square-necked cotton sweater, pull on socks, and then brown, low-cut boots.

Before I bound down the steps I stop at their rooms and take a deep breath. "Jambo, my children. I went to Africa. It felt like I met 'us' there. I miss you."

Deep breath. Downstairs I go. The aromas from below beckon me along with the sounds of the Italian and Spanish music playlist Erica made and loaded on my iPod. Roy has made a good choice. I love the flavor of this music. I also imagine that just by listening and humming and singing along I will someday master Spanish.

In response to me noticing that the place settings are no longer on the counter nor is the dining room set, he tells me I don't have to worry about setting the table, he's got it.

He loads up the plates and asks me to grab the salad. Sliding the parlor door open with his foot, he says he will return for the garlic bread. All I can say is, "You amaze me."

He's made over the parlor. The first thing I notice is the fireplace. Happy tears roll down my face. He's unsealed the flue and made it all work again. There's a crackling fire! My drop-cloth-covered bed is gone, replaced by a table, beautifully set, and two green, high-backed, soft dining chairs. He's rearranged the furniture in a manner that the room feels both bigger and more cozy, like a true parlor. The room sparkles and smells of fresh paint, the wood fire, and a dinner I can't wait to eat.

He holds my chair out for me. Toasting me with a really nice Chianti, he says, "Welcome home, Jes."

We sit at the table for hours, savoring the meal and, I'd like to think, the pleasure of each other's company. I tell him about the trip, omitting, for now, the footprints. He tells me about the renovations at The Grange and what he's accomplished here. I'm delighted, and a little surprised, that he's also made sure that the fireplace in my bedroom now works.

He shares that the move into the new house is scheduled for this week and everyone seems happy with the space. The voting on the names for the new house is to be on Tobias' upcoming birthday. Roy runs down the list of entries and hints that Sonia has been lobbying hard for her recommendation. "Casa Verde," the green house.

I still like "the Eves," but begrudgingly admit I like Sonia's idea. It fits well with all the "green," energy thoughtful, touches.

I insist on cleaning up the kitchen and he insists on helping. We make short work of it. He's a tidy cook, something I envy. He shows me that the bathroom under the stairs is complete. I'm delighted that he used the excess materials from The Grange's new house and that everything is made out of the recycled materials. He's given me a proper toilet, saving me the "gift" of one that composts, although he did consider installing one. I thank him for that and admire all the other elements. CC's influence is now here and appreciated. I'll have to tell her.

The travel, the time change, and the sheer enormity of the experience is creeping up on me and I am fading fast, but I want to give Roy the little carved bird before he goes.

"Come upstairs a minute." I take his hand. "I brought you something." As we climb the stairs, I suddenly feel awkward. I'm inviting him to my bedroom? I open the duffle bags and slide out the tissue-wrapped bird, telling him the story of the birds and about all of the "Uncle Sams." He seems to delight in it.

"I'm so glad you like it. I'm so glad you did this tonight. I was disappointed when you weren't there to pick me up. I thought, maybe, I had mis-stepped."

"Jes, I'm a man of my word and I'm not going anyplace. This was a good night, thank you."

He takes my shoulders and leans in to kiss my cheek. I turn, ever so slightly, and our lips meet, just for a moment, and I breathe him in.

"Good night, Jes," he says, pulling back. "Sleep well. I'll turn off the lights and lock up. You are exhausted. I've left a folder in your office with all the receipts and the last invoice. Let's go over it tomorrow and set up a timetable for the balance of the work."

I hear him call goodnight to Gabler as he checks the kitchen door, turns off the lights, and turns the key locking the front door. For the first time in too long I am upstairs and choose to sleep in my tidy bed. It feels luxurious. As I reach to turn out the light, I notice that Roy has laid a fire to be lit at some future date.

The text beep comes just as I am closing my eyes. I see I've missed multiple texts from Sonia and Erica, I scan through them quickly. Erica texts saying she was out with one of her friends and they got in a car accident, she was OK, but wanted me to pick her up. Sonia frantically texting saying she was crazed about the accident and that she was rushing back from Calvert County, could I pick up Erica.

Texts from each of them, frantic and scared, all while I relaxed. The last texts from both of them, Erica's saying thanks, but she is home and safe. Sonia's so much more primal, "I was so scared, I was so scared. Thank God she is safe. We are home now."

We text back and forth a bit. Sonia says that she and Erica are not speaking. They have a difference of opinion about Erica's decision to go out tonight. Sonia emphasizes that Erica needs to understand about *her opinion.*

I apologize for not being there for them. Sonia actually apologizes for trying to interrupt my evening. Clearly, she knew, and did not let on, Roy's plans.

"The house looks quite good. Do you not think? S."

"Nothing short of amazing. Thank you and Roy for getting this done."

"So, did you have a good night ;-) S."

"Yes, very. I am so glad you are both OK. I was scared, just reading the texts. I will see you tomorrow. Can't keep my eyes open. Love you."

the naming

Waking up in my bed feels as lavish as falling asleep in it. Roy's "parlor trick" of a make-over has made it impossible to stay camped out on the first floor any longer. I've officially been reinstated in a proper bed. Clever man.

Getting up I remake the bed, smoothing the comforter, feeling the richness of the quilt my mother made beneath my fingers. I go quickly through the mail and walk through my greatly transformed house admiring Roy's work, the neatness, order, and the cleanliness he's brought to it. Roy has pre-set my coffee maker and the strong smell of rich, shade-grown, home-brewed Tanzanian coffee fills my kitchen and mug. A small dusting of snow has blanketed the neighborhood, leaving it looking unspoiled and new and the house feeling cozy. Checking the notes I made before the trip, I decide that I need to be thinking most about "wrong-headedness" before returning to The Grange.

Catching a look of my reflection in the mirror, I have to admit, but maybe not to Sonia, that I finally feel more comfortable in the Sonia-esque running outfit. Checking that the snow has mostly left the sidewalks and streets, I am eager to run, I pull up the lightweight ankle support, and caress Adam's note on the back of the door. Closing it behind me, my rock-star mom iPod strapped to my arm, earbuds in, I set out to run, focusing on "wrong-headedness."

It feels good to be able to keep a steady pace after so many weeks. Waiting at a stop light, running in place, smiling, I notice my footprints in the dusting of snow, so temporary. Africa seems so far away, yet I can still feel the outlines of the footprints on the ridges of my fingers.

The run, as it did in the old days, helps me sort things out. Clearly, the stereotyping of The Grange women and my pre-conceived notions need to stop. I think that I basically have to simply experience them, stay in the moment with them, and see where this goes. The big takeaway to the wrongheadedness is that they themselves don't think they are "done." And, maybe I'm not either.

After the run and a quick shower, I decide to head to The Grange to see the results of the move into the new house and, in truth, to do my own lobbying for my suggested house name, The Eves. Before I go, and having no desire to actually grocery shop, I find the jar of beans from the M and M, put together the ingredients, pull out some frozen chicken, and toss it all together in a slow cooker. Assuring Gabler that I won't be late tonight, I check her food and water, and I text Roy. *Let me treat you to a very simple dinner tonight. Bean soup, leftover garlic bread and salad, and a good beer. My place, 7:00.*

With my small gifts, the quilt squares, and my notes, I take the comfortably familiar route to The Grange. Unsure of where everyone will be this morning, I decide to head to the old house first. When I enter the side door, I find Tia alone in the kitchen. She genuinely welcomes me back as I give her one of the bags of coffee.

Immediately, I notice that except for the dining table, the kitchen has been all but cleared out. Gone are the Hopi jar and spoons.

Tia looks out of place. I ask, "Are you OK?"

"I honestly don't know," she answers, looking bewildered. "Suddenly, the whole new house seems like a very bad idea. I haven't said as much to CC. It would break her heart to think I didn't love everything about it. I actually do love everything about it, except it's not here, it's not home. When I lie in bed at night, or in the quiet of the day, like just now, I can almost hear the voices of my ancestors and all that came before me. My parents made them so real to me that I feel they are still here. I can tell you about almost every meal that was served on that table. I can tell you who fell down the side steps. I can tell you whose hearts were broken and who was overjoyed at what news. Mostly, there is something about being in the house you were born in, the house where your mother died. It's ridiculous I know, we are moving just up the cliff a bit, but I feel like I'm leaving my mother behind. I don't want to."

She looks up to me with pleading, tear-filled eyes. If I had either the power to let her stay or the power to bring Joan back, her wish would be granted. But I lack both the words and the power to comfort this ache.

"Tia. I am so sorry. I remember when my mother died, my dad stood in the kitchen and said over and over, If I just keep everything as it is, it will be OK. I don't think that ever worked for him, but I so understand what you are feeling. Your dad reminds me so much of mine. The first time I met him in your mom's studio he asked me not to touch anything. I knew he wanted to keep everything the same and he thought that would make everything, somehow, OK.

"When my dad died, I had to close the house and sell it. Like this, it was my childhood home. To this day, one of my favorite going-to-bed pastimes is imagining going up the driveway to the house, opening the front door and going through each room. I visualize everything, where it was, what it looked like—a small Lenox swan in the living room, cream-colored canisters in the kitchen, a lamp from India on the dining room sideboard, the smell of my father's coat in the hall closet. I imagine going into each room and visiting again. I see my mother ironing in the basement, hear my father playing Burl Ives, see my cousin's wedding. What's most remarkable is that in my mind I can do this at any period of time and multiple times simultaneously. I can have my twelve- and fourteen-year-old cousins playing baseball in the backyard at the same time their older versions are helping me put in a car stereo system in the garage, and still older versions of all three of us sneaking drinks in the basement while we have big, lofty discussions. I visit when my bedroom was pink and when it was blue. When the kitchen was paneled or when it was wall papered. I can call up the smallest detail—when the corner of the living room had a black-and-white TV with the rabbit-eared antenna, when it housed the huge Hammond B3 organ, and when it held the china cabinet. I can line up each of the cars we owned over sixty years and imaginatively park them in the driveway as if they are still there. With each image comes a flood of different memories and sensations. We ate Eskimo pies in front of the black-and-white TV, I listened to my cousin and dad play the organ, and I can feel the weight of the china, and hear the sound of it being put away after a Sunday dinner.

You are just going up the cliff a bit, but I know what it is like when you take that last personal item out of the house and pull the door closed behind you. You can come back here. You are leaving your mom and all the others here to greet you only when you imagine them. We're all different, but maybe while the memories are still fresh you can recreate the house and all the pieces for you to revisit anytime you want."

"I like the imagery, Jessica. In truth, I'm surprised I feel this way. I simply don't want to go, but that ship has sailed. Seriously, thanks. What you said helps me understand my dad. I've been so frustrated with his obstreperousness about the move. He's insisting on keeping mom's art room exactly the same. He knows we need to start total renovations on this place. But he did let us move one of her two chairs over to The Eves solarium but was insistent that everything else stays in place. I've been mad that he wants to keep this place a freakin' museum or shrine to her. I've been so caught up in all of this that I violated my own personal mantra, 'seek first to understand.' Thanks. Jessica, I think I get it now."

What? Did she just say *The Eves?* My heart jumps for a second. I'm just about to ask her when Tobias comes in.

"Get what now?" Tobias asks as he rounds the corner from Joan's studio.

"Nothing dad. I just love you and I'm sorry I wasn't as patient as I could have been during this whole move, and for a while now."

Tia plants a kiss on him as he passes her coming towards me, arms outstretched, welcoming me home. "Let me hug you girl! That was one amazing trip you took. Joan and I always intended to go on safari, but never made it. I'll want to hear everything. I'll drive you up to The Eves and we can leave Tia to finish things up here. Tia, child, do not touch one thing in your mother's room."

He winks at me and still has one arm around me. I love the sense of it. Tia looks at him and is about to say something when I look beseechingly at her to let it rest, to understand.

"Thanks for the coffee, too, Jessica," she says as our eyes meet in agreement. "Why don't you take it up to The Eves with you and brew some for my dad."

Still from within the comfort of Tobias' arm I look at both of them and ask, "Did you really both refer to the new house as The Eves? I thought a decision wasn't being made until next week on Tobias' birthday. Are you really taking the name, calling it 'The Eves'?"

Tobias speaks first. "It really wasn't even much of a decision. Almost as soon as we saw the submission, we all got it. I think we all loved it for so many, and different reasons. We liked the play on words between the eaves of the house and the lovely *virginal* Eve-like women." He looks at Tia, knowing he is riling her. She, unrestricted by me, rolls her eyes.

"We probably won't tell Sonia until next week. We've been enjoying her lobbying, bringing food, making more visits than normal, trying to teach us all a bit of Spanish so 'Casa Verde' rolls off the tips of our tongues. None of us is above being pampered a bit. Plus, in truth, as Tia says, it's fun to mess with her. That girl really does believe she can control the world and, while she does a pretty good job of it, it's nice every once in a while, to remind her that none of us does."

Tia picks up where Tobias leaves off. "The house became *The Eves* from the moment we read it, Jessica. We've already had Roy make a really smart-looking sign with the name. We plan to place it in the front corner garden when spring comes. We'll also put in Sydney's homeopathic plants. Seriously, it's the perfect name."

I am delighted beyond words! I got to name the house! Everyone liked it for all of the images and plays on words that I imagined. "I'm so, so glad you liked it and picked it. I won't say a word to Sonia, I promise. More important, most important, you mentioned Sydney. How is she?"

"Not as well as we would all like, I'm afraid," Tobias answers. "She's feeling better now that the chemo is over, but her markers aren't where they should be. She'll be monitored over the next few months and then decisions will have to be made. Come on, you can see her up at The Eves and you can make me some good African coffee."

We leave Tia to her chores and, hopefully, her imagination. Hopping in the golf cart, we head up past the llamas and sheep toward, to my glee, *The Eves!* Tobias makes an unexpected right turn before we get there, however, and loops back down the path, past The Grange house and up a bit of a hill. There, in the crisp winter light, trees bare against the sky, sits the cemetery. Tire marks in the remaining snow from this morning announce that Tobias has already been here today. Parking the cart, we follow his earlier footprints and stand together in silence listening to the wind before continuing.

Tobias, putting his arm around me again, talks as we begin to wander among the graves. "I like coming here and visiting with them all. Sometimes I bring my coffee and I tell them about all that has gone on. Sometimes I ask them questions. So far no one is talking. But I'm a patient man.

"This cemetery tells the story of this land in many ways. You've got all the white folks over there a bit further, behind the gate. We keep their graves nice and tidy for them, but no one visits. All of their stones have their names, their lineage, age at death, and dates of birth and death. Sometimes there is a verse. The earliest ones are slave holders and their kin. I imagine them a different lot. I'd like to give them the benefit of my doubt, but I often wonder what their conversations with St. Peter were when he met them at the Pearly Gates. I talk to them, too, and I always thank the last two for this land. An amazing single gift, as you've heard me say.

"Our lot is different. Here you can trace us all back in time, although the earliest graves are unmarked and, even the oldest stones here mostly say simply what they did, the year they died and, maybe their age at death."

We pass graves marked "Chinese cook," "Negress," and one marked simply "kitchen boy 6 years of age." "This one makes me sad," he continues. "I wonder about who he was, and if he's buried near his parents. You'd think a place like this might be haunted, but everyone seems to be at peace."

As we walk, he introduces me to his parents and grandparents, cousins and aunts and uncles. He points out that some of Gene Martin's family is here too. As we walk past the stones, he seems impervious to the cold as I begin to shiver beside him. He's moving slowly and keeps eyeing the too newly dug grave several stones ahead of us.

I get the sense he is delaying, as if a delayed arrival will keep Joan alive a bit longer.

When we arrive, he sighs deeply and brushes the last of the snow from her stone. His eyes keep darting across the stone and grave, checking, taking in the enormity of her presence here. I read the etched words.

Joan Eve Thatcher
Beloved by all.
Now, born into eternity.
She lies here, still.
Until we are reunited in the Lord,
Love always.

"Tia decided on the inscription. I wanted it to be something splendid but couldn't bring myself to say anything. I am so grateful for Tia. I don't think I could walk this part of my journey without her. She's made it possible for me to keep going and it gives me peace to have her with me. I don't think I've made it very easy on her these last few months. The move is the right thing, but it's hard to imagine sleeping in a place that I haven't stared at the ceiling with Joan. Tia's ready to move on. I don't think she understands that I don't want to leave them all behind.

"Come on, you're beginning to shiver. I'll have you up at The Eves in a minute." I smile up at him. "It's a good name for it, Jessica. Has a nice ring to it, don't you think?"

He winks at me as he kisses his hand and touches the stone in good-bye.

The Eves, indeed!

deirdre

During the short ride to The Eves I take Tobias' hand that's resting on the seat between us and squeeze it.

"Thank you for that, and for being so kind to me. I want to tell you all about Africa, the feel of it, the smells. The vocabulary of it alone was amazing to me. I think, I hope, that the journey was a life-changer."

"It's all a life-changer, Jessica. Every day, it is a journey, remember, not a dress rehearsal."

As we pull up to The Eves a "Gentle Ben's Movers®" truck with a logo of large brown bears carrying a china cabinet is parked at the front. Underneath the words it says, 'Martinsville College students *on the move.*'

"Sonia idea?" I ask Tobias, grinning.

"Well, Sonia and Gene. Gene wanted to give the students, mostly boys, skills and jobs, and a respect for others. Gene pitched me the idea, I donated the first truck. Sonia started the project, but Ali now manages it. Gene and I mentor the boys. I like how the work changes them. I like watching them learn and plan their futures and grow into men. This is the third year Gentle Bens has been in business, and it's turning a profit. Mighty proud of it. Got my granddaddy Benjamin's name on the truck, too," he says, satisfied.

He tells me that Gene is inside as he drops me at the front of the house before bringing the cart around back. As he does, I call after him, "Remind me to tell you about Orion!"

Opening the front door, I find organized chaos. At Ali and Gene's direction furniture is being moved about, put in place, then repositioned. Interesting that Tobias didn't mention Ali was here too. Even with Sonia not being happy with Ali and the affair, I can't help but being excited to see her, to catch her energy, and watch her be so enthusiastically bossy.

More students are loading boxes into the elevator while others are moving boxes on the second floor. Noise from the kitchen indicates that there are more students unpacking there. It's a hard place to hear yourself think at the moment.

There are excited quick "hellos" and "welcome backs" but I'm clearly in the way. Ali is on a mission. She hurriedly tells me that Sydney has taken off for the library at the college trying to get some work done in the quiet there, and that Jan is establishing herself as chief cook and bottle washer by setting up the kitchen. The other oldies are off in various rooms trying to escape the noise. She warns that I particularly shouldn't disturb Margaret Mary, who is showing great disdain for the composting toilets. "She's not amused, even by the brand name. Go figure. How can you not be amused by a 'Loveable Loo'?

"We have to catch up later. I want to hear all about your trip.

Africa—you were so brave! We're staying on the boat tonight, care to join us?"

My eyes quickly go to Gene's and he just as quickly averts mine. Ali catches this and winces. I issue my apologies, telling her I have other plans and head to inspect the mystery of the composting toilet. As expected, the kitchen is bustling. Joni Mitchell's version of *Both Sides Now* is blaring. Unsurprisingly, Jan is singing along. Someone else is whistling the tune. Jan already has the Hopi jar and spoons on the cooking island. There are boxes everywhere, packed, unpacked, and empty. She's on a ladder arranging dishes in the upper cabinets as students bring them to her. She descends quickly when she sees me. Almost missing the last rung, she explodes with welcoming laughter as she reaches out to grab me.

We hug and greet, I tell her I brought coffee, placing it on the counter. "I brought you this too," I tell her and take one of my spoons from Ngorongoro out of my satchel and hand it to her. She's instantly still and the room seems to calm as she rubs her hands over the wood, feels the grooves in the shaft, and fingers the little red and blue beads at the top of the handle.

"This is a fine addition, thank you! What shall we cook with it, eh?" With that she slides the spoon into the jar amidst the others. "Looks like it belongs here. We will cook something fine together with it. We didn't know we'd see you so soon. Can you stay for dinner?"

With that, the whistling stops and a voice, coming from a pair of legs protruding from under the sink says, "She can't. She has dinner plans. Greetings, Jes."

I bend down to pop my head under the sink to be greeted, of course, by the ubiquitous Roy. "I didn't know you'd gotten my text. I'm glad you can come, but it really will be simple and it's mostly your leftovers from last night." As I straighten up, I catch Jan with arms crossed across her chest, raised curious eyebrows and a wry smile across her face. I can only shrug my shoulders and smile back as I go off to finish my inspection of the new place.

In the solarium CC is posting instructions in large print on the inside of the bathroom door that say simply, "It's a toilet. Use it. Dump peat moss. Done."

"This is harder than I thought it would be," she says. "Really, you'd think it's pretty basic. No fuss, no bother, no smell, fabulous for water conservation, amazing humanure for our gardens. I guess they'll adjust. Hey, I'm sorry. Welcome back. How was your trip?"

"Good, really good. Thanks for asking. It looks like the move is going well, well except for the toilet thing. The solarium has shaped up really nicely."

I leave CC to finish and continue to chuckle about the Loveable Loo. On my way back to the great room to report to Ali I notice that off in one of the alcoves, glass doors shut, Deirdre is sitting quietly knitting, eyes closed. I decide to escape the din and my current uselessness and visit with her.

Knocking softly on the door and opening it, "Hi, Deirdre, mind if I join you? I'm not much use to them today." She opens her eyes and smiles, inviting me in, but she looks like I've disturbed her. "Am I interrupting you? A penny for your thoughts?"

She seems to visibly try to focus on me. "Oh, it's Jessica, isn't it? I haven't heard that expression *a penny for your* thoughts in years. I should tell you a story about that sometime, it would be a nice little story for your project. Oh, what was I thinking? I think I was thinking about my boys. I dreamt about them and their sister last night and they were so very tiny, and cute, and active. I like it when I dream of them that way.

"You know what's odd when you get to my age? It's like I'm missing two sets of totally different people. I miss the little boys that I raised, and I miss my two grown boys who turned into such fine men. The first set I get to see and re-experience only in my dreams, the second set I don't get to see nearly enough. I don't dream about their grown-up selves. It's hard for me to remember them, the way they look, or the sound of their voices. I don't like that I'm not really an important part of their lives, don't like it at all."

I'm struck that for the first time in our brief meetings she is not the ever-ebullient person she portrays to everyone. Equally striking is the evidence of a memory issue.

"They had a sister, you know," she tells me, as if I had this knowledge already. "An older sister by a wee bit. She died of polio. It was really quite horrible. I don't dream of her. Did someone say that Sydney might get polio, poor dear, that and the cancer? You went on a trip, didn't you? Tell me about it while I knit, it's so very noisy and confusing out there, sit with me."

I'm taken aback by the difference in her. I don't know how to process the new knowledge of her dead daughter, I surprise myself when I tell her, "I like your image of two sets of children. It makes sense to me. I know I wake up so content and at peace when I have dreams of my children, Ryn and Adam, when they were little. I ache to know them better as the adults they are becoming. Two separate sets of the same people. I get that."

She asks me how the name Ryn came about, noting that it's unusual. I explain how we came to call our Cathryn by her nickname. Although a non-sequitur, this prompts her memory into a different area. "Did I ever tell you that as a child I was always called Penny? Didn't you ask me something about that just a minute ago?

"My Irish parents, thinking I was the most beautiful of baby girls, named me Deirdre after the fabled Deirdre, the most beautiful woman in all of Ireland. That Deirdre died of a broken heart, so much so that the name in Ireland actually has come to mean 'sorrowful.' My grandmother, God bless her soul, however, called me Penny from the moment my mother came home from the hospital with me and the name took over. You see, dear, I was the first Farley to be born in America and my family wanted to do it up right.

"When my mother shared the news with my father that she was expecting, he was excited and nervous. He feared for his wife and he feared for, what he naturally assumed, would be his first-born son. At that time, everyone was still giving birth at home. The landlord, who also worked as a janitor at Physicians Hospital, brought home a pamphlet for my father about a new 'maternity department' at the hospital. It touted that the new department was the safest place for any expectant mother and her babe. My Dah feared my mother giving birth, and he feared the tenement fires that plagued so many of the places where his countrymen settled here in America. The pamphlet lured him in with its promise of fire-proof construction and modern equipment. He was determined to safeguard his newly forming family. The challenge was the price.

"My father knew he could never save enough for a private hospital room, but he thought he could save enough for my mother to stay in a ward bed. He had just six months to raise enough for the flat-rate services that would include a seven-day stay, the use of the labor and delivery room, all normal supplies, nursing care, and laundry for the baby. I can still hear my father telling the story over and over and saying, 'Oh how grand it was to be, to bring the first Farley son born in America onto this Earth in a modern hospital!'

"The price was very dear, don't you know? The $75 for a private room and all the services was unthinkable. However, with the luck of the Irish, and hard work, my mother would have a seven-day stay in a ward, if he could only set aside the $40 needed. In 1935 that was more than a tidy sum.

"My father was good at doing figures in his head. He calculated that he had about one hundred and eighty days to save twenty-two cents a day. Twenty-two cents a day, every day. My mother and grandmother took in more laundry. My Dah worked extra shifts at the docks, and my grandfather limited his trips to the pub. Still it was hard. Each day, each week, they counted their pennies, sliding coins around the white Formica kitchen table putting them in piles for the necessary expenses. They needed $19 for the monthly rent on their two–bedroom apartment on Fourth Avenue and 69th Street. It was the largest of their expenses. They cut back on lots of things, including the amount of ice they used. I can't remember how much everything cost, except I know Dah stopped his half-hour weekly violin lessons. At twenty-five cents, it was a luxury he could no longer afford. He never took another lesson. Imagine that, twenty-five cents making such a big difference.

"And, that's how it started, my parents and grandparents saved pennies, literally pennies. Although I was not the son my father so dearly wanted, I was the first Farley to be born in a hospital. Christened Deirdre, called Penny for all my life until I met Bob Stalzer who thought I was the most beautiful woman in all of Brooklyn. He took to calling me Deirdre. It amused me that the tall, handsome, Irish-German, soccer-playing boy from two streets over thought me beautiful. He was the one still turning heads with his handsome good looks until the day he died.

"It's a nice story, isn't it dear? I don't understand why the young people today can't seem to save their money. 'A penny saved is a penny earned' my father would always say with that great twinkle in his eyes.

My boys have no patience for my stories. Maybe their sister would have liked them. Hard to imagine such events just eighty and a wee bit of years ago. Such a nice memory. You know, I was sorrowful, powerful sorrowful, when the boys' sister died, but I had the little boys and Bob. I was never truly broken hearted except when Bob died."

Deirdre then told me how when Bob died she met Joan at the church and started helping out there to fill her days. Joan told her about The Grange and invited her up to see the place and the animals. Deirdre fell in love with the mule Oliver and the feel of the barn. She said it reminded her of her grandparents' place on Staten Island in NY. One thing led to another. Deirdre talked to Joan about how she dreaded the idea of moving north and moving in with one of her sons. She thought it was the beginning of a slippery slope to lost independence. She and Joan had heard the same from their friends and seen the decline in those that didn't, somehow, build full lives for themselves. Together they hatched the idea that there should be a place, a place like this, where there could be not only independence but vitality.

"The rest," as she said giggling, and mimicking Erica "is her-story. Joan and I seemed to have stated something!"

Deirdre was so engaging that I hadn't noticed the passing time or that the noise from the great room had ended. Looking through the glass door panels I notice that all the movers had gone. Gene and Sydney are together, talking on the newly arranged furniture. Sydney is sitting with her feet tucked under her legs, black jeans, red silk shirt, matching shade of red lipstick. Gene, in jeans and denim work shirt, has his arm outstretched across the back of the couch, close enough to almost touch her.

It's later in the day than I thought, and I should be getting back. What a gift this place is, the invitation to the boat, an invitation to dinner here, the openness of the women, the intrigue of whatever might be being said on that couch. I say a silent prayer of thanks to Sonia for the gift to me of this place before I refocus on Deirdre.

We sit together and she tells me about her Aunt Lily teaching her to knit as a child. Deirdre remembers her as having a very long neck and pursed lips, sort of like the llamas, she giggles. She talks in great detail about the fiber project, her love of the sheep and llamas, how she cares for their dietary and medical needs, and her plans for expanding the herd, the possibility of adding Angora goats. She mentions she's interested in the fiber, but that CC is still doing some research for her on goats and sheep living together and about goat cheese, something she personally thinks disgusting.

She seems more focused now, her energy returned. It's as if the clouded memory conversation hadn't happened. She's amicable, bright, and cheerful, every bit the Sleeping Beauty Fairy Godmother I imagined in our first meeting. She asks if I know how to knit, promising to teach me the process from the start, how to shear the animals, how to prepare the wools and fibers, dying and knitting. She promises that I will be knitting a sweater by next Christmas.

I can't imagine, but she can. She leans into her knitting bag and digs to the bottom. "Take these dear," she says handing me a pair of thick wooden knitting needles, "these are the needles I learned to knit with, a present from my Aunt Lily. It will be nice to have you use them. Please stop at the M and M and pick out the fiber that attracts you the most. Just tell them to put it on Miss Deirdre's tab."

"Deirdre, this is amazing. I'm really, really touched. I don't know how good I'll be at it, but I'd like to try. Thank you. Thank you for these, and your sharing. I hope you will keep telling me your stories as we knit."

"You are welcome, dear."

As I am about to close the door to the alcove she stops me. "Jessica. You offered a penny for my thoughts when you came in. It was so noisy, and we have all the new things to get use to here, I lost my train of thought when you came in. I know I'm getting confused. I know the others notice it. It's frightening. I sometimes can't remember words. Names are worse. I'm afraid I will forget Bob and my children and the grandchildren. Today I couldn't remember my daughter's name. It was Deirdre," she says, pained. "Deirdre, because Bob thought she was the most beautiful baby he had ever seen. But he always called her Penny," she laughs. "His Penny from heaven. That is what I was thinking about when you came in. But, her story and mine was all confused in my head. I should have been able to keep it straight. You need to write about us."

A deep breath and a single tear rolls down her cheek as she goes back to knitting.

two chairs

As I gently close the door behind me, I have to wipe tears from my own eyes. Getting old is not for the faint-of-heart. Sydney and Gene are still talking in the great room. She gives me an almost imperceptible shake of her head indicating I shouldn't disturb them. I turn away and enter the kitchen. Roy is presumably off on another project. Jan is humming away as she continues to bring order to the kitchen. She tells me I have to plan on dinner later in the week and make sure I bring Sonia and Erica with me. They want to do something special for Tobias' birthday but haven't made any firm plans yet. Besides, she says conspiratorially, you'll want to be here for the big name reveal, and so will Sonia.

I smell coffee. Tobias! I forgot all about him and making him coffee. Jan tells me she's taken care of it and that Tobias is waiting to take me back to the old house. I silently wonder how The Grange house so quickly became just 'the old house.' I see why Tia doesn't want to leave it behind, relegated to some obsolete status.

In the solarium I find Tobias in his position. Resting in the one chair he brought over from Joan's studio, wallet behind his head, long legs outstretched, eyes closed. He's not asleep. His hand is gently conducting the Mozart playing through the speakers. Still, I don't want to disturb him, so I whisper softly that I'm just going to take one of the golf carts back to the house and that he can stay here. Without opening his eyes, he smiles in response, nods, and goes on conducting. "The key is on the hook just there by the door. Good to have you back."

I haven't driven a golf cart since James golfed decades ago in Sarasota. This one quietly zips along, responsive to my stops and starts as I get use to the pedals. The llamas trot over to the fence and I give them a wide berth as I pass. The sheep are huddled together against the fence, their wool getting heavier as winter goes on.

Back at the house, it doesn't seem right to leave without checking in on Tia. She's not in the kitchen so I call her name and hear her from the studio. She's sitting in the one remaining chair in Joan's studio. Joan's presence is so strong here. I look at the trio of her portraits and nod a silent hello to her.

"Hey, I just needed to check on you before I go. You ok?"

"Thanks, Jessica. Sure. Dad isn't the only one who likes to come and sit here. Frustrated as I get with him, I do understand. I don't want her to be gone. I feel so stupid. From our birth, all that is guaranteed in life is death. We can't ever seem to get our heads around why someone dies. How can that energy just leave us?

"Jessica, I don't know if you've spent much time with Elizabeth yet. She can be a bit of a downer, always worrying, always thinking she's 'done.' She really has some words of wisdom though. I was talking to her about the move and how I wish we could just live in both places, stupid as that sounds.

"You know what she said? She said, 'Tia, you can no sit in-*a* two-*a* chairs.'" I smile as she does an impersonation of Elizabeth. "Meaning what, Elizabeth, I asked her. She explained that it's simply impossible to try to sit in two places. She's wicked smart, as CC would say. Elizabeth went on about how we can't stay in the past and be fully in the present, let alone see or plan for the future. You can't have your heart in two places. You can't live life indecisively. You are either in one chair or another. You can't sit in two chairs at the same time.

"The new house, your Eves, represents me renewing commitment to life and a future with CC. The new place is her dream. Elizabeth is right, I can't sit in two chairs."

I inelegantly segue, "Speaking of chairs, your dad's conducting music from the one you brought up to the new house from this room. It looks good up there and he looked happy to be resting in it. He looked content. It was a good thought for him and for you. I haven't spent enough time with Elizabeth. She's really been kind, sending me emails from time-to-time. She senses, more than most, that I need to figure out parts of my own life. She's always there to listen. As your dad would say, this isn't a dress rehearsal. I need a lot of work to get this journey right. The women, your mom among them, are somehow helping me sort out so many life lessons."

"They are interesting, aren't they, Jessica? I like having these old ladies around me. When my mom came to us and told us she wanted to really open this place up with all the projects and the oldies I was dead set against it. CC and I had crafted a nice life here. We were open about our lives but did not live under a microscope. No one in the community bothered us. I just wanted to continue living with the woman I love, with the family I love, and be content. Then mom got sick. Deirdre and Margaret Mary were already here. Jan was coming down a lot but hadn't moved in yet. They made it so much easier, cooking, picking up on chores, making Momma happy, easing our stress and sorrow.

"One day when Momma and I were sitting together she asked how I thought this was all going and if I liked the women. I shared my feeling about it being better than I thought, that they were more interesting than I imagined, and that they all seemed to be both the same and unique. I remember telling her 'but they're not you Momma.'

"You know what she said then? She said that no, they weren't her, but she was so glad that they were here. She said they were angels sent to watch over me and my dad when she died. Angels."

Tears well up in both of our eyes.

"Tia, really? I so, so wish I had gotten to meet your mom. She left so many gifts."

"She sure did. Sometimes I'm not sure if the oldies are good angels or bad angels but I'm happy to have a set of other mothers. Hopefully, I'll have years before I run out of them!"

We both laugh out loud. I tell her Jan's invited me back later in the week and I'll see her then.

On my way back to DC I call Sonia and ask if she and Erica are back on speaking terms. She tells me that she's grounded Erica. She admits it's probably only an excuse to keep her close to her after the scare of the other night.

It was such a full morning it's hard to sort out what to share with her. I tell her about Deirdre, and she confirms that everyone has noticed the confusion, but no one has mentioned it to Deirdre yet. I ask if she knows what's going on with Gene and Sydney. She admonishes me for being nosey but then shares that she knows they have been spending regular time together over the last month. I omit that I know that *The Eves* has already been selected as the name for the new house. It's hard to keep it a secret from her, but it's not mine to tell. Besides, I don't want to sound too gleeful.

As I cut through Anacostia, and pass the Big Red Chair, I tell Sonia about Tia and Elizabeth's 'two chairs' comment. She's quick to respond.

"Of course, Jessica, this makes perfect sense to me. It is just what I told Allison. She texted me over Christmas. She and Malcolm were on their sailing trip. She texted that she was missing Gene. This was very upsetting to me. I texted her back 'Allison, I am very tired of this. You cannot wear two pair of shoes. You must decide what you are doing with your life. You have the most perfect of husbands for you. Do you want to throw that away for Gene? He is a very, very good man, but he is not your husband. Those shoes are not yours.

"This is what I told her Jessica. You cannot wear two pairs of shoes. It is obvious that you cannot sit in two chairs. Allison cannot. Tia cannot. You cannot either, Jessica.

"Why do people need to be told this? Live decisive lives, this is obvious."

We ring off. She promises to come to dinner in a few days and also go to the dinner at 'the new house.' I'm left with her scolding of Allison ringing in my ears. I know that speech. I've had Sonia's alternate version raged at me. I guess we will see what unfolds with the others. For me, I have to get home, ready dinner, and set the table. For the first time in a very long time, I'm setting a table with two chairs.

two truths and the lie

As I pull up to the house, I snag a close-by parking space, head up the steps, grab the mail, open the door to the lovely Gabler on her perch atop her small staircase, stop in the kitchen to check on the soup, and head upstairs to change and go through the mail.

The house smells good and looks so good to me. I'm sure I would have gotten around to the cleaning eventually but the surprise of this, along with stopping and not restarting *The Washington Post* after the trip, leaves the whole place looking tidy. It's time I started reading *The Post* online anyway.

In my office I pay attention first to Roy's receipts and invoices, along with the proposed plans. I go through these, write him a check, and know I will agree to most of the proposed work. I like having him around. Next, I tackle my email. There are the usual ones from students who were unhappy with a grade they received for last semester and from the ones enrolled in the upcoming semester wanting to get the syllabus ahead of time. I always wonder if they are trying to impress me with feigned interest or if they really will start the readings. At least they are better than the ones I get from the "helicopter," or the more recent descriptor, "lawnmower" parents. The ones who try to be involved in everything, trying to mow down all obstacles and challenges for their children. They write, telling me how eager their child is to take my class, and would I please send them—*the parents*—the reading materials. Ridiculous. Are the parents going to read the materials, write the papers, and then complain about the grade? These emails I simply shake my head at and write a straightforward response that encourages them to have their child contact me directly. I'm glad I just missed that generation of childrearing where the parents and children are in some intense symbiotic parent-child dance. Or am I?

Lastly, there isn't much in snail-mail except a card, *the card*. Tucked inside a bunch of circulars, I almost missed it. I knew it would come, I just didn't expect it so soon upon re-entry. Nothing will be unplanned about James' Christmas greeting. Like a moth to a flame I open it. The card depicts a beautiful, pastoral scene with shepherds going toward a manger, the Christmas star overhead. The little stack of photos slides out as I open the card revealing James' message. "Dear Jessica, *we* had a lovely Christmas visit. Did you?"

There they are, my children. One could say *bucolic*. James always could play on my love of words and uses it now.

I can't avoid James' eyes as he leans in toward the camera, grins and looks fiercely at the lens an arm around each of our children. He looks well, still handsome. He doesn't even look stressed. Prison hasn't changed him. The thought crosses my mind that he has probably figured out how to manage illegal drug trafficking even there. I have to stop myself. It doesn't do any good to be bitter.

Both James and Adam have beards. I think Adam is looking more like his dad as he grows into manhood, but he has my mother's brilliant blue eyes. Adam looks really healthy. He must be running again. Ryn is glowing. There's a man in the picture by her side and I wonder at this, of course. Slowly, I go through the other pictures trying to take in every subtlety. What does their body-language tell me? What are they wearing, are there rings on their fingers, how happy do they really look, is there some secret code someplace in the picture I should try to understand? Adam is wearing a sweater I gave him years ago. Ryn is wearing an orange top, her favorite color. Am I supposed to read into this or just be pained that I'm not in the picture?

Its four o'clock. Surely, it's not too early to check on the soup, set the table, and have a vodka. I take the photos with me.

Gabler joins me in the kitchen as I freshen up the salad, add some seasoning to the soup, and decide to make some basil cheddar scones in lieu of the left-over bread from yesterday. The vodka tastes good and stiff as I work. I decide to set the table in the parlor, lay a fire, and move some candles from the dining room onto the new little table.

Back in the kitchen, I pour another drink and feel, already, that I am on a slippery slope with this. Opening the back door, the chill comes in as I decide to carefully maneuver down the rear steps to get some holly leaves and berries for the table. How long has it been since I had Christmas decorations or holiday greenery in the house? I know exactly. It was the Christmas before that fatal phone call

"Live *decisively*," I hear Sonia say in my head, and I add it to the growing list of life-lessons I'm capturing for The Grange Project. I should be incorporating them into my life, developing mantras for more focused and peaceful living. Instead I pour just one more vodka and tuck the bottle under the counter. I tune my iPod to *Pavarotti and the Three Tenors*, grab some papers from the dining table along with the photos, and head upstairs again to write "live decisively" in my notes.

At the top of the stairs I stop at their bedrooms and talk to their empty beds. Again, I apologize aloud. "I'm sorry. I felt I had no choice. I know you don't know this part of the story. I *decided* to cooperate with the investigators because I thought it would save you. Yes, I *decided* to testify, but do you remember I didn't have to? The courts had enough evidence. I'm not the one who convicted him. Forgive me. Please."

Thinking about Sonia's comment, I know that that time, just before the trial, was the last time I lived decisively. It didn't work out that well.

In response to Erica's ringtone I slide the phone out of my jeans' back pocket. "Hey sweetie, what's up?"

She says she's calling because her mom wants to know what I'm wearing. "You know her," Erica goes on, giggling and mimicking her mother. "When you are dead, they will not care what you said. They will remember only how you looked. Of course, that is *in her opinion.*"

Ever since the night I got back from Africa, and Erica and Sonia had their scare and subsequent fight, Erica has become very clear about labeling things in people's opinion. It's become a joke between us.

"Thank you, Erica. Please tell your mother that *in my opinion* I don't actually believe she believes that. Tell her I am wearing something appropriate to have a friend in for a casual dinner."

"You're not wearing sweats are you, Aunt Jessica? Tell me you are at least wearing skinny jeans, boots, some cute top, some jewelry— something big and showy or elegant like your gold locket, gold hoops, and makeup. Oh, please promise me you are wearing makeup!"

I laughingly agree to her demands. I change into an outfit that I think both Sonia and Erica would approve. I'm fastening my gold locket around my neck when the text from Roy comes in announcing he will be late and that I should eat without him. He reinforces that he really, really wants to come by tonight if it's still all right with me. I respond that it is fine and head to my office. It doesn't feel fine at all. I feel so out-of-step with him. I don't know where this is going at all. I decide to add the new stack of pictures from James to the others in the desk. Doing so, I realize that the folder is right next to the one I've been keeping for Roy's work.

Dread fills me. I realize he still doesn't know the truth. He only knows my "story." If tonight is going to go at all well, I have to tell him. They aren't dead, just dead to me. The lie made such sense at the time. There are lots of cultures where the kids are "dead" to the parents, to the community. Like Tevye's daughter Chava in *Fiddler on the Roof*. Like the Amish and shunning. The lie seems so inane now.

It's a cold night with a gentle wind. The neighborhood is quiet. I decide to brace for the impending talk by going out on the roof. I'm sober, but I want to be very clear-headed. I drag blankets out through the window and snuggle into one, sitting up, my back against the house, observing from my perch. It's nine when I hear Roy coming up the street whistling. Seeing me up on the roof, he walk-runs towards me from the other side of the street, no coat, just a corduroy jacket. I call down to him and he asks for permission to come aboard. With a "permission granted," I instruct him to bring us two mugs of soup, unless he's really hungry, in which case we can do a full meal.

A few minutes later he taps on the window from inside my office. He opens it, and hands me the steaming mugs with two spoons. He hops ably through the opening to join me. Closing the window behind him he sits on a blanket, draping just the top of it around his shoulder.

We sip and slurp on the soup and chat about the day. The smell of a wood fire from one of the houses adds atmosphere. He compliments me on the soup, saying it hits the spot. I tell him I think he's quaint for using that expression and that I'm glad he likes the soup. It's easy to be with him, I don't want to ruin the moment. I like the warmth of his hand on my leg as we chat.

"So," I begin. "You should be really proud of The Eves." At the mention of the name he cocks his head, challenging me with his eyes. "I know about the name. Tia and Tobias told me. I didn't want to pretend with you that I didn't know."

The first truth.

"I'm also really proud of all your work there, and here. Your bill and your recommendations for the rest of the work are fine, really good. I want you to keep working here. If I'm really being honest, that's in part because, to paraphrase you, I *might* like you a 'considerable amount.'" He squeezes my leg.

Truth number two.

He rambles for a bit in response and then there is silence. It's time.

I reach for his hand. "It's been a very, very long time since I've let anyone close. The loss of Ryn and Adam. It was just more than I could handle. I'm not proud of that."

I explain to him that the car crash was real. That the hospital called me, they saw from the cell phones recovered at the scene that they had called "mom's number" shortly before the crash. I rushed to them.

"By the time I got there, they had been treated. They were both in ICU. All night I'd go between their beds, talk to them, pray for them. Ryn held my hand tightly throughout the night. Her hand felt so little. Adam wouldn't meet my gaze and would flinch when I touched him. By morning, Adam asked me to go and Ryn said she thought that was a good idea.

"I went back the next day and the next. Hospital staff told me I couldn't see them. I sat outside their rooms for two more days before the staff made it clear I shouldn't be there. I haven't talked to either of my children since that night. They were both jury and judge, deciding I had destroyed their 'perfect' father."

As I talk, I take my hand away and feel my fists clenching. I tuck them deeply underneath the blanket. My nails cut into my palms, as I tell him I've lied. A really huge, and now really stupid, lie.

After a few minutes, Roy takes in a deep breath, "I'm sorry, Jes. I knew they were alive. I'm sorry. I knew. I shouldn't have pretended I didn't. It was wrong to pretend, but it seemed so important to you to keep me out, I didn't want to intrude."

"How? How did you know?" Fists still clenched, fighting for control.

"There were lots of things. The first time I left invoices for you there was an email to them on your screen. I didn't think you'd gone so far as to be writing to them if they were really dead. Then, there were the small handprints you left under your iPod the first night we talked. I wondered at why you brought them out. I put them back on top of that chest in the closet the next day.

"A while back, Tobias asked me if I'd ever met any of your *three* kids. This evening before I left The Eves, Deirdre told me to say hello to your babies, especially the one with the funny name. There were so many openings to ask about this, but you seemed to need, well, need the lie. Tonight, you must have dropped this on the steps. It's date-stamped 12/24, this past Christmas, just a few weeks ago. I've wanted to ask, Jes. Is this them?"

He slides a photo of just Ryn and Adam, mugging for the camera, out of his jacket breast pocket. I nod, silently at first, and then, uncontrollably sob. Tears cascade. I keep trying to say, "They are alive. Alive!" but I'm gulping simply to breathe. He holds me until the rattles have subsided, but I'm still shaking.

Slowly, he takes my hand to lead me over the window threshold just as the wind shifts. Suddenly, you can hear them. "Listen, lions" I tell him, trying to steady myself.

"I know," he replies. "A westward wind. Now, take my hand."

The smell of the wood fire is coming from my own house. Before coming out to the roof he'd lit the fireplace in my bedroom and laid out two glasses and a bottle of brandy on the little table at the foot of the bed.

"Sit here," he gently orders as he pours me a brandy. "You are still shaking. I'm going to draw you a bath."

He takes off his jacket, puts it on the back of the other chair, and smooths the shoulders. I do as I am told. Sitting staring at the fire, sipping the brandy, glass in one hand, other hand balled in a fist, shaking.

A bit later he's brought the mugs in off the roof as well as the blankets, neatly folded. I hear him go back down the hall and turn off the water. He comes back for me carrying my robe from the back of the bathroom door across his arm. Laying the robe on the bed he kneels at my lead-like feet and takes off my Erica-ordered boots and socks. Taking the glass from my hand he pulls me to a stand and ever so gently, as if he has done this a thousand times, unbuckles my belt, untucks my shirt and begins to unbutton it. He runs his finger, and then his lips down each area of exposed skin, his eyes checking with mine each time.

Naked, except for my gold locket, he asks if I need to take it off. As I shake my head no, he puts the robe over my shoulders for the short walk to the tub. Only the night light and skylight illuminate the room as I sink silently, still with balled fist, into the perfectly warm tub. Roy brings our glasses and sits on the commode. I'm not even aware of the flab of my skin or the droop of my breasts. I'm dimly aware that I like the sense of him nearby but otherwise I'm not really sure what I'm feeling. I've stopped shaking but I can't seem to un-ball my fist. I feel like I've never been here before.

Roy finishes his brandy, then mine. He rolls up his sleeves, takes a cloth from the rack, and begins to wash me. My eyes find his and he tells me to just be still. "Just be here, don't think."

Before the tub cools, and before the fire in the bedroom begins to fade, he instructs me to get up as he drains the water and guides me out of the tub, toweling me dry, completely. There's a tingling in my body, in all the right places but he makes no more advances. I feel too otherworldly to act on my own. Back in my robe I head down the hall and sit in my bedroom. I can hear him tidying up the bathroom before he joins me. Entering the room, he stokes the fire and turns down the bed, just on one side.

"Come on," he says, hand extended reaching for me.

"Stay," I tell him as I slide off my robe and slip into bed

It seems to take him a long time to decide. He sits on the end of the bed, staring at the fire, hand on my leg through the covers.

"Jes, I told you. I like you a considerable amount. I don't want this to be about sex. This is probably not the night for me to be here."

"Maybe it's exactly the right night," I say beginning to shake again. "But I can understand if I've scared you away. I've scared my-self pretty well tonight."

"I don't scare easily, Jes. I'm not going anywhere."

Sometime after that he obviously decided. I must have fallen asleep. When I roll over in the night the room has grown cold, the lights are off. There are only embers in the fireplace. He is in bed beside me! I roll toward him for warmth and realize he's naked. I love the feel of his skin. Peace washes over me. I never remember having this by simply lying with a man. He stirs in his sleep, pulling me closer.

The next morning starts with unneeded apologies and welcomed thanks for the night before. He traces the half-dollar size, round locket around my neck and asks about the inscribed initials, clearly not mine. I tell him it was my mom's. That she had given it to Ryn, but that it is mine until I can pass it to her. He notes the little dents in it and I smile sharing that as an infant I had played with it as it hung around my mom's neck and bit into it and that Ryn and Adam had done likewise leaving the little dented teething marks my mother and I so cherished.

I point out the picture on my dresser of the three-year-old girl perched on a stone ivy-covered wall, clearly in a photography studio. She's dressed in early 1920s attire, ridiculously huge bow on the top of her head, broad collared shirt, skirt, and little button-up-the-sides shoes that come to the middle of her little girl leggings. The gold locket is around her neck. My mom.

Unexpectedly he throws back the covers, pops out of bed, grabs the picture from the dresser, closes the flue, and gets back in bed all in one seamless short motion. Not so short that I don't have time to admire his body, the firmness of his ass and legs.

After admiring the picture and placing it on the bedside table, he opens my locket revealing the picture of my mother, as I knew her, on one side and a very young, smiling Ryn and Adam on the other. Closing it reverently he begins to kiss between my breasts where the locket rests, just over my heart. He goes up to my shoulder, lingering on my neck. Suddenly, my fist clenches. He works down my arm with lips and tongue. With his fingers he slowly unclenches my fist, kissing the little crescent cuts made by my nails.

Exquisite tension, then, peace.

the blur

The next weeks fly by in a blur. Sonia and Erica approvingly comment that I am walking around smiling a lot. The semester started with an improved class schedule the Dean and I worked out. My university teaching is packed on Tuesdays and Thursdays. The rest of the week I work on the dissertation re-writes and The Grange Projects. There have been multiple visits to The Grange, and I have a few more conversations under my belt with the women. I've drafted a letter to Ryn and Adam that I just want to read one more time before I send. Mostly, Roy and I are surprised, delighted, and a bit amused at "dating" at our ages.

Life unfolds. The new space is so comfortable, just the right balance, *in my opinion,* of the old and the new. It's perfect with small areas and large. It feels like a comfortable home, not a communal living space. The eco-friendly features are seamless. Tobias' birthday was the first official dinner and that felt just right, too. It was a low-key event at his request. Low key, that is, if you consider there were fifteen of us for dinner at the bamboo-constructed, spacious table that can hold twenty.

The evening was flawless except for some uneasiness I sensed from Malcolm. He seemed to be trying just a tad too hard to be jovial with Gene. Later, he avoided sitting anywhere near him at dinner. Presents were kept to a minimum. I gave Tobias one of the carved birds I brought from Africa. Allison and Malcolm gave him a "coupon" for going out on *The Tug* with them any time he pleases. Sonia and Erica gave him a deck of "conversation cards." Like playing cards, they have various words, phrases, and topics designed to prompt conversations. Tia and CC gave him a photograph of the three of them with Joan picnicking down below the cliffs on the beach. It was the last photo ever taken of her.

Sonia took the naming of the new house "The Eves" in stride, only feigning abject disgust that her Casa Verde wasn't chosen. I think she's actually proud that I'm engaging here, engaging in anything.

The Grange Project finally has focus. During my visits I've asked if the women would mind showing me their new bedrooms. Margaret Mary is the first to say yes. When I visit with her, she has simply placed the items in the same order as from before, just in a larger space. The room is still starkly simple.

"I like this room," she says. "I like the light and how it plays on the walls during the day. The other room felt so familiar, though. When I entered the convent in the early '40s they called our rooms 'cells.' Did you know that? It sounds peculiar now but there was something so Spartan and pure in how we tried to live. That's why I picked the small room under the stairs in The Grange house. I've been thinking quite a bit about how we, as nuns, lived in community. I realize that this sense of Spartacism is, at least in part, CC's motivation for all of what I thought of as ridiculous innovations here. Now all the ecological soundness makes sense, I quite love this place. You see, Jessica, none of us is *done*."

When I am invited to Elizabeth's room, I have no way of comparing it to what she had at the old house. Here at The Eves her room contains a walker and a chair that helps her stand, a bed for Pavarotti, and newspapers and books everywhere. The room somehow feels heavy and cumbersome. The furniture is not so much arranged as simply dropped in place. NPR is playing on the radio. She invites me in and, with difficulty, lumbers to her chair, Pavarotti going to her side.

"I try not to make him-*a* work when we are in here together. He has a lot to support and move around all the other times. After my stroke it just made sense to get help. He's been perfect."

"I was listening to NPR in the car on the way down," I tell her. "I didn't know you would be a fan. I was figuring you to be a Pavarotti listener. I thought of you when I played 'Three Tenors' the other night."

Her response takes me by surprise. "Thank you for thinking of me. I think of you when you are not here, too. I've never liked opera though. I know Tobias loves playing it, but it has never been something I've enjoyed. I guess I'm not a good Italian in that area. My parents never understood my aversion to it."

"You don't like opera, but you name your service dog Pavarotti?"

"Jessica, he is a *Rott*weiler. When I got him, I was calling him simply 'Rotti' but soon it turned into Pavarotti. It was a good play on words. You and I share a love of words, Jessica. It's one of the things that attracted me to the law. The power of the words we write— the words we speak." She takes Pavarotti's ear and tugs it gently.

She takes note of my locket and pulls a remarkably similar locket from beneath her shirt. Like mine, the distinct color of 18-karat gold. Like mine, hers is initialed. Like mine, it is the traditional gift given to newborn Italian baby girls of a certain era and of a certain means.

As we smile at each other, a deepening bond growing between us,

I think of Joan's comment to Tia. *Angels to watch after us when our mothers are gone.*

Indeed.

Elizabeth is all about business this morning. She thinks she has found a way to focus my interest in this place and she's right. She suggested I start writing articles about the changing face of The Grange, getting word out about its development as it relates to the physical, sociological, and ecological. From her chair-side table she digs through a stack of newspaper clippings and finds an article with a web link for The Council for Green Buildings and the annual contest that honors design and construction using eco-friendly and sustainable materials.

"Write about-*a* this," she urges me. "Write about-*a* us. This is an interesting phenomenon, I think, us all living together, learning, and changing. Even Margaret Mary no longer complains about the Loveable Loo."

Later, in the kitchen, Jan has piles of books out on the dining table, accompanied by recipe boxes, and a propped-up iPad. Deirdre is there as well going through Tobias' "conversation cards," tossing them as she reads through them into a wide-mouthed glass vase. "A penny for your thoughts this morning, Deirdre?"

She recognizes my inference, remembering our conversation from a few weeks back. Good.

"I've convinced Tobias that these cards are a very good idea. He thinks we all talk more than enough, I am sure, but this will focus our conversations. Goodness knows, dear, we live together but we don't really know each other that well yet. Look, here's a card that reads 'match the adjectives below to the people in the room.' Doesn't that sound like fun?"

Jan looks up from her work. "We put up with her," she says, laughing at Deirdre.

"You can laugh all you want, Jan Kiley, but the rest of The Eves all voted, and tomorrow 'Breakfast Bowl Banter' begins. If you don't like it, you should just be happy that the others didn't also approve my suggestions for 'dinner dialogues' and 'loquacious lunches.'" She can't control her own giggling at the positively pleasant plosives.

Trying to remain neutral on the breakfast banter, and also trying to understand the relationships that are building here, I control my own laughter and introduce my idea. Elizabeth's idea really, to write about The Eves. They approve and suggest I talk to CC, who had wanted to write something for the local paper about going green at The Grange but hadn't gotten to it.

Jan suggests that there could be peak opportunities for writing if I wanted something more than just the living green focus. She's working on fleshing out a calendar of events for the year. The Eves, as they apparently now refer not only to the building but to themselves, have approved having Tobias' birthday be an annual event that will live on in perpetuity as the day commemorating the starting of The Grange Project.

Tia has asked that the next big event be an annual "Mothers' Day Planting of the Crops." Her request was based on the fact that each year she and Joan planted the small family garden on that day, hands digging in the fresh warm dirt, with full smells of the forsythia and lilacs around them. Everyone agreed to this, thinking it fits in nicely following Earth Day in April. It's often too early for large-scale planting in April. By May, Mother Earth has warmed up enough to plant. The Harvest, of course, scheduled already. The only other event they are considering, and this is what has prompted all Jan's digging this morning, is a possible "Juneteenth Celebration."

"Juneteenth, really? What's that?" I ask.

"Well we got quite the story on that when Jan proposed it," Deirdre responds. "Let me see if I can tell you. Jan, tell me if I am remembering this." She continues, her voice altered, like a narrator setting a stage. "The story is filled with murder, intrigue and injustice. Picture it—it's 1865, two years *after* Abraham Lincoln signed the Executive Order freeing the slaves. For two and a half years after Lincoln's order, in Texas, slaves remained slaves. It wasn't until a general—I don't know his name—arrived in Galveston and announced the war had ended and the slaves were free. No one knows why it took two years to get the news. That's where the murder and intrigue fits in. In any event, dear, there was, understandably, a large celebration. The general arrived and read his proclamation on or about June 19ᵗʰ and that's how we got Juneteenth."

"Very well done, Deirdre," Jan says looking pleased. "That is indeed how we got Juneteenth, the oldest nationally celebrated remembrance of the ending of slavery in America, and an official state holiday in Texas.

"Deirdre, I think you should help me plan it and convince the others that we should do it. It will be a lot of work, but I want to open it to the whole community, not just the Black folk. I want it to be a communal event anyway, with everyone bringing food. If we don't make it too formal, hopefully, we won't have to get a lot of permits and such. Elizabeth is checking on the legal end of things to see if it can work. The whole theme of Juneteenth has been gathering together, doing a little thanksgiving, focusing on education, and highlighting achievements. We Eves are doing all that anyway, why not put that all in the context of a great barbeque topped off with strawberry soda?

"Jessica, we should have documentation on how this place is evolving. If it's not written down, it's all too quickly forgotten. When you are back up in DC, check out the Smithsonian website. They've been doing Juneteenth celebrations for years. If this gets approved by the others, you'll definitely want to include it in any writing you do."

The Smithsonian? I don't know about Juneteenth. Why, I wonder. I thought I took Ryn and Adam to every activity I could at our wonderfully free, amazing museums. Missed this, I guess. At that, I hear Adam in my head teaching and scolding me about my lack of understanding of "white privilege."

Driving out today I decide to stop at the M and M. I haven't picked up the fiber for my knitting lessons and I've carried my quilt squares in and out of my car and house more times than I can count. This, however, is not the day to add those efforts to the list. I just need more coffee. Articles are already taking shape in my head. I've always been lucky when it comes to writing. Book and article titles come to me. I can see the way the type sits on the page. After a few hours or days, or, in the case of my dissertation, years, I can pretty much sit down and simply write. The words come easily, the internet access points, both common and university-access related, make the research needed pretty easy. I can't remember if it was my kids or Erica that started calling the immense amount of information instantly available on the Internet "magic," but it has become a part of family folklore that continues today. Erica can frequently be heard saying, "Bringing you, from the magic of the internet..." and then adding the factoid or piece of information that is relevant.

Elizabeth has given me the application for the green building award and thinks it should be accompanied by an article. I want to shop that idea around to see if I can find a publisher. The Calvert paper would be an easy sell, local news, global perspective, but I'd like to see if I can shop it to Washingtonian or Baltimore magazines. *Smithsonian* magazine feels like a better fit given all the aspects of the story, but it's much more of a stretch. I can see the title already, "Living Gray and Green in America."

the same
and then some

Days turn to weeks, weeks to months, and Roy, the ever constant, now says he loves me. In response I tell him, "I like
you a considerable amount." I don't return his "I love
you." I'm not being cruel, not playing hard to get. I just can't say it.
I see the way he tries to respond to my "considerable amounts" by making a joke. I know he wants more. More than I can give, at least right
now. Always, always, there is the sense of loss, the sense of need, the sense
of desperately wanting to somehow heal this split with Ryn and Adam.

Roy has been more than patient. I do like him so very much, a
considerable amount. Why can't that be enough for right now? Besides, what does love, falling in love, and being in love mean at this
age? Does he experience the same giddy "butterflies in your

stomach" that I did when I've fallen in love decades before, but don't feel now? Does he have that sense of desperation to see me, as if you can't breathe until you are together? I've had that. I finally came to understand that wasn't love, it was what it is called, desperation. Does he feel and value what I do? With him I have near perfect contentment, satisfaction, peace. I love our bodies together, how our hands reach for each other in the night, that my head fits perfectly on his shoulder. There's the pleasure of watching him cook, the knowledge that I will always win at Scrabble and he will almost certainly win at cribbage. The pure smile that comes to my face as I hear him enter with his "greetings, greetings," is that love?

It seems so different at this age. There's no denying, nor need to deny, our pasts. There's an understood delusion that we still look young, that my breasts don't sag, and his stomach doesn't protrude, and that we actually both look beautiful waking in the morning. We know, understand, and manage our own finances. There is no naïve thinking that our lives stretch forever before us. We value each day. We appreciate and worry about the very real finite nature of declining health, long-term care, assisted living, and nursing homes.

We talk about everything except what love means. I'd hate for him to think there are not butterflies, that I am not desperate. It's wonderful to have someone who so avidly cares about the progress I am making at work, with my writing, and running. Pick a topic, Roy will be interested, and I am interested right back. It is always delightful to be together. I love the sheer fact that there is no drama to it. It just is. I love playing at lustiness, feeling wanted, prized, and desired. I want to fool myself that time will just stop, and we will always be exactly as we are, no older, no less hale.

It's fun to be a couple. I had so forgotten that aspect of dating. We see Malcolm and Ali and have spent the night on the boat. They continue to be both the most hardworking and likeable of people. You always feel immediately at home with them. Gourmet meals and casual ones are created effortlessly from whatever Ali has on hand. It's always a party with rich conversation. One night we took some of the 'conversation cards.' It made for a really good night!

More recently, we've been spending time with Gene and Sydney. Yes, Gene and Sydney! I'm so pleased. It started on moving day at The Eves and with Sydney's barely perceptible shake of the head asking me not to interrupt their conversation. It seems that when Gene made the decision to leave Martinsburg College, he had job options, life options. Enter Sydney the life coach. He was honest with her about Ali being a large part of the motivation to leave as well as his embarrassment that the two of them had let themselves go someplace they had no right to go.

Gene and Sydney talked over several sessions about what he saw as his life plan, life options, desires, and needs. He was clear that he wanted to stay on the land, committed to Tobias like a son to a father, committed to keeping the tradition of this land and to having a hand in the ongoing development of it. He also liked the security aspects of his work and had offers to transfer those to both the Calvert and St. Mary's police forces. What became clear to both of them was that they actually had an awful lot in common. Through email exchanges and golf cart rides along the cliffs, the life coaching stopped and the living a life with each other in it started.

I was right, they do look stunning together. Gene's as easy to be with as Malcolm. He's a man's man as well. There's a seductive attractiveness about him that isn't in any way uncomfortable. He's just someone you want to talk with. He's quick with a story and a helping hand. He smokes a cigar, but only on occasion. He looks very wistful when he says how he and Malcolm used to go fishing, rum drinking, and cigar smoking, "before." Just before. He's very open about how much he misses Malcolm.

I hope that somehow the tensions between Malcolm, Gene, Sydney, and Allison eases. I can't imagine that as possible. The ever-optimistic Roy tells me "never say never," stranger things have happened. Selfishly, I want it to improve because, in so many ways, they have so much in common and the six of us would have great fun. It's hardest on Sydney, I think, trying to straddle the relationships. I worry about the tension of that for her.

I've been so busy lately that I have to carve out special time for just Sonia. Our friendship is the constant. I think this is true for both of us. We continue to check in almost each day even if it is just a short text. What we cherish is the conversation, the connectedness, the absolute sense that we have each other's backs, even if at times Sonia can be still pushing me from behind.

Her latest mission for me is to not give up on Ryn and Adam. Both Sonia and Roy approved an email to them before I sent it off. I am hoping it won't be received as just more of the same. This one is simple.

> Dear Ryn and Adam,
>
> I start each day and end each day with the same thought and hope – that you are safe, that you are happy, that you know that you are loved, and that there is a path back to being the three of us.
>
> I have apologized before, but I know that somehow, still, I am failing you. I continue to be sorry. Sorry for so much. Please, please consider meeting me. Meet me any place and any time. I will make it happen. There is nothing more important. If it is easier to start with an email, even a text, that too is ok.
>
> I loved you from the moment you grew under my heart and I love you still.
>
> - M

It's been several weeks since I've sent it. Nothing. I've added a new approach. I forward them things that remind me of them, an online article or cartoon, a magazine that looks like it might appeal. I try not to overdo it. So much reminds me of them. It's hard because it's been too long, I don't know their current interests. If I send Ryn some of the fresh salsa she likes from the store around the corner, or Adam seeds for his garden, how do I know they haven't given up an enjoyment in those things? How do I know how they will be received? Will they think me manipulative or crazy? Will my gifts be, at any level, welcome, or even acknowledged? So far, no.

The tension of this is so uncomfortable. Even my friends with good relationships with their kids talk about the strangeness of connecting with their adult children. There is a whole generation of children who think it just fine to text or email rather than call or visit. I hear many adults say they have to watch what they say to their kids. It seems, collectively, we are a generation of parents who feel we must walk on eggshells around the landmines of whose whereabouts only our children know.

I certainly feel I'm walking on eggshells with Ryn and Adam now. Carefully tiptoeing around my pain and their—their what, disappointment in me, their own pain? I don't know. Now, however, I try to find something each week to send them, a cute or funny card simply signed love, and, simply - M. No other words, no demands, nothing more than I am here. I love you. Maybe someday it will make a difference. I just want it to feel normal again, to be connected to them. Never say never, as Roy says.

Sonia and I continue our runs. As the days are getting longer, she now shows up after work in one of her dozens of stiletto shoes. I love how the staccato clicks of the stilettos echo her speech pattern. "I am here, it is time to run. Quickly, we must change."

With that she transforms herself from Dr. Cortez to Sonia the sleek runner, girlfriend, confidant. We've taken to running through the zoo, usually with some decided topic between us. She'll want to bounce an idea for a new project off of me or focus on an Erica issue. I in turn, share my submission for both the green housing award application and the article to Smithsonian. She's a good mental foil for me, challenging me in all the right places.

Erica runs with us on weekends at least as far as the zoo's southeast entrance. We leave her there as we push up hill to the lions and all the way to the main entrance and the elephants before we head back toward Erica. The last few weeks she's been meeting a boy, one thoroughly scrutinized by Sonia. Sonia allows them this time together knowing that we will be close by and will be returning to the same spot in about thirty minutes. It's hard to believe that Erica is ready for dating even though she obviously has been for quite some time. It's fun to watch young love. As the three of us run back to my house, Erica with her iPod shuffle playing in her ears. She is singing along, "Te ammo, Te ammo." I love you. I love you.

It's different at that age.

Thankfully, Sonia has reconnected with Ali now that things are more obviously, and appropriately, on track with her and Malcolm. Like Sydney trying to maintain her relationship with Ali, I was always skirting around telling Sonia that Roy and I spent time with Ali and Malcolm. Now things are more comfortable between us.

Being with Sonia is simply my cornerstone. When I am with her, and with Roy, I am doubly blessed. Two corners in place, waiting for two more.

things happen in threes

Allison calls early one morning asking if Roy and I can have dinner on The Tug on Friday night. The days are certainly growing warmer and with sweaters we'll be really comfortable on deck, although we'll probably eat in the salon. She shares that she's invited Sonia to bring Erica down as well. She's using the ploy that she is going to cook an Argentinean meal and wants Sonia's reaction to it.

"Jessica, you know Sonia. She couldn't stand it. She told me, 'Allison, you cannot cook this meal. I will do it.' Ha! That is exactly what I wanted from her, although it's not so easy for me to give way in my own galley. I want to see how she makes empanadas. I can never get them right, and my chimichurri sauce is nowhere near hers. This way she'll cook, and we'll drink good red wine, relax, and learn Sonia's secrets."

As always, she tells me we should bring our things if we want to stay overnight.

I text Erica, *"What's mom making for Friday night? Can I bring anything?"* She texts back with the menu and says that Sonia might ask me to pick up a Dulce de Leche Pionono at Tango's on DuPont Circle, but she's going to see if she has time to make it ahead of time.

My mouth is already watering. The Dulce cake is a rich jelly-roll-like sponge cake filled with caramelized sweet milk. Sonia usually dusts hers with confectioner's sugar. Rarely, she also has the traditional caramel sauce with it. The rest of the meal will be amazing. I have turned over my kitchen to Sonia on many occasions in order to benefit from her cooking, but I've never made any pretense that I could copy her skill. It strikes me as odd that she would cook in Ali's galley. I decide to call Sonia.

"You're not actually going to cook on *The Tug*, are you?" I ask, already anticipating the answer.

"You know me, Jessica. I do not share my secrets with others who will copy them. In this thing I am not a generous person. Besides, the empanadas are better if made ahead of time. If I get everything done ahead of time, and of course I will, I can then relax and drink the Malbec wine you will bring with you. I have already texted Roy asking him to bring some. I will let him and Malcolm grill meats under my supervision."

It's a great evening. Sonia walks onto the boat with perfect baskets filled with all that's needed for our Argentinean feast. Erica's eyes are wide in anticipation and she snatches some empanadas before they are reheated. Sonia tells her she should not do this, and that she should not serve herself first. "Mom, stop being so pissed. It's just one empanada and you made like a zillion."

"Erica, how many times do I have to tell you, do not use the word 'pissed.' It is very unattractive. There are very many words for being annoyed." Erica rolls her eyes, and as Sonia and Roy go to the car for yet more food, she snags a cold empanada for herself and hands one to Ali.

Ali chimes in with, "You really shouldn't say 'pissed,' at least in front of your mom, okay? But thanks for the empanada. How does she do this…the crusts are amazing and the beef and onion filling, oh my…what's the spice?"

Stopping her before Erica can answer Ali, I interject "She's never going to tell you. Just enjoy them."

To say the rest of the evening was a gastronomical success would be an understatement. The grilled meats with the side of chimichurri sauce melt in our mouths. The grilled vegetable skewers with the perfectly placed Argentinean accent of one boiled potato at the tip are done to perfection. Sonia made time to bake the focaccia-like fugazza bread with oregano, kosher salt and richly piled with sweet onions. Of course, she has also found the time to make the Dulce de Leche Pionono, decadently including the caramel sauce on the side. Roy and Malcolm readily have seconds and avail themselves of the sauce. The Argentinean-perfected Malbec was drunk in great quantities by all of us save Erica.

Roy has to be up early to help Tobias at The Eves, so all of us decide to over-night in harbor on The Tug. Roy and Malcolm good-naturedly deal with the slumber party nature of the late evening. Erica is patiently amused at the sloshy nature of the grown-ups.

When Roy decides to turn in, I ask him to make sure he wakes me when he's up in the morning. I've decided to go up to The Eves in order to observe Breakfast Banter. Surprisingly, Erica lets me know she wants to come with. Sonia and Ali decide to finish cleaning things up in the morning. With that Sonia, Erica, Ali, and I settle in on deck listening to low music and the unclear conversations carried across the water from other boats that are taking advantage of the winter's thaw. The moonless night is perfect for searching for shooting stars and for "catching satellites" as they arc across the sky. It's hard to tell who is more fascinated by this prospect, Sonia, or Erica. James and I used to "catch" them when we'd take the boat out at night in the Gulf. At first, you think they are a plane, then realize they are too high. When you find one, and if you can try to memorize where you see it in the night sky, you then try to find it again in about an hour and a half as it makes its way in that short span of time back around the earth to you. Erica both spoils some of the game and enhances it by quickly downloading the Star Walker app. With ethereal heavenly music as the filler we can lie on our backs and instantly identify constellations and their individual stars and determine that in about fifteen minutes we should be able to see the International Space Station appear as a dot overhead.

At some point in the night we fall asleep, and then later wake each other up to go below. As I slide into the berth next to Roy, he murmurs what a good night it was. Indeed, I tell him, nuzzling into his chest.

The early morning is glorious, despite the late night and the too-oft drunk Malbec. The day is one of those that promises summer's warmth is around the corner. Roy has promised to help Gene and Tobias with getting the fields ready for planting. A good breakfast up at The Eves under his belt is the order of the day. Spending time with the Eves is the order of mine. We gather up the sleepy Erica and head to The Eves.

In contrast to my routine of speeding up the drive to The Eves, Roy takes the driveway slowly, and carefully pulls to the back side of The Eves. As the three of us get out of the car we can see through the solarium doors that the household is up and active. Tobias is reading the paper, chatting with CC about whatever he's reading. Deirdre is knitting. Elizabeth is reading, most likely *The Wall Street Journal.* The smell of good Tanzanian coffee fills The Eves as we enter. There's also the smell of bacon and something rich, something baking.

Roy sets things in motion with his "greetings, greetings," and coffee is suddenly in our hands as we're asked to set the table and call everyone in. Sydney appears, leading Gene, hand in hand. He's looking a bit sheepish. Apparently, they haven't spent the night here before.

Deirdre, delightful Deirdre, says "Oh good morning dears. Really Sydney, Gene knows his way around by now you don't need to lead him." Jan and Margaret Mary exchange glances.

There's a knock on the door and Tobias answers it. From the solarium we hear a "Good morning, son." Gene informs us that one of the kids he mentors is joining them to work in the barn today. I set another place. Thirteen at table again, I hold my tongue. I didn't realize I was this superstitious.

Jan has cooking for groups down to a science. Seamlessly, bowls of eggs, plates of bacon, and coffee cake come to the table. The coffee cake is delicious, warm, cinnamon, and streusel topping. "Jan, is this Bisquick? I used to make it every Sunday! I haven't made it in years. Did you notice they dropped the recipe off the box?"

While we eat, the conversation just flows. Jan confirms that it's the old Bisquick recipe and promises to send me a link. Gene's mentee seems a nice kid. Erica is certainly taken with him. I try to remember what that type of flirting is like. As we are finishing, Deirdre gets up and pulls the vase with the conversation cards toward her, reaches in, and shuffles them about. Selecting one, she pulls it out and announces that "Today's breakfast banter will be 'things unexpected at my age.' Oh, won't this be fun!"

"You say that every morning," a chorus of voices responds.

"Do I now? Well, it is fun, today more so because we have the pleasure of having Miss Erica with us." Erica gives a grand acknowledgement of her presence to all. "Besides," Deirdre continues, "I learn something every day. It's good to do that."

"I agree, Deirdre. I try to do that myself," responds Tobias, getting up from the table. "What's unexpected for me at this age is that I still can't wait to get Oliver set up to plow." Then, to the other men he gives an aside. "The banter is probably a bit more than we'd enjoy this morning. Gentleman, shall we?"

The four of them head out to the barn with Erica shamelessly putting her hand, telephone hook-shaped, to her ear and mouthing "call
me" to Gene's protégée.

"So, Miss Erica, what happened to zoo boy?"

"Aunt Jessica, keep up, that was so last weekend."

"Ok. Deirdre, I'll start," I announce. "What surprises me at this age
is that Erica thinks she can meet a boy, twenty minutes later be asking
him to call her, and think that that's going to be okay with her mother!"

"Aunt Jessica!"

"Come on, let's move the banter to the Great Room," Elizabeth
says, saving Erica further scrutiny. Jan brings in a big decanter of
coffee and clean mugs and the usual accompaniments. My statement
has set off comments about dating propriety that spans back over a
hundred years to stories about the Eves and their parents.

"What surprises me at this age," chimes in CC, "is that I am still
lucky enough to love and be loved by the great love of my life." She
leans into Tia on the couch and kisses her squarely on the mouth,
one of the few outwardly demonstrative shows of affection I've seen
between them.

Erica erupts with an idea. "OMG, you two should *so* be getting
married now that you can. We could have the wedding here. Mom
and Jan could cater it. Are you going to get married?"

"Probably not," responds Tia. "But we've talked about it. We'll see."

"What surprises me at my age is that you can get married, and
that I think it's a good thing," comments Margaret Mary.

Uncharacteristically, Elizabeth chimes in, "Are you surprised they
can get married or are you surprised that you think it's a good thing?
Because it would surprise me that you think it's a good thing, Margaret Mary."

"I do think it's a good thing, Elizabeth. It's a surprise the law took
so long to meet up with mores. There's really not that much that
surprises me at this age. Did I mention the lack of pubic hair?"

"What!? OMG, you're, like, all bald? Bush-less? Gross!"

"Not all of us Erica and it's only in *your opinion* that it's gross." I caution her.

Jan shares that she's surprised that she almost never hears from her daughter when they used to be so close. Deirdre says that she doesn't see her boys enough and it surprises her because they took such care in helping her get started here. She wonders if this was so they could avoid her having to move in with them, when she thought she was doing the avoiding. She talks about how they do the obligatory things like send presents at the right time, or call on the right occasion, but she recognizes this for what it is, duty.

"You two have so much in common with Aunt Jessica. She never hears from her kids at all."

"No, no I don't, Erica." I must have said this in a defensive tone that I didn't intend.

"Oh crap, are you pissed I said something? I thought we were all OK about talking about that again."

"Erica, don't say 'pissed,' remember? And, no, no I'm not angry. It's ok. It just doesn't get any easier."

This seems to be the great conversation stopper. Most of us wander off, leaving Jan and Deirdre to ponder what went wrong in their broken mother-child relationships. Erica and I go into one of the two alcoves. The one on the north side of the house has become the game room, the one on the south the quiet room with computer hook up, bookcases and comfortable chairs. Even though the whole house has wireless access I find there's something substantial about sitting at a desk.

Checking my email, I scan the in-box, jumping immediately to the one from *Smithsonian* magazine. I'm disappointed, but not surprised, that they've turned down my "Living Gray and Green" article. It was a long shot.

I continue to scan and see one from Green World Solutions. Ever since I entered the contest proposing The Eves worthy of the best green and sustainable award, I've been getting way too many unsolicited emails. I open it anyway and turn to Erica asking if she can quickly go get CC.

"Why, what's up?"

"Come and look over my shoulder!"

"OMG! I'm on my way."

"Don't tell her!"

Erica and I stand and hold hands as CC reads every word of the email printout I hand her.

> *Dear Ms. Barnet;*
>
> *Thank you for submitting "The Eves: A time of Re-creation" for the Mid-Atlantic Green and Sustainable Housing Award. It is our pleasure to inform you that the committee found your submission clever and captivating and exceeding all criteria for recognition. Indeed, the committee point value ranking of your submission placed it amongst the highest values awarded to any First-Place awardee to date. Congratulations to you and the entire team at The Eves.*
>
> *You will not be receiving any paper communication notifying you of your award based on the committee's own commitment to keeping green. However, please find attached materials to be completed for the distribution of the cash award and links to the forms we would ask you to complete. Among the forms, please pay special attention to the request for biographies of the individuals cited in your application including the concept designer and architect(s) as well as the instructions and information needed for further press releases and photographic uploads.*

Again, congratulations. Your First-Place award, as well as the names and information of the other awardees, will go out to the press networks today. We have listed Ms. Cynthia Newbury as the point of contact for press inquiries as noted in your submission.

We also want to inform you that one of our committee members serves on the board of Retired Persons International (RPI). She has taken the liberty to share your draft article "Living Gray and Green" with the editors of that organization's publication with the caveat that it is already under consideration. In the unlikely event that your article is not immediately picked up by the other publication, I have attached the contact information for Dr. Marianne Vesay and the RPI editors. Ms. Vesay indicates they would be greatly interested in publishing your work.

Sincerely...

CC looks up from the paper, eyes filled with tears. "Thank you. Oh my god, thank you. I don't know who to tell first. Tia and Tobias are up at the barn, Roy's there. Malcolm didn't come over, did he? He needs to know right away. I can't think! I just wanted all of the oldies to have a place of their own, a place of renewal. This is so much more than I could have hoped. Let's go up to the barn. Erica you'll need to drive the cart. I can't even think. Hot damn, we won! There is a story here!"

"More than one," I tell her, as both Erica and I hug her.

jubilation

Jubilation abounds! So does an awful lot of work. I gratefully take the publication offer from RPI, with its international and immense circulation. Since theirs is an electronic publication, news spreads quickly about 'our' little corner of paradise. *The Washington Post* has sent a request for an article. They want a spin on The Grange and how it has changed over time. With some help from Tobias filling in my historical gaps, it is pretty easy to churn out "The New Grange Movement" article incorporating the full complement of things that are happening down here. That article, with a much more diverse audience, prompts more interest. Deans of Students, eldercare facilities, state and federal agencies are all interested in what is going on here.

Malcolm and Roy are busier than ever. I'm ghostwriting responses for CC, who has more requests for information than she can handle. There seems to be as much interest in Tobias and the women as there is in the sustainable materials and green nature of the house. Of course, the award is exciting and well timed for Earth Day. However, it is also the end of the semester already and I've got papers to grade and record, graduation to help plan, and my first dissertation review.

It's hard to be overly stressed though. There is no more beautiful place on the planet, in my opinion, than Washington, DC, in the spring. The cherry blossoms are notoriously stunning, but it is the total combination of brilliantly red tulips in front of white monuments, skies that have lost their winter gray and turned to brilliant, cloudless blue. Daffodils along Rock Creek Parkway dotting the hills and calling attention to the majestic cemetery that sits high on one of them. Trees are just waiting to explode into full-leaf, while the giant magnolias in pinks and whites are displaying their large showy flowers and the dark-barked red bud trees have their minute, deep pink flowers creep along and cover each branch and limb. Pear blossom trees are everywhere with their magnificent and dainty white flowers that fall away like so many snowflakes when their time has come.

Good news just keeps coming. Sydney is in full remission. This allows a whole new level of ease for all of us, but most importantly for Sydney and Gene. You can watch them visibly relax into their deepening relationship.

Roy and I too continue together. He understands that I really do like him a considerable amount. I'm not going any place either. There are nights when my fists still clench but those seem fewer and further apart. Roy, now more than the vodka, keeps my demons at bay.

Then, out of the blue, there is the inquiry, and the world tilts on its axis.

inquiry

From: JWStengle@ao-po.sy
To: JMBarnet@google1.com
CC:
Subject: Inquiry
17:22

Dear Ms Barnet

I hope this email is not an intrusion. My name is Jesper Stengle. I was born in Oslo, Norway on 11 December 1977. I was surrendered to adoption by a foreign woman. I am inquiring if you are my mother.

Please forgive the abruptness of how I say this, I have been searching for a very long time and it appears that you are a good, how should I say, candidate. I wrote to you three years ago and got no response.

I would like you to know that I am not asking anything from you. I am a grown and independent man. I am writing you again. If you would consider a response to me, I would be very grateful.

Respectfully,

Jesper Stengle

Breathless, literally. I have to tell myself to breathe.

Hit [**REPLY**]. Think better of it.

Hit [**PRINT**].

Text - *"Sonia, pls come."*

An hour later she is in my parlor, I am pacing and drinking. Not pacing my drinking. I hand Sonia the email and she gasps, eyes growing wide.

As she reads, my mind races. He wrote me three years ago? That would have been at the height of everything. I probably just deleted the email not recognizing the address. I wouldn't have read it and forgotten this, right? How do I know it's him? What do I do? A million questions run through my head. What if he wants to know about his birth father? Do I have to, finally, tell James? Oh, God, what about Ryn and Adam? I am so hoping that something in my new approach with the kids will open the door to communication. Will this be just one more opportunity for them to hate me? What does this Jesper want? What if it's him? What if it's not?

"Jessica, you are getting overly worked up. This is not the time to be drinking and it is not the time for hasty responses." Taking the glass from my hand, "First, we need to answer him. It is the polite thing to do."

Her saying that "we" have to do this makes this situation somehow manageable. We go up to my office and Sonia sits at my desk. Before she hits "reply," she reads it again. "How honest do you want to be, Jessica?" I simply nod. She types. I read over her shoulder.

Dear Mr. Stengle,

Thank you for your email, it was no intrusion. A surprise, yes, but no intrusion. I do not recall receiving correspondence from you earlier, as I am sure I would have responded. As to your specific inquiry, may I ask why you suspect I am your mother, as well as why you are opening this conversation after so many years?

That said, I must say there is a possibility that I gave birth to you, that you are my son. I did give birth to a beautiful boy on that date, in Oslo.

You said you have been searching for your mother, your birthmother, a long time. Thank you for letting me know that. How would you like to proceed?

You should know that I have wondered about the son I gave birth to, always. I always pray that he is happy.

Jessica

Sonia turns to me. "What do you think?"

"I don't know, what am I supposed to say to him? Do you think it might sound too formal, like I'm putting him off? I've thought about this, hoped for this, and now what?"

Sonia looks at the printed email again. "I didn't realize he was so close to my age. I guess I always thought of him as just a bit older than Ryn."

"Great, Sonia, remind me that I could almost be your mother! Now I feel old on top of everything else," pausing, "Let's hit 'send.'"

Sonia stays a while and we try to imagine what might lie ahead. After she leaves, I call Roy to say good night and tell him what has happened.

"You don't sound happy about it, Jes. Are you OK?"

"I think so. It's complicated. How could he have found me? What does it mean for him to find me now? It's just really unsettling. The time difference doesn't help. I've checked the computer dozens of times for a reply."

"Of course, you did. Well, try to get some sleep. I love you, sleep tight."

"Thanks, you too. I like you a considerable amount. Talk to you in the morning. I wish you were here tonight."

We ring off. It's after midnight. Unable to sleep, I get up to re-check the computer. We sent our email hours ago, nothing. He wrote at 17:22 his time, 5:30 in the afternoon. Maybe he was just finishing work. I wonder what he does. What is the time zone change? I think it's five hours, like London, no, it's six ahead of us. When we hit "send" it would have already been 11 o'clock there. Of course, he wouldn't be answering.

Looking at my inbox, there's a sweet good night note from Roy. "I love you Jes, thank you for liking me a considerable amount. This is a very good thing. There is hope for us."

No other emails. Then, it pops in, time stamped 06:22.

Dear Ms Barnet

God morgon! Good Morning. Takk! Takk! Please excuse me, I am excited. Thank you, thank you very much for writing back to me. It is a possibility that you are my birth mother, and you wrote back. This is more than I wanted to let myself hope. It is a way to, to use your word, proceed.

Let me tell you, first, to allay your concerns, I am fine. I was and am happy. Thank you for saying you wondered about me. I never knew if my birth mother ever thought about me. And this matters. This makes a difference to me. Takk.

I had a good childhood. My parents adopted many children. I was their last. I went immediately into a big family. I have many sisters and brothers and nieces and nephews. I am not married.

My parents were older when they adopted me. My father died ten years ago. My mother is still alive and is in her mid-eighties.

You, perhaps, remember how difficult the foreign adoption process was in Norway until a few years prior to my birth. It was unheard of, really. In the year of my birth, there were less than 30 such adoptions. That should have made the searching easier, so few women to try to identify. The laws were so strict on trans-national adoption. Women who could not meet the legal requirements simply officially abandoned their newborns. This makes the parental search for these adoptees much more difficult. I was such an abandoned baby.

"Abandoned." The word both stings as I read it and confirms that it's him. I reach out to touch the screen. I was so naive when I went to Norway thinking I could just hand my baby over. The laws were strict, requiring involvement and releases by both countries. 'Abandonment' was my only choice, and a far better choice than the one James gave me. Gave Jesper.

It is my mother's search for a place to 'retire,' a place that suits her intrepid nature that made me find your name again. A companion of hers found the article 'The New Grange Movement' on the Internet. Mother very much wants to find or, more humorously, start something that would be as stimulating as The Grange sounds. You would have to meet my mother to understand the humor of this, but let me leave it, for now, that she is an amazing woman and I am blessed that she found me.

When you did not respond three years ago, I assumed either I had identified the wrong person, or you wanted to stay in secret. Then there was the peculiar confluence of the Grange article, and your name as the by-line.

I want to also assure you I want for nothing. I am not seeking anything from you emotionally or financially. My parents were people of means. I am a well-established documentarian. You could go to my web site, if you have interest. jesper.stengle.no.

What I seek is a history. When you are adopted, at least for me, regardless of how well loved you are, you know that the older generations of your family are not your history, not your lineage. Their stories are not your story. Their illnesses and reasons for demise are not yours.

I look at people both here and in the United States when I travel there, and I wonder are you my mother, my father, my half-brother, or sister? I think you can understand this. In searching for you I found an article you wrote many years ago, it was on women and DNA. Quite simply, I do not know who I am.

If you would please consider corresponding until we are sure, I would be most grateful.

Respectfully, <u>yours</u>? ☺

Jesper

Cute, clever, child-like.

I hesitate, only for a moment before going to his website. This silences any last doubt. His picture beams out at me. Although there is something different about the eyes, this is an older version of Adam. If Jesper was sitting on a train across from me, I'd be staring at him because of the likeness. I reach to the screen and trace his face, the bridge of his nose, the eyebrows, the lips, and under his chin. It's been thirty-eight years, four months, and a handful of days. I know he has ten fingers and toes.

Text - *"Sonia, Roy, it's him."* Joint responses.

"Amazing, are you OK? You do not need to decide anything now. – RLG"

"Of course she does, Roy. What are you going to do now, Jessica? S"

What indeed, I ask myself.

not lost in translation

The irony of it being almost Mother's Day when Jesper reaches out to me while my own Ryn and Adam remain silent isn't lost on me. I wonder at Jesper's timing. The "magic of the internet" teaches me that although Mother's Day is celebrated almost universally in May, in Norway it's early February. Coincidence then.

In my email back to Jesper I tell him that I believe I am his mother. I also ask for some time to process all this. He has been searching for a long time. In my mind this day would never happen. While I am so very glad he found me, I would not allow myself to search for him. I knew that I had "abandoned" him and did not feel I deserved finding him. I need some time, a small bit of time, to figure out how to move forward. I want to be very sure, I assure him, that I simply don't muck this up. I tell him all of this. He is gracious, but you can hear the edgy eagerness in how he responds. I ask the he just let me get through a big celebration I am involved in at The Grange in a few weeks and he agrees.

After our email exchanges, I head down the hall to their bedrooms, vodka in hand. As I face them, Ryn's is on the left at the top of the stairs, Adam's to the right. Ryn was always her younger brother's ever-protector. If he headed too close to the top of the stairs as a toddler, or if Adam thought the always-feared monster was ascending from below, she was there for him. They idolized each other then and always.

As I have done for years, I go into each of their rooms, smooth the bedspreads and make some small, unneeded adjustment to the placement of something that hasn't been touched since the last time I dusted or came in here—a favorite book, doll, trophy, or an art project. These have become relics to me, holy icons of those who choose to be dead to me.

I breathe in their presence and remember only happy times, reading books, picking out prom dresses, sorting baseball cards. Even the times when they had problems—a stomachache because Ryn hated her fifth-grade science teacher or when Adam had a migraine and came home sick from school. It was all good because we were family. We were *three*. We were so close. How does the lack of that closeness not leave a gaping hole in them that needs to be *desperately* filled? Filled? Is it selfish to think it should be filled by me?

Then, as I did countless times when they were tiny, I lean with my back against the small hallway wall that separates their doorways and slide to the floor, knees to my chest. I talk out loud to them. I'd do this after they had both been tucked in bed and well snuggled, but when one of the three of us was not quite ready to say a final good night. I'd sit there on the floor to be close to both of them, neither the favorite. Sometimes I'd read, sometimes we'd recount the day, or plan a new one. Slowly, I would hear their responses grow sleepy and their breathing become regular. Even then I would sit and be at peace just a bit longer.

Tonight, my ears long for those sounds as I talk aloud to their empty beds. Tonight, I imagine the little versions of Ryn and Adam. "Tonight, my children, I will tell you a story. It is not an easy story to tell. This story is not hearsay, this is really true. A very long time ago, before you grew under my heart, before Papa and I loved each other well, Mama took a long, long trip. On that trip she gave birth to a little, tiny, boy. That little tiny boy grew up to be a man, a man almost forty years old. I've seen his picture. He is your brother. Not a half-brother, a full brother, a big brother. He looks a lot like Papa and like you, Adam. Ryn, I think he has your eyes. He takes photographs like Cousin Erica and makes documentaries too. His name is Jesper.

'Jesper.' It sounds like a nice name doesn't it? The magic internet taught me it was the most popular name for a baby boy in Norway when he was born. Yes, Norway, very, very far away. Yes, Jesper, like the name of one of Baby Jesus' visiting three kings. It means 'keeper of the treasure,' or 'the gift.'

"This is all I know about your brother. I don't know what to tell him about you. About us. He found me on the internet, but since you have Papa's last name I don't know if he knows about you. What would you want him to know? What do you want to know about him? Papa doesn't know. If I tell you, you will want to tell Papa and I don't think that's a good thing. If I tell Jesper, he will want to know about all of you. He has so many questions."

Saying this out loud makes me stop. I can refer to Jesper as their brother, but it sounds to me like a betrayal of them to call this man my son. *They* are my children, not this Jesper. Silent. Silent, and selfish, and scared. What if Jesper forms a bond with James and the kids? Can I risk losing the barely found Jesper to them?

He's not really mine to lose.

It seems too late to be able to control any of this now. The lies and webs are too hard to untangle as I've learned with Roy. I continue my story, speaking again to their empty beds, the empty rooms, and the empty house, with them as close to me in spirit as though I could go in and tussle their hair and give them another kiss. I fill in what I think their responses would be.

Gabler finally joins me, meowing into each of their rooms before she settles into my lap. We both yawn.

"I want to go see your brother and talk to him. Is that OK with you? It makes me nervous.

"Do you remember a long, long time ago I told you the story of the beautiful Pandora? According to the Greeks, she was the first woman on Earth.

"Yes, Adam, Pandora is like Eve but that's in a different story.

"Pandora was created from water and earth at the order of the mighty Zeus. Each of the gods gave her great gifts. At one-point Zeus was mad at, *hmmm*, I can't remember who, and he retaliated by giving Pandora away to be married.

"No, Ryn, I am not going to give you away to anyone. Anyway, remember that in the story Pandora opened a box in her husband's house.

"That's right, Adam. It was a jar, but most people think it was a box. Anyway, she opened the jar. Do you remember what happened next?

"That's right, it was filled with many sad and bad things that escaped and couldn't be put back in the jar, and these bad and sad things filled the earth. Do you remember that there was one thing left at the bottom of the jar that didn't escape? *Hmmm?*

"Yes, yes, Adam, it was 'hope.' That's right, too, Ryn, a different translation, but still just right, 'expectation.'"

Hope, expectation, the keeper of the treasure, the gift. Jesper.

Yawning and getting up, "Good night, my children. Sleep tight, be safe, both the little and big versions of you."

mother's day

Despite my dread, I know I need to be at The Grange for Mother's Day. All of the Eves, and most of their children and grandchildren, will be there. I'm dreading many parts of today including watching all the happiness between generations of mothers. Wanting to be a good sport, and wanting to participate fully, I pack a Mother's Day orchid from my collection for each of the Eves. In my mind the group has fully expanded beyond "the oldies" of Jan, Elizabeth, Deirdre, and Margaret Mary. Tia and CC, and even Sydney, are so much of the fabric of the place they also are included in who I think of as the Eves. At my request, Sonia is going to pick up lilac and forsythia bushes for me at Johnson's Nursery in Wheaton before she drops Erica off with us. Nora, the gardener, promised she'd set some that are in bloom aside for me. A special gift to Tia on this day.

Roy and I tuck the orchids, the just-dropped-off plants, and Erica into the back seat of the car. Erica will spend part of the day with us photographing the festivities. Sonia will join us later after giving a short talk at one of DC's Latino centers for young mothers.

Roy tries to slide a small gift-wrapped box in the backseat without me noticing. I don't say anything. Whatever it is, it won't be from Ryn and Adam. I try to shake this thought from my head before we start out. Roy is just being sweet, knowing today isn't going to be easy.

"What did you get your mom for Mother's Day?" Roy asks. When Erica replies, "Nothing," we both say that's unacceptable.

"Come on back into the house. We'll pick her out something from my gifting closet," I tell her. Erica always has been amazed that I have extra gifts in the closet where I keep the gift wrap. It always seems magical to her that at a moment's notice I can pull out a present for almost any occasion and for any age group. In truth there are a lot of items to be re-gifted on the shelves, but many are things I just see and pick up for just such occasions. It all began because I always wanted to have little things for the kids if they got sick or stayed home from school on a snow day. Erica picks out an emerald green and gold silk scarf that will look stunning on Sonia. I know because I bought it for her upcoming birthday. Erica decorates a gift bag, tucks the scarf in and we're off for Mother's Day at The Grange.

On the way down, we talk about all that will go on today. From all the emails it's clear that Tia has put her emptiness on the occasion of her first Mother's Day without Joan into great preparations. There's a host of activities and two planting projects, one at The Eves for the homeopathic garden and one in the same acre we harvested last October. Is it really just seven months ago?

When we pull up to The Eves, Roy jumps out, opens the door for Erica and reaches into the back seat as she gets out, handing her an orchid. He tells us that he has things to attend to, and so excuses himself. Erica and I get the rest of the orchids and plants out of the car. They are amazingly well received to *oohs* and *ahs* by everyone. The orchids make a great centerpiece for the table laden with breads, meats, salads, pies, and cookies. Tia is so pleased at the plants that will surround her herb garden.

Jan has selected a loop of Bob Marley and Simon and Garfunkel music to be played today. Upbeat, fun tempos. She's singing, "Gee, isn't it great to be back home, home is where you want to be" and adjusting the tables. She gives us warm hugs, but I notice there is some edginess about her that I can't put my finger on.

Tia has everything in readiness. Outside tables are lined with gardening gloves and tools of various sizes and hues. Jars of seeds and seedlings are in abundance. There are colorful and cute rubber children's boots, some with frog's eyes on the toes, to be chosen at will. Tia's scheduled the horticulture students from the college to shear the sheep and llamas at two different times during the day using. Art students from the college will be doing face painting in the barn. Elizabeth will be overseeing tile painting on the side porch. There are piles of clay baked tiles, made from this land, and left over from the various bathroom and kitchen backsplash projects. These are now re-purposed for family art commemorating this day, or simply to paint for the sheer fun of it.

The Gentle Ben movers will be running the golf carts about. Food will be available throughout the day. Families can help themselves to the more than ample assortment of food laid out in the kitchen. Beverages are on the porch.

At Sydney's request, Tia's arranged for Gene to run the Oliver-led mule cart around the property both for transporting people about and for the pure joy of it. In truth, it's also to give him a role in the festivities that will allow him to meet and mingle with Sydney's children and grandkids in a manner that builds rapport between them in preparation for introducing him as the man she's dating.

Dating. Dating sounds like such a stupid word to describe what this means at our ages. Dating, boyfriend, beau… really, we're old! What is the appropriate term for the man you trust, look to, enjoy, are sleeping with, rely on, and like a considerable amount? It's something Sydney and I have discussed often. Elizabeth points out that the courts use the word "paramour," but that doesn't suit us either.

Up at The Eves, Roy has installed the sign that will officially identify the building with its given name. He sweetly designs a little unveiling of it for me. Everyone gathers at the corner of the house. Roy has the sign covered with a drop cloth and he's already planted a mass of beautiful daises around its base. As if I am launching a ship, he asks that I pull away the cloth and pour the contents of the watering can he hands me over the beautifully hand-crafted sign, and onto the daisies to the applause of all.

"They aren't daisies, Jessica, it's Feverfew," Sydney informs us. "You dry it, turn it into a tea. It's good for everything from fever to allergies to arthritis to migraines."

CC of course loves this. I'm getting a little overwhelmed.

As I inspect the seedlings and seeds waiting to be planted, I break off one of the Feverfew leaves, roll it in my hand and smell it. Citrus. Most of the plants I either don't recognize or don't recognize for their medicinal properties. The exceptions are the pink and purple coneflowers, *Echinacea*, a pink cousin to the Black-Eyed Susan I've grown these for years, almost impossible to kill, drought resistant, showy. I vaguely remember they have an antibacterial or digestive property to them, but I'm sure any tincture I'd make of it could be deadly.

Erica asks all of us to assemble on the ramp leading up to the house so she can capture all of us and the sign in the photo. Me and my other mothers, my friends, and the man I probably love.

Taking it in, I will it to be a good day.

I think about my own mother and miss her today. In fact, I miss her more and more. I worry about the hurts I caused her, the ones I probably can name and the ones I never knew about. How would she have reacted to this rift between me and the kids? I wish I had the counsel and wisdom of her age and the kindness that accompanied it. I remember so many little things about her now. Appreciating them more now than when she was still here. When I was little, she would always urge me to be nice, even in the face of nastiness. "Jessica Marie," she would say, "be kinder than you need to be. It takes so much less energy than being mean." Did I learn that? Did I pass it on to my kids?

I've told her in my head about Roy and this place. I wonder what she would have thought about this day, what it would be like to be here with her. In my family she always made sure we made such a big deal out of Father's Day. Mother's Day itself was downplayed. I should have honored her more. Unfortunately, I carried forward the tradition, teaching Adam and Ryn that it was never important to celebrate Mother's Day in any special way.

Roy takes me out of my reverie, surprising us all when he asks for permission to make a small presentation. He's taken the liberty to make another sign. Everyone looks to Tobias and CC and Tia, but they look as in the dark as we are. Roy runs up the steps of the porch and brings forward another drop cloth covered sign and asks Tobias to do the honors. It matches in beauty and craftsmanship the one for The Eves. This one says, "Joan's Acre." Multiple sets of eyes fill with tears as Tobias puts his hand on Roy's shoulder.

"I hope it's OK," Roy states. "I thought we could put it down below in the harvesting acre. It deserves a name."

In reply, Tobias says, "Thank you, son. Thank you."

Just before the families arrive, Tia goes over assignments. The plantings at The Eves will be supervised by Sydney and Jan, the ones at Joan's Acre by Tobias and the horticulture students. They are equally important but the one below has to guarantee, to the extent God allows, as Tobias says, a crop worthy of the student harvest in the fall.

As each of the families arrives, Erica poses them on the ramp for an official family photo. She has a great knack for getting the people in the right spot and capturing the right moment. I've agreed to help out as she directs me and to take email addresses so we can forward the photos later.

Deirdre and her boys and their wives flank her, the perfect set of four grandchildren in coordinated outfits stand in front holding little wooden cages filled with baby chicks. One of the boys contacted CC asking if he could add chickens to Deirdre's menagerie. The boys wanted something easy for Deirdre to care for if the sheep and llamas became too much for her. CC happily agreed, noting that it's been a long time since they've added new chickens to the brood. Malcolm and Roy constructed a straw-bale chicken coop behind the house. Once these chicks get to a certain size, they can free-range and will start laying in a few months.

Margaret Mary's family is large, multi-colored, and spans so many levels of children, grandchildren, and greats. It's an impressive sight. I never get them straight, but they fill the ramp and each of them seems genuinely happy to be here today. Margaret Mary looks proudly over them.

Jan's daughter Brenda has come. It's actually painful to watch. Jan is so thrilled she came, but the rest of us wonder why she has. The tension is so palpable between them. Jan is trying too hard. Brenda is barely answering her eager questions aimed at starting conversation. When it comes time for their photo, it feels so awkward that Jan asks Tia and Tobias and then, belatedly, CC, to join the two of them in their family photo. Somehow all of them look out of place.

Sydney's family arrives. Honestly, each of them is as handsome or as beautiful as she is. Her two sons are strong and athletic looking. Their wives, stunning. Her daughters look just like her and they've married handsome men. The gene pool continues to the five grandchildren. I'm meeting too many people right now to figure out which kids go with each of the four couples. They all seem extra celebratory, rejoicing I am sure, the gift of Sydney's remission this Mother's Day. As they assemble for their portrait, Gene moves behind Erica to take it all in. Sydney looks so serene, so peacefully happy in the center of her brood. She reminds me of the portraits of Joan. When Erica and I preview the images she's captured, you can tell that feeling is captured, that and the fact that Sydney's eyes are fixed squarely on something just beyond the lens. Gene.

I love it.

All this while, Elizabeth is rocking on the porch, taking it all in. As the others move off to the various activities, I go to sit with her, stroking Pavarotti's ear. "Whatda ya hafta do, *eh*, Jessica."

"Hey, you two, look over here." It's Erica about to take our picture. Just before she does, Elizabeth reaches and takes my hand. Then Erica runs up the ramp to us, pops on my lap, and leans back, taking a selfie of the three of us. "Gotta go, pictures to take." She's gone in a flash, flagging down one of the Gentle Bens for a ride and, undoubtedly, some flirting.

Roy and I have our assigned roles for the day, but Tia has made sure that in each person's schedule she has built in time for everyone to enjoy and relax throughout the day. Roy and I decided to walk to the shearing of the sheep and llamas. We're both mesmerized. Roy, of course, wants to try his hand at it. Deirdre is overjoyed on this occasion. She's like a child on Christmas morning waiting for the fibers to be gathered starting another cycle for her of wool and fleece sheering, gathering, tending, dying, spinning, weaving, and knitting. Sweaters by Christmas she's promised!

The llamas seem to take it in stride as they are tethered and the hand shears separate blanket-like sections of their fleece from their newly sleek bodies. The sheep go kicking and bleating. Each sheep is placed on a blanket and made to sit squarely on its bottom, feet off the ground. In this position, held in place by one hand of the shearer, the sheep are immobile and look quite indignant. The shearing goes quickly, and in almost one piece each sheep yields its wool.

From here we go to the barn and watch the face painting. The art students are far more capable and creative than I was with Ryn, Adam, and Erica. I simply painted their faces with small designs and animal noses. These students use sponges and textured brushes, turning the kids' faces into masks worthy of appearing in *Cats* or *Lion King*.

"Come upstairs," Roy beckons me.

I haven't been in the loft since the harvest. I'm instantly drawn to the walls, the colors, the handprints that people made here. The gallery lighting isn't lit but sun beams in through the skylights. You can hear the giggling and happy voices of the students and families below. "This is for you" Roy says. "I hope it's OK."

It's the small box he's brought with him. It makes me nervous. Thankfully, bigger than a ring box, smaller than a shoe box. Inside there are two small wooden hands. Traced from their handprints, carved into the wood, and painted. One red, one blue.

He takes the look on my face for me not knowing exactly what these are. He begins to explain, but I cut him off, holding them to my heart. "I know. I know exactly what they are. I know every line on their palms. These are perfect. Thank you. How did you know how to do this?"

"Jes, I don't know how you'll feel about this, but I made copies of the handprints when you left them on the counter that day. I thought you could hang them here. I've put little hooks on the back. I've checked with CC, she said it would be fine. It's up to you to decide."

"Oh, oh, that's a tough one. Can I just hold on to them for a while?" I slide them into the side pockets of my jacket, liking the weight of them there. "Come on, cute man. We better get out of here before I get melancholic. I'm doing really well so far today."

Melancholia at bay, at least for the moment, we head to The Eves for an early lunch and to check in with Tia. Our chores don't start until about two, so we have time to eat and visit. She's making To-bias some lunch and an early-in-the-day highball. She offers me something to drink, but I decline.

Erica pops in, exuberant about the pictures she's taken. She's heard from her mom who is getting ready to leave DC and head down here.

"Hey, Erica, can you text her? Ask, if she hasn't left yet, can she go by my place. I think I left my cell phone in the house when we went back inside for her present. If she can, can she bring it with her?"

Jan comes in to put some hot items out on the tables knowing that soon families will start wanting food. Paul Simon's *Mother and Child Reunion* is playing and it's hard not to sing along with Jan. Upbeat tempo, beat bopping around the kitchen. "...no I would not give you false hope on this strange and mournful day...." Our eyes meet. The lyrics seem about right to Jan and me, we continue, and it feels good. "The mother and child reunion is only an ocean away," Jan sings.

"It's notion, not ocean, Jan," I correct her.

"No, it's not."

Erica chimes in, "You are both wrong. Once again, through the magic of the internet, I bring you proof—the word is motion!" She says as she holds up her cell phone and presents the results of her web search.

"Like the word 'motion' makes sense? I thought it was notion, too. Is there anything you can't instantly know?" asks Tia prodding Erica.

"Leave her be, child." This from Tobias. "Einstein himself said he never bothered to memorize anything he could just look up."

"Here's something interesting," Erica reads from her screen. "Paul Simon himself didn't really know what the lyrics meant. He just made them up because he got this idea from a Chinese restaurant."

"What are you talking about?" Tia asks.

Erica replies, "He thought it was hysterical that the menu had an item that combined chicken and eggs. It was called 'Mother and Child Reunion'! Ha!"

Jan leans over to her and takes her cell phone away.

After lunch Tia and Tobias decide to take Oliver and the cart over to the cemetery, giving him a break from the constant attention of all the kids. It makes sense to me that they would want some quiet time themselves today. Erica, not getting that, asks if she can go too.

Tobias purses his lips, but says, "You sure may, child, and you might as well bring your Aunt Jessica, too."

I kiss Roy goodbye and the four of us climb into the cart. Tia, gloved-handed, ably drives. Tobias goes up top with her. Erica and I sit in the wagon, feet dangling off the back. The Chesapeake glimmers to our right, and sailboats slide through her waters as we bounce along. You really couldn't ask for a more perfect Mother's Day, unless of course you were missing your mother, or the children that made you one.

At the cemetery we sit in silence for a while. My eyes, and the tight hand on her arm, tell Erica that she too needs to be still for a bit. Finally, Tobias says "Your mother would have really loved this day, Tia. She would have been so proud of what you and CC have created. I'm proud of you."

"I miss her so much," Tia says.

"I know you do child. I know you do. You've created something lasting here for her. And, maybe a little bit for me, even though there won't be any more Tobiases on this land."

This is a special moment between them. I'm feeling like we shouldn't have come. Erica, not so much. She takes this exact opportunity to say. "OMG, Tia, you and CC should *so* get married, adopt a little boy, name him Tobias, and then he'll have babies someday…"

The explosion of laughter from Tobias makes it all alright.

As we turn Oliver back toward the houses, Tobias asks to be dropped off at The Grange House. He wants to spend some time in Joan's studio. We can hear him chuckle as he notices that Roy has placed a sign stating "The Grange House" by the side kitchen door.

When we get back to The Eves, we see Sonia's car speeding up the drive. I'm not sure she's even put it in park when she leaps out and rushes to me handing me my cell phone. "Read," is all she says.

Taking the phone, I'm surprised she doesn't chastise me for never activating a lock code. "Sonia, what's up," I say tapping the screen and bringing the phone to life. My heart stops. *Hi Mom, thanks for the gifts and cards. Adam tried to call. We are both fine. Happy Mother's Day. —Ryn.*

half full

Sonia and Erica walk me into the house. Roy and CC are there, families have begun to wander in, the kitchen is filling quickly. I simply hand Roy the phone with the display showing. His eyes wide, he makes excuses to CC, telling her we have to go. She graciously tells us that everyone else can handle our few chores for the afternoon and we should indeed go.

I surprise myself by refusing. "Really, I just need some time. I'm going to walk. I'll be back. I'm fine, really. I just need to walk. Walk and breathe."

Roy and Sonia each want to come with me, but I tell them I need to go, right now, and alone. I slide my phone into my back pocket. Shoving my fists into my jacket pockets I find their carved wooden hands waiting for me. I grip them as tightly as I can, walk away as fast as I can, all the while trying to maintain sure footing and trying not to lose it.

My mind is racing faster than my steps.

Adam called, actually called? Ryn reached out?! She knew I would want to know they were fine. It's Mother's Day. Adam didn't leave a message. What would it have said? Ryn didn't sign it "love." What's the message in that? Did she text because she didn't want to talk or because Adam's phone call didn't get picked up? She said they got the gifts. She didn't say she *liked* the gifts. It's been three years of missed holidays and birthdays and *everydays*. Half full, half empty. I'm so happy. I'm so angry. So scared. This is a start. This is going to be hard to finish.

I need to quiet my mind. I wish I had joined Tobias in an early-in-the-day beverage! I want to pick up the phone and call each of them. What are the first words you say after three years? Jesper flashes to mind. What are the first words I say to him?

I hear my mother's voice in my head. "Jessica Marie, before you speak think about what it is you want to accomplish. Think about the result you want."

With everyone down at The Eves by now I head into the barn. The face painting tables are empty. The barn has the smell of fresh hay and manure. Tia must have brought Oliver in after she dropped us letting him settle for a while. He raises his head and nods as I come in, shifting his weight from hoof to hoof. We both need a little peace right now. His long glance draws me forward and I slide my hands out of my pockets, caressing the smoothness of his face as he nuzzles into me. I can feel my heart rate slowing, my breathing become easier.

When I feel calmer, I decide to go upstairs to the loft. Taking the little wooden hands out of my pockets, I put them on the bench next to the hammer and nails Roy must have left. The handprints of others surround me. Each of these, regardless of the age of the maker, was made by someone's child. Each of them has a story, someone they loved, didn't get along with, wondered about, kept secrets from, and shared secrets with.

Taking the phone out of my back pocket, I stare at Ryn's message again, shaping a text of my own. "Fabulous to finally hear from you…." No, delete "finally"–it sounds like I'm scolding her. Is "fabulous" too strong a word? Do I sound too eager? God, am I going to ponder every single word and wonder if it's OK?

Yes.

What is it I want to accomplish?

To have them back. To have them back at any price. The price I've paid for the last three years has been too great. There can't be anything more costly. What else do I want to accomplish? To have them understand my side of the story. And, if they don't want to hear it?

I said at any price.

I prepare to text back.

Ryn, my daughter! I love you, and love that you texted today! Thank you, very much. I am so sorry I missed Adam's call. I would love to hear his voice, and yours. Perhaps we can talk very soon. I hope so. I know it won't be easy for any of us. I would like to try if you and/or Adam are ready. It is good to know you are both ok. Thank you for that, too. Much love, again, my daughter. –M

Before I hit "send" I read it several times for any triggers that could send off a bad reaction. I think, I hope, it's OK. I hit [Send].

Next.

Adam, you called! How wonderful, son. Ryn says you are good and I am so happy. If you are ready, I would love to hear the sound of your voice and to talk. It will not be easy, I know. This time apart hasn't been easy, I assume, for any of us. It is your decision. Please know my heart waits for you both. Much love, – M

It sounds more emotional, still "safe" though. At least I think so. I hit [Send]. Wait.

Nothing back, but I don't really expect it. They will want to talk together and decide if individually or collectively they want any more than they've already tried. Maybe they also emailed? Checking my phone quickly, nothing. Already I'm greedy for the sound of them. I want more.

I should write to Jesper.

> Dear Jesper, today is Mother's Day in the United States. You have come to my mind very often today. I do not know where your and my journey will go, but I would like to continue communicating and set up a time, somehow, that we can meet. Meanwhile, please tell your mother how joyful I am that she found you. –Jessica"

At almost sixty years old, am I really becoming a mother of *three*? What would that mean? I so thought I was "done." I don't know how to create this part of my life—dating, estranged children, a once seen son, a career that is limping along, and this place, what the hell is it about this place that is unlocking things in me as I unlock things in it?

If I stay away much longer the others will surely worry. Retrieving the little wooden hands, I decide. Picking up the hammer and nails I hang them, fingers touching, at the top of the stairs. When I descend, I touch them in the same way as you see Orthodox Jews give a light touch to the Holy Scriptures encased in their threshold mezuzahs. Then a kiss on their fingers, blessed for having touched them. I pray a silent prayer of thanks for the gestures of all three of my children, even as I grow uncomfortable with the foundation-rumbling events that will surely soon occur.

When I return to The Eves, Erica has her tripod in place and is posing everyone on the wide front steps of the house overlooking the fields. To be more precise, Sonia, bedecked and looking beautiful in her emerald green scarf, is ordering everyone into places. It's always amusing to see Sonia control the world.

Roy and Sonia catch my eye. Nodding, I assure them that I'm OK.

As I watch families move into their places with disheveled hair, muddy knees, and painted faces you can look for the gaps—Joan, Sydney's deceased husband, Deirdre's dead daughter, the absent Ryn and Adam, the awkwardly missing Allison and Malcolm.

Or, you can look at the whole. Tobias, amidst all these people, overlooking his land. I know he can see a ribbon of Rt. 4 and the M and M from the top step. He's flanked on one side by the celebrating Tia and CC, and on the other side by Jan and Brenda, who appear to be amicably talking. Beneath them there's Gene, standing just behind Sydney and her family, joking with one of her sons. Deirdre is to their left with grandchildren all over her. Margaret Mary's entire brood is to Sydney's right. Elizabeth is sitting in a chair, front and center, Pavarotti lying at her feet. Roy, kneeling to her right, calls to me with both his arms wide open. Erica sets the self-timer and starts us all on a countdown to ten. She and Sonia run and kneel to Elizabeth's left.

Just for today, I choose to not see the gaps.

As we all get frozen for this moment in time, looking out over Tobias' land, I smile for the camera and chose to think of Joan, and all the others, even those up in the cemetery, standing just behind the tripod and looking at the marvel of this day through Erica's lens.

It's Mother's Day. Indeed.

mea culpa, mea culpa, mea maxima culpa

When Roy and I arrive back at my place we are amazed that there, on the porch, is my large suitcase. Five months and, judging from the baggage tags, twelve countries later, there is my Africa-bound suitcase, wholly intact. Ridiculously amazing.

By later that night Erica has already sent a link to everyone so they can view all the Mother's Day photos. I sound redundant, even to myself, saying how much I like the way she sees things through her lens. The family portraits, in my opinion, will be long cherished, used for holiday cards, and shared widely. I print out the selfie she took with me and Elizabeth, and one she caught of Roy and me trying to hold a sheep to shear. I'll give this to him next month for our sixth-month anniversary, framed with a note that says something pithy like "shear happiness together."

Clearly, though, I missed out on a lot of the day. The pictures of the little kids running through the fields, rolling down the hills, and playing in the dirt can't help but make you smile. Tobias and Roy setting up the sign for "Joan's Acre" are touching. Once again, Erica's chosen to capture this mostly by shooting tight, just showing their hands.

Somehow, I entirely missed that Margaret Mary's children had gotten permission to redo her old room in the Grange house. Tia must have shared that they are starting renovations and updating that house after years of beloved use. Margaret Mary's children latched on to this and created a whole new space for her. There's a wonderful group of shots of her and her family in the now brightly lit room under the stairs. They've set up a chair with a magnifying rack so she can continue to do the fine needlework and embroidery on quilts squares. They've also installed a large quilter for the actual assembly and finishing of the quilts.

Just before the large group photo at the end of the day, there are three fabulous shots of Sonia and Erica. Two of them mugging for the camera, the third is the two of them, nose to nose kissing, eyes wide open. These I will print on good paper and frame for them in one of those multi-picture frames. It will be a great gift for Sonia's birthday now that she already has the green scarf.

The photos that resulted from the twenty rapid-fire, self-timer shots are great, capturing the expanse of the moment, the little quick glances, the inevitable rabbit ears behind heads, and one with me staring at the text that had just come through.

Mom let's talk. It's from Adam, copied to Ryn. I texted them right back with a simple *Yes! When? Anytime.*

Several hours later, still no response from either of the kids. Roy and I talk about all of this as we lie in bed, Gabler at our feet. The simple joy of how our bodies feel together is what I think I love most about being with him. The nights we are apart leave me incomplete. Being honest with myself, I have to admit that, after all these years of being solo, he fills the spaces I didn't know I had. I suppose we will have to address living arrangements pretty soon.

As we talk, I tell him I'm feeling very conflicted about this coming up with the kids now and how it feels rubbing up against connecting with Jesper. There's no question in my mind that he is my son, however, Ryn and Adam are my children. There's no replacing that. I need to focus on Ryn and Adam and work to fix us.

I start to get up for a nightcap. "I'm sorry, I need to quiet my mind. I need sleep."

He pops out of bed instead, puts his pajama bottoms on and calls to Gabler. "Come on Beast. We might as well pour her a drink and see where this goes."

Coming back to the bedroom, he hands me vodka, neat, in my favorite glass. Danny Wright's quiet piano music is now playing from the kitchen. "Roof or parlor?" he asks."

"The parlor's fine," I reply, knowing it's closer to a second vodka. "Then back to bed."

By morning, Jesper has written!

God morgen, Jessica.

I hope you had a very happy Mother's Day. My mother was very touched that you sent her your thought about her finding me. As I said, I am very lucky to have this family.

I also am so very eager to know, and I have hesitated to ask, if I have other family that you will tell me about. Is my birth-father from Norway or am I actually an, how do you call it, 'All-American?' Do I have any half siblings? I bring this up, in what I hope is not an intrusive way, because you wrote on Mother's Day and I didn't know if you have other children.

Your offer to set up a meeting is most welcome. I am not sure, however, how we can make that happen in the short term. I am going on a four-month assignment to begin a documentary on the art of indigenous peoples. I will be travelling for all of this time. Regrettably, the art of your Native American's is not included in our itinerary. Upon my return, there is a one month editing turn-around. I do not see how we could have a good visit before the end of October. Please do not take this for any hesitancy on my part. I am very eager to meet you.

Would it be possible for us to set up video chat in the coming weeks before I embark?

More confidently, yours,

Jesper

There's an email from Erica and one below it from Ryn. I shouldn't, but I do, give Erica's short shrift. She's sent me something about a school project. It's photos of feet and shoes. It's not her best work. It doesn't evoke anything. I write back.

> Hey sweetie, I'm in a rush this morning, sorry. I think you might want to rethink this one. The shoes and feet thing seem shallow. Sorry, give me a call if you want to talk about it. Love you.

Then, from Ryn—

Hi Mom,

Adam and I have to be in DC next week on business. We'll be there for a week. We've asked Aunt Sonia if we can stay at her place. It's been so long since we've seen her. Erica must be huge by now.

Anyway, we are wondering, if you have time, can we meet someplace and talk. Let us know your schedule. -Ryn

I notice she has copied Sonia. Thankfully, the phone is already ringing as I re-read this. It's Sonia. She cuts me off before I can say a word.

"Jessica, I just saw the email. They wrote to me. They asked to stay with me. I did not invite this. I will tell them, of course, that they can stay here, but only if it is OK with you. I must also say, this arrangement has to be alright with you. It is your chance to finally fix this."

"Jesper wrote this morning," I tell her, as I try to gather my thoughts and calm my hurt feelings. "He can't meet until at least October, but he'd like to Skype or some-such before that."

"Jessica, do not avoid the topic. This is immense."

"It is immense, Sonia. Do the kids not see how much an email like that hurts me, or do they know exactly?" I hear my voice getting out of control. "Do they delight in knowing they have the power over all this, deciding to stop all communication for three years, suddenly choosing to spend their time with James, and now they are sending texts and emails as if it was yesterday when they cut me from their lives? They haven't seen *you* in such a long time? They're eager to see Erica? They want to set up a goddamn meeting with me someplace. They don't want to come to the house? They are staying with you for a week? Exactly how long have you been keeping in touch with them?"

"Jessica, stop it. They are not mothers. They are not parents. They do not understand the hurts that are written on our hearts with just a single word. You know this. This is not new. They will know this someday, but this is not that day.

"Staying with me and Erica makes it easy for them. We are safe to them. You would want that. You are a dangerous emotional place for them to be, at least right now."

"What's that supposed to mean? I'm their mother. You are not even a real aunt," I practically shriek into the phone, far more unkindly than I would ever want to sound.

I must have startled Roy because he comes into the room carrying Gabler. I point to my computer screen and his eyes grow wide as I mouth that I am on the phone with Sonia.

"Jessica, do not ask me this thing." My silence tells her that I will sit and wait until she tells me. "It means that they think this is all *your* fault. Ryn's email to me said, wait, I will read it to you.

> Hi Aunt Sonia, I know it's been a long time. We hope it's OK to write. It just got too hard and too crazy to know what to do three years ago. We're sorry. Everything is still all screwed up with mom. I don't know what she's been doing with sending the cards and gifts recently. We guess she's sorry for cutting us off three years ago, but WTF! She stopped coming to see us, stopped communication. What does she want from us now? Does she have any idea how hard it was for us to lose dad and her at the same time? Does she have any idea how hard it was to have to make her insignificant in our lives after how close we were? In any event, we are going to come to DC next week, can we stay with you and Erica? Please. We'll be there about a week. We've missed you. Hugs to Erica, she must be huge!

"Jessica, Jessica, are you there?" I hand Roy the phone as I vomit into the waste basket.

Fault? I cut them off? I cut them off? I could no more cut out my heart. They thought I was the one who caused this? They needed to make me insignificant?

Altar boys in fresh black cassocks with their crisply ironed white surplices, high-polished shoes, and butched-up hair appear before me, bending and swaying from side to side, pounding their chests in supplication, uttering the words from the Catholic Latin mass: "Mea culpa, mea culpa, mea maxima culpa"—these swarm before me just before I pass out.

"Through my fault" – I am sorry. "Through my fault" – I am sorry. "Through my most *grievous* fault" – I am so very sorry.

dog days of summer

The next week of waiting to see them was difficult. The entire time I felt as if I'd been hit by a train. I doubted I'd actually had a heart attack, but the aftermath from my discussion with Sonia left me feeling that way. I can't seem to go for any runs, even walking seems an effort. I feel like I'm made of glass and might break with every step.

Knowing that the kids think that this has all been *my* fault is bad enough. I am devastatingly crushed. The realization that the one thing I had worked hardest for their entire lives, that they were safe and happy, I had also unwittingly, single-handedly, destroyed. My children were not happy. They did not feel safe with me. How could I have, in any way, shape, or form, made it possible for them to think I would want them out of my life? I hurt my children. It doesn't even seem melodramatic for me to feel that I hurt my children in a way, far worse it seems, than in any Greek tragedy. Hurt the two people I love the most on this earth.

Even a week later, I can't wrap my head around it. This all happened because I wasn't clear about the intent of my actions. Because I didn't tell them at the time of the trial, or to this day, about their dad's drug abuse, the illegalities, the wire fraud, or, most importantly, that he was ready to throw them under the bus.

When the kids come to town and we finally meet, it is even worse than I could have expected. I have things planned to say but the sheer sight of them brings me to tears. The opportunity to hug them, even as briefly as they allow, is a tonic. I open with an apology, an apology for everything. I start right out with saying I didn't know they thought I had cut them off. I thought they were the ones who were done with me. Even with the apology I can tell that this *mea culpa* raises their suspicions, puts them on guard, and feels like I am accusing them.

Sonia is right. They are not yet parents. They can't know how I can read them. I know them. I have studied them since they grew under my heart. Ryn loved to stretch inside of me, pushing her heels under my ribs. As an infant she had the most dramatic and sweet stretches. I miss seeing those still when she wakes or prepares for a run. Adam was quiet as he grew inside me. He had a rhythm. I knew when he was awake as he quietly stirred, rolling gently from side-to-side in my womb. He's quiet still, thoughtful, watchful, and gentle with everyone but me these days. I know them, but apparently not well enough to not misstep as I watch them grow tense within moments of our meeting.

I try to explain, with further *mea culpas*, citing chapter and verse from their own words on the night of the accident, they were "denouncing me as the mother they knew," telling me that they "didn't want anything to do with me," that they were the ones who asked me to leave them at the hospital.' What was I to think? I accepted all this rather than have them know James was willing to see their work destroyed.

They retorted, in their own version of the truth, with equally heartfelt tears. I had "written them off just because they supported their dad." I listened with silenced responses as they ticked off their litany for how this happened. They thought I had gone crazy, "suddenly turning on their dad" (because I didn't want them to be implicated in the case). I left town "abandoning" them that first Christmas (because not once in eight months had they communicated with me). I wrote to them saying that I had "changed my will" making Sonia my executor and power of attorney (because I thought I was a burden to them). I'm not sure I heard all they said. As they were talking, I kept trying to figure out how to fix it. Seeing them in so much pain was worse than any pain I had suffered. Never was there a clearer moment, one more true than this. I could understand the sentiment of wanting to take the pain your children suffer and bring it on yourself.

We left clumsily. What had happened between us three years ago, and in the interim, was far too big to say all this was simply a misunderstanding, a miscommunication. Did I really think we could pick up where we left off? How could both of our versions of the story be so clearly true to each of us and ring so hollow for the other? How could they not even recognize their part in how this happened, or recognize my pain, or take any responsibility for it? There were no apologies from them.

It should have been obvious to me before. It is suddenly so clear. One of the things I absolutely assumed about the three of us was unconditional love between us. I realize that a big part of what I have been missing is that unconditional love from them. I miss the absolute comfort and ease of being able to pick up the phone, to not watch every word, to hug or touch an arm or shoulder, to brush back a piece of hair from their faces, to simply be together. They still have my unconditional love, at any price. It's not even a choice, it just the truth.

I asked if I could see them again before they left town. They said they'd let me know. I felt my heart constrict at their words but managed a weak, "great," in response.

With the semester behind me, and an upcoming sabbatical to finish my dissertation, I'm free from university responsibilities. The next few days, and then the summer, crawl by in a series of vignettes.

Before she leaves town, Ryn texts and says she and Erica are going for a run at the zoo. She asks if I want to meet her up by Nancy the elephant, saying we could sit and talk for a bit. She remembers! We love Nancy. We would always take extra time to watch her. When we'd hear the lions at night we used to strain to hear if we could ever hear Nancy trumpet. We didn't. This is a good omen. She's chosen this spot!

We meet and try to act normal. I ask her the type of questions a mother asks—is she happy, how's work, who is the boy in the Christmas pictures her dad sent. I get guarded answers and her surprise that her dad sends me the pictures. I ask if she wants to come by the house with Erica after their run. She replies simply, "No, I'm good. Thanks. Hug Gabler for me." With the briefest of hugs, she's gone with a call over her shoulder that she'll call.

A day or so later Adam texts and asks if I can meet him at the butterfly house in Wheaton Regional Park. My heart leaps that he's chosen this place, a special, magical place that for a few months each summer is filled with butterflies that sweep and alight in the enclosed botanical garden. It's a place Adam particularly loved as a small boy and as a poetic teen. He remembers, and my heart sings!

When we meet in the parking lot, I ask if it's alright for me to take his arm. He says neither yes nor no, so I slide my hand into the crook of his arm and feel his arm stiffen, although he doesn't pull away.

He stops our stroll through the gardens and asks if we can sit on one of the benches. I try to reconcile the image I have of seven-year-old Adam leaping across the stones in the koi pond and the decidedly sullen young man at my side. He tells me this is all fucked up. He tells me that he's glad he saw me but that he needs time to "recover from being my son" before he sees me again.

I don't remember what else was said, if anything else was said. When we part in the parking lot, I tell him I love him, that I can wait, that I am sorry, that I want him to be OK. I remember an awkward hug and the sight of his car pulling away, but all I hear are his last words to me. He needs to "recover from being my son."

Throughout the summer there are occasional texts or emails cautiously crafted. Now it is the gaps I see, not the whole. I keep sending little gifts and cards. At Summer Solstice I send them each a card marking the longest day of the year, one we used to celebrate with late night fun and firefly catching. I make several offers to have them come this way again, knowing they must be here for business from time to time. I tell them I will meet them in a city of their choice. I tell them they would love The Grange. I don't tell them I'm sorry anymore, but I am. I don't tell them about Jesper.

Jesper writes regularly. I am grateful. I am so interested in his work. He reminds me of Erica, capturing experiences through his documentarian work. I realize I envision him as a small boy showing me his art work that I will want to hang on the refrigerator, trying to reconcile that with the fact that he is just a handful of years older than Sonia, a grown and quite capable man.

In one of our exchanges he expresses frustration at what he is filming, the art of indigenous peoples. He asks if I had ever visited Froger Park and the sculptures when I visited Norway. I hadn't. He sends me a link to the appropriate website. I "tour" the vast acreage and the hundreds of sculptures. I ask him which ones he likes, and he says all of them, but he especially likes the woman dancing with wild hair and wild abandon. I tell him that I love the ones of the old women, especially those on the central piece at the monolith. It is fun to have these easy, ready exchanges with him.

Sonia and Erica have now left to spend the summer in Argentina, something they do every few years. I know Sonia was right about safety and the reasons my kids stayed at her house. Still, I was jealous of the time she had with them and the ease of it. She tells me she had many stern talks with them, trying to get them to see things my way. She and I had many silent runs before she left. Time and distance serve a purpose. If I'm honest, I am glad they are away.

Sydney and Gene come up to the Hobart house on several occasions for doctors' checks and for weekends in DC with Roy and me. We give them what I consider my special nighttime tour of Washington. I give them the history I know, and make up some along the way, telling them it is hearsay. We go to all the monuments, including the relatively new one with Martin Luther King walking out of a huge block of granite. DC hosts free outside summer concerts on almost any given night and we partake in them. The two of them are beautiful together. This now goes well beyond their collective looks. They have a synchronicity between them that is electric. When they spend the night with us, I pull out the trundle from under Adam's bed like I have done when the kids had sleepovers or when my mother stayed with us. After a while they tell me it's not necessary. They are quite comfortable in a single bed. They profess their love easily. This makes me feel pressured to answer Roy's frequent "I love you" with more than I ever do.

Gene loves his new job with the Calvert Police. Sydney worries about his safety. He worries about, but never mentions, that the cancer is lurking. They are coupled, and this is a very good thing.

I spend more time at The Grange and do some half-hearted attempts at writing. Elizabeth is my ever-present sidekick in the quiet alcove, reading her Italian newspapers, *Wall Street Journals*, and legal journals as I attempt to write. She seems to have an urgency for me to focus, to write, to hone my thinking. When I am thinking of giving it all up, she gives me what Tia and I now call "the two chairs lecture." She tells me I cannot-a sit-a in two chairs, I must choose the life I want.

Elizabeth is there for my sidebar comments, the questioning of a spelling of a word, or for thinking through of an idea. On occasions, she sends Pavarotti out with me as I stroll the cliffs in thought, knowing I must come back to her and continue.

I'm not convinced any of the writing I am doing is very good. My head and heart are with my children. Surprisingly, the Mother's Day article I have written does get picked up by the AP and circulated to many papers. Jesper lets me know he has seen it and has shared it with his mother who thinks even more about wanting to live in a place like The Eves.

After I met with the kids, I respond to Jasper's emails sending him a link to Erica's photos. I also told him about Roy, not wanting him to think the man in the photos was his birth father. I told him that his birth dad was indeed an American. I told him I took the only option open to me for the baby I carried. In the telling, I think I made it clear that his father never knew why I chose to go to Norway—to guarantee my child's safety. Jesper will understand that his birth father has no knowledge he exists. I told him that he has two siblings. Full siblings that came many, many years after he was born with no knowledge, at least yet, that they had an older brother. In asking him to respect that they didn't know, I used the trite expression, saying "It's complicated." I know that I can't, and shouldn't, try to control this.

Deirdre has taken to setting up her spinning wheel in the barn in anticipation of the next harvest. She thinks the students will like to see and learn about a program she wants to do for them. She wants to call it "From Sheep to Sweater." She's funny. Funny and smart and most days pretty focused. Throughout the summer, to the rhythm of the pedal of her spinning wheel, with her excellent instruction, and under the watchful eye of the patient Oliver, I learn to knit, knowing that my children's handprints hang just above me.

Margaret Mary asks me to bring my quilt squares and I carry them to her for the umpteenth time. This time we lay them out. They are muslin squares started when Ryn was just in Brownies with the promise that we would someday make a quilt. They are crewel work embroidered with designs, some by Ryn, some by me. There are frogs and paintbrushes and the things a child likes. Margaret Mary deftly arranges and rearranges them telling me I need more squares. She asks me to think of Ryn today and make squares that represent her now. I'll have to ask Sonia. She's the one who knows my daughter best right now.

Margaret Mary and I pick out background fabric that will connect the squares and a marvelously rich indigo patterned backing. She explains that she likes to leave a message or a saying on the back of the quilts she makes and asks if I can think of something. It's simple, I tell her immediately, "A promise kept." From that point on I work on additional squares for Ryn and start some for Adam. It won't have the same significance, but I like to keep it even between them. Especially now. The sad truth of the matter is that even if things had not gone so horribly wrong between us, in the three years that transpired, things would have shifted between us anyway. They've turned from children, to young adults, to the adults I don't know today. Making the new squares is painful guess work. Yet, each stitch is pulled with love. I can feel, with each tug of the needle, my desperate attempt to mend things.

When I am feeling very brave, I ask Margaret Mary to tell me about adoption from her point of view. I tell her about Jesper and the conflict I feel—the hope of getting to know a new son, the fear that he too needs to recover from me due to "abandoning" him at birth. We talk about her multi-hued family and how ridiculous she felt at times creating this family history about her Irish parents being the "grandparents" of all these kids, or that she was now the grandmother and great-grandmother of the next generation of equally multi-hued babes. She comforts me by saying that her kids seem happy straddling two worlds. For some the wondering about the missed opportunities, or the sense of loss, is harder, Mary Margaret assures me, each knows that they came to her for a reason. In a myriad of ways, she comforts me throughout the summer as we assemble Ryn's quilt. She tells me, "Jessica, you need to forgive yourself for so many things in this life. I am not telling you not to examine your life and your actions. What I am telling you is that if you live a life where you are kinder than you need to be and keep a solid compass, you will be the best person you can be on any given day." I smile at the near verbatim echoing of my mother's own words.

I try to remember that.

Of all of the Eves, Margaret Mary is the most surprising to me. Everyone's original impressions of her are quite wrong. She is demanding, has standards, but she is not haughty, hard, or cruel. One day I build up the courage to tell her this and her response is surprisingly delightful. "Miss Barnet, my demeanor is a cultivated skill that has served me well. You should have seen me as Sister Lucia!"

Jan expresses disappointment that Juneteenth didn't come off the planning page this year. It was just too much to take on. In addition, she and Margaret Mary get into a bit of a pissing match about the quilts. Jan insists that African American quilts be included in the celebration. Margaret Mary thinks this a great idea but balks at Jan's insistence that the quilts were used historically as communication and road maps for the Underground Railway and thus are a vital part of Black history. Margaret Mary insists that there just was no historical basis for the quilts doing anything of the sort, that these quilts were known to be historical family records but that no quilting history showed the use Jan purports. Jan takes umbrage at this, especially after Margaret Mary tells her that, in general, the first reference to the quilts being used for the Underground Railroad were part of a fabrication in a 1987 video. The debate rages for most of the summer as each does furious research.

As a compromise between the two, Tia and CC install a wonderful wall-mounted water feature. It's a large flat fountain made up of the tile paintings done on Mother's Day. It looks very much like a patchwork quilt of all the families' artwork and history. The water slides over the tiles, bubbles in the basin and is recycled to once again slide down. Margaret Mary says she will not contest that Jan's tile depicts the Underground Railroad. In any event, Juneteenth is on the calendar for next year.

Jan and I plan meals and cook with the spoons. I tell her about Africa and Robert, and the footsteps and the spot where man, or maybe just woman, learned to stand erect and walk with two others. This makes her prod me to become the storyteller she imagines me to be. She invites me to her room. She's chosen one on the second floor. We take the elevator and pass Roy's plastic panel reminding us of the straw bale construction. She's taken all the orchids I brought for the Eves on Mother's Day to her room and gotten books on propagation. Everywhere there are attempts in various stages of success. I get out my phone and gave her the phone number of "The Orchid Lady" from the mall in Sarasota as well as a link to Selby Gardens so she can get good information. Jan has a notion about getting students involved in growing the plants and giving the orchids as gifts or selling them. She's still not sure how she wants to proceed. She is just fascinated by the flowers.

In her room she's recreated the bookcases, displaying the Native American pottery. We talk about the orchids. I reach for the Cordero storyteller and, suddenly, the story I want to tell spills out of me. Jan sits on her mother's bench and listens as I tell her the story I have in my head about the love between mothers and their children, and about the gift of "other mothers." I add that this may all be a coming-of-age story about women as they age. As Jan listens and leans forward. When I finished, she says to me, "*Aliksa'i*, child, this is delicious."

As I limp through the summer, using the love of others, the story I want to tell takes shape, not as an article but as the book Elizabeth first envisioned. The writing comes easily. The story that now needs to be told oozes out the tips of my fingers, on to the keyboard, and on to the screen. I write best when I was at The Eves. Roy and I find ourselves spending more and more time there.

One night we went out on *The Tug*. It was just Malcolm and Allison, Roy and me, and Tobias. He had to be coaxed to come but the lure of staying overnight and watching the cliffs wake up was too great. Ali cooked a great meal while all three men fished off the back. Wine and conversation flowed. Tobias told us stories about his youth and of his father and grandfather. Malcolm told us the story of falling in love with Ali the first time they met.

As the sun set, Roy played Taps for us as Malcolm took down the American flag he flies when he sails. There were no tears and Tobias didn't sing. His eyes were fixed on the top of the cliffs, though, at about the point I imagine the cemetery to be. In the dusk I thought I saw him mouth the words "Good night." It's been almost a year since Joan died. Maybe it gets easier, but I doubt it. I think it just gets different.

When darkness fell Ali and Malcolm went up top to check weather and charts, and to smoke cigars together. While I was cleaning up the galley I could hear the murmur of their voices, their laughter, and the occasional banter about the Ravens and how preseason play was going. Roy sat with Tobias on the open-air deck while Tobias pulled out his banjo, played, and hummed.

When I joined them, bringing Tobias a highball, Roy went below to make up a bunk for Tobias and turn in to read. Tobias insisted that he wanted the bunk in the salon, leaving the forward cabin to Roy and me. He wanted to make sure he was awake to see the dawn. He told us he might just spend the whole night right where he was on one of the couches out here.

Ali and Malcolm came down from up top. With their goodnights they confirmed the time of sunrise and the beautiful morning promised the next day.

Alone with Tobias, I tell him I'd missed Orion overhead all summer. My knowledge of summer constellations extends only to the Big and Little Dippers.

"Jessica, Orion will be back," he told me as he continued to pluck. "You just have to wait for him. Things happen in their own time. You'll see. The bonus of the summer sky is Sirius. The brightest star in our galaxy. Look for it."

Upon his instruction, I got up and located it, pointing. "Sirius?"

"That's right, Jessica. Sirius, part of the constellation Canis Major, actually consists of two stars, but the Greeks didn't know that. Canis, the dog constellation. It's where we get the expression the dog days of summer. Myth has it that Sirius was Orion's hunting dog. I always think of it as him leading Orion back to us. It will happen Jessica, but tonight you should go to bed with that man who loves you so much. Besides, I have a woman to talk to," he tells me nodding up to the cliffs.

When I go below Roy has fallen asleep. I slide in quietly next to him and find my spot, the place where my head fits so nicely on his shoulder and I can hold his left hand. As I listen to his regular breathing I tell him, finally, that I love him. Love him a considerable amount.

"I know you do Jes, and I'm glad," he says squeezing my hand tightly.

In the morning, very early, Tobias awakens us all with the clang of the ship's bell and the pronouncement that the cliffs are waking up.

They are a sight to behold!

second harvest

Suddenly, it is fall. Sonia and Erica are back. Erica is starting her junior year of high school, getting a driver's permit, looking at colleges. It is so good to have them back. The history of us creates one of those few friendships where each time you meet is like yesterday. We pick up where we left off with our runs and texts and chats. I've forgiven Sonia for the uncommitted crime of being there for my children when they were not ready to have me.

I've finished my dissertation and am just waiting for the final suggested edits from my advisor, and questions from the readers. The oral defense is rescheduled, as Sonia suggested, for just before Christmas. This leaves the long winter break to finish the book and send the final edits to the proposed publisher.

Gabler and I, along with Roy, decide to move down to The

Grange the last half of October and the beginning of November. It is the second-prettiest time of year in the mid-Atlantic. We want to enjoy the rich colors and as much boating as possible before the weather turns.

It's hysterical to watch Roy each morning try to participate in the "breakfast banter." He proves single-handedly how different men's and women's brains work. After a few weeks he's up and out the door early, helping with the animals and fields.

These days, I try not to read too much into things, but I still frequently over-think things. Both Ryn and Adam at least acknowledge my gifts now. There have been a few correspondences where they send me things that remind them of me. They've said they aren't coming for any holidays, but maybe they are talking about coming to see this place in the New Year. I've tried not to make a big deal of it, telling them they are welcome anytime. They each say thank you. Tobias promises, "Everything in time." I let myself go with the flow.

Knowing that they aren't going to be with me has made it easier to accept an invitation to finally meet, face-to-face, Jesper. The video chats have been good. We cover hard questions and are building rapport. I am always eager to talk with him. However, I can't quite get over the hurdle that he is not just this very nice man, he is *my son*. We can't figure out what he should call me. I tell him that I will be coming to Oslo around the time of our American Thanksgiving. I will stay until 12 December, the day after his birthday. The word birthday feels full and rich to me.

The preparations for Harvest kick into high gear. "Joan's Acre" is ready for the students from Anacostia. The barn is set up for the ritual of the hands. The day of the event we get shattering news. Sydney's cancer is back. She tells us this in the same breath that she tells us that the polio injections have already been scheduled for Thanksgiving week. For a few moments, our world stops. She's already told Gene.

Somehow, the day still unfolds, and it is as magical as my first Harvest. What a year it has been! Towards the end of the day, Deirdre meets each student, gleefully asking them if they had "peak produce picking." They laugh and take places at the tables. Tia now takes Joan's spot. Tobias looking content, his hand gently resting on the back of the chair. I sit with Elizabeth and she squeezes my hand. Sydney joins Jan and Allison. Once again, I marvel at the discussions, the interactions, and the beauty of the Harvest. Taking it all in I notice Oliver shifting his weight and pulling back and forth in his stall.

Excusing myself from the table, I go to eavesdrop on the other tables, making the rounds. Done with that, I go around the corner, pick up a handful of oats and move to nuzzle Oliver. He seems agitated, probably because of all the commotion. He keeps pushing me away from him shaking his head toward the room. Sydney seems to notice as we catch each other's eye.

"Come on," I motion to her, knowing the barn loft will already be set up. She missed the last Harvest because of the chemo. Who knows if she will have another chance? As she climbs into the loft you can see the sense of awe come over her as she takes it in.

"Is your handprint here?" she asks.

"Nope, wasn't ready." I walk over to the little wooden hands Roy made. "Here, here are my kids. The red one is Adam, the blue one Ryn's."

"You know Jessica, tomorrow isn't promised. We should both do this, ready or not."

Together we review the colors laid out by CC. Dipping our hands in the paint we pick a spot on the wall, overlap our palm prints, and leave a mark on this place. Then I go back to the paints, dip my right hand one more time, walk to the spot where I've hung their small wooden hand cut-outs, and place my purple-dipped hand so that the paint on my fingers is touching the little wooden hands. I place a small tiny pinky fingerprint on each of their prints. We've made a mark on the land. One way or another, I have made a mark on their hearts.

Tomorrow isn't promised. There is only hope.

reach

The morning of my trip, as I get ready to leave, Deirdre pulls the word "reach" out of the Breakfast Banter Bowl. The conversation gets off to a sleepy start as the Eves move into the solarium. Margaret Mary rolls her eyes, reaches for the dictionary, and finds the page defining "reach." She reads aloud synonyms for reach. "Touch, stretch, grasp, arrive at, get to, attain, achieve, influence." They all go around and around citing their accomplishments, noting what they've attained or achieved. I notice, half listening, that the topic doesn't seem to be getting much traction. I can't go perk up the conversation though, too much to do today before leaving for Jesper!

My vacation preparations are spread all over the house this morning, especially in both alcoves. I've been working in the little alcove near the solarium all morning. My anxiety at meeting Jesper is eased by the bubbling of the water feature and the Eves' babbling about 'reach.'

I hear the sound of a car grittily speeding up the gravel drive announcing Sonia's arrival. Getting up to get more coffee, I see Sonia wave as Erica pops out of the car. She has no school today and she, very sweetly, wanted to be here to say good-bye and good luck for my trip. She is, increasingly, like her mother in beauty and in style. She bursts upon the scene this morning with positive energy interrupting both the rhythmic water sounds and the stalled conversation on "reach." With good mornings to everyone, Erica's arrival pulls me back from future to present.

She's a quick study. "Bad brainstorming banter?" she asks me, moving her head to indicate the solarium discussion.

"Very clever, little one. The topic is 'reach.' It doesn't seem to be working for them."

"Reach?" she says moving to the solarium. Her energy enters with her, and all of a sudden, the topic takes off. A few minutes later, I can hear the volume rise and the Eves all talking, interrupting each other, sparring, laughing. Erica rejoins me in the alcove.

"How'd you do that?" I ask her.

"Sometimes I don't think they listen to themselves. Remember Margaret Mary telling you about wrong-headedness, or Jan singing 'Both Sides Now?' They were already talking about the whole 'reach' thing then, *in my opinion*." She says these words with deferential Sonia-like emphasis, "They had too much focus on the end, the arrival, what they have done so far, not the impact they have going forward.

"Dag, didn't Margaret Mary yell at you about that too? All I did was say that they should think of this like the reach of a long arm. I told them I think they are actually always talking about reach. They talk about how they can reach back in time, like, one hundred and fifty years, to stories that their grandparents or parents told them, or taught them. That means their grandparents and parents still have reach into today. And, they have their own reach of at least, like what, a hundred and fifty years into the future. As long as their kids, and their friends, and *we* keep talking about them, get influenced by them, learn from them. Like, how old would Tobias' grandfather be now, kazillion? I bet I'll be telling my kids about the cliffs 'waking up.' I got that from him, and Orion, from you. That's reach."

I simply stare at her. "You're brilliant, amazing really," and I pull her to me and kiss the top of her head. I won't be able to do that much longer. She's grown in these last months.

"Not really," she says pulling away and smoothing her hair. "It's kind of like your lame question about what you want on your tombstone. I just asked what they wanted to be remembered for, what lessons they are leaving for the future, what would they want their kids to know, what do they still have from their parents, what *reach* they expect to have. It's all in the wording Aunt Jessica. You know that. W*ords* matter." She winks at me. I know she is playing on my love of words and downplaying her mother's comment that it does not matter what we say, only how we look.

I take her hand. "Let's go listen. Make notes for me, Ok? I'm way too overloaded to add whatever they come up with to the book before I leave."

We go back toward the solarium and listen. I can see Erica making mental notes. I'm sure she will email them to me while I'm gone. *Reach* might be a good name for the book, if it ever gets completely finished and I stop finding more things, like this, to add!

Erica and I return to the alcove. "Thanks, email me your thoughts on that, OK?"

"Sure, look for the subject line '*eves* dropping.'"

"Really? Ouch!" She's quick.

She's suddenly serious. "Can I talk to you about something? I was thinking about what you said about shoes." She plops cross-legged into the rich, blue, easy chair, and hands me a thick envelope. "And, about books."

"Tell me what you are thinking," I ask, eager to hear from her.

This reminds me of when Adam would come home from school and share his day. Linking that time and this is less painful now. I want to believe there is hope for me and Adam, me and Ryn. Separately and together and, maybe, just maybe, if things go well, with Jesper. For today, it's a blessing, really, just to have Erica want to share these things with me.

"So," she says suddenly all business, "I think the idea I had about a photo book of just shoes and feet is a good one. I want to explain it to you better than I did last time. Here's what I was thinking. I got the idea at first from mom's closet. You know what a shoe freak she is. Ridiculous! So, I started taking pictures of her shoes, then her feet. Then I thought back. Do you remember that photo I took of CC's ankles and sneakers, and the one of Tobias' shoes and cane? Maybe I have a shoe thing like mom and didn't realize it. I started doing an internet search and there are lots of things for people who have a shoe fetish, like wine bottle holders in the shape of a shoe. I don't get it, but it means there might be a market for what I want to capture."

I don't dispute her argument. Maybe I just don't get the whole shoe thing.

"I was going to give up the idea because you thought it was shallow. It pissed me off. I mean ticked me off. You're as bad as the oldies sometimes. Do you ever listen to yourself? You are always saying things related to feet, like, *getting your footing, wrong footed, misstepped, walking on eggshells, two left feet, sure footed, not a leg to stand on*. Then, when I thought of you and THE footprints I was really pissed. Sorry, ticked, that you thought it was shallow. This is for you. I need you to tell me if it's shallow."

From out of the envelope I slip a beautifully bound, high gloss covered book. The cover picture is the Latoral footprints, *my* African connection. Title of the book: *FEET* by Erica Cortez. Dedication: 'to jb who ticked me off enough to do this project.'

Looking up at her, amazed, I ask, "How did you do this?"

"Anyone can get anything published Aunt Jessica, you know that. I just sent it away to one of those photo-book companies. I'm submitting this for my photojournalism final. We had to create a book."

The photos are really good. She's chosen black and white, again. The ones of Tobias' and CC's feet are included. There are baby feet. Feet standing at a gravestone—probably Tia's, bare feet, shod feet, dog feet on a lap, calloused feet, boots with frog eyes, sneakers with the shoelaces being tied, foot in a leg brace—mine, feet on a ladder. There's one page with three photos—sheep feet, four llama feet— two stomping, and Oliver's hooves deep in mud. There's a striking one of a pair of stilettos one already on, the other with a foot poised to go in, or just sliding out. You are left with the feeling of what role will the wearer, obviously Sonia, take on today. There doesn't seem to be a theme to the book, but you get a feel from it, a focus. It leaves you wondering.

I think Erica is worried I don't like it because she interrupts my flipping through the pages. "If you think it sucks, I could maybe get these together before the end of the term." She hands me a second envelope.

Before I open it, I say, "Wait, slow down, Erica. I should piss you off more often," a nod to her using "ticked" for me "These are really good. What exactly was the assignment that led you to create FEET?"

As I open the second envelope, she explains that it was "to create or inform a feeling using just one body part."

I want to push her thinking. "I think it does that, but what feeling do you want to convey with this work? What feeling do you get?"

I don't give her a chance to answer because I am already looking at the contents of the second envelope. Color photographs of arms and hands. I don't know about her having a foot fetish, but she clearly has a body part thing. She's included the picture of Joan's empty chair, hands holding Oliver's reins, a hand reaching for one of the wooden spoons, hands spinning and weaving, Roy and my hands intertwined, Sonia's hands mid-expression. I love these, dozens, and dozens of pictures.

"These really inspire me, Erica. I really do like the other, but these are so much stronger. These have, OK, for lack of a better word, 'reach.' I get the feeling that all these hands are telling a story, I love the sense of touch that I get from them. The hands are working, making an impact, touching, even if it's only touching air. The way you've shot these, in my opinion, makes the viewer want to reach into these photos."

"You really think so? Can you help me sort through them? I'm only allowed to have thirty for the project."

As we pour over her photos, it seems the breakfast banter has reached its natural end as Pavarotti and Elizabeth walk past us. Elizabeth puts her hand on my shoulder as she passes and, to mine and Erica's head shaking, utters, "Whatda ya hafta do" as she goes into the game room and closes the doors. Through the glass doors I can see the two of them, Elizabeth staring out the windows tugging on Pavarotti's ear.

"I'm sorry Erica, do you mind? She's been really cranky the last few days. I need to see if I can fix that, get a run in, and finish packing before Roy gets here. We should still have some time to go through your photos." I kiss the top of her head, deliberately tussling her hair, and begin to head to Elizabeth. "Hey, Erica?" I stop to ask her. "When I'm gone for these few weeks, can you be extra nice to Elizabeth? I worry about her feeling so alone."

She gives me a nod and I head to Elizabeth. With the game room doors closed the room is already overly warm, heat turned up to ward off the fall chill just beginning to envelop the house and fields. Elizabeth is staring out at the fields, freshly plowed under, waiting for winter to come to Southern Maryland. Although I've come in specifically to check on Elizabeth, I set to busying myself with trip preparations, packing books and my knitting needles in my duffle. I'm hoping to avoid a prolonged discussion.

"Whatda ya hafta do," she sighs as I enter. I ignore her. I know now that this is never really a question, but her catchall statement, similar to "alas."

She leaves her non-question hanging in the air, waiting for me to give her my full attention. She lets her pause go on for too long. She wins.

"Okay, Elizabeth, I'll bite, 'what do you have to do' about what?"

"I didn't think it would be-a like this," she states, matter-of-factly, as she does most things.

"Be like what?" I ask, sitting on the window seat indicating she now has my attention.

"This sense-a of-a waiting to go on a vacation."

I'm exasperated. Why is she bringing this up hours before I leave for the airport? She's waiting? Ridiculous! It has been such a busy year getting ready for my doctoral orals, finishing up the interviews for "our" book, planning the trip, all of the oldies moving into this house—none of this felt like waiting around.

Elizabeth knows, better than the others, how important this trip is to me. She's the one who urged me to go. 'Go find your family, make decisions, you can no sit-a in two chairs,' she counseled me. Now she resents that I'm going? She is, in so many ways, the subtle power behind everything that has transpired here. Why doesn't she see that?

I'll be back in four weeks, defend my dissertation, and then I'll have the winter holidays here.

I try to practice patience, but for the moment I am indignant that she is questioning my leaving for a vacation. I know she resents the sense that she is being left behind with the others when she so wishes so was able to make this trip with me. I get that, but I resent her resenting it. Somehow, we are in a struggle. I don't need right now.

As she always does, she reads me in a heartbeat.

"Not your-a vacation, silly girl, mine. The one with no-a suitcases. The one that lasts forever." She pauses, "When the leaves fall, old people think of-a going on vacation."

With emphasis she levels her eyes at me and says, "I didn't think it would be-a like this. As if one place would be different from another, any less lonely, any less-a desolate. It feels like a very long wait."

This "vacation" metaphor line had been a long-standing joke between us. She says she is ready to "go on vacation." I simply refuse to acknowledge that she really wants "to go." *I* may be heading to Europe for a month, but I am not ready for *her* to go anywhere! She has become too important to me in the last year. The mother and friend I didn't know I needed. Still need, even at almost sixty years old.

I have even grown to enjoy her calling me a "girl." I am no longer so insecure that I need "woman" status, and I am just old and vain enough to like that I look young next to the women living here.

How could this past year feel like waiting for her? We had done so much since this whole project began. Every day seems full. And she has been waiting? Had I listened so poorly, missed so much, been so selfish? I look at her more squarely. With one of the other women I might have taken one of their hands, but not Elizabeth. She is of a strong Northern Italian, closer, stereotypically, to the stoic German type. She laughs easily but at the core she is solid rock.

"Remember when we started?" I ask. "I was such a mess and you were the one who first listened and pulled me along. You thought the book concept was solid and did a lot to convince the others. You created most of the interview questions for the book. I owe you so much. So much has changed. You are really the one who helped make all this happen, don't you see that? Our projects are making a difference to others."

I can hear myself pleading like a little girl. "Elizabeth, after all this, I am not ready for you to 'go on vacation.'

"We have a real story to tell. Besides, when I get back, I still have the last interview to do—yours. You can't put it off any longer. I don't have that piece in place, and you are going to be part of the story, like it or not. Please, drop this feeling like you are just waiting around. You've never been good at waiting anyway. It's a journey, remember? So, "no-a vacation for a you!" I kid her, mimicking the insertion of the 'a.'

She's returns to looking out the window. It doesn't appear that I've captured her interest at all.

"Elizabeth, I know I haven't shared the book draft yet. I've been saving it for right now. Here. Here's the prologue to *our* book," I say the 'our' with great emphasis. Read it while I go for my run. We'll discuss it before I go."

She takes the papers, complete with my margin notes. I watch and wait as she begins the prologue, hoping for a hint that I got the beginning of the story right.

"And, so, our-a book begins," she says aloud, *"Our Mothers' Stories."*

She looks at me and settles into the story.

This story begins many years ago at exactly 12:01 a.m. on December 7th, the moment my mother died.

With my mother's last breath, she inhaled Death and all that may come after it. In that last sigh of an exhale, the story of my mother was forever lost to me.

In the release of that single breath she let go of an eighty-year journey and of the roles of wife, mother, grandmother, sister, aunt, godmother, friend, mentor, artist, fundraiser, and event planner, as well as a host of other roles that left in their path only love, respect, longing, and an appreciation for the gifts she shared. She was, again, simply, Magnolia D'Alessandro Barnet, a child of God.

I was there at her side. My father had just risen from their shared bed to check on her. For the last few days, as her fever raged, she lay silent in the arms of coma. He leaned over, kissed her, and then, in a moment, the long eleven months of battling cancer ended. She slipped, ever so peacefully, into eternity.

If you've walked this part of a life with someone, you know that it is a privilege. You also know that you don't know how you will react.

With my father now downstairs, the men from the funeral parlor came to wrap my mother in the heavy black plastic sack to take her away for preparation. As I watched them get ready to take her, I was only thinking that I still needed her risotto recipe. The men stood by respectfully as I looked at them waiting for them to direct me as to what comes next. To them this was a routine call, made too late at night, causing them to exchange the warmth of their winter beds for black suits and ties needed only for the short ten-minute ride to the funeral parlor.

I didn't want to give her to them. I knew they wouldn't care for her as our family had cared for her these last months and weeks. I knew they would have no idea of the grace, dignity, and kindness she shared until consciousness left her just days ago. They wouldn't have a sense of the amazing wife she had been. They wouldn't see past the cancer-havocked body of an eighty-year-old woman to the woman who, just months ago, was still brilliantly beautiful, with eyes of the most lustrous blue. They didn't know the stories she had told of her girlhood with long curls and an oversized bow in her hair and a gold locket around her neck. The image of that little girl now stares back at me each morning from my dresser, a life of promise ahead of her. One that ends here in this bedroom.

The men from the funeral home don't, and couldn't, know who she was.

Was? Oh, God, how quickly the word "was" slipped into my thoughts? I sensed the men were eager to take her and get back to their beds! I hurried and lay down along-side her, understanding at my core that this is the last moment I have to be her daughter.

I assured her aloud that it would be ok, that the men would care for her. This was so unnecessary. She was already safe. There was no one more prepared to leave those she loved so well, no one more trusting that she would lie in the arms of a God she loved and served.

I told her, not yet wanting her ears to be deafened, that we'd see her tomorrow, and reassured her that she would be alright.

In truth, it is I who needed the reassuring. I realized that so much was lost in her passing. There is so much I wish I had asked, gotten answered, written down.

In the months and years since her death I have found real gifts in the kindnesses and wisdom of older women. Often, I vowed that I would start the book I envisioned in the moments after my Mother's death cataloging the life lessons that she and other older women wanted to share with those they leave behind. Aunts Marthy and Mary died without me taking the time to even ask their thoughts. My Aunt Lilly and I spoke of a writing project often. We agreed to begin it together, but she had the good sense not to wait around for me to come by and sit with her. After two years of waiting, at ninety-six, she too left this Earth.

Now it is, finally, time to write.

I know that the younger generation is not interested in taking the time to listen, let alone be ready to care about the stories that go before them. I reassure myself that someday they, like me, will care. I can no longer trust that there is time for the conversations. Now is the time to talk, to listen, and to write so our stories will be waiting for them when they are ready.

What unfolds over these pages is all true, reflecting the ever so common confluence of chance meetings that become the fabric of our lives. Every aspect of what is here is part and parcel of women searching, seeking, and satisfied. These are the stories of women determined to control their own destiny, even in the final chapters of their lives. These are our mothers' stories. The ones they needed to tell, and the ones we were not ready to hear. These are our stories, from both sides of the mirror. Sooner or later, if we live long enough, we will look in the mirror and wonder who that old person is staring back at us, or be surprised as we watch our mother's hand come out of our own sleeve as we get dressed. It won't be long before we find ourselves sitting in their chairs as we run out of time to tell those behind us what is important, real, or imagined.

I hope I capture their stories fairly, or, as my ex-husband would say, "warts and all." If I get it right, you will recognize me and you, and your children and mine, and your friends, relatives, and the women in your community. You will, I hope, argue, agree, aspire, and analyze. You will, I hope, hold conversations. The conversations help write the next story, and the ones that come after.

Once upon a time, all of our stories began with "once upon a time." We were young girls who dressed up in crinoline skirts even when we played in the mud. We dreamed of being princesses and mermaids. Then we were girls. It never occurred to us until we read psychology books in college that the only older women we saw in story books were evil and old—the archetypical Freudian foils for a child's battle against their parent.

Somehow, we still became women, with little in the way of role models. We took on the roles of mother, caretaker, community worker, nun, nurse, teacher, lover, partner, and breadwinner. In the early '70's we girded ourselves in manly suits and took on "a man's world." We over-proudly thought we were the first generation of women to balance career and family, have affairs, divorce, have women lovers, or to have crises of faith.

The reality was, of course, that there were countless role models at our fingertips. As babies we crawled to them and used their legs to gain our own footing. We only needed to reach for the hems of their skirts and our role models were there. Through twists of history no one had written the personal stories of how our mothers made their journeys, largely because we didn't take the time to listen. Even today, in our accomplished selves, we don't have a road map.

Now, we are women, and while our children may not be ready to hear our individual stories, perhaps they will value the story of the whole. There are still so many voices that need to speak, and there are ears that will want to listen. These are our stories. They begin like the old stories…

…Once upon a time, we were girls… and, we still believe we are.

Jessica Barnet

The Grange, Calvert County, MD

I hear the deep intake of her breath as she mouths the last line and raises tear-filled eyes to mine. Before she can comment, I raise my hand, interrupting what she is about to say, "Elizabeth, I am going to be sitting a very long time on the flight from Dulles to Oslo. I really need to fit in this run before Roy picks me up. We will have time to talk when I get back, I promise. Please, sit with it for a bit. I *so* want to hear what you think and if I got this right."

With that I turn from her and make a quick check for final trip preparations. I jot a quick note and slide some things into an envelope for Elizabeth.

Checking my papers for my "note for the run" I strap my iPod to my arm, support sock on my left ankle, 'tricked-out,' elite cross trainer running shoes at the door.

I am ready for my run.

elizabeth

I wait until Jessica leaves and I hear the door close behind her to tell Pavarotti, "Up." From the front windows I watch as she runs down the drive and makes the right turn, north on Route 4. I watch as she stops for a minute, reties the laces on her left running shoe, pulls up the support sock, and adjusts her headphones.

In truth, I am angry because she is going on vacation. It seems so unfair that my aging body and my fears, real and imagined, keep me in place. I want to go on vacation—both kinds, and I can't do much about either one.

With chagrin, I turn to find the envelope she has left for me. The prologue of the book is perfect. Although I am sure she will want many rewrites, I am awestruck at how she captures the feel and sense of urgency for the conversations and stories.

The envelope she's left feels heavy in my hand. It contains a stack of papers with margin notes for both her doctoral defense and our book. There's a packet labeled - oral *her*-stories and "my playlist." Inside there are also gifts, an iPod player, and a note.

Elizabeth,

I know you. <u>You can't wait</u>. I've put the iPod on "pause." Listen, it's my favorite piece of music!

This probably sounds, like Roy would say, "hokey," but my mom always gave me her gold locket when she'd go on trips, telling me to keep it for her until she got back. Look inside the envelope. Mine is inside. Can you hold it for me?

We'll talk when I get back from my run. I need to hear what you think!

I love you –j.

Sliding the locket out of the envelope and into my pocket, I go to the player console in the solarium, insert the iPod and hit the play button. I feel the surge of a full-bodied cello and orchestra. Yo-Yo Ma's *Gabriel's Oboe* washes over me and fills The Eves. The oboe, haunting, the *"ill-wind of the orchestra."* Next is *The Falls*–equally eerie, breathtaking. The music draws the others and we sit, quietly enjoying the sounds, the feel of the composition.

Jan gets up to make cocktails, Deidra picks up her knitting. Sydney is working on something on her tablet. Erica has photos spread across the floor. I begin to sift through Jessica's papers. We are all interrupted by a call from Roy. He's been trying to call Jes and can't reach her. He's worried, of course, that he's going to be late getting to our place in time to pick Jess up for the airport. Traffic is heavy on Route 4. I tell him there is no need to worry, that Jessica got a late start on her run, that her phone is right here next to me, that I am sorry I didn't answer it the first few times he called. Everything is fine, just drive safe.

The calm of the afternoon is noisily interrupted as Ali speeds up the drive, gravel flying under tires. Jessica's playlist continues through in rotation. I watch Allison get out of the car and brace herself against its door. Her eyes are wide with shock and disbelief. I know then, with gut-wrenching clarity. Even before she reaches our door, pain rushes in ahead of her.

She tells us it happened on Route 4, just past the store. Gene was called to the scene. He had tried Sonia but didn't want to leave a message. He called Ali asking her to come to us. He told her all the right things. "She couldn't have suffered. It happened in an instant. She probably never saw the truck."

It happened in an instant. An eternity, and a minute later we hear Roy's voice, "Greetings, greetings."

two years later: what's past is prologue

I didn't think it would be-*a* like this. Not after all that had happened. Two years later, there is still a story, and now it is mine to tell.

The minutes that followed the accident moved in ploddingly painful slow motion. Roy's "greetings, greetings" hung in the air surrounded by our collective shocked, disbelieving faces. As Ali turned to tell Roy, Erica blurted out "Aunt Jessica is dead," and collapsed in sobs into Roy's arms. He looked beseechingly at Ali and then at me, begging with his eyes that this not be true. Looking around the room he then gasped, "Oh my god, does Sonia know yet?"

Erica grew up a lot in those few minutes, deciding that she should be the one to tell her mom. She calmed her voice, called Sonia, and asked her to come to The Grange as soon as she could. It was important. She didn't want her mom to be alone when she heard. Sonia was uncharacteristically silent when Erica told her. We sat for hours in the solarium, Sonia rocking Erica in her arms, Tobias with his arm around Roy's shoulder as they stared out at the bay.

Almost immediately after her death, I surprised the others and myself by deciding to take the trip Jessica could not. I instinctively knew that she would want this for Jesper and, I think, for me. I knew she thought I could do more, that she was frustrated with me that last morning. Simultaneously, Roy, too, felt compelled to complete this trip for Jessica. The rapid trip planning kept our abject grief in control, but just barely. When our eyes met, the anguish in Roy's eyes would tear at my heart. I wonder if Jessica ever knew how well loved she was.

I don't think I could have made the trip without Roy. His knowledge of languages and his skill at negotiating any situation was a life saver, as was, of course, Pavarotti. We decided to fly to Oslo via Reykjavik and see if we could find CC's nephew's handprints, the ones that inspired the Harvest handprint project. We couldn't find them, but we agreed to tell CC that we had.

Meeting Jesper was nothing short of a profound experience for Roy and me. Jesper selected Frogner Park and the Vigeland Sculpture Garden for our meeting. Even with Pavarotti's assistance I knew I would be unable to walk the long distances. Roy anticipated this, of course, and secured a motorized cart I could drive. Just coming through the gates of the park inspires awe. There is simply no other description. Frogner consists of a vast eighty acres, a fifty-seven-foot-high sculpted monolith, the gardens, the fountain, the children's play areas, and over two hundred, simply and unabashedly, naked statues of granite and brass. Moving among the sculptures you experience the absolutely palpable feelings coming from them of joy, agony, shame, haunting, delight, compassion, sadness, wonder, and anger.

The morning of our meeting Roy and I were anxious and up early in preparation. The anxiety of the meeting was intensified by the sense of waiting for the day to even begin. With a nine am sunrise and a three pm sunset the shortness of the days at this time of year gives us a sense of urgency. We got to the park early enough to scoot around the sculptures. Roy liked all the ones of the trees around the fountain—the people in them. I loved the old women around the monolith, their unpretentious, saggy bodies, simple, compassionate, and haunted forms. These are the ones Jessica had pinned to her bulletin board and picked out for our book cover.

Jesper suggested that we meet at one of the park's most popular statues, "The Angry Boy," located by the waterfall and bridge. That seemed about right given that meeting us was not the same as what he had hoped for in finally finding Jessica. The angry, stomping, raging child in bronze waited with Roy and me for Jesper's arrival.

Roy and I warned each other not to look too closely for likenesses to Jessica. We had disagreed with Jessica's feeling that he looked like Adam. We saw so much of her in all the pictures. Even with our cautions, however, we both knew it was him as he strode toward us from across the park. Perhaps it was that he looked like a young man on a mission amidst rambling tourists. But both Roy and I thought it had something to do with how he walked, the way he held his head. When he stood before us it was unnerving to see him so closely resemble her in life. He had her eyes, a ready smile. He has her mtDNA too, I thought. He was tall and lean. He wore glasses similar to the ones we see on Ryn in the photos. I wonder if Jessica would have pointed that out. He had a beard, similar to the one we've seen on Adam in photos in her files. I could imagine Jessica wanting to reach out and touch it, trying to feel both of her sons.

When he greeted us, with a firm handshake, and what I think of as a stereotypical Danish or Swedish cadence to his words, he said simply, '*Hel-lo, I am Yhes.*' I had to take Roy's arm to steady him.

How did it not occur to either of us that Jesper would be short-ened—*Jes.*

We answered as many of his questions as we could. We hoped to ease his palpable sorrow at losing her after he had searched for so long and anticipated so much. We tried to convey that even though they had never met, the emails and video chats had brought her great joy and great hope. For him, it was simply unfair. We told him over and over how very excited she was knowing he had reached out to her, knowing that she was a day away from seeing him, that her note for that last run said, simply "Jesper!"

We didn't discuss his birthfather. I had set that up as something I was not willing to talk about. I do not think Jessica would have kept information about James from Jesper, but I was unsure what she would share.

When I am feeling very mad about her not being with us, I like to think that Jessica would have sent James pictures of all the fun she and Jesper had in their planned month together. But Jessica would be kinder.

Jesper wanted to know about The Grange and the Eves that he had begun to learn about from, and here he gulped when he said, "my mom." We answered all his questions and expressed our great delight in knowing that he had thought, if the visit had gone well, that he would come to the States to see her again.

He was, to me, like his mother, instantly likeable, bright, engag-ing. He had her sense of humor. She never saw those things in her-self, yet everyone else did.

Jesper seemed to take an immediate liking to Roy. That pleased me.

We did not need to share anything about Ryn and Adam. Jesper was well-skilled at tracking people down and had reached out to them as well. I didn't want to know if they had reached back, but I hope they did or do. It would be nice, I think, for Jessica to know that they were *three.*

As our time came to an end, I took his hand and passed him the

small, thin package I found in Jessica's suitcase when I unpacked
her. The gift was wrapped in the Sunday comics and had his name
across the front in fuchsia crayon. He kept looking at it and back at
me as he unwrapped it. The picture book by P.D. Eastman, a child's
book, *Are You My Mother?*

Roy and I sat holding hands as Jesper read about the adventures
of the baby bird that leaves the nest in search of its mother. The baby
asks a hen and a cat, and a myriad of animals and things, "Are you
my mother?" And each says, "I am not your mother." Finally, the
little hatchling gets dumped back in its nest and he finds her waiting
for him. I am, I am your mother the mother bird says proudly. I could
see Jessica had written something on the final page but couldn't read
it. Jesper sat and laughed out loud, tears running down his cheeks.

When we returned to The Grange, I wrote an end to Jessica's
book. I tried hard to incorporate all her notes and comments, as well
as Erica's memories of the breakfast banter conversation about
"reach." The small Norway section, I think, rings hollow in contrast
to the other sections, but the others don't seem to think so, and the
publisher was eager to get it to print.

Jesper stays in touch with us, especially Sonia and Erica. I haven't
figured out the dynamic there. I know Erica is enamored of Jesper's
work. The thought crosses my mind from time to time that Sonia is
actually enamored with Jesper. It would be hard not to be attracted
to him, so like his mom.

The reason the Norway section of the book does not satisfy me is
because we omitted the meeting of Jesper. Despite this, it has surprised all of us that "our book" has generated a bit of a cult. In truth,
as Deirdre would say, The Grange has become quite the location for
those seeking. They are seeking so many things. Peace and stimulation,
the answers to questions that their mothers could have answered if they
had taken the time to ask, or tell, or listen. Visitors to The Grange, and
to our website, want guidelines on how to create sustainable

communities, and how to enjoy the journey not the "vacation." And so many aging baby boomers are now interested in the way we live that Tia and CC have started a new environmental education project "Living Gray and Green˚." It was written up in *The Calvert Independent,* then *The Washington Post.* A reporter from *Smithsonian* is coming out next week to do a story on us. Jessica would be amused.

We finished all the renovations, or so we thought, until Roy decided we needed to put in another water feature. The reflecting pool he designed is crisp and clever, like Roy himself. As you approach The Eves it stretches north and south across the western lawn mirroring the sky, welcoming you to a place of reflection. While looking in all aspects like a reflecting pool, with places to sit comfortably, to think, and to write, it is actually exactly twenty-five meters in length and four meters in width, designed specifically to accommodate two regulation swim lanes. It's surrounded by paving stones with solar panel insets, so it is warm even at this time of year. As I write, Gabler is curled up on the desk. I can see Pavarotti and Sydney doing laps. The chemo treatments did not work. However, bizarrely to me, the polio injections to her brain brought about an almost instant "cure." Sydney glides through the water, strong, whole. In the interest of being honest, describing Pavarotti's frolicking next to her as him doing "laps" is probably a stretch.

It wasn't in the original plan that Sydney would stay with us, but so little of what is planned happens. What is it that Deirdre's father said? "Gang aft agley." Man plans and God laughs. This is a good laugh. Sydney and Gene have moved into our original house. They have converted Jan's upstairs room into a place to grow orchids and use the rest of the house as a Bed and Breakfast. It's a much-needed accommodation given the popularity of this place.

In keeping with tradition, the hospitality students from the community college help manage it, clean, prepare the meals. Each evening cocktails, including "highballs" are offered.

Even with the pool completed Roy is still unable to sit still. He is now drawing plans to expand the Mikado Mercado. It continues to be a viable place, all tied up with the various departments at the high school in Anacostia and with the students at the college.

Roy's here most of the time now. I can't say exactly why, but none of us question it. We like having him close by. We sit together in the evening sometimes and it feels like at any minute Jessica will just come around the corner from her run.

A little under two years ago we lost Tobias. He got his wish and didn't have to wait any longer to rejoin Joan. He died around Christmas, just after we got back from Norway. Just that morning Tia and CC presented him with the official papers granting that all the property is now secured as a land trust. Along with the papers, they gave him a Roy-made sign renaming the land "Tobias' Grange." Tobias seemed to like the fact that his name, along with all the past Tobias Thatchers, would stay on this land.

He slipped away from us ever so peacefully, in the solarium. He leaned back in the soft armchair we brought over from Joan's art studio, put his wallet behind his head, had *La Traviata* playing on the stereo, and closed his eyes. When Tia turned to bring him his highball, he was gone. It was that simple. He was the smartest man I ever knew. He knew how to pick people, especially Joan. Knew how to accept people too, not an easy thing at any age. Mostly, he reveled in learning something new each day. He's resting now next to Joan. Tia folded his hands in the box and made sure his wallet was tucked behind his head.

The "Tobias' Grange" sign greets you, coming southbound, as you make the left from Route 4. It is placed across from the M and M, very close to the spot where she was hit. Even in winter the area around the sign is well planted and well lit, by solar power, of course. Roy makes sure of it.

Amazingly, despite everything else that has happened, the falls, hip replacements, medications, and health scares, the rest of us are all still here, even Margaret Mary. At age ninety-four, we're fairly sure that nothing will kill her.

Erica has become a regular. It's hard to believe, she's finished her first year at college. She submitted her book of hands and arms and called it *Reach* for her photography class final project. Sonia was against it, given that it wasn't new work, but she mellowed on that when she saw that both her professor and Jesper suggested she get *Reach* published.

Sonia didn't have to endure Erica going away to school. Losing Jessica has been hard enough on her. Watching her be so lost leaves me to wonder who really helped who out during all those years of their friendship. In any event, I think Erica knew that if she went away to college it would be more than her mom could handle.

Jessica had come to me, after Sonia had done her Will. As we talked things through, I wrote up her Last Will and Testament, designating that Sonia and Erica have the use of the Hobart Street townhouse for as long as they wanted it. The rest of her significant estate went to Ryn and Adam. We never would have anticipated that she didn't have time to redo her Will to include Jesper.

I helped Sonia set up the townhouse as a rental property for college students and that's where Erica and her housemates are when she is not with us. There's something satisfying in the townhouse turning back into its use before Jessica owned it.

It's good to have Erica's energy here, and I'm glad that Sonia encourages it. Sonia is so busy running for the state senate that she appreciates the other mothers surrounding her daughter. Sonia comes here often to get a break. We are a haven to her too, although we debate her politics on many occasions.

The past two years have been good ones. Perhaps we've now accumulated enough drama between us that we get to rest awhile. We've added a few more sheep and llamas. Tia is brewing some plan to do fun and educational activities with the llamas. She's created a list of seasonal, and what she calls, "target market" events that she wants to explore. Between her and CC they have envisioned everything from "Lesbians and Llamas" to "Lullabies with Llamas." They figure we're close enough to Baltimore, Annapolis, and DC to attract tourists and residents for casual day trips where families and friends can get a break, walk a llama packed with lunch through the fields, eat, listen to music and go home.

CC and Tia brought up their idea during "breakfast banter" the other morning. I just wanted a quiet cup of coffee, but Jan started off, "We could have relaxing strolls with the llamas and call it 'Loafing with a Llama.'" Gene says he will post it on the B and B web site as a happy-hour offering—"Libations and Llamas." Deirdre pipes in. She feeds on this and giggles as she asks that "Liturgy and Llamas" be added to the list of activities to capture the religious market. All you have to do is take one look at Margaret Mary's face to know she thinks this is all a bad idea. She's thinking, and says aloud, "Liability, litigation, and lawsuits with llamas." She's still the skeptic first, but she's smiling. CC picks right up on Margaret Mary's thinking and jots a note to consider a program where "Lawyers and Llamas" can be added to the "Llama Lline-up."

They just don't stop, and that's one of the reasons I love them. It's true, I've come to love each of them, *warts and all*, as Jessica would say.

We'll see if this llama thing comes off the page. Even if it doesn't, our fiber business keeps growing, keeping our hands busy with spinning, weaving, knitting, and teaching the students over at Martinsburg. Our newest llama is named Lilly in honor of Deirdre's aunt, who taught her to knit and weave. We think she'd like that. Our current mule, Oliver, is getting up there in years, so we've purchased another mule and named him Tobias. It wasn't right not to have a Tobias at The Grange. The two mules will be double-teamed for the spring planting. We can't figure out if Oliver will be helping Tobias or Tobias will be helping Oliver and it doesn't matter. In any event, Jan has decided that it is time to pull out an African American saying from the '70s. She intends to have "Each One Teach One" T-shirts for everyone for our next Juneteenth celebration.

Two years, so much has happened.

Jan and Ali are away on a consulting trip at the moment. The orchid project that Sydney, Jan, and Ali started, now incorporated as Orchids for Others*, is being recreated in other communities, yet another Tobias Grange operation that raises money to support high school youth. This new work keeps Jan from finishing the cookbook Jessica urged her to write, but it's in the works. She and Sydney, along with the students at the college, have a publisher and are working to finalize the recipes. These will be featured at monthly themed dinners up at the B and B. Sonia has submitted recipes, giving up her enchilada secrets. The book, *Spoons: Our Mothers' Favorite Recipes*©, will sport Erica's picture of Jan's hand reaching for one of the spoons from the Hopi pottery piece on the cover.

We still have two empty rooms at The Eves. In time, I imagine we'll fill them. For now, however, Tia doesn't want her Dad's room touched.

I think of Jessica often. I wondered if she was listening to the same piece of music we were when her ankle gave way, when she rolled into the traffic, when she was hit by the truck. It sounds so matter of fact to simply write it that way, but that's what happened, and that's what I wonder.

I found her note for the run about Jesper, the lessons, and the written playlist folded and tucked into her passport as we were preparing for the funeral. I keep them tucked away there. I imagine she was going to work on them while waiting for the plane. She'd be formulating yet another question to wrestle with as she crossed the Atlantic.

Ryn and Adam didn't come to the funeral. I sent them their quilts for Summer Solstice. Adam's wasn't quite finished, so Margaret

Mary and I finished it. We agreed on the colors of red and black and brown and green. For the panel in the back we chose the simple expression "Out Biking."

I never heard from Adam, but I got a "thank you" note from Ryn asking if she and Adam could come visit sometime. I imagine they'll have questions. Maybe they'll just want to be where she was, and maybe meet Roy. It's been just over a year since she wrote, but when they have time, we'll welcome them.

Sonia keeps in touch with them. She's invited them to spend Christmas with her and Erica at the Hobart Street house where they grew up. Erica's roommates will be away, and they can have their rooms back for a few days. Maybe they will remember how they went out on the roof and listened to lions. Maybe they will realize what they gained and what they lost in having Jessica for their mother.

That first spring after her death, on a Saturday, just as the earth was warming up, Roy, Sonia and Erica, Malcolm and Allison, Sydney, and Gene the tension finally gone between them all—took The Tug out with Jessica's ashes aboard. Tobias had offered to have them distributed or buried on our land, but we didn't own her, so we opted for the sea. They positioned The Tug just under our cliffs and anchored. That night Pavarotti and I stood useless guard watching nightfall settle over the ship. I was wearing her gold locket and I wear it still, next to mine. I will pass it to Ryn when the time comes.

As the sun set, Roy played Taps, and my heart broke just a bit more at the collective missing of her. As the bay went to blackness, we could hear them laughing and talking, and we could hear the occasional strands of music from her playlist carried over the water.

In the morning, as the sun rose, and the cliffs woke up in splendid color, they set Jessica free to travel.

It was Mother's Day.

They all had to hurry back to take their places at our celebration. The day was hard and empty for all of us, so many losses. But we go on, we begin. We are not yet finished.

Two years. You let go. You learn. You go on. You reach.

She would laugh at the irony that she never finished her interview with me and that she was the one who got to "a go on-a vacation." I don't. I never got to tell her how much I liked what she had written, that I thought she got our story spot on, that she was more than a daughter to me. For that reason, I finished her book. For that reason, I miss her more than most. I want to believe that people will remember not what she looked like but what she said and did. Sonia is wrong, it does matter.

These last years were unanticipated. I am not sure what comes next. Leaning heavily on the desk, I push myself up and scoop up the cat. "I don't know, Gabler. *Whatda ya hafta do?*"

It is, at last, a question.

Elizabeth Jacobi, age 82
The Eves@TobiasGrange.org
Calvert County, MD

coda

I am sitting here wanting memories to teach me,

To see the beauty in the world through my own eyes.

I thought that you were gone, but now I know you're with me,

You are the voice that whispers all I need to hear.

Excerpted from Wanting Memories
Dr. Ysaye M. Barnwell

Listen to it in its entirety by Sweet Honey in the Rock at:
https://www.youtube.com/watch?v=vW2TpW4gCt8

— Dr. Ysaye M. Barnwell
Professor, vocalist, activist, community supporter

THE LESSONS

1. First do no harm (Hippocratic Corpus)
2. Go with the flow.
3. To thine own self be true.
4. There will be occasions to say "please", "thank you", and "I'm sorry", every day — do it.
5. Seek always to understand
6. Live decisively
7. You cannot sit in two chairs or wear two pairs of shoes
8. Never say never
9. Be patient with yourself and others
10. Love one another as I have loved you (Lesson 23 — Luke 22:1-38; John 13)
11. Don't be selfish, share widely of yourself
12. Think before you speak, what outcome do you desire from your statements and actions
13. Do good work
14. Seek to find the reason in all that happens, be responsible for your part in it
15. Don't be bitter, bitterness is of your own making
16. Sometimes there are no second chances; but give others a second chance
17. Be kinder than you need to be, it takes so much less energy than being mean
18. Don't hide your gifts, use them, challenge, them, hone them — give them wildly away
19. Learn something new every day
20. A penny saved is a penny earned
21. Watch how a (man) treats his mother, it will tell you all you need to know

22. Listen to others. even the dull & the ignorant: they too have a story (The Desiderata)

23. Write it down. You'll forget too quickly and so will others

24. Pay attention to the little things. the big things will take care of themselves

25. Be safe. have fun. this is a journey — not a rehearsal...

THE PLAYLIST

1. "On Children," Sweet Honey in the Rock
2. "Gabriel's Oboe," from The Mission, Yo-Yo Ma
3. "Hello in There," Better Middler
4. "Mother and Child Reunion," Paul Simon
5. "Both Sides Now," Joanie Mitchell
6. "Speaking of Happiness," Gloria Lynne
7. "As If We Never Said Goodbye," Danny Wright
8. "At This Point in My Life," Tracy Chapman
9. "Slipping Through My Fingers," from Mama Mia
10. "Everybody Hurts," R.E.M
11. "Amazing Grace," by anybody
12. "Both Sides Now," Judy Collins
13. "Les Misérables Medley," Danny Wright
14. "A Sunday Kind of Love," Etta James
15. "Alucinado," Tiziano Ferro
16. "At Last," Etta James
17. "Grazie, Prego, Scusi," Adriano Celent
18. "Dime," Willie Colon & Ruben Blades
19. "Don't Go to Strangers," Etta Jones
20. "Take My Love Precious Love," Nina Simone
21. "Come on Home," Mary Chapin Carpenter
22. "Children Found," from *Hotel Rwanda*
23. "Heroes and Heroines," Mary Chapin Carpenter
24. "Take Me as I Am," Wyclef Jean
25. "Thank You for The Music," from *Mama Mia*
26. "Wanting Memories," Sweet Honey in the Rock
27. "Travelin' Thru," Dolly Parton

author's notes

The Eves is a work of fiction that I imagine could be true. Jessica's townhouse is a very real place in Washington, DC, and the renovations, much as I would like them to be. Calvert County, Maryland is a place steeped in history, still with working farms. Martinsburg, The Grange, and Martinsburg Community College are fictitious places, but I wish they weren't. The Eves, especially, is a place that I wish existed. I would gladly take my place among such women.

The Eves is sandwiched between two literary pieces, one by Kahil Gibran, the other by Dr. Ysaye M. Barnwell. Each is sung a cappella by Sweet Honey in the Rock. Dr. Barnwall was a long-standing member. Stirring and haunting, they are appropriate bookends for the story. They set the stage with music and they carry the main messages and central themes of the book.

The main pieces of this book came together, as they all do, in parts. First, there was Bette Midler's cover in her 1972 *Divine Miss M* album of John Prine's, "Hello in There." There was no reason that, at age nineteen, I should have been so impacted by hearing...

> *If you're walking down the street sometime and you should spot some hollow ancient eyes, don't you pass them by and stare as if you didn't care. Say, "Hello in there. Hello."*

I was transformed by the song. Never since have I walked past an older person without saying hello and wondering about their back story. Second, and most important, the account of Jessica's mother's death is autobiographical, and very close to the story of my own mother's passing. From that moment on, this story needed to be written. When you are a writer, it is like childbirth—once the seed has been sown and taken root, you have little option but to birth the story.

A few months after my mother's death, while wandering in Albuquerque, New Mexico, the "Land of Enchantment," I was, indeed, enchanted by a whimsical Native American Indian "Storyteller" sculpture. Originated by the Cochiti, and now copied by members of various tribal nations, these are clay figures of men and women, often with many children on their laps, backs, in their arms, and at their feet. These are the storytellers, the keepers of oral histories, myths, legends, and traditions. I purchased a very sweet and inexpensive figure in the old market, and it's been on my desk ever since, waiting patiently for me to tell this story.

The book is filled with double entendre, not because I planned it. What evolved in the writing was that so often there are two sides to every story. The characters give us true lessons by which to live, or not live, our lives. The characters are still learning themselves. Their stories are not finished, even for those who do not make it alive to the end of the book.

I hope I have captured fairly, and with great respect, the stories of those who will think they recognize themselves here. I hope I have opened a door for conversations that will happen between those we first love and those we love fiercely.

It is impossible to bring anything to success alone. I'm particularly grateful to Chad at Writing Nights (wrightingnights.org) – who has the skill, wisdom, and vision to bring *The Eves* to reality. Special thanks to all those who read my drafts, cheered me on, and to Marilyn who demanded I give birth to the Norwegian part of this story. This first-time novelist could not have asked for, or received, better support, criticism, cheer leading, and guidance in the birthing of this novel than my Sarasota Book group and my friend and fellow author Saralyn Richard.

Special thanks to the prototypes for Elizabeth Jacobi, for letting me be friend and "daughter;" and for the ever-likeable Kim Stephanic, the inspiration for Allison Beck. The very first reading of the book took her breath away and she kept reading as I wrote. To Sharon Barrett, Tonia Essig, and Pier Ormond who shared color and philosophy and let the white girl know when she was "not all that." To my sisters, Barbara, and Susan, who know more about reconciliation than I do and were patient enough to teach me. To my brothers Bob and Rick, for cheerleading, challenging, and helping in real ways. To Lauren Sammon for her brilliance in artistic design and to Ivica Jandrijević and Elena Brighittini for the cover art.

There are no words strong enough, or well-crafted enough to capture my love and thanks to my mother for the many gifts she left behind, to my dad for his hanging in long enough for me to dig deeply into this story, or to my children for simply being astounding. I am humbled and blessed to have found my personal Roy Gillis. I like him a considerable amount. He is the other side of my coin, for which I am most grateful.

This is not hearsay. This is really true. I hope my little storyteller is happy.

Grace Sammon
April 2020

book club discussion guide —basic book banter

1. Did you like the book? Why, why not?
2. What did you learn from the novel?
3. Which character do you identify with most? Least? Why?
4. Who did you like the most? Least? Why?
5. Erica, in many ways, is the turning point for the novel. In what ways do you agree with this statement?
6. We don't get to meet Ryn and Adam, what do you know and feel about them?
7. What do you think of the themes of honesty, truth, fact, fiction and lying throughout the book?
8. Jessica has kept a huge secret, in fact, she lies. How does this make you feel about her?
9. Sonia never lies. What does this make you think about her?
10. Sonia says that she believes that in large measure we can write our own stories, change the ending. What evidence do you see of this in the book or in your own life.
11. What role do individual's perceptions play in the storyline? Does it make sense? How do you know the truth of an event?
12. Jessica seems to get stories and information from the other characters that they don't share with each other. Why do you think this is?
13. Jessica tries to define what love, falling in love, and being in love means. Is she in love? Do those things mean different things at different points in life?

14. Is Jessica religious? Are the others? What role does religion play in the story?
15. What do you think of the lessons Jessica chooses to catalogue?
16. Jessica states on several occasions that she felt she didn't deserve something. How does that play out for her?
17. If you were to sum up the message of each character what would it be?
18. How does the theme of regret play out in the book?
19. There is no interview with Elizabeth. What do we really know about her? We don't get to hear the conversation about 'reach.' What is the 'reach' of each character?
20. Why do Jessica and Elizabeth have the bond they do?
21. Why does Erica feel so connected to Jessica?
22. Do the characters have a moral compass?
23. Does Jessica decide her future, or does she let others shape her future?
24. Do we know Jessica, or do we have other's impressions of her?
25. How important is Jesper?
26. What do you think will happen between Jesper and the rest of his 'family?'
27. The last few chapters of the book are unexpected. How does this position the characters for the future? What is the lesson of those chapters?
28. Do you have a favorite line or scene from the book?
29. What do you think happens in the coming years for the characters?
30. The novel follows a musical path—overture, theme, and coda. Does this work for you? Why, why not?
31. The core of the book is the bond between mothers and their children, "other mothers," and the life lessons we share or miss. Discuss this.

book banter bonus

MEAL MUSTS:
- Morning book club? Make Ethiopian coffee, fruit and Bisquick coffee cake.
- Dinner? Make Jan's Key Lime Ginger Curry meal, Roy's meatballs and peppers, or Sonia's Argentinean dinner.
- Make sure to have a variety of non-alcoholic beverages. As appropriate, have vodka, Chianti and Malbec wine, and the ingredients for a Tobias' 'highball' on hand.
- Need dessert? Make Roy's apple pie.

CONVERSATIONS CREATIONS:

One of the goals of writing *The Eves* was to generate conversations beyond book club, beyond the book. Think about the prompts below and open a dialogue! Consider a brunch, dinner, or event where everyone in the group brings index cards with conversation starters on them or purchase 'table topics' or other cards from amazon.com. You could start with some of the ones listed below.

1. Centuries ago, Tobias' family is given a "single gift" that changed the future for many people. What are examples of single gifts you've been given—that you hope you gave away?
2. Should children be told the truth, or be oblivious to the details of their parents' lives and vice versa?
3. What role does, should, or can lying play in people's lives?
4. What boundaries should there be between children and parents?
5. If you had just ten minutes to have a conversation with someone

now, who would it be? What would you say? Why is this 'the conversation' you would have over other possibilities?

6.   Tell me about being a child.

7.   What are three good things and three hard things about your childhood?

8.   What are three good things and three hard things about your adulthood?

9.   What taught you more, or made you who you are today, the good things or the hard things?

10. Would you want to live in a place like The Grange? Why, why not?

11. If you went to The Grange, what would you bring with you?

12. What would you want to leave behind?

13. What's on your playlist?

14. What would you want said on your tombstone?

15. Are there things that you would want forgiveness for or offer forgiveness for?

16. What don't you know and how will you learn it?

17. What have you left undone?

18. What have you left unsaid?

session
with sammon

What gave you the inspiration to write *The Eves*?
The narrative of Jessica's mom's death is very autobiographical, although I was not thinking of her risotto recipe at the time she died. The profound understanding that at that moment all of her stories were now lost to me was stunning despite the time we had to prepare for her death. The other big piece was bearing witness to the struggle I see in fellow adults in their relationships with their grown children and the horrible feeling of not feeling part of their own children's stories. It seems to me that the book connected those experiences.

How autobiographical is the story?
There are certainly parts of me and those I know in the book. I've told you the core, the impetus for the start. The story itself, however, is quite fictional. Carl Jung, the great German therapist, says that when we dream each of the people in the dream actually represents a part of our selves. That's probably true to some extent when you create characters. There are parts of me in each of the characters. I have to also admit I've stolen heavily from personal experiences and conversations, as well as the experiences of those around me.

Can you give an example?

Sure. I have a good friend with a boat. She and her husband are among the most likable people in the world. *The Tug* is modeled after their boat, and so are the characters. They are the prototype for Allison and Malcom, but their stories are not my friends'. Another example would be the quilt and the handprints; there are real examples of this in my life. The best example is the harvest. I had the great privilege of being with my son when he participated in a similar project. He lived 'off the grid' for six months and then there was this wonderful harvest. It is absolutely my imagery from there that created The Grange.

Your writing creates such clear pictures of The Grange and the house on Hobart Street, where do those images come from?

I owe thanks to my children for so many of those images. I've already mentioned the harvest. The house on Hobart Street is conjured from a house my daughter lived in and that I would love to remodel the way Roy and Jessica did. And yes, you can hear lions from the roof! I think it's the fine details in a story that make it rich, believable. I wanted readers to feel they were sitting on the window seat with Jessica, that they knew where she kept the vodka in the kitchen, that they could hear the smack of The Washington Post on her porch.

How long did it take you to write *The Eves?*

I started it five years ago and wrote the first two and last two chapters, then put it away. A potential agent at the time said she thought Jessica was too self-centered and she didn't understand where I was going with the novel. I was discouraged, but the women kept roaming around in my head. I didn't have much choice but to finish the book. Once I decided, it took about three and a half months.

You wrote the first and last chapters, then the middle? How does that work?

I've heard most authors write from start to finish and are surprised at where they wind up. That's never worked for me in any of my books. I know where I want it to start and end up. In education we call it 'planning for the end in mind.'

Did you know what would happen in the middle to get you to the end?

Absolutely not. For me, the middle is the hard part. I had some high points. I knew Jessica would go to Africa, for example but there were so many parts that were just fun to uncover as I wrote. I didn't know about the decision Sonia would make regarding Erica. There were also unexpected and never anticipated things, like the character development of all the ladies. The character of Jesper was fully unanticipated, demanding some rewriting in the final chapters necessary. Those things changed the last two chapters, but not by much.

Is writing easy for you?

Yes and no. I'm really blessed with the ability to have words spill off the end of my fingers onto a page. I'm much better that way, actually, then when I'm speaking. The easy part is that I get such a charge out of the process, the characters talking in my head, the ability to create tension and resolution, the opportunity to help people learn. You can have great fun as an author. There are things in the book that make me, and probably only my siblings, giggle or nod. For example, the phone number of the driver Jessica texts in the 'Re-entry' chapter is my childhood phone number, the locket Jessica wears, and the picture of her mother are actually descriptions of my mother's locket. You can make things live again or be important again in your writing. I like that part a great deal.

What's hard, sometimes, is the attention to detail. When I read through one of the drafts, Erica was fifteen on one page and several paragraphs later I state she's sixteen. There were times where it was hard to tie the two ends together. There were big things like what had to happen for Jessica to change, and little things like why Jessica bought the can of beans at the M and M. I didn't know why I had her buy them, then it just made so much sense that she would have used them to make the soup in 'The Naming' chapter.

You mention helping people learn as something you like about the writing process. The book is filled with that from the harvest, to the sustainable/green house, to lamb shearing, to the Leakey foot prints, and so much more. Why is that important?

As an educator, and simply as a person, I think it's so important to keep learning. In *The Eves* I'm very much guilty of what they accuse many first authors of contriving. Namely, a book that has everything I know in it. It was great fun to also do research. I didn't know how to shear a lamb, or about the regrets of aging parents, or about Paul Simon and the lyrics to Mother and Child Reunion, or a host of things. 'Through the magic of the Internet,' as Erica says, you can find out an awful lot.

I wanted the experience of reading *The Eves* to be similar to, say, listening to NPR. In fact, it was the inspiration for a few of the lines in the book. One set is when Elizabeth and Jessica first meet in her room and they talk about listening to NPR. The other is when Jan and Margaret Mary have a dispute about the use of quilts in the Underground Railroad. I wanted to provoke thought, conversation, being informed. It was important to me to create that dynamic because I think most readers are really smart and they want to not only be entertained but to learn.

What's it like to have people read your work?

Honestly, it's the most naked and hardest thing I do. Opening your-self up, even for praise, is a very humbling process. It's also really fun. I didn't realize how much I'd enjoy sharing the experience of people reading *The Eves*. When someone says they are on page twenty or the chapter about Africa and are loving it, I get excited for them. I want to know where they are in the book, what they hope happens, what makes them sad or happy or mad. It is for me, like Jan says, delicious! It's also somehow silly, it's just a book. So many people have such amazing gifts. I just gather words.

How important is age, race, and sexual identity in the story?

I want to say it's critically important and not important at all. When I was writing the plot summary for review, the document where you have to describe the characters, I had a very hard time labeling them, Black, White, Latinx, Native American, lesbian, etc. Part of that points up my privilege, or advantage, as a white author. People as-sume the character is white unless otherwise categorized. I wasn't comfortable with that. Their individual ages, traits, experiences, and cultural background certainly give them their richness. These, com-bined, are the sum of the whole. But I also wanted the book to feel seamless as if we could get the feel for them without the labeling.

Do you have a favorite character or a least favorite?

Oh, that's a tough one. I like them all for so very many reasons. I love Tobias. I can hear his voice in my head, and the actor that would play him on the screen. He's very much like my Dad, who I miss dearly. Jessica isn't my favorite, but I can feel her very inti-mately. Sonia just makes me laugh and I love that. I wish I got to know Tia, CC, and Jesper more. I'm particularly glad Jesper showed up.

You mention the book going to the big screen, do you think there will be a movie?

Wouldn't that be lovely? Let's see it become a full-fledged, well-received book first. However, to be honest, I wrote with the idea of a film or cable series, not because I was being grandiose, but because I got such a visual and palpable sense of the experience. I could see it as a movie or a Netflix experience and wrote with images of certain characters in mind.

You mentioned, just now, being honest. Talk about the theme of that in the book.

Well, without giving too much away, Jessica is living a lie. She does this because it makes her life easier. At the end we learn that Elizabeth and Roy tell a lie as well. I think that a lot of us are less than honest with ourselves and others and I wanted that tension and honesty to come through in the book. There is also judgement around Jessica, is she a bad person because she is living this lie, or do we have sympathy for her because it helps her survive.

Another theme is how differently different people look at the same event, can you talk about that?

That was much harder to write about, probably because it's just so true, so honest. We all know that no two people see the same thing the same way but there is something so very 'off' with the way Jessica sees things. She mentions early on in the book that Roy sees things she doesn't. That gets echoed in a statement about Sonia and Erica as well. Most profoundly, I think, is what Jessica believes to be true about her and her kids. Certainly all the other characters see Jessica much differently than she sees herself. This raised for me the question of what is true and how do we ever know it. Is personal 'truth' real and how much does it matter when it differs from another's?

Is there another book in you?

When I finished *The Eves,* I thought my little storyteller was quite happy. However, I've started another novel called "the egg." It's about two sets of sisters and two pandemics and how a single decision can change the course of our history. I'm looking forward to seeing where this leads!

about the author

Grace Sammon grew up on Long Island, New York. She spent many years in the Washington, DC area where she raised her two children, and established and owned an educational consulting firm operating in 32 states.

An accomplished author and public speaker in the area of education, *The Eves* is her debut novel.

Grace lives on Florida's west coast with her beloved husband and a small herd of imaginary llamas.

next steps

Thank you for reading *The Eves*. I really hope you liked it and are as sorry as I am that it is over. Let's stay connected!

Here's what you can do:

1. Write a review on Amazon and Barnes and Noble. This is a great way to let me and others know what you think. It will also help build a following for *The Eves*.

   https://www.amazon.com/dp/B0897V7WSM

2. Visit my website and send me an email. Let me know that you'd like to be part of my email subscription list, receive updates, and be eligible for future giveaways. Invite me to virtually visit your book club and discuss *The Eves*. I love to talk about this book and how it impacts people's thinking.

When you visit my website you will also find "extras" such as links to music that inspired *The Eves*, recipes, and a some PDF downloads that will make ongoing conversations and book clubs more enjoyable.

www.gracesammon.net
grace@gracesammon.net

3. Follow me:

ON FACEBOOK
https://www.facebook.com/GraceSammonWrites/

ON INSTAGRAM
https://www.instagram.com/GraceSammonWrites/

ON TWITTER
https://www.twitter.com/GSammonWrites

ON LINKEDIN:
https://www.linkedin.com/in/grace-sammon-84389153/

4. Keep an eye out for my upcoming book *The Egg*. It's the story of two sets of sisters, two pandemics, and how a single egg changed the course of our history.
Here's the opening:

> *Of all the things I learned about my mother to be true is that she buried both of her parents in the backyard next to the family cat. But, I am getting ahead of myself. First, comes the story about the egg.*

It will be a fun journey to see where this story goes.

Thanks again for reading and sharing the story of *The Eves*. I hope we stay connected!

Grace Sammon
May 2020

Made in the USA
Columbia, SC
24 June 2020